KU-527-664

THE KILLING JOKE

ANTHONY HOROWITZ

LARGE PRINT

Oxford

9030 0000 463 653

First published in Great Britain 2004
by
Orion
an imprint of the Orion Publishing Group Ltd

Published in Large Print 2005 by ISIS Publishing Ltd,
7 Centremead, Osney Mead, Oxford OX2 0ES
by arrangement with
The Orion Publishing Group Ltd

The moral right of the author has been asserted

British Library Cataloguing in Publication Data
Horowitz, Anthony, 1955–
    The killing joke.– Large print ed.
    1. Suspense fiction
    2. Humorous stories
    3. Large type books
    I. Title
    823.9'14 [F]

ISBN 0–7531–7347–6 (hb)
ISBN 0–7531–7348–4 (pb)

Printed and bound by Antony Rowe, Chippenham

For Jill — thanks for the laughs.

CHAPTER
ONE

There's this guy, goes into a bar . . .

CHAPTER
TWO

His name was Guy Fletcher. He was thirty years old, reasonably good-looking and thoroughly pissed off. You'd have to be pretty pissed off to choose the Cat and Fiddle, one of the most inhospitable pubs in North London if not the entire world. This wasn't a cheery riverside inn with a smiling landlord and a choice of real ales. It wasn't even a place to come for a quick half-pint and a chat after work with your mates. The Cat and Fiddle was a dark, dirty hell-hole situated in a street of garish plastic signs, garbage toppling out of bins and graffiti scrawled across the walls, just round the corner from Finsbury Park tube station. The building looked as inviting as a butcher's shop and smelt like one too, thanks to its neighbours, both of which were butcher's shops, with windows full of grey, damp meat hanging on improbably large hooks, being gently cured by the exhaust fumes from the passing traffic.

A lot of the local pubs had been prettified over the years — given stripped pine floors and almost edible food — but not this one. The Cat and Fiddle wore its brass horseshoes, fake flintlock pistols and collection of antique beer mats with pride. The carpet was quite possibly the original, Victorian or even Georgian, discoloured and made rancid by generations of spilled drinks. The pebbledash wallpaper was nicotine yellow. The sort of people who came to the Cat and Fiddle never went anywhere else. Indeed, to look at them, you'd think they never went anywhere at all. They had a hopeless sort of look, as if they had been trapped there for ever.

Guy was different. He had chosen to come here, wandering down from the more elevated surroundings of Muswell Hill, because he wanted to be alone and because he knew with certainty that there was no chance at all that he would bump into any of his friends. He was going to get drunk. And here was another advantage of the Cat and Fiddle. If he did manage to get so pissed that his speech blurred, he wet himself on the way to the toilet and vomited over the fruit machine, he would blend in nicely with the crowd. They might even invite him to join the darts team.

There was just one problem. Guy didn't terribly like alcohol. He never had done, not since, aged eleven, he had shoplifted a bottle of cherry brandy with two friends and wound up winning the Edgware General Hospital (under-thirteen) record for the longest time attached to a stomach pump. He had learnt the obvious lesson: that cherry brandy, like almost everything containing cherries, is either naff (Black Forest gateau) or (Coca-Cola) just nasty. But since then he had failed to find any alcoholic drink that appealed.

He ran an eye over the various pumps that stood to attention behind the sodden towels laid over the bar.

Adnam's or Waddington's? He drank beer occasionally but not with any real pleasure. In truth, he didn't really understand it.

Here was something that began life as a spiky, alien-looking and otherwise useless plant, then had to be put through a series of bizarre, almost ritualistic processes to produce — what? A liquid that came with the colour of cold tea, tasted of chemicals and required a massive, bladder-stretching intake before it had any effect. Bottled beer — German or Belgian — with its fanciful names and even more fanciful prices was worse. As far as Guy was concerned, it was just a little bit sad that the Germans, who had produced Bach and Goethe, were still capable of holding summer festivals where they dressed up in leather trousers and braces and made complete fools of themselves all on account of a cold drink.

He didn't mind a glass of good wine, although how he hated the po-faced language of that. "A good wane". It was impossible even to say it without sounding middle class. And it bothered him that he didn't actually know what a good wine was. He hated going into off-licences where the rows and rows of bottles seemed to sneer at him quite wilfully, just like the imported French shop assistants. The labels told him nothing. One bottle might come with a picture of a poplar-lined avenue and distant *château* — but the stuff inside had probably been pressure-hosed into a huge silver juggernaut. Some transport company from an industrial zone outside Paris that carried diesel or fertiliser Mondays to Thursdays and then, after a quick

4

rinse, wine for the rest of the week. And what about the people who could judge a wine by its legs, its bouquet, its robustness? They were all, invariably, complete wankers. Guy had never been able to detect honeyed undertones or the scent of gooseberries in anything. He sometimes wondered if the whole thing hadn't been invented by the French (typically devious and underhand) to sell what was, at the end of the day, only a fermented grape.

Anyway, wine was out of the question at the Cat and Fiddle. Anything served here would have the delicate bouquet of white spirit and would be corroding the inside of the cardboard box it came in even as it was poured.

He glanced up at the spirit bottles, hanging upside-down in a row. The Cat and Fiddle specialised mainly in cheap brands he'd never heard of. Who would have suspected there was a vodka called "Shooting Tsar"? He decided to give it a miss. His eye travelled past the Bailey's to the gin, and for a moment he was tempted.

Gin and tonic. Here was a drink with echoes of Noël Coward and faded royalty. He liked the fact that it was a collision of two mysteries. The recipe for Beefeater gin, he had read once, was a closely guarded secret, known only to the most senior member of the Beefeater family. He could imagine a terribly old, white-haired man on a life-support machine in some private clinic, lifting his head to address the waiting family.

"You add juniper berries, the zest of three lemons and . . . and . . . and . . ."

Tonic water — that was the other mystery. Didn't it contain quinine, a drug that the Victorians had taken to combat malaria until they discovered that it was even more lethal than the disease itself? Gin and tonic. A drink redolent of scandal and depravity and yet, to the whole of suburban England, there was nothing nicer.

But it was out of the question at the Cat and Fiddle. Ask for a gin and tonic in the wrong tone of voice and he could end up with a broken nose.

In the end, he went for a Scotch. That was safe. A single, gruff syllable. "Scotch." Then: "A double." He liked the sound of that. It made him feel better already.

Guy was getting drunk because he felt his career was going nowhere and because his girlfriend, Kate, had just gone somewhere . . . that is, out of the house and his life. He was drinking to forget that although he was now thirty and had been thirty for the last eleven days, he was living in a cramped flat only half a mile away from the street where he had been brought up. Three decades and he'd only managed to make it up Park Road, left at the traffic lights and left again into Mapletree Close. Some progress!

He threw back his first double, noticing that the glass had not been washed. Or maybe the dishwasher had managed to fuse somebody's lipstick into the rim. He gestured at the barman, who was bald and drab with a face that would have done him well if only he'd considered a move into the funeral industry. "Another." It came in the same glass. There was something faintly depressing about the way the optic measured out the right amount, down to the last drop. Maybe he should have chosen a cocktail bar where the bottles were thrown and spun and where this self-pitying descent into oblivion would at least have been given the colourful veneer of a circus act.

He looked around him.

The lounge bar of the Cat and Fiddle was crowded. This wasn't difficult as the room was very small. Guy could make out fifteen or twenty people through the clouds of cigarette smoke that hovered over them like ectoplasm. It was the usual mix of London Underground workers, aggressive builders, dead-eyed old-age pensioners, tarty girls and tattooed boys. A man with a fat lower lip and a Popeye arm was throwing a dart at a board. Thunk! Double twenty. Like all darts players, he just looked bored. Three of the long-term unemployed were playing pool on a table whose green baize had worn to the consistency of old paint. There was a fruit machine in a corner, its lights flashing and endlessly rearranging themselves. Come on. Play me. Win twenty pounds. An old woman with bright red lipstick was feeding it with pound coins. So far she hadn't won anything. Perry Como was playing on the sound system.

Guy (on his third double) fitted in well enough. In his faded jeans, plain T-shirt and very old leather jacket, he could have been a drug-dealer, a minicab driver, a dozen things rather than the moderately successful actor that he actually was. Successful in the sense that he was seldom out of work. Moderately, because he didn't get the work he actually wanted. His clear blue eyes, roguish smile and fashionably untidy fair hair would have made him a perfect hero or even the perfect hero's best friend who tragically gets mown down just when you think everything's going to be all right. Unfortunately, these parts were never offered to him. Too often, the parts that did come his way had the word "bit" attached to the front end. He was the suspect who never had anything to do with the crime, the messenger upstaged by his own message, the love interest who was neither loved nor particularly interesting.

It should have been otherwise. Guy was well-built, with a square face and broad shoulders. He looked as if he could look after himself, which, in fact, he couldn't. That is, he couldn't cook, couldn't sew, couldn't programme a video or sort out a glitch in a computer, couldn't even maintain the Kawasaki 600cc motorbike he had bought at a knock-down price from a friend who had, indeed, been knocked down. (There was an opportunistic side to him — but at least he had the good grace to feel guilty about it.) All in all, he did not look like an actor, which, in the Cat and Fiddle where acting was almost certainly synonymous with homosexuality, was probably a good thing.

"The fuckers don't know a fucking thing."

"Fuck 'em."

"Fuck the lot of them."

The conversation in the pub was a soft, semi-incoherent babble punctuated by fucks. Somebody spoke to the old woman at the fruit machine and she screeched, briefly, with laughter, then added another coin. A very thin man with a grey, twisted face, as lifeless as an old tea-towel, slumped forward on to his table, a cigarette trailing out of his lips. Another dart thudded into the board.

"Same again." Guy had reached his fourth double and the room was beginning to spin.

This performance, this one-man adaptation of *The Lost Weekend*, was pathetic. He knew it. But what else was he to do? Kate had left him. After four years — well, three and a half anyway — Kate had told him . . .

"I'm sorry, Guy. I really am. But I just feel that the way we are together . . . our relationship . . . it isn't going anywhere."

"Kate . . . what do you mean? What are you talking about?"

"I can't breathe. I do love you. It isn't your fault. I just feel I need my own space."

"No, Kate. I can't accept that. I don't believe that."

"Guy . . ."

"Tell me the truth!"

"I've told you . . ."

"Kate . . ."

"All right. I'm shagging Martin."

Was that what she had said? They'd both been a little drunk when they'd had that final, stale row. But sometimes, when he played it back in his head, it sounded like a bad sit-com with himself, uncharacteristically, in the main part.

And how had Martin got into it? Martin of all people! His best mate five years before at the Clairemont Theatre School! Guy was dumbfounded. Martin Mayhew was a slob. That was what Kate had always said. He had no idea about personal hygiene. And Kate couldn't stand him. At least, that was what Guy had thought. In fact, the two of them had been seeing each other while he had been in the middle of the worst job he'd ever had: a three-month stint in a daytime soap where the sets were as shaky as the scripts and the director — well into his sixties — was often shakier than either. He'd actually rung her once. He was shooting a steamy scene with an actress and he was worried about it. He wanted to tell Kate that he was only doing it because it was in the script, that he didn't fancy the actress and that there wouldn't be any tongues. And all the time . . .! It wasn't fair.

And, while he was thinking about it, what did it all say about his career? Three months shooting total dross in a suburb of Manchester had certainly been the low point of the millennium — but work had been thin on the ground and his agent had persuaded him that it wouldn't do him any harm. Since nobody watched the programme, nobody would know he had been in it. And it had been no more demeaning than waiting in a restaurant or a stint in telesales . . . both of which he'd done in his time. Hadn't they all? And yet he'd had a good year up until then. Guest spots in *E for Emergency*, *Policemen's Wives* and *The Manchester Murders*: all prime-time shows. Two fairly substantial scenes in an English film, which was being pitched as the next *Full Monty*. Even a series of advertisements for a new coffee.

A good year. Or so it had seemed at the time. Now, savouring the suddenly acrid taste of the whisky, he

10

wondered. Just how solid a career was he building if its high spot was his role as the hero of a Nescafé commercial? And as for the film — who did he think he was kidding? Every English film was pitched as the next *Full Monty*. At script stage, in casting, production and right up to the release. It was only when it finally crawled onto the smallest screen at the local Odeon, met a barrage of venomous reviews and retired, hurt, to the bottom shelf of the video shop that anyone would admit that it was actually a pile of crap. But by then, of course, the producers would have moved on. Working on the next *Billy Elliott* . . .

Moderately successful or barely successful?

On the set of the *Full Monty* fiasco he had stood next to Ewan McGregor — who had managed to be both cocky and dull — and had felt the distance between them. At that moment he had experienced an uncharacteristic surge of . . . well, it was professional jealousy, really. Envy. Bitterness edging on psychopathic hatred. He was never going to make it to Hollywood. He was never going to be paid millions for making movies as irredeemably awful as *Attack of the Clones*. He was just going to have to stay in Muswell Hill with Kate.

Without Kate. She had gone.

He became aware of the group of builders nearest to him. Why did he automatically assume they were builders? Oh, yes. They were dressed in overalls and had quite enormous buttocks. They were standing at the bar, smoking, drinking, telling jokes.

"... and so the man's zipping up his fly and suddenly he's feeling guilty, so he says, "I think there's something you should know. I'm not really Jesus Christ." And the nun says, "I think there's something you should know. I'm really the bus conductor.""

And they all laughed. Big, retching laughs that spilled the beer and turned a few heads round them. Even the thin man with the cigarette woke up briefly. For his part, Guy just felt depressed. He had never understood jokes. Of course, he'd swapped stories with other actors. Bad directors, worse scripts, terrible disasters involving inexperienced stuntmen or special effects that had gone horribly wrong ... There were plenty of laughs in that. But that was real life. Shared experience. Jokes were something quite different.

Why did people tell jokes? Mainly because they were pissed. After a certain amount of alcohol — cherry brandy or whatever — normal conversation became difficult and jokes more or less looked after themselves. People who didn't know each other told jokes. They were useful to fill in awkward silences at dinner parties. Guy had had an uncle who was always telling jokes. Dear old Uncle Sid lived on his own in a single room in Battersea and was still laughing the day they cremated him.

"I heard this great joke the other day ..."

Guy had always found it just about impossible to laugh at jokes. Laughter surely comes from the unexpected and yet a joke both demands and expects laughter. It is therefore by its very nature self-defeating. And yet he always felt the dreadful need, the obligation

12

to tell one back, like a missionary exchanging beads with a tribe of cannibals. He'd heard a joke and so — God help him — he'd have to tell one, which meant searching desperately through his memory for any joke he could remember while at the same time knowing he would mangle whatever it was he happened to find, screwing up the opening and probably forgetting the punch line. He was an actor. He could speak funny lines . . . even those written by Shakespeare or Shaw. But jokes defeated him. And so he listened to these braying voices with a growing sense of annoyance. Didn't these people have anything else to talk about?

But now that they'd started, they meant to go on. He looked at them over the top of his whisky glass. The leader was a man in blue overalls that were struggling to hold the various contours of his body — like a badly stuffed duvet. He had a spatchcock nose and narrow, watery eyes. The other was an apprentice, about eighteen, with a single earring and acne. The third had his back to Guy. All he could see was a thick neck, more blue overalls and those overripe buttocks.

It was this man — the third man — who told the next joke.

"Why is Selina Moore like a Ferrero Rocher?"

For a moment, Guy experienced a sense of total clarity, the taste of the whisky and the sting of the cigarette smoke snatched away.

They were telling a joke about Selina Moore!

Of course, they didn't know. There were very few people in the world who knew the truth about him and Selina Moore, England's most successful and most glamorous Oscar-winning actress. He had never met her but she was everything to him: the centre, the very pedestal of his life. She was everything he had ever aspired to be. He loved her.

And, for that matter, he was also rather fond of Ferrero Rocher. He had actually appeared as the youngest of the guests in the original advertisement for the oversized chocolate, the now notorious ambassador's party, which had become a laughing stock in every country it had been shown, curiously without doing any harm to sales.

Just one week ago, Selina Moore had died. She had been killed when her plane crashed into an orphanage in south-west France. And now these men were telling a joke about her.

"Why is Selina Moore like a Ferrero Rocher?"

Guy waited with a sense of dread. Could it be something to do with the gold paper, the layer of wafer, the hazelnut in the middle?

The answer came.

"Because they both come out of France in a box."

Haar, haar, haar, haar. The joke wasn't even slightly funny but it got the same, ponderous laughter. And weren't Ferrero Rocher made in Switzerland anyway?

"Excuse me. I knew Selina Moore." Guy looked round to see who had spoken and realised, with a queasy sort of thrill, that it was himself. He had stepped forward and now he was right among the three men, in their face, so to speak. He had accosted them. It was incredible. He had only drunk eight whiskies, surely not enough to bring on a death wish.

"You what?" the youngest one asked, putting down his pint. There was a moustache of froth on his upper lip. The other two were looking at him curiously, as if he was something unhygienic.

"She was a brilliant actress. She was fantastic. Did you see her Desdemona at the RSC?"

"What the fuck do you want?" the man who had told the joke asked. Now that Guy could see his face, he was a nightmare. Twisted nose, crooked teeth and cauliflower ears. Guy realised he had probably seen very little of the Royal Shakespeare Company's 1989 season.

But he couldn't stop himself now. He was too drunk to negotiate his way out. "She was a great actress," he said. "She did a lot of charity work. She was someone who tried to make a difference." And then, insanely, "Eleven children got killed in that plane crash. I don't think it's something you should be making a joke about. That's all."

"Who the fuck gives a fuck what you think?" the leader asked.

"Wait a minute! Wait a minute!" The joke-teller, whose sense of humour had rapidly evaporated, held up a hand. Guy noticed that he had knuckles like oyster shells. "I'm talking to my mates. Who said you could fucking eavesdrop?"

"It's just that Selina was —" Guy began.

The joke-teller hit him. Not with his fist. He simply leant forward and Guy felt something unbelievably hard smash into the side of his face. He jerked back, knowing that he had been head-butted. Warm blood

15

cascaded over his lip. His knees crumpled —
fortunately, for if he had remained standing he might
have been hit again. He fell on to the floor, taking a
bar-stool with him, and the crash brought a few
seconds' silence to the Cat and Fiddle though not to
the juke-box, which was now playing "Stand By Your
Man". The three builders finished their drinks and
walked out together, heads held high, obviously pleased
with themselves. The barman shook his head wearily.
The woman at the fruit machine laughed again. Life
went on as normal.

CHAPTER
THREE

From *Hello!* magazine.
An interview with Selina Moore

I'm meeting Selina Moore at her beautiful house in Marlow, overlooking the Thames, where she has settled down following her recent marriage and return from Hollywood. The house was converted from a nineteenth-century watermill and Selina spent half a million pounds converting it back again. Why? "I always wanted to live in a watermill," she explains, with a disarming smile.

Marlow seems the perfect setting for this quintessential English rose — "A tea rose," she quips. Tea is her favourite drink. It is hard to believe that she will soon be sixty. Her husband, Edward, wandering into the room, mentions that she is actually sixty-five. But on this warm summer's day, with the river burning gold in the setting sun, she looks ten years younger.

Selina, of course, leapt (dived, cartwheeled and somersaulted!) to fame as the leather-clad heroine of cult TV series *The Interceptors* back in the seventies. The poster company Athena once boasted that it sold more images of her character, Tabitha Strong, than even its famous sand-streaked buttocks. Fidel Castro was rumoured to be a fan and a Cuban TV critic who panned one episode was, allegedly, executed. Her decision to quit at the end of the third series stunned the entire nation and sent the share price of Yorkshire TV crashing.

From television to classical theatre. The critics sneered but her performance as the Duchess of Malfi was a sell-out at the Old Vic with even the ticket touts fighting to get tickets. Cleopatra, Medea, Hedda Gabler and Saint Joan followed. A well-known theatre critic famously compared her power and beauty to that of a waterfall: theatrical Niagara.

In 1984, Selina was unable to resist the call from Hollywood . . . not when it came with a seven-figure cheque and a three-picture deal. The first of these, a remake of *Love Story* with Dustin Hoffman, won her an Academy Award. Further successes followed, including *Tetrix*, the first major motion picture based on a computer game.

Selina Moore rose to the very top of the Hollywood pile but then came the shock announcement of her retirement, her return to England and her marriage to the Bishop of Rochester. She has said that she intends to spend the rest of her life doing good work and has already given much of her wealth to charity.

We pass through the conservatory and into the grinding room where Selina serves us home-made lemonade and we can watch the waterwheel turning. She is barefoot, dressed in a simple off-the-shoulder dress, which has, indeed, slipped off her shoulder. I ask her to tell me why she has returned to England.

18

SM: I just realised there wasn't anything more for me to do. I was still getting offers. I'd been asked to play the love interest in the next Hannibal Lector movie. But I was missing England. I just wanted to come home.

Hello!: You have a beautiful home.

SM: Thank you.

Hello!: Do you really think you'll never act again?

SM: I never say "never" about anything. Right now, I'm determined to give something back. I once endowed an award for the Clairemont Theatre School in London and now they've asked me to become a governor. And then there's my charity work . . .

Hello!: Elton John has asked you to help his AIDS foundation.

SM: I love Elton and he's doing such great work. But I'm also very concerned about the Amazon rainforest. Sting wrote to me about that. Did you know that an area the size of London will have been cut down before we get to the end of this conversation? And that's assuming we don't overrun! And then there are the donkeys in Spain. I know they may not seem as important as the destruction of the eco-system but I think it's dreadful the way they're treated and I'm determined to do something to help.

Hello!: Can we talk about your marriage? It must have come as a great surprise, marrying so late.

SM: A surprise for whom?

Hello!: For everyone.

SM: I met Charles [*the Bishop of Rochester*] in San Diego — he was officiating at the ordination of the world's first lesbian bishop. I think it is very important that the church moves into the twenty-first century with perhaps a little less emphasis on God and more on the issues that really matter. Charles and I met at the party afterwards and ended up talking into the middle of the afternoon. He's a very spiritual person. I think that was what attracted me to him. But he's also very private. Bishops are a bit like actors, in a way. Of course they're out there in the public and people want to know about them but they're entitled to a private life.

Hello!: Do you regret not having any children?

SM: That's not something I want to talk about. I adore children. I think they're just like adults in a way, only smaller. I would have liked to have had children of my own. But it wasn't to be.

Hello!: Tell us about your plans for the future.

SM: My plans for the future? I don't know where to begin! Well, I suppose the most exciting thing in my life — apart from my wonderful husband — is my autobiography, *Strong Woman* which I plan to start writing very soon. Right now, I'm still doing the research. And there's still things to do in the house. The kitchen is a disaster, for example. There's no Aga, which is extraordinary considering the house has river views. But to be honest with you, I'm still worn out from the wedding. We had five hundred guests . . . and all those thank-you letters! So next week I'm going on holiday. There's a little hotel I know in the South of France. Charles has a synod, unfortunately, so he can't make it and I'll be flying there on my own.

Hello!: *Bonne voyage!*

SM: *Merci.*

CHAPTER
FOUR

The next morning, Guy woke up with a throbbing head and a sense that one side of his face had somehow got stuck to the pillow. The whisky had left his throat dry, his mouth sour and his stomach nauseous. He got out of bed and staggered, naked, into the bathroom. He leant over the toilet and urinated, at the same time examining himself in the mirror.

He had always hated the mirror. He had gone with Kate to Ikea, a vast warehouse on the North Circular Road. With its multiple showrooms, it had reminded him of the world's biggest film set for the world's most boring film: the story of a Swedish family with twenty-three bathrooms and nineteen kitchens. Scandinavian design in lethal combination with North London salesgirls. It had taken an hour to buy the thing, and when they had finally lugged it home, of course it was half an inch bigger than the space it was intended for. He should have smashed it. If he wasn't superstitious, like all actors, he would have.

He wanted to smash it now, but only because of what it showed.

"Mirror, mirror on the wall — who's the biggest arsehole of them all?"

He looked dreadful . . . and he was meant to be filming at eleven — a good part in a new adaptation of John Buchan's *The Thirty-nine Steps*. Guy had already shot half his scenes and suspected that Continuity might notice a slight hiccup when he suddenly turned up with a face that had turned in parts yellow with coagulated blood rimming his nostril and an eye that was not only black and half its normal size but, more significantly, half the size of its neighbour. All in all, it was remarkable that one head-butt could do so much damage.

He brushed his hair and cleaned his teeth, which didn't improve how he looked or how he felt. Then he went into the kitchen and made himself breakfast. It was strange how much bigger the flat felt without Kate. He didn't have to wait for the toilet. He didn't have to step into the bathroom to let her pass down the corridor, stop running the hot water when she was taking a shower, or squeeze himself into the kitchen table so she could open the fridge. The two of them had shared this tiny space for eighteen months and he saw now that they'd developed an intricate ritual in that time, like bumblebees about to mate or something. He wondered what sort of architect had converted the building. A very small one, presumably.

He opened the fridge and took out some orange juice, which he swigged straight from the carton. Then he made himself some toast. He looked around the small, neat kitchen: the pine spice rack, the saucepans hanging from the ceiling. As if he wasn't gloomy enough already, that was something else he had to consider. Half the things in the flat belonged to Kate in the sense that she had paid for them. Including the toaster. Would she be coming back to collect them? At least the leasehold was his, the mortgage in his name alone. Kate had paid her share of the bills but he had never asked for rent. Perhaps she would leave him some of her furniture *in lieu*.

As he ate, he thought back to their first meeting at the Clairemont and it seemed to him that the kitchen dissolved in a series of wavy lines and suddenly he was there . . .

. . . a twenty-two-year-old drama student, standing in a shabby corridor looking at the notices on a board. The first week of his first term. Everything still quite new and strange. This was when he could still smell the mustiness, the makeup and old scenery in the air. A movement behind him and there she was, looking over his shoulder. God — she was already the ultimate actress. Long black hair sweeping over her shoulders as if groomed for a shampoo ad. The physique of a Bond girl, with eyes a deep Russian blue. A slightly boyish smile, perfect for any of Shakespeare's sex-change comedies.

"Hi," he said.

"How are you?"

"I'm fine. I'm Guy Fletcher."

"Kate Evans."

"Is this your first term?"

"Yes."

Not the most memorable first conversation. It was remarkable, in fact, that he could still remember every word of it. Later on he learnt that she had come to the Clairemont straight from Aberystwyth, where she had studied English and art history. She hadn't enjoyed herself there. She had spent three years being soaked by torrential rain or enormous waves, the two often saving time by meeting in the middle. At least the university had a theatre, even if half the plays had to be in bloody Welsh. That was where she had spent most of her time.

Guy fancied her but he didn't quite trust her. She was too assertive for his taste, talking about Brecht and Stanislavsky in the pub round the corner or working late into the evening on the play she was directing, starring in and had also written. He went to see it and, like everyone else, was annoyed to discover that it was quite good. In the envious, insecure world of a London drama school, Kate could all too easily have been disliked. She already had an agent — and not just any agent but a name. At Clairemont, such conspicuous success before she had even finished her first year was considered *de trop*. There was something a little tasteless about it . . . like an Oxfam worker with a liking for *foie gras*, perhaps. Or a nurse in a hospice winning the pools.

Guy decided to ignore her. She was much too classy for the likes of him. In his first year, he began a serious relationship with a red-haired girl called Peta, who only slept with him when she had worked out that they were astrologically suited. Guy had lied about his age, making himself a Taurus to suit her Pisces. The relationship ended spectacularly at the surprise party she threw on his birthday — the main surprise being

25

that it was nine months too early, and he moved on to Jane, who laughed at everything and even managed to make him smile when she told him she was leaving him for Torin. Torin was another good friend; blond-haired, Irish, unbelievably lazy. Torin seldom got up before lunch but was said to be so good in bed that none of his girlfriends would have wanted him anywhere else.

That had been the early summer of his life: Clairemont and the years afterwards. Knocking around London with Jane and Torin — and with Jack and Paul, two provincial lads who had both come out a few days after meeting each other. It was a time of terrible part-time jobs, of gossip in Soho cafés, cheap films at the Prince Charles, designer-clothes sales in strange back alleys and endless packets of Marlboro Lights. And then there were the scams. Getting into first-night parties, getting into premières, wangling introductions to people who might, just might, help their careers. Scrabbling through life on the most tenuous of threads. Friends of people who knew people. Grabbing the moment. Living in hope.

One evening they had gone to see a new musical at the Shaftesbury Theatre: a location that was already bad news for any musical show in town. The Shaftesbury, despite its name, was not on the part of Shaftesbury Avenue where it needed to be. It was out of sight of Piccadilly Circus, too far away from the centre of the West End, isolated on a sort of concrete island with traffic converging to form an arrowhead on both sides. The Shaftesbury managed to be both cavernous and cramped, and musicals that came here were often big, expensive and unloved. This musical was called *Dunkirk!*. The exclamation mark had been borrowed, with faint desperation, from *Oliver!* or *Oklahoma!* or any other one-word musical that had actually made anybody money.

"Why on earth are we going to a musical called *Dunkirk!*?" Guy asked, when the project was first suggested.

It was a stupid question. Wasn't the answer obvious? They had free tickets! New productions were frequently "papered" with hundreds of tickets given away to create the illusion that people actually wanted to see it. And there was something else.

"Kate's in it," Paul said. Guy looked puzzled. "You remember her. Kate Evans. That play about lesbians in the PLO . . . Everyone always said she'd go far."

"She got as far as Nuneaton," Jack muttered archly. "A winter season."

"I remember her," Guy said.

"She's in the chorus," Paul told him. "But she's got a couple of solo spots. And she can get us into the first-night party afterwards."

That decided it. Jack, Paul, Jane, Torin and Guy put on their most stylish, which was to say their least crumpled, clothes and went to the opening performance of *Dunkirk!*. The poster for the show ("Five days in May that changed the world") showed, curiously, a poppy floating on the surface of the sea, suggesting that the producers might only have a fleeting acquaintance-ship with historical iconography. This was confirmed by an early sighting of Kate in the first act, dancing as a nurse during the Blitz, which, according to the libretto, had come before the evacuation of the British Expeditionary Force. She was spotted a second time in Act Two, hiding behind a fisherman's jersey and beard and also in the final reprise of "With A Stiff Upper Lip And A Song In Your Heart" during which the miracle of Dunkirk was depicted on stage, the little boats never having been littler as the director attempted to reproduce the first great turning-point of the Second World War using puppets.

The party was at a nightclub just down the road and was filled with Norwegian businessmen, who were the show's backers and who (as was often the case) still had no idea just how dreadful it was and how quickly they were going to lose all their money. Guy and the others had enjoyed every minute of *Dunkirk!*, watching with a disbelief that became ever more hilarious as it went on. By the end, they were sucking in their cheeks to hold back the laughter and they said nothing at the party, afraid even to meet each other's eye. There was a certain etiquette involved with first nights. Nobody asked you what you thought and if they did you certainly didn't tell them. You were, after all, eating their food and drinking their wine. You could leave the excoriation to the critics next day.

Guy was on his third or fourth glass when Kate arrived, glowing with excitement, unable to suppress the pleasure of being at her own first-night party. She was looking even more beautiful than he remembered and he had to admit that, despite the almost total lack of merit in *Dunkirk!*, she was still a working actress,

28

and in the West End, even if that wasn't likely to last too long. He'd only got five lines in a soap so far. He was in no position to sniff.

And then suddenly the two of them were face to face and he had drunk a couple more glasses of wine and so had she because she was challenging him with those amazing blue eyes that seemed to have a touch of humour he couldn't remember seeing before.

"What did you think of *Dunkirk!*?" she asked, sweetly.

Guy considered. "By and large I'd say that the British forces were incredibly lucky that Hitler decided not to advance his tanks and heavy artillery," he said.

"I meant the musical."

"It was great."

"Tell me the truth."

"Well, coincidentally, I had a great-uncle who lost both his legs at Dunkirk."

"And . . .?"

"I'd say he got off more lightly than the audience."

She laughed, and when the party ended at about three in the morning they shared a taxi home. It turned out they were living quite close to each other in almost identically depressing rooms in Kensal Green. Guy ended up spending the night with her, and six weeks later they upgraded to a shared top-floor flat. *Dunkirk!* closed on the day that the first month's rent became due.

It was incredible, really, that they had stayed together as long as they had. Actors in long-term relationships play a complicated game of leapfrog where you can never be sure who's going to be the one up and running and who's going to be bending over with their arse in the air. When Kate had been in *Dunkirk!*, Guy had been out of work. That changed a few months later when he landed his first good role in a long-running television series. They spent their life congratulating or commiserating with each other. When they were both in work, it just came down to who had the most lines.

In fact, a graph showing their joint progress over three years would have looked like two intertwining snakes. Their employment was fairly steady if unspectacular and as their twenties slipped gently by they found themselves resembling more and more an ordinary married couple, although with more sex and fewer arguments. Sometimes it troubled them that they were becoming boring, but they had to agree that it was happening in a perfectly pleasant way. They talked about children. And when interest rates were low enough, they stuck their necks out and took a mortgage on a flat in Muswell Hill.

Guy remembered how uneasy Kate had been about the whole thing: the mortgage, the insurance forms, the removal van, the journeys to Ikea, the bottle of champagne with the compliments of the building society that had arranged the mortgage. She never said anything and they never discussed it but even on that first night, having sex surrounded by a bed that Guy hadn't yet assembled, she was awkward, not entirely herself, and he was relieved that she was currently working, even if it was only a corporate video, a training film for the NHS.

And it was about a week later that Martin Mayhew, who had been his best friend at Clairemont, struck gold with a fringe play about police corruption. It had a new writer, a hot director and a really quite surprising amount of buggery, and the critics went ballistic. Suddenly Martin was on TV and in the papers. The same Martin who had picked his nose and never changed his sheets. But now he was well dressed, well groomed and articulate. Suddenly he was a star.

Cut back to the present.

"Martin, you're a shit," Guy muttered, as he opened the fridge, sniffed the milk and dumped it in the sink. The milk came out in a watery rush followed by a solid lump, like something out of a fifties science-fiction film. He realised he was going to have to be careful. His life was already sad: it was on the edge of becoming squalid. He took out a jar of Coffee-Mate, mixed a spoonful with water and poured it over his cereal. It didn't make him feel any better.

Could he really blame Kate for leaving him, he wondered. She had gone for her share of what they had both set out to achieve. Not fame and wealth — although both were always welcome — but excitement, adventure, the unknown. After all the insecurity and the anxiety, not to mention the boredom of an actor's life, just getting a job isn't enough. And when it is, perhaps that's the time to do something else.

It was nine o'clock. Dressed in leathers and carrying his motorbike helmet, Guy left the house. As he closed the door he noticed the flicker of net curtains over the window next to the front door and knew without looking that Mrs Atwood had been waiting for him to go.

That was the other thing about his flat. It was on the first floor, sandwiched between two neighbours who seemed to vie with each other to see who could make him feel more unwelcome. The top floor was taken by a man who worked for some sort of charity and who was otherwise unremarkable apart from the fact that he was four feet tall. In the twenty-first century it was inappropriate to call him a dwarf but that was what he undoubtedly was. Guy knew very little about him, although when they passed in the doorway or on the stairs he seemed unusually bad-tempered and unfriendly. He and Kate referred to him as Grumpy although his name was actually Johnny Peters. He was on his own. When he was in, he was very quiet. But most of the time he seemed to be out.

Mrs Atwood had the ground floor. She was also single and had been living in the house for more than twenty years. She had been there before it was converted. She had been married then, but nobody knew anything about Mr Atwood. She was a plain, dumpy woman with a grudge against Guy, a grudge against Johnny Peters, in fact a grudge against life. She was always spying on them. Mrs Atwood had taken Neighbourhood Watch as far as it could go. A leaf couldn't fall, a letter couldn't arrive, without her taking note.

This was the household that Guy left behind him as he walked over to his bike and sat for a moment, breathing in the air. It was the end of May, and what felt like ten months of winter, of drizzle and grey skies, had finally stepped aside to allow in a touch of late spring and early summer. There were no maple trees in Mapletree Close. The name had actually come from the Victorian civic engineer who had built the undistinguished row of terraced houses. Nor was it even a close any more. One of the houses had been bulldozed back in the sixties and the road continued through to Poplar Drive. But it was a beautiful day and Guy could smell the blossom wafting down from Muswell Hill. Perhaps everything was going to be all right after all.

It wasn't.

An hour later he found himself at Borehamwood, sitting in a square, empty office, face to face with Nigel Jones, director of *The Thirty-nine Steps*.

"For God's sake, what have you done to yourself?" Nigel was about fifty years old, wearing a puffa jacket with so many pockets that by the time he had found anything he invariably had no further need for it. Like every British television director, he was fighting against an absurd budget, an impossible schedule and a crew that was permanently on the edge of mutiny. He looked as if he hadn't slept for a week.

"Someone hit me," Guy explained.

"Where? Why?"

"In a pub. They were drunk."

Nigel stared at him in horror. "Guy, I don't know what to say to you. I mean, I can't possibly shoot you looking like that. You must know that. I don't know why you even bothered showing up."

"I thought you'd be able to do something with makeup."

"Makeup? You don't need makeup. You need a sack. I mean, for fuck's sake! You look like the Elephant Man." Nigel grimaced. Guy had been unable to wipe away the congealed blood without making his nose bleed again. He felt as if a cork was coming out of his left nostril. "Jesus Christ! We've got the dinner scene this afternoon. We've got everyone on standby . . ." He turned to the production manager, who had been sitting with him when Guy came in. "Is this an insurance claim?"

The production manager shook her head.

"Well, what am I supposed to do?"

"I'll look at the schedule."

Nigel turned back to Guy. "You might as well fuck off home. There's nothing I can do."

"I'm sorry," Guy said.

"So you bloody well should be." Nigel shuffled out of the room. The production manager was already head-down in a pile of photocopied sheets. She had been friendly to Guy when he had first come on to the set. She had even got him a trailer with a washbasin and its own plug. Now she didn't want to know.

That afternoon he went to Notting Hill Gate to see Sylvie.

The office was a few minutes' walk from the station, over a shop selling second-hand books. Guy rang the bell and climbed a single flight of stairs so narrow that he almost had to go up sideways. The steps were, he realised, intensely theatrical . . . just as the door at the top looked like a prop from a play. The door led directly into an office that was like no office at all, with oversized sofas, unwashed glasses, red velvet curtains and — on the edge of incongruous — a large chandelier. And there was Sylvie Graham, sitting behind her antique desk, pretending (surely) to be studying contracts through her half-moon spectacles with a ginger cat asleep on her knees.

"Guy, my dear!" He had telephoned ahead, of course. Nobody came here without asking first. She seemed pleased to see him. "Come and sit down and tell me what happened. Eric!" She called out the name and a second later another door opened and a small, bald-headed man with a moustache and a terrible, tight-fitting, pastel-coloured jersey looked in. "Look who's here!" she said.

"Guy Fletcher." Eric always announced every visitor. It was part of the opening ritual. In case Sylvie had forgotten their name.

"Let's have some tea."

Sylvie Graham had been Guy's agent ever since he had left the Clairemont. She was a round, motherly woman with unruly grey hair and an always benevolent face. She had represented at least a dozen actors who had gone on to become household names, but she had one problem: whenever anybody became famous, they immediately dumped her. Sylvie belonged to the Peggy Ramsay school of agents, an elegant, old-fashioned school that had long been superseded by a new breed of quietly spoken young men and women with Armani suits and hands-free phones connected to the side of their head. She was a name but no longer an influential one, and it was well known that the clients on her books were either starting out or frankly washed up. Sylvie's furnishings spoke of the Palladium, of Gielgud and Olivier, of nights — and knights — at the Garrick club. Ambitious actors preferred grey partition walls and doors that might open to Hollywood.

In her sixties, she still acted the part, dressing extravagantly and drinking white wine from ten o'clock in the morning until well into the night. It was rumoured that she had been an actress herself but that a performance of hers had been so savaged by the critics that she had never acted again. She had been married four times. Two of her husbands had died. Two of them she had divorced. She kept photographs of them all (three in black-and-white, the most recent in colour) in heavy silver frames. She was now single but had a close, rather impenetrable relationship with her assistant, Eric.

Eric had his own office on the other side of the door. It was little bigger than a cupboard . . . Indeed, he had once told Guy that it *was* a cupboard that Sylvie had converted for him, and Guy didn't think he was joking. With Eric you could never be sure. The two of them — Eric and Sylvie — had worked together for thirty-five years.

"You poor thing!" she exclaimed, after Guy had told her what had happened. She rattled the porcelain, searching for the sugar tongs. She must have been the only person in London who still had sugar tongs. "I never go to public houses myself. I can't stand them. You should join a club. Groucho's or Century. They're almost as bad. In fact, now I come to think of it, Groucho's is perfectly horrible. But at least if you get punched it may be by somebody important."

"Have you spoken to Nigel?"

"Yes. He rang me just after you did." She dropped three lumps of sugar into her tea, using the tongs, one lump at a time. "I'm afraid it's not good news. They've decided to recast. It doesn't make any sense but that's the way they want to play it. They've got somebody else in for the dinner scene and they're going to reshoot the stuff they've already done." Guy's face fell. "Don't worry about it, dear. Nigel's just having a fit of pique. But it'll blow over and — you'll see — he'll hire you again because he thinks you're good and because he fancies you. Don't look at me that way! You know it's true. He said he wanted the fee back but I told him to get stuffed. It wasn't as if it was your fault."

"Well . . ."

"Let's not discuss it because, if I might be just a little bit frank with you, you might need to hang on to the money. The BBC's not going to be too pleased with you at the moment and there's not an awful lot around. Anyway, looking at you, I'd say it's probably going to be a couple of weeks before you're handsome again."

"What about radio?"

"Radio's a club and I'm afraid you're not a member of it. We have tried — but I think we both agreed you're not very good at it. You don't have a radio voice." She sighed. "What was it that got you so upset in the first place? You said it was something to do with a joke."

"It was a joke about Selina Moore."

"Oh." She stopped, the teacup half-way to her lips. "Was it a very horrible joke?" she asked.

He told her the joke. Even as he spoke, he realised he wasn't actually telling it. He was relating it. There was a difference.

There was a pause and she nodded. "It's not very funny," she said. "But is it really so offensive?"

"I don't know. I'd had a couple of drinks. Maybe I overreacted." Guy considered, and suddenly a thought tumbled out of nowhere and slipped into his mind. "I wonder who invented that joke," he said. He had spoken the words simultaneously, at the exact moment the thought had arrived. But now he found himself continuing: "Where do you think jokes come from?"

"I'm sorry?"

"Jokes. Where do they come from?"

Sylvie shrugged. "I suppose they come from television, don't they?"

"Well, some of them might. But not that joke about Selina. Somebody must have sat down and worked it out."

Sylvie's eyes narrowed over her cup. Her lips were pursed. "Not necessarily . . ."

"Somebody must have! Think about it, Sylvie. Why is Selina Moore like a Ferrero Rocher? It would have to take a pretty twisted mind to put those two together. A really great actress and a fucking chocolate!"

38

"I seem to remember you liked the chocolates well enough when they were paying your rent."

"That's not the point. I'm just saying . . . somebody must have thought it up. That's all. There must have been somebody who actually invented it."

"But why?"

"I don't know. But it might be interesting to find out."

Sylvie looked at him doubtfully. "Darling, you've only been out of work a few hours. You're not setting off on another of your flights of fancy. Are you?"

"What are you talking about?"

"You know perfectly well what I'm talking about. The lottery, wasn't it?" She corrected herself. "Premium Bonds."

"That wasn't a flight of fancy. It was an idea for a radio play."

"A radio play that you never wrote."

"This is different, Sylvie. Come on! You know about Selina. You know how I felt about her."

"Well, of course. She was your mother."

And there it was. As simple as that.

His mother.

Guy hadn't found out until he was eighteen. He knew he was adopted. His foster-parents had never made any secret of it. His foster-father, Alistair Fletcher, was a chartered accountant and was unable to have children . . . something he blamed on his work: he had been doing the annual returns at Sellafield nuclear power station. Guy had decided to find out the truth about his background at about the same time that he had decided to be an actor and, with the new legislation, it hadn't been difficult.

Selina Moore! The two words on a typewritten form in a North London register office had, in a single second, made sense of his life. Sylvie was one of the very few people who knew the truth. He had told her because he had thought it would impress her and had immediately regretted it. He had told his foster-parents — who had been strangely unimpressed — but no one else.

"You know, Sylvie," he said, "when I was a kid, going home from school, sometimes I'd go past a film set. And I couldn't stop myself staring. I'd sit on the top deck of the bus and I'd press my face to the window, looking at the trailers and the lights and all the rest of it . . . and somehow I knew I had to be there. I started going to the theatre when I was fourteen. All my mates were going to football matches. I preferred Shakespeare."

"It was in your blood."

"She made me what I am. Literally. And I never even met her."

"You should have written to her, Guy. She was only on the other side of London. Henley or somewhere."

"Marlow." Guy had read dozens of newspaper and magazine articles about Selina, including a fawning piece in *Hello!* magazine, following her whirlwind romance with the Bishop of Rochester. "I was going to write to her," he said. "I started lots of letters. But I was too scared to post them."

"Scared?"

"Scared of being rejected. I mean, she'd already rejected me once ... when I was too young to understand why. I suppose I was scared of being rejected a second time. And now it's too late. Selina's come out of France in a box."

Sylvie frowned. "The important thing is not to get depressed," she said. "This business with Nigel is unfortunate but it's not the end of the world. Why don't you drop him a line to apologise? A bit of brown-nosing never hurts. In the meantime, I'll have a call-round and see if there's anything going. Just let me know as soon as you're presentable and, for Heaven's sake, try to avoid builders and bars!"

Later that afternoon, Guy found himself sitting back at the flat with a tube of Jaffa Cakes. Now, there was a conspiracy every bit as sinister as the Premium Bonds. Ten years ago, the orange jelly on a Jaffa Cake had stretched, definitely, right across the sponge. But every year it seemed to shrink another millimetre, like an oasis drying up in the desert. The chocolate was getting thinner too. The manufacturers were obviously doing it on purpose, cheating the public and hoping nobody would notice — but how far were they prepared to go? And thinking it through, how long would it be before there was no orange and no chocolate at all? Could it happen that, one day in the far future, they would be able to get away with selling an empty tube?

Despite all this, he knew he was going to have to guzzle his way through the lot. Once you began, you could never stop. There was something about the experience of eating a Jaffa Cake that made resistance futile. Outside, the sun was still shining. Guy's thoughts were fractured. He wanted to think about Nigel Jones and the letter he was supposed to write. But he couldn't get the joke out of his mind.

Why is Selina Moore like a Ferrero Rocher?

He remembered seeing her in *The Devil's Disciple*, her last theatrical outing before her retirement. It was a tedious play, even by Shaw's high standards, but he had spent more than twenty pounds on a seat in the front row. It was the nearest he would ever get to her. She was playing Mrs Dudgeon, all greys and blacks, but he could see through all that, through the character to the flesh and blood. He remembered her eyes (the same colour as his), the way she moved across the stage. He had wanted, right then, to reach out to her, to take hold of her. His adoptive mother had always been a good woman and a kind woman but she had never been very physical, as if holding Guy had reminded her that he would always be alien to her. She had been a peck-on-the-cheek sort of mother. But this woman, barely a metre away from him, was the real thing.

Everyone at Clairemont agreed. Selina Moore had undoubtedly been a beautiful person in every sense. Only a few of her films had been an embarrassment, she hadn't cried at the Oscar ceremonies, and she had led a blameless private life, the only tabloid sensation being her late marriage and sudden retirement. Her death had been on *News at Ten* and — the ultimate accolade — had been followed by a repeat of one of her old films, hastily fitted into the schedule. Guy wished he had been able to go to her funeral. He should have been there. He had never been part of her life. Surely they could have found room for him at her death.

And what sort of person — still he found himself asking the same question — could have found something funny in her dying? What sort of person could have found something amusing in the notion of a wonderful actress, a major international star, a mother, falling out of the sky on her way to a well-earned holiday in the south of France? The pilot and four other passengers had died with her. And then there were the children, for Heaven's sake! There were flags flying at half-mast all over France. The French president had cancelled his Easter holiday.

And yet somebody, somewhere had sat down and read the story on the front page of their newspaper and their response had been to make up a joke.

Guy made himself another coffee and ate the last two Jaffa Cakes. He wanted to do other things but he couldn't get it out of his mind. It wasn't just the sickness of the joke, finding humour in death. He could understand that well enough. It was the perversity of it, the equation of the actress, dead and in her coffin, with the luxury chocolate. Who had done it first? he kept asking himself. Who had come up with that particular twist?

Was there some fat kid in an attic who had seen the news on television? Had he been eating a Ferrero Rocher at the time? Had he somehow made the connection and come stamping downstairs to tell his mother? The mother could have told her husband. And he could have been the foreman or the crane operator on the building site where the men at the Cat and Fiddle had been working. Maybe it had happened like that.

The telephone rang. Guy hoped for a moment that it might be Sylvie. Whenever the telephone rang, he hoped it was Sylvie. In fact it was Kate.

"Guy?" She sounded embarrassed. He wondered if she was calling him from Martin's flat. "I thought you were filming today."

"I was. It got cancelled."

"Well, you see . . . the thing is, I wanted to come and collect some of my stuff."

There goes the toaster, Guy thought. He heard the wail of an ambulance on the line. Of course she wasn't in Martin's flat. She was in his car — probably a brand new BMW, damn him. She was on her mobile, on her way over now. And if he hadn't been there, what would she have done?

"Where are you?" he asked.

"I'm driving over."

So he had been right. "You thought I wasn't here," he said. "You were just going to drop in and help yourself to whatever you wanted."

There was a brief pause. "I was only going to take a few things that were mine."

He felt the rising anger but he forced it back down again. He'd always been a soft touch, he knew. At the same time, what right did he have to stop her? They'd had fun together. The sex had been good. Why spoil it all now?

44

"I'm just going out," he said. "I won't be back until six."

"Right."

"Are you OK, Kate? I mean . . ."

"Yes. I'm OK. How are you?"

"I'm all right. But I miss you."

God! Guy had heard this somewhere before. He had spoken exactly the same lines a year ago, recording the one play he'd ever done on the radio, something for BBC Radio 4. A Second World War drama. Sylvie had been right about his voice talents. A few seconds later a bomb had fallen on his character.

"What was that?" Kate asked.

"I can't hear you," he said. "You're breaking up."

"Guy?"

"Take what you want. 'Bye."

He rang off and went out.

He meant to go to the cinema. He had noticed that Truffaut's masterpiece, *Day for Night*, was showing at the Curzon. He had always loved that film, the way it invested movie people with such tenderness and humanity. He could have sat in the darkness and lost himself in the illusion of it all.

Instead he went back to the Cat and Fiddle.

CHAPTER
FIVE

The Cat and Fiddle looked even more dilapidated in the middle of the afternoon. Like most of Finsbury Park, sunshine only showed it at its worst. It had done its best to keep the daylight out, with small, ill-placed windows and dirty panes, but the light had stolen in anyway and showed up the faded decoration, the general dirt and stickiness. There was now only a handful of people drinking and smoking but they included the thin man and the woman with red lips who had been playing the fruit machine the night before. Nobody was talking, as if they were too ashamed to be there during working hours. The juke-box was silent. The bald barman was nowhere to be seen.

Guy went over to the bar and perched on a stool. Its unwashed, plastic surface clung tackily to the fabric of his trousers. A girl came over to him. She was about eighteen, drab, with peroxide hair and a bored face. He wondered how long it had been since she had left school. To look at her, you might wonder if she had ever gone at all. Guy ordered a lime and soda and a packet of crisps.

"Cheese and onion, beef and tomato, smoky bacon, chicken or plain?" she asked.

"Plain."

She nodded, as if that had really been the only sensible choice.

"I wonder if you can help me," he said, when she brought him his change.

"What do you want?"

"Do you know the barman who works here? He was here last night at about ten o'clock? Aged about fifty. Not much hair. He was wearing a brown suit."

She shrugged. "No," she said.

Guy persisted: "The thing is, you see, I'm trying to track down three men who were here. They were builders by the look of them. About my age. I got the feeling that they were regulars."

"Regular what?" she asked.

Guy gave up, already feeling a little foolish. He sipped the lime and soda, which had been served so warm that the few slivers of ice in the glass had already melted. It had been a mistake coming here. He would finish the drink and leave. But then the woman with the lipstick spoke: "They was the ones that nutted you."

"That's right." Guy turned to examine her, noticing for the first time how infinitely sad she looked, like a princess out of a fairy story, transformed into an old crone and forced to drink lager-shandy in Finsbury Park for eternity. Her face was withered. Her eyes were bright and black, like steel bearings.

"What do you want to see them for?" she asked.

"Well ... I ..." Guy faltered. "It's difficult to explain."

Why did he want to see them?

He wanted to ask them where they had heard the joke. That was why he had come here. But even assuming he could persuade them to tell him, what good would it do him? They would probably have heard it from someone else on whatever building site employed them. So what would he do, then? Go and ask the person who had told them the joke where *he* had heard the joke and then follow it back all the way along the line until he finally arrived at the fat boy in the attic, or whoever it might be?

Yes, he realised. That was exactly the idea.

Could it be done? Guy couldn't see why not. It was like the play he had once seen — *Six Degrees of Separation*. Everyone was connected to everyone else in the world . . . you could get to the Pope with just six links. What he had here was exactly the same thing but with a lifeline, an invisible thread. Jokes. Of course, it wouldn't be easy. The workmen might have heard the joke from the foreman who might have had it from a relative in southern Iraq. Good old Uncle Abdullah and his laughing camel. What would Guy do then?

But he might as well try. It might be as productive as searching for the end of a rainbow or the last figure in *pi*, but doing it would fulfil a need, a longing he couldn't quite define. He would start out, and see how far it took him. It probably wouldn't take him anywhere at all.

The old lady was squinting at him. "I know you, don't I?"

This was something that happened occasionally and always brought with it a sense of pleasure, which he felt duty-bound to hide. "You may have seen me on TV," he said.

"Do you read the news?"

"No. I'm an actor."

"Oh." She was unimpressed. "What have you been in?"

"I was in *Policemen's Wives*." That had been his last broadcast appearance.

"I've seen that! I like that!" She examined him, then shook her head doubtfully. "I don't remember you, though. Were you a copper?"

"No. As a matter of fact, I got beaten up." It was true, now that he thought about it. The TV makeup department had done almost as good a job as the men he had met the night before.

That brought the old woman back to the subject. "I wouldn't go looking for them if I was you, dear," she said. "I don't think they'd want to see you again."

"Do you know them?" Guy asked.

She fell silent.

"I only wanted . . ." He didn't know what he was going to say to her but suddenly he had a brainwave. "I wanted to apologise to them. I was a bloody fool last night. I spoiled their evening."

"They certainly spoiled yours. That's a horrible black eye you've got."

"I thought I should offer them a drink."

"Do you want to offer me one?"

Guy swallowed. The woman was eyeing him most peculiarly. "Certainly," he said. "What would you like?"

"I'll have a whisky mac."

"Right."

He ordered and paid for it. There seemed to be a sort of complicity between the old woman and the bar girl, who winked as she slid the drink over.

The woman's name was Mrs Lovejoy. As she told Guy this, she gave a little kiss of a smile. "I don't often get bought drinks," she said. "I used to, though. I came here when this place was first opened. I was married then, but everyone used to buy me drinks. It wasn't the Cat and Fiddle either. It was the Crown. It had real class." She nodded. "I was in the same business as you."

"You were an actress?"

"I worked down at the Regal. I used to sell refreshments. Butterkist popcorn. They don't make popcorn like that any more. And Kia-Ora. Do you remember Kia-Ora? It was lovely. I loved it there. All those wonderful films. Burt Lancaster! Steve McQueen! That was when men were men and you didn't have all these homosexuals and pretty boys and God knows what! Some of these young people you see on the screen! I can't tell whether they're boys or girls. And they can't act. Not what I call acting, anyway." She sighed. "I used to see all the films. I'd turn the light off on my little tray and I'd sit at the back. I had my own seat. Sometimes I'd see the same film seven times! But I was never bored. And then one day they knocked it into a bingo hall. I don't know why they did that. I suppose people weren't coming. But they didn't come to bingo either. And bingo! That was nothing. It was all just numbers. It was a complete waste of time. They've demolished it now. The whole building. Sometimes, when I'm out doing my shopping, I can't even remember where it was."

"About the men who were here . . ." Guy tried.

But Mrs Lovejoy was having none of it. "Everything's changed," she went on. "Even this place. The Cat and Fiddle. It used to be called the Crown. That was when it was run by Les Farleigh. He was a real gentleman. But then he got cancer and that was the end of him. And he wasn't even a smoker. I've been smoking twenty a day since I was this high and I'm as fit as a fiddle." She sounded almost disappointed. "My father was bombed in the war, blown out of the kitchen. But you'd have been amazed how people helped. That was when neighbours were neighbours."

"You knew the men who were here last night," Guy tried again. Now that Mrs Lovejoy had started talking, it seemed she wouldn't stop. She probably lived on her own. He felt sorry for her.

Mrs Lovejoy emptied her glass in one gulp. "Of course, there weren't so many blacks then," she announced suddenly, and Guy felt his stomach heave. He didn't feel sorry for her any more. "These days, I sometimes feel like I'm living in a foreign country."

"Please, Mrs Lovejoy —"

"It's all right, dear. I know. You're not allowed to say it, are you? I hate the way they try to stop you saying things, this government. They want to control what you think, but they can't do it, can they? They can't stop you thinking things, even if you're not allowed to say them. Do you want another drink?"

"No. I'm fine, thank you."

"I'll have the same again."

Guy ordered it reluctantly.

Mrs Lovejoy took out a cigarette and lit it. Her fingers were as withered as her face. The knuckles were swollen and ancient. Lighting the cigarette caused her pain. Guy could see it. She blew out the match. "Ron Meadows," she said.

"I'm sorry?"

"He comes here most nights. He was the one who hit you. I know his mum. She works three days at Budgen's. Ron's her oldest boy. He's a nice lad."

"Yes, he was very charming," Guy agreed.

"You sure you're not out to make trouble?"

"No. Really."

"The other two are Dave Brown and Sam . . . I don't know his other name. He's the youngest. You'll find them on the Seven Sisters Road. Just on the corner after the bridge. There's a house they've been doing up. It feels like they've been there seven years!"

The woman laughed. It was strange how the years fell away from her at that moment, how the old crone gave way to the princess. "Seven years," she said. "On the Seven Sisters Road."

Was this how jokes began, with a grotesque old woman playing with words after too many whisky macs?

Guy already knew this was a mistake. But he set off anyway.

CHAPTER
SIX

It was a three-storey town-house, narrow and a little lopsided, wedged between a launderette and an undertaker. It was surrounded by scaffolding that reached all the way to where the roof should have been. Someone had begun converting the attic but at the moment there was just a gaping hole, half covered with plastic. Broken fittings and bare wires sprouted out of the walls. Builders' detritus spilled onto the street. A wheelbarrow lay on its side next to a half-filled skip. The front door was ajar but there was no sound of any activity coming from inside. Guy tried to look through a window but the glass was coated with dust. If he wanted to find the men, he would have to go inside.

It seemed like a very bad idea, walking into this semi-derelict building, out of the safety of the street. Guy had a vivid imagination, particularly where physical harm was involved. He had a pain threshold so low that if it entered a limbo-dancing competition it would easily win — and he could already see himself in Casualty with multiple stab wounds from a Black and Decker all-purpose drill or lying in the gutter waiting for an ambulance big enough to accommodate both him and the ten-metre length of scaffolding sticking out of his back. Would his next television appearance be on *999*, the series that re-created grotesque and improbable accidents for a mid-week audience? These builders were violent people. They had already proved as much. He doubted they would be happy to see him.

And yet, at the same time, he was in control of the situation. That is, if he talked to them, he could make sure that he was standing next to an open door. And he'd come here to apologise, hadn't he? With a bit of luck, the builders might even be charmed. He had walked quite a long way down from the pub. He might as well go in. And surely Ron Meadows wasn't going to commit murder on somebody else's property, not if it meant getting blood on the new plasterwork.

He took a deep breath and opened the door.

The house was a mess. It was hard to tell whether it was being pulled down or erected. The corridors were lined with plasterboard, the floors an arrangement of loose wooden planks with gaps everywhere exposing a network of pipes that didn't seem at all connected. Light switches hung out of the walls on a tangle of red, blue and brown wires. The building had electricity. Naked bulbs, hanging at odd angles, lit the way forward. What it didn't have, though, was a way forward. A line of scaffolding, supporting the ceiling, blocked the passageway. There was a staircase, but it was covered with debris, impossible to climb. There was so much cement dust in the air that when Guy breathed in he could feel it clinging to his lips.

He went through a doorway with no door and into a room where the wreck of a fireplace slumped out of a

54

hole in the wall. Another jagged gap led into the kitchen, which, at least, was in a better state of repair. In fact, it was the only operational room in the house. It was where the men took their tea-breaks. He could hear them now, the three of them from the Cat and Fiddle. Trying not to make any noise, Guy went over to the gap and looked through. There they were, sitting on upturned crates, dunking digestive biscuits into mugs of tea and smoking. An incredibly dusty radio was spitting out the traffic news. Just looking at the three of them, Guy knew that his first thoughts had been quite correct and that coming here had been a mistake. They weren't going to tell him anything. If they even saw him again they would probably give him a good kicking.

But no harm had been done. At least it wasn't too late to change his mind.

Guy turned to leave and the sleeve of his jacket brushed against a loose nail, lying on a plank. He caught his breath. That had been close! Any noise, and the three workmen might have discovered him. The nail rolled to the end of the plank and dropped into the air. Guy reached forward to catch it and his sleeve caught a second plank, unbalancing it. The plank shot up. Its far end hit a pile of paint cans, which clattered explosively to the floor. At the same time another dozen planks, all cunningly interlaced with the first two, came crashing down bringing with them scaffolding, wires and plaster. When the dust settled and Guy opened his eyes again, the workmen were standing in the gap, staring at him with a look of surprise that was rapidly turning to disgust.

Ron, the head-butter, was the first to speak. "What the fuck?" he demanded.

The second man — Dave — had been rolling a cigarette. He licked the paper and closed it up. "Fuck!" he said.

The boy with the earring said nothing.

"Hello!" Guy said.

The three of them had stood up, forgetting their tea. Guy felt a bit like Clint Eastwood in *For a Few Dollars More* — but without the gun or the courage. He noticed that a Stanley knife had appeared in Ron's hand. From the look of the house, it was the only tool he had handled in recent weeks.

"I expect you're wondering why I'm here," Guy said.

"Too fucking right," Ron agreed.

Guy searched desperately for a good reason. "Well, the thing is, you see," he said, "I felt I ought to apologise."

"You what?"

"For last night. When I woke up this morning, I realised I'd made a fool of myself. Talking the way I did last night . . . I was completely out of order. So I thought I'd come and say I was sorry . . ."

The three men stared at him incredulously.

". . . and offer you all a drink to make up for it."

There was a long silence.

"Are you taking the piss?" Ron asked, as hostile as ever, if not fractionally more so.

"No, no! Not at all. That business with the joke, I must have had too much to drink." He was burbling now. "Selina Moore was somebody I knew so I was a bit thrown but, actually, now I think about it, it was quite a funny joke. I'd love to know who told it to you. Just out of interest."

"This is private property," Dave said, speaking very deliberately. "Why don't you piss off out of here before my mate sticks that knife right up your public-school arse?"

"Grammar-school arse," Guy corrected him. Keeping his eye on the Stanley knife, he began to back out of the room, nodding and smiling as if he had just finished an unusually cheerful and intimate audience with the Queen. There was a movement behind him and he groaned inwardly. It seemed that someone else had arrived. His escape route was blocked.

But the newcomer wasn't another builder. He was a middle-aged man with floppy grey hair and a long face. He was carrying a leather attaché case and a copy of *Metro*, the newspaper given away free on the London Underground. He had brushed into a wall and there was plaster dust on the arm and shoulder of his expensive suit. "What's going on?" he asked.

"Not very much, Mr Cooper." The atmosphere in the room had quickly changed. The three builders had become if not more friendly then more ingratiating. Guy guessed that this must be the owner of the house. While he was there, at least there would be no bloodshed.

Cooper turned to Guy. "Who are you?" he asked.

"I'm nobody," Guy said. "At least, I know . . . Ron and Dave and . . . Sam. We all met at the pub and I just looked in to say hello."

But Cooper wasn't interested. "So, is the central heating in, then?" he asked, a faint crack of desperation in his voice.

Ron Meadows shook his head. "I'm afraid not, Mr C. It's these small-gauge pipes you've chosen. We're still waiting for a part that's got to come in from Scandinavia. It should be here Thursday. With a bit of luck we should have it done by the end of next week."

"And the wiring?"

"The electrician's not feeling any better."

"The plumbing?"

"No point getting the plumber in until the electrician's had a chance to look round. Just trying to save you money."

"Have you managed to do anything?"

"We've knocked through upstairs. And the windows have arrived."

Cooper grinned feverishly, clutching at straws. "That's good!"

"Not so good, I'm afraid. They're the wrong size."

"What?"

"They got the wrong measurements."

"But didn't you send them the measurements?"

Ron Meadows looked slightly offended. "I sent them the measurements, Mr Cooper, and they was the right measurements. But they're saying they was the wrong measurements."

"They would say that," one of the others muttered.

"But you said they were reliable!"

"They are reliable. Nine times out of ten. I been on the phone to them but . . ." He shook his head. "We're going to have to recut the frames. It shouldn't hold us up too long." His eyes brightened. "We've done the tanking."

"You did that last week."

"Oh."

Cooper stood there, his shoulders suddenly limp. The suit and the newspaper made him look cartoonish. Like something out of one of those old Ealing films. "This is all a bit of a joke, isn't it?" he said, in a helpless voice.

"We'll get there, Mr C. You've always got to expect the odd hiccup or two. We'll get there in the end."

"Yes. Yes . . ." His voice trailed away. The three builders looked at him sadly. "Well, I just thought I'd look in," he said.

"Nice to see you, Mr Cooper."

Cooper shuffled out of the room. Guy followed, keeping close. And that's the end of the fat boy in the attic, he thought. He would never find out now where the joke had come from.

The two of them stood together in the street. Cooper put down his case and took out a packet of cigarettes. He lit one. "Four months," he said. "When I bought the house, that's how long they said it would take."

"When was that?" Guy asked.

"A year and a half ago. There's always something. Things don't arrive. They're the wrong size. They're sick."

"Why do you stick with them?" Guy asked.

"I paid them a deposit."

"Up front?"

"Twenty per cent. In cash. I must have been out of my bloody mind." Cooper began to walk away, pulling his briefcase along with him. He was heading back towards Finsbury Park. Guy found himself walking in step with him. "They were recommended," Cooper went on. He sounded amazed. "I have a friend who's an architect. *Had* a friend who's an architect. The bastard! I keep thinking I ought to get rid of them and start again but they've done so much damage now that it would cost twice as much to get someone else and, anyway, all builders are the same. They just take the piss. I sometimes think they'll be there for ever. I sometimes think . . ." He shook his head. Some things were better left unsaid.

"I'm sorry."

"It's funny, isn't it? How things go. You make one telephone call. It doesn't seem to mean a lot. You're choosing Bloggs Brothers or Smith and Son. And you don't know at the time you might be ruining your life." He stopped, aware that he had said too much. He examined Guy, noticing his injuries for the first time. "What happened to you?" he asked.

"One of your builders hit me."

"Ah." He didn't seem surprised. He was almost amused. "Well, they're not very nice people. I have spent time with them, God help me. I've been down the pub, tried to jolly them along. Buy a round of drinks, swap a few jokes. That sort of thing. I thought I could get them on my side but it didn't make a jot of difference. What always gets me is that they have a reason for everything. The pipes are too small. The

60

doors are too big. They can't get the parts. If I ran my business like that . . ."

But Guy was no longer listening. "Jokes?" he said.

"What about them?"

"Well, nothing, really. It's just that . . . I'd be interested to know. You didn't tell them a joke about Selina Moore, did you?"

"The actress?"

"Yes."

"Why do you ask?"

"No reason." There was a troubled silence. "I thought it was a very good joke," Guy lied, trying to reassure him.

Cooper was evidently puzzled, wondering what Guy was getting at. But he thought about it, saw no harm and answered, "Yes, I suppose that was me. I bumped into Ron a few days ago. Bought him a drink. He likes jokes, so I told him a couple and that was one of them."

Cooper had stopped walking. He took out a set of car keys and pressed the fob. There was an electronic bleep from a Saab parked on a yellow line. Guy realised they were about to part. That they would never meet again.

"I wonder," he said, "just out of interest, you don't remember who told you?"

CHAPTER
SEVEN

Cooper had heard the joke from his dentist, a man called Silberman who had a surgery in East Finchley, not far from Muswell Hill. Guy rang him and discovered that his wife worked as his receptionist and that both of them were Hungarian. Mrs Silberman had a thick accent and only a fleeting acquaintanceship with the English language. It proved impossible to explain what he wanted and in the end he found himself making an emergency appointment to have his teeth examined. Perhaps it wasn't such a bad idea. Since his meeting with Ron Meadows, some of them had been distinctly wobbly.

Which was how he found himself sitting for thirty minutes in a small, square room with an assortment of uncomfortable chairs, an industrial carpet and an aquarium. He wondered about the aquarium. Why did so many dentists keep fish, which didn't, in fact, have teeth? Wouldn't rats or even rabbits be more appropriate? There was a circular table with an assortment of magazines so old that they even included *Punch*. That took him back to his childhood. Dentists had always subscribed to *Punch* — a last laugh before the pain began. He thumbed through a copy, quickly realising that wherever jokes began, it wasn't here.

About a dozen people came and went. They sat glumly, as if they were at the funeral of someone they hadn't known well. Mrs Silberman, a grey-haired woman sitting behind a hatch, called out their names and they left the room and didn't return. Finally, she called out Guy's name. He got up, went through an archway and into the room opposite.

It was the surgery. Silberman was a very tall man with white gloves and too much hair on his neck. He reminded Guy strongly of someone — Christopher Lee perhaps — out of a Hammer Horror film. Give him a hunchbacked dental assistant called Igor and the picture would be complete. Silberman had a great tombstone of a face, thick eyebrows and dark, inquisitive eyes. His mouth was covered by a green, surgical mask.

"Pliss sit down," he said, through the cloth, the words heavy and indistinct. At the same time, he gestured towards a fiendish-looking chair.

"Actually . . ." Guy began.

"Pliss sit down." Mr Silberman wasn't used to addressing people who were still on their feet.

"Well, all right." Guy lowered himself on to the black leather surface and was about to continue when Silberman reached out and touched a button. At once the back of the chair crashed down while the front shot up and suddenly Guy was horizontal. A light came on, blinding him.

"Now, what seems to be the trouble?" Silberman asked.

"Actually, my teeth are pretty good."

"Allow me to make the judge of that." Silberman had a few well-practised if inaccurate phrases and this was one of them. His fingers, coated in latex, pulled at Guy's lower lip. "I do not think we have met," he said.

"Awa wekadenned cha why Amanka Cooker."

"I'm sorry?"

Guy turned his head, releasing his mouth. "I was recommended to you by a man called Cooper."

"Michael Cooper? Yes?"

"He's just bought a house on the Seven Sisters Road."

"He told me. Yes. Do you floss?"

"I'm sorry —"

"You will be very sorry if you do not floss. You have quite a dangerous building-up of plaque. And some gum disease."

"Well —"

"Can you open your mouth, pliss?

Guy opened his mouth and Silberman began to probe, first with a mirror, next with a metal pick. "This won't hurt," he said, and jabbed upwards. Guy just managed to stop himself screaming as a huge spasm of pain shuddered through his body.

"There is no loose tooth but you have a filling you need to be replaced," Silberman said, a few minutes later.

"Hot ingay, hango," Guy said.

Silberman removed his instruments and Guy swung his legs off the chair. His mouth felt as if it was full of blood. He was amazed that there were still dentists like Silberman around. Weren't they supposed to give you laughing gas or something?

"You know, Michael thinks you're a first-rate dentist," he said.

Silberman beamed.

"He told me you have a great sense of humour. That you make visits a real pleasure."

"I always believe, yes, in keeping my patients at their ease."

"You mean, while you brutalise them?"

"I'm sorry?"

"Actually, Michael told me one of your jokes. Something about an actress called Selina Moore."

"Selina Moore? Selina Moore? Oh, yes!" The dentist had taken off his surgical mask and somehow Guy wasn't surprised to see that he had teeth that were simply too perfect for the face they were in. "Why is Selina Moore like a wooden box of Ferrero Rocher?" Silberman frowned a little, realising he had blown the punch-line.

"It's a brilliant joke," Guy said. "Where did you hear it?"

"I'm sorry?"

"You must have heard it somewhere. Unless you made it up."

Was this the answer? Was this huge Hungarian dentist the source of all jokes?

"No, no, no. I didn't make it up. I heard it, I think, when I was playing golf."

"Where do you play?"

"St Albans."

"And who were you playing with?"

But now Silberman was suspicious. Guy was asking questions that seemed incoherent and possibly even insane. "I would recommend you to get that loose filling looked at," he said. "It's on your upper third."

"I'll remember that," Guy said.

There were two golf courses in St Albans and both refused to give details of their members — not even their names — over the telephone. Guy drove over to them. He was already beginning to see that following the joke was going to involve physical travel, that he couldn't do the whole thing from an armchair in London. It was too awkward to explain what he wanted over the telephone. But the weather was good and, anyway, he needed an excuse to use the motorbike, which, like him, spent much too much time resting.

The first club was expensive and unfriendly. Guy explained that he wanted to join but was told there was an eighteen-month waiting list and that he would need to be recommended by at least two members. He tried Silberman's name and learned that no Silberman belonged to the club. At least that had achieved something. The second club was smaller and closer to the town. He knew he had struck gold, quite literally, when he mentioned Silberman's name to the club secretary and she smiled painfully, revealing three gold crowns. Yes, Mr Silberman was a member there, she said. He hadn't played much recently, although he had been there a week ago with a certain Mr Penderville.

There were five Pendervilles living in the St Albans area. Guy called them first, using his mobile phone. Angus Penderville ran a hairdressing business, "Hair Today", in St Albans high street. He had never played golf in his life. James Penderville was out. Nigel Penderville was so helpful and chatty that Guy found it hard to get him off the line. But he was eighty years old and bedridden. The fourth Penderville — Marcus — was a vet and this time Guy struck lucky. He had gone to school with Silberman and still saw him regularly, either to play golf or to get his teeth checked or, indeed, both. He agreed to see Guy after he had finished his lunch-time surgery and Guy went round to his clinic, which occupied the ground floor of a small, terraced house.

Once again Guy found himself waiting, this time behind a variety of different species. It took an hour and the magazines here were even worse than in Mr Silberman's surgery: *Country Life*, and a couple of issues of *Hello!* so out-of-date that several of the celebrities featured had died. Really, Guy felt, *Goodbye!* would have been the more appropriate title. He spent the time staring balefully at the receptionist, a plump, plain woman who lavished so much affection on every single animal in the surgery that he knew somehow she wouldn't have children of her own. It was a sad and somehow demoralising spectacle. Certainly it was the only time he had ever seen anyone trying to baby-talk a stick insect.

It was almost three o'clock when the last casualty — an Afghan hound missing great chunks of fur — had sloped out of the room. The buzzer went and the receptionist showed him into the surgery where a small, bald, serious man in a white coat stood in front of a raised table with an open book of animal diseases. He was studying a cross-section of a dog's ear. "How can I help you?" he asked, looking in vain for any sign of a pet.

Guy had thought this through in the reception area. Both Cooper and Silberman had been, in different ways, suspicious of him. It was already obvious that to many people this quest of his might seem strange. He would therefore need an explanation, a motive that people could understand. And he had thought of one. He launched into it now.

"I'm a student at London University," he explained. "I'm doing a postgraduate thesis on popular culture with particular reference to the geographical dissemination of anecdotes and jokes. The aim is to put jokes into their social and economic context. As part of my paper, I've actually taken a model and I'm attempting to track it back in a linear way. The model in this case is a joke about the actress Selina Moore and a box of Ferrero Rocher chocolates. Mr Silberman told me that he had heard this joke from you. I'd be very interested to know where you heard it from."

It sounded good. Guy almost believed it himself.

"Jokes?" Mr Penderville said. He had a dry, brittle voice. Guy couldn't imagine him ever being remotely funny. "It seems a very strange thing to want to study."

"Well, not really. It's a bit like . . . urban myths and legends."

"I don't see the connection."

Penderville went over to a sink and washed his hands. Guy wondered why he was in such a bad mood. Had he had to put the stick insect down? "I probably heard the joke from Joyce," he said.

"Joyce?"

"The girl outside. The receptionist."

He had wasted an hour, but at least Joyce was still there and agreed to come for a coffee with him. Her full name was Joyce Colman. "Miss Colman", she preferred. Guy had been right about that. She was unmarried and devoted her life to animals and to people less fortunate than herself . . . wherever she could find them.

They walked down the high street to a baker's shop with a few plastic tables on the side. Miss Colman ordered tea and a doughnut from a waitress who obviously recognised her. Guy had a cappuccino. It came out of a machine that squirted the liquid, unappetisingly, out of a series of pipes.

"So you're a student," she said.

"Postgraduate. Yes." Guy felt awkward lying to her. Miss Colman had the look of a woman who had been lied to all her life.

"I've never heard of anyone studying jokes." She took a bite of her doughnut. Red syrup oozed over her fingers. "It was a joke about Selina Moore?"

"Yes."

"Well, I'm not sure who told it to me. It could have been at the youth group . . . that's Mondays. Or the Samaritans on Tuesday. Wednesday I do Scouts and they're always telling jokes, but I could have heard it at the animal shelter. That's Thursdays."

"You do a lot of charity work."

"I like to help. Maybe one of the nurses told me."

"You do hospital visits?"

"I see my mother on Fridays. She has Alzheimer's, poor thing. She doesn't even know where she is, half the time."

Guy sipped his cappuccino. It tasted more of the machine than of coffee. "So you don't remember who told it to you?" he asked.

"No. Actually, I didn't think it was a very nice joke. That poor woman. She was a wonderful actress. But Marcus does bring out the worst in me."

"Mr Penderville."

"He left his wife recently and we've been seeing a bit of each other. He took me for dinner at the Harvester last week and he would insist on ordering a whole bottle of wine and one thing led to another . . ."

The angry vet and his spinster receptionist having hot sex after a night at the Harvester. It was a mind-boggling thought.

"What I mean is, we began telling jokes." Miss Colman had coloured slightly and Guy realised he might have misconstrued what she'd said. "Some of them were rather *risqué*." Her eyes suddenly brightened and she stopped, the last piece of doughnut half-way to her lips. "I remember now. I heard it at Scouts."

"This must have been a Wednesday night."

"That's right. Exactly one week ago. Yes." She smiled. "You know what Boy Scouts are like! They're always telling jokes and some of them you wouldn't want to tell your mother although, as a matter of fact, I do. I like telling Mother jokes when I visit her. She doesn't laugh at them. She only drools. But I think she enjoys them."

"Do you know which one told you the joke?" Guy asked.

"Now who was it? It could have been Michael or Gary — they're dreadful those two! Or was it Billy? I'm sure it was Billy. No. It was Michael!"

"I don't suppose . . ." Guy began.

"What?"

"Well, it's Wednesday today. Do you think I could come along and meet the pack?"

"You mean the troop."

"Just for a few minutes. It really would help me with the research."

Miss Colman considered. "Well, we don't normally allow outsiders. These days you have to be so careful, especially where children are concerned. But I don't suppose it will do any harm since I'll be there with you. But we don't start until six. And there's a charity shop

I work at until then. We're collecting for the victims of landmines."

"Perhaps I can give you a hand?"

"No. But you can meet me there at half past five when it closes. The hall's very near. We can walk there together."

The church hall was large, empty and smelt of cigarette smoke. There was a raised stage at one end with a pair of tatty curtains. The windows were covered with metal grilles. About a dozen boys had turned up for Scouts. None of them was dressed in uniform but all of them had bits of it — either the navy trousers, the blue shirts or the woggles but never all three.

"Boys. This is Guy Fletcher," Miss Colman said. "He's going to talk to you about jokes." She smiled at Guy. "I'll leave you to it." And before he could stop her, she did, disappearing through a set of swing doors next to the stage.

Guy drew a breath. He had never seen quite such a malevolent-looking gang of children. They looked more like muggers and football hooligans than Scouts. There was a fat, ginger-haired boy, poking his nose. Two black kids, lithe and suspicious. A tiny boy missing most of his teeth. He was the one who spoke first. "Go on, then, mister. Tell us a joke."

"That's not quite why —" Guy began.

"What did the boy in the wheelchair get for Christmas?" someone shouted.

"I don't know," Guy answered helplessly.

"Cancer!"

They all laughed. And that let loose a torrent of jokes, the boys crowding in on him, competing to be the loudest, the dirtiest, the unfunniest. Guy felt himself being pushed back towards the stage and held up his hands, trying to stop them.

"Wait a minute!" he said. "I'm here because of a joke about Selina Moore."

They all knew it. Three or four of them shouted it at him. Two Asian boys had started a fight, punching at each other's faces. Guy looked round for Miss Colman, but he was on his own. "I just need to know who told it first!" he shouted.

That stopped them.

"It was me!" The ginger-haired boy stabbed a finger into his chest.

"No, it wasn't. It was Tariq!"

"I never!"

"It was Darren."

"Darren's a wanker!"

"Fuck off!"

"It was Bob."

"I told it! I told it!"

"Bob Galton. He told me and I told Michael."

"Yeah — it was Bob!"

Gradually, the name of Bob Galton rose to the top of the cacophony. By now, one of the Asian boys had a bleeding nose. The ginger-haired boy was in tears. Two of the Scouts were on the ground, trying to strangle each other. But it was generally agreed that Bob Galton had first introduced the joke.

73

The trouble was, Bob wasn't there. He was off sick. Guy wasn't surprised to hear it. He was feeling a little sick himself.

Bob lived a mile away on a council estate. His full name was Robert Ian Galton. Miss Colman had given Guy his address. She knew very little about the family but thought the father might drive a bus. Either that or a taxi.

It was dark by now. Guy was beginning to feel increasingly uncomfortable, tracking round the back end of St Albans like a detective without a corpse. He wondered how long he could keep this up. He found himself standing on the outside terrace of a block of flats, four storeys high, each terrace a giant step built out of prefabricated concrete. All the windows were made of pebbled glass, the sort you get in public toilets. There were net curtains everywhere. The block was called Casterbridge and stood between Egmont and d'Urberville. The developer or town planner had evidently been a fan of Thomas Hardy. He rang the bell.

The front door opened and a woman came out.

"Mrs Galton?" Guy asked.

She had been doing housework. She looked tired, with a downturned mouth and hopeless eyes. She was wearing an apron and slippers, a small woman with greying hair and a weather-beaten face. At least, Guy hoped it had been the weather. "Yes?" she said.

"I was sent here by Joyce Colman. At Scouts . . ."

"What do you want?"

"It's about Robert."

"You'd better come in!" But she was suspicious, not inviting.

He went into a tiny hall with a violently patterned carpet in perpetual warfare with the wallpaper. There wasn't much space for the two of them and much of it was taken up by an odd-looking vacuum cleaner leaning against a table, all multicoloured plastic fittings and silver pipes. Guy had never seen anything quite like it. It was like something out of a nineteen-fifties television programme; the prototype of some future invention that would never in fact be built. Its motor was still running. She turned it off. Now Guy could hear a television, playing in one of the rooms. "What's he done?" she asked.

"He hasn't done anything. I just wondered if I could have a word with him."

"You say you're from the Scouts?"

"Yes!" He hadn't actually said that but it might be easier if that was what she believed. "I've started helping out. I was there this evening. I was sorry to see Bob hadn't turned up."

"He's in bed. He's got flu."

"Could I talk to him?"

"Why?"

Guy could see this going terribly wrong. He hadn't just stepped into this woman's house. He had stepped into her life. And he had no right to be there. "Well, the thing is, we believe he told the other boys a joke."

"What joke?"

"It was a rather tasteless joke about an actress. We wondered where he might have heard it."

"Why?"

"Well . . . we want to know."

"Why?"

He was talking himself into a corner. Frantically, he searched for a way out. "We were just worried that Bob might have been in contact with some people who . . . tell unpleasant jokes. It's not as if he's in any trouble or anything." He tried a reassuring smile. "We're just thinking of him."

And then a door opened and a tall West Indian man came out wearing a sleeveless T-shirt and jeans and smoking a cigarette. There was a tattoo of an octopus on his left shoulder. "Who are you?" he demanded, seeing Guy. He had large white eyes, brimming with hostility.

"He's from the Scouts," the woman said. "He wants to talk to Bob."

"Why?"

"He wants to know where he heard a joke."

"What joke?"

"I don't know. Something about an actress."

The man frowned, screwing up the bottom half of his face. He glanced briefly behind his shoulder, then at Guy. "You with the Scouts?" he said.

"I help out a little," Guy replied.

"You got any ID?"

"What?"

"Identification. I don't know you. You could be anyone."

"Well . . ."

There was a long pause. Then Galton spoke again. "I don't know what you're doing," he began. "I mean . . . you know . . . what time of day do you call this? Walking into people's houses just like that, asking stupid bloody questions!" Strangely, his tone wasn't particularly aggressive. Even Guy had to admit the man had a point. "Maybe I should give the police a call," he went on. "Tell them that there's a man who claims to be from the Boy Scouts trying to talk to my son."

"I'm not! Really! There's absolutely no need —"

"And how's he supposed to remember where he heard a bloody joke anyway? Kids hear jokes at school all the time. You got some sort of problem, kids telling jokes, you talk to the teachers. All right?"

"Absolutely, Mr Galton. I'm sorry to have —"

But Galton had already gone, turning his back on Guy and walking away.

A few seconds later, Guy was back out on the terrace. As the door slammed shut he noticed the flicker of a curtain. He looked up and saw a thin, dark-haired boy looking down at him. So near and yet so far! For a moment he was tempted to call up, but thought better of it.

He got on to his motorbike and drove off without looking back.

In a way he was glad that it had ended so quickly. Guy saw that the whole thing could have become an obsession. What had Sylvie called it? A flight of fancy. She was right. But how far would he have been prepared to fly? Would he really have gone bombing back up the A41 the following morning to engineer his way into a school playground and somehow find the next link in the chain? He had to admit that he very probably would have. There was a trait in his character, a strange desire to spend inordinate amounts of time in pursuit of something essentially worthless. If he wasn't careful he might turn into a trainspotter or start collecting matchbox labels.

Well, it was over. And he was glad. Really he was. The fact that it was his mother who had been insulted by the joke was irrelevant. She hadn't even known he was alive.

That evening he found himself in a Chinese restaurant — the Singing Duck — in Wardour Street with four ex-students from the Clairemont; Torin and Jane and Jack and Paul. All his friends were getting to the age when they needed the obligatory "and". Torin and Jane were even talking of getting married. Guy sighed. It didn't seem that long ago that Jane had been going out with him. Now she was sitting with her hand resting on Torin's head, her fingers caressing his hair. Jane had just been cast as a French countess in a Channel 4 Dickens: *A Tale of Two Cities*. For cost reasons, both cities were being played by Prague. Jane was flying out the following day and this dinner had been arranged to wish her luck.

And so here they were, the five of them, arranged around a table in the corner. The table had a rotating centre and it made Guy think of their changing fortunes, their shifting relationships. They weren't even

78

actors any more . . . not all of them. Paul had spent his last year at Clairemont wondering why he was there and a year later he'd made the decision to move into finance. He was, of course, the only one earning any real money — but it had changed things. He was no longer one of them.

Guy glanced at Paul, sitting opposite him. There were touches of grey in his hair — so soon! He had come straight from work and had been wearing a suit and a multi-coloured tie but Jack had insisted he take off the tie, pronounced it "ghastly" and given it to one of the waiters. Now Paul was studying the menu with a hurt look. It was he who had chosen this restaurant and Guy wondered, a little ungraciously, if he would pay.

"Why don't we just throw a pair of dice?" Jane suggested. "Order whatever numbers come up."

"No way," Paul said. "The last time we did that we ended up with duck's feet and five different sorts of rice."

"All these places are the same," Guy said. "I sometimes think that all Chinatown restaurants share the same kitchen. It doesn't matter where you go. There's a huge kitchen somewhere underneath Soho and all the restaurants are connected."

"Is this another of your lunatic theories?" Jack asked. He was twenty-six, fair-haired and strikingly handsome. Six months in the gym had just paid off spectacularly because it looked as if Calvin Klein might be about to use him in a new underwear poster.

Only Paul wasn't entirely happy about it. "All those middle-aged men lusting after you on the Underground."

"That's crap."

"Calvin Klein ads aren't about underpants. They're about tearing them off the boy who's wearing them. Anyway, you're an actor, not a model."

"An out-of-work actor."

"Did you really go all the way to St Albans?" Jane cut in.

She had changed too, Guy thought. She was softer, rounder . . . older. In a year or two she'd probably be a mother. She looked like one already. "It's not that far," Guy said. He was beginning to regret telling everyone what he'd been doing that day.

"You really are extraordinary, Guy. I think you need help."

"Thank you."

"If you *had* managed to get into the school, how would you have got the kids to talk to you?" Jack asked.

"Bribe the little bastards with lollipops," Torin suggested. He caught hold of Jane's wrist and lifted her hand out of his hair.

"You need to get a job!" Paul said. "You always go a bit crazy when you're out of work, Guy, and this is exactly like the last idea you had. The Premium Bonds thing."

"That was a perfectly reasonable idea. If you actually think about it . . ."

Everyone groaned. They had heard it all before.

"Jokes are interesting," Guy said, "and nobody's ever written anything about them, apart from Freud. He took a joke as a model and wrote a book about it, trying to work out why it was funny."

80

"And was it?" Jack asked.

"No. Not even remotely. The book is completely impenetrable but I don't think Freud had much of a sense of humour. It's strange. There have been lots of books about urban myths but none about jokes."

"They're not the same thing," Jane said.

"I bet they're related. Anyway, I'm sorry I didn't get any further. I could have gone from A to B to C to D. I could have gone all the way to Scotland. Or even out of the country." He drew a line with his chopstick across the tablecloth. "That's something to think about. Do jokes travel? Do they cross boundaries? Or does every country have its own sense of humour?"

"They wouldn't have made jokes about Selina Moore in France," Torin said. "Wasn't it a French orphanage that she hit?"

"They made jokes about 9/11," Paul said. "They were doing the rounds only a few days after it happened. And the funny thing is, the jokes actually started in New York."

"Such as?" Jane asked.

"Well . . . they weren't particularly funny. Why is American the best airline? Because they fly direct to the office. That sort of thing."

"That's sick!"

"I said it wasn't funny. But I suppose Guy does have a point. Who'd make up a joke like that?"

"Are jokes made up at all?" Guy asked, warming to the theme. "Or do they sort of develop? If I'd been able to follow the Selina Moore joke, would it have changed? Why is Selina Moore like a Camembert?

That's something else that comes out of France in a box."

"Who really gives a fuck?" Torin asked.

Guy shrugged. A waiter arrived to take their order, dressed in black and white but with a multi-coloured tie. The conversation moved on.

Ten minutes later they were talking about a director they all knew whose modern-dress *Romeo and Juliet* had just opened at the Theatre Royal, York, to poisonous reviews. The critics had particularly loathed the fish-and-chip man who had appeared as a ludicrous interpretation of the friar. By and large, the five of them didn't take pleasure in other people's misfortune but the director had always been a prick and had never cast any of them so he deserved what he got.

And then Danny arrived, the last member of the party. Danny was always in a hurry, always late. He was a fat, cheerful man who dressed and behaved larger than life and who was convinced that he would be famous before he was thirty. He only had six months to go. Currently he was in Westcliffe-on-Sea "doing an Agatha", as Christie's tedious, almost unactable plays were known in the business. Rehearsals had already begun. His play opened the following week.

"Sorry I'm late!" he exclaimed, as he approached the table, brushing between two diners and knocking over a glass of wine with his shoulder-bag. "Fucking director wouldn't let us go and I missed the train. God, it's a bloody journey. Westcliffe-on-Sea to Fenchurch Street. Sounds like something off a fucking Monopoly board and it's right in the middle of nowhere. God, Guy, you look awful. What happened to your face? Don't tell me! Kate nutted you. Found out you were screwing a Labrador. Can't say I blame her." He sat down, found an empty glass and raised it. "Anyway, here I am. Don't worry about starting without me. Oh, and by the way, you remember that actress who gave all that money to the Clairemont? Well, I just heard this most wonderful joke . . ."

CHAPTER
EIGHT

Danny had heard the Ferrero Rocher joke from the actress who had the title role but no lines in *The Body in the Library* at Westcliffe-on-Sea. Guy knew her slightly and called her the next day. In the course of a ten-minute phone call, he learnt that the director was crap, the play was a disaster, the theatre was ugly, the town worse, and that she had heard the joke from her boyfriend who worked in the City.

"Do you think you could ask him where he heard it?" Guy asked.

"Are you playing Chinese Whispers?"

"Sort of."

Five minutes later, she called him back. Her boyfriend had been told the joke by his boss. His boss had been told it by a hairdresser at "Prime Cuts" near Liverpool Street station.

Guy had his hair cut there. He had begun to notice that every hairdressing salon in the world had a name that was some sort of pun. Was it regulatory, he wondered. Something that came with the licence? The man who cut his hair was called Frank and came from the old-fashioned school of white jackets, manual clippers and "something for the weekend" when "something for the weekend" hadn't been available in seven colours and eleven flavours from your local chemist or public toilet. He told lots of jokes.

Guy came out with hair that was shorter than he would have liked and the description of a man who cut sandwiches in a greasy spoon just down the road. Frank went for lunch there every day but didn't know his name. In fact, it was Kailash.

Kailash made Guy a cheese and pickle sandwich and sent him to an Italian restaurant on the Old Kent Road. He had a mate there, Sammy, who worked as a waiter.

Luigi's was one of those Italian trattorias that had sprung up all over London in the seventies but which had surely outstayed their welcome. All the familiar icons were there: the hors d'oeuvres sweating slightly on a wheeled trolley, the handwritten menu with so many dishes that they just had to come out of the deep freeze, the hard little bread rolls that came with chilled, over-salted butter. All the waiters were Italian, apart from Sammy who pretended to be. Guy went into his student routine and was directed to the manager, whose name really was Luigi and who had heard the joke from his chef. Unfortunately the chef was at home. With food poisoning.

Guy had nothing better to do and it was a pleasant day. He got back on his bike and drove over to Enfield where he found the chef sitting in a tiny, rectangular garden, watching a television that had been propped up on a wheelbarrow. The garden backed on to a railway line and every four or five minutes a train rumbled past, on its way in or out of London. The air smelt of rotting vegetables and diesel but the chef — whose name was Carlo Ponti — didn't appear to notice the noise or the fumes. He seemed to be a genuinely happy man.

He had heard the joke from his neighbour, Ali, who worked as a traffic warden. The two of them spent hours talking over the fence. They were friends, living in each other's pocket gardens. Guy spoke to Ali's wife but she didn't know the joke and Ali wouldn't be home until at least eight o'clock. Guy went off in search of him.

He spent the next two days in an increasingly frustrating game of Hunt the Traffic Warden. He found Ali overseeing the clamping of a BMW near St Paul's — but it was now that he discovered that traffic wardens regularly exchanged jokes with each other when they were out on patrol. Ali had heard the joke from Phil, who had heard it from Jasminda, who had heard it from Sue. This particular length of the chain only ended with Mike, who had heard the joke from his brother, Henry, and it had been he who had first introduced it to the traffic wardens' world.

Henry was a plumber, living in Hertford. Thirty pounds for a call-out and twenty pounds plus VAT for every fifteen minutes he was there . . . Henry admitted he had a strong sense of humour. He had heard the joke from a customer, before he had presented his bill.

From Hertford the trail led to Sandridge, Redbourn, Chaul End, then back to Bishop's Stortford, Royston and the village of Wimbish Green. The joke had been told, respectively, by five postmen, two teachers, a garage-forecourt manager, nine car mechanics, a Lloyds Bank cashier, a post-office clerk and a landscape gardener.

The landscape gardener's name was Fairfax. Guy realised he was travelling further and further now. Soon it would be impossible to get back to London without stopping overnight, not unless he wanted to exhaust himself on the motorways. But he was enjoying himself. It was difficult to explain, but the further he went, the more he felt he was achieving something. He was beginning to think he might actually find the author of the Ferrero Rocher joke. It could happen any time now.

He managed to track Fairfax down to a small, wooden office — actually little more than a converted shed — at the back end of a garden centre. Fairfax was short, grey-haired and asthmatic. He chain-smoked, wheezing audibly every time he took a breath. Guy hoped his plants were healthier than him. He was a friendly man. This was something Guy was beginning to learn about the British character. By and large, people were amenable; glad to help. And the fact that his business with them was utterly eccentric only seemed to help. In a way he was surprised that, even in these hard-edged, stressful times, the spirit of the Ealing comedies lived on. Would he have got as far as this, he wondered, if he had been living in Germany, say, or Belgium? And, for that matter, would the joke?

"Ferrero Rocher! Yes. I remember that one," Fairfax rasped. "My dad told me. Over the phone."

"And where does your father live?"

"Stoke-on-Trent."

Guy felt his stomach sink. He had expected this to happen sooner or later. Stoke-on-Trent was miles away — the other side of England. Even so, he was probably lucky. The father could have been living abroad.

"Are you going to drive all the way over there?" Fairfax asked.

"I suppose I'll have to."

"It seems a lot of work for a university paper." Fairfax lit another cigarette. "But maybe you won't have to. You see, now I think of it, I also heard the joke from one of my gardeners."

This was a new development and something Guy hadn't considered. Since Westcliffe-on-Sea, the joke's progress had been linear, a straight A to Z. But he should have realised that the pattern might become much more complicated as some people would pass on the joke twice or three times.

"This is what happened," Fairfax continued. "I told the joke to Harry Collins. He's getting on a bit but he still likes a good laugh. But the thing is, he already knew it."

"He'd heard it from someone else?"

"That's right."

Harry Collins lived just ten minutes away. He had a tiny terraced cottage, so covered with ivy as to be almost invisible. Fairfax had telephoned ahead and Harry invited Guy into a square room with a sagging ceiling and furniture that was too big for the available floor space. The labourer was about seventy years old and still working. He was a small man with big, permanently muddy hands.

"I don't remember where I heard the joke," he said. "I've got a terrible memory. Ferrero Rocher? It might have been Bill Fairfax. Yes, that's who it was. That's who told me."

"No, I don't think so, Mr Collins," Guy said. "It was you who told him."

"Was it?"

"That's what he said."

Then the door opened and a very old woman came in with three cups of tea. She was hunched over the tray, almost weighed down by it. This was Mrs Collins.

"Who told me that joke?" Collins asked her.

"Which joke?"

"Ferrero Rocher."

"I did!"

"You didn't!"

"Yes, I did. I heard it when I was doing the shopping and I told you when I came back."

Guy's spirits rose. "Can you remember where you heard it?" he asked.

"Oh, yes. From Janice Richards. Saffron Walden. She works in the cake shop."

And so to the cake shop, the shoe shop, the bookshop and the greengrocer's. Then the dress shop, the post office and the "Cut and Run" hair boutique. The joke had zigzagged its way up and down the high street but the point of entry seemed to be the library. The librarian had heard it from her sister, Marion, who lived in the village of Ickleton and who did the flowers at the local church. She had been told the joke by the vicar.

"I didn't tell the joke because I thought it was funny," the vicar said. He was an elderly, patrician man, embarrassed to have been caught out by Guy. "As a matter of fact, I was talking to Marion about humour generally. I told her the joke as an example of a joke that isn't actually very funny."

"That's one of the reasons I'm interested in it," Guy said. "Would you mind telling me where you heard it?"

"From Ray Cranbourne. You'll find him in the graveyard. He looks after the graves."

There were, in fact, two of them: Ray and a plump, moon-faced boy who might have been retarded. They were laughing together as Guy approached and, of course, he thought of Hamlet.

What is he that builds stronger than either the mason, the shipwright, or the carpenter?
The gallows-maker; for that frame outlives a thousand tenants.

Well, it was a joke of sorts, still unfunny five hundred years after its creation. Nobody told them quite like Shakespeare. Grave-digger clowns. Was that where jokes began?

But no. Ray had heard it from his postman, who had heard it from a lady, who had heard it from . . .

Guy now found himself parallel-tracking the M11: Duxford, Stapleford, Great Shelford and Newnham before turning off via Rampton (a little further north) to Cambridge. He was starting to set standards for himself. Four "scores" in one day was a good average. He would set off each morning from London at about seven and try to get back while it was still light. Some days he missed his targets altogether. He still preferred not using the telephone. He liked the unpredictability of each encounter. And, anyway, he had nothing else to do. Sylvie still hadn't called with any job offers. And the sun was out.

A late-afternoon meeting with a painter-decorator brought him to Cambridge. The painter remembered that he had been told the joke by the landlord of a pub where he had been working, the Bear, which was situated on the river Cam. Guy thought he would just be able to fit it in before returning to London, but when he got there he found himself parking his bike in front of an irresistibly pretty building with thatched roof, beams and river frontage. There was also an advertisement in the window, a special offer: "Bed and Breakfast £25". Guy decided to stay the night.

It was the right decision. The girl who showed him to his room told him that the landlord, Mr Patterson, wouldn't be in until eight o'clock. Guy had a shower and slept for an hour before going downstairs.

The Bear was a traditional countryside pub, but a countryside of frolicking lambs, sunshine and children leaping off haystacks rather than recalcitrant farmers, mud and foot-and-mouth. Everything about it was perfect. There was an open fireplace big enough to stand in. An uneven slate floor. Photographs of village life before the invention of the motor car and the beginning of village death. There were eight or nine people drinking there when Guy came down and he got the immediate impression, even from the comfortable silence, that they all knew each other, that they came here most evenings and that the Bear had become their second home. Only one man sat alone, slightly apart. Guy noticed him as he walked over to the bar. The man was middle-aged, dressed in a cheap grey suit with a shirt and tie that looked as if they had been bought together in a gift pack. He was eating a toasted sandwich and reading a paperback. Guy supposed that he often ate alone. There was a practised ease about the way he held the sandwich and turned the pages at the same time, never looking up. He had to be a salesman of some sort, a man who spent a lot of time on the road.

The landlord had arrived by now and brought over the menu personally. John Patterson was a tall, red-faced man with unruly black hair and oversized sideburns, dressed in a faded sports jacket and cords. He was obviously proud of the Bear. He walked as if he was one himself.

"Are you going to eat?" he demanded. There was something about the way he spoke that suggested it would be a mistake not to.

"Yes," Guy said.

"Tonight's special is steak and kidney pie. It's home-made. All the food here is home-made." He glanced at the salesman, who had done himself no favours by ordering the toasted sandwich. "Soup of the day is leek and potato."

Guy ordered the pie and a pint of beer. The pie was more expensive than he would have liked and he didn't really want the beer but it seemed the right thing to do. "Are you Mr Patterson?" he asked.

"That's me. Yes."

"I met a friend of yours this afternoon. Roy Ingles."

"Roy? Oh, yes! What did he want?"

"Actually, he was helping me with a project. You see, I'm a student."

"At the university?"

Which university? Of course — he was in Cambridge.

"Yes. I'm doing a postgraduate thesis on popular culture." And out it all came for the twentieth time. The origin of jokes. The social and economic context.

Patterson listened, bemused. "Well, that's the first time I've heard anything like that," he said. "Which joke is it you were trying to track down?"

"Why is Selina Moore like a Ferrero Rocher?"

Patterson screwed a smile on to his lips in the way people do when they're meant to find something funny. "I don't know," he said. "Why is Selina Moore like a Ferrero Rocher?"

Guy frowned. "No," he explained. "I'm not telling you the joke. It was you who told the joke to Roy Ingles."

"Did I?"

"That's what he said."

"Why is Selina Moore like a Ferrero Rocher?"

A small, round woman — a real Mrs Tiggywinkle — had come out of the kitchen carrying a bowl of soup.

"Because they both came out of France in a box," she said.

"Oh! That's right! Yes!" Patterson threw his head back and laughed, and Guy felt a twinge of something like pain. It happened every time anyone laughed at the joke. It hurt him. It really did.

Maybe that was why he didn't notice the man in the suit. The salesman. He had stopped eating and stopped reading his book. He was listening to everything.

"Where did you hear it?" Guy asked.

"I don't remember."

The woman — presumably Mrs Patterson — had served the soup. She returned to the bar. "Sally told you," she said.

"Did she?"

"I was here at the time. Honestly, John! Don't you remember anything?"

"Sally Lockwood?"

"There were four or five of you here. Last Friday. Matthew and Jamie and Chris and you. You were all telling jokes — and that was one of them."

"Sally Lockwood." Guy made a note of the name. "Do you know where she lives?"

"Somewhere in Cambridge, I think. But she's got a shop in the town centre. Sally's Pantry. You can probably find it in the phone book."

"We buy a few bits and pieces from her," Patterson said. "You're having the pie? That's hers."

"I thought you said it was home-made."

"That's right. It was made in her home. So you're going to ask her where she heard the joke?"

94

"Yes," Guy said.

"And what then? You keep following it, it could take you the rest of your life."

The man in the suit had heard enough. Leaving the toasted sandwich to get cold, he stood up and left the room. Guy noticed him then. But he didn't think anything of it.

The man went over to the tiny reception desk and glanced at the guest book, which Guy had signed when he checked in. Guy's name was there, and next to it the registration number of his motorbike. There was a public telephone on the desk but he didn't use it. He had his own mobile phone. He took it out, checked for a signal and pressed a single button. He was connected at once.

"This is Naughtie." He paused and looked round, making sure there was nobody in sight. "I think we may have a problem," he said.

CHAPTER
NINE

Sally's Pantry was in a narrow, twisting street in the middle of Cambridge. Guy could see at a glance that this was the sort of shop that sold nothing he would really want to eat but, then, it was surrounded by shops that sold things nobody really needed to buy. They were all there: humorously shaped teapots, soaps with flowers in the middle, hand-carved wooden puzzles. Give your nose a treat — scented candles, pot-pourri and about a hundred varieties of incense. Guy found a parking zone just round the corner, next to King's College. He left his motorbike surrounded by bicycles, and went to find Sally Lockwood.

The shop was small and smelt of cheese or coffee — it depended where you stood. There were no well-known brand names on the shelves. Even the simplest items — biscuits and crisps — came from Austria or Denmark with brightly coloured crowns and coats-of-arms on the wrapping to justify the high prices. They looked as if they had been there for a long time. The delicatessen counter included cured ham, obscure cheeses and home-made pies like the one he had eaten the night before.

There was a very old man ahead of him and Guy watched as he was served a slice of cheese barely thicker than the knife that cut it. The girl behind the counter didn't seem to mind. She weighed it, wrapped it and delivered the cheese with due severity even though the paper and the bag must have eaten away most of the profit margin. At last the old man went.

"Can I help you?" the girl asked, with a quiet desperation, as if she already knew with some certainty that she couldn't.

"Are you Sally Lockwood?" Guy asked.

"No. Sally isn't here," the girl said. "You just missed her. She's gone home."

"When will she be back?"

"Not until tomorrow."

This was something Guy hadn't expected. It was only eleven o'clock. He wasn't going to be able to kick his heels in Cambridge all day and, even at the special rate, he didn't want to pay for a second night at the Bear. "Can you tell me where she lives?" he asked.

"Does she know you?" The girl was sensible and efficient. She wasn't going to give Sally's address to just anyone.

"Not exactly," Guy admitted. "I'm a friend of a friend. John Patterson at the Bear."

"I don't know him."

"He buys food here."

"Well . . ."

"I just want to meet her," Guy said. "Do you think you could possibly ring her? It'll only take five minutes of her time."

"I don't think she'll want to meet you," the girl said. "Her mother's not well. That's why she's gone home. She won't want to be disturbed."

Another customer came in: a woman in a Barbour jacket. She ordered four slices of salami and a small tub of olives, and while the girl turned her back to deal with it, Guy leant over the counter. He had noticed a number of letters tucked into a space next to the till. He thumbed through them quickly. Four were addressed to the shop but the fifth had Sally's name and a personal address. He made a mental note of it and left.

Sally lived twenty minutes' walk from the shop, in a wide, grassy area that was just outside the city centre and seemed completely removed from it. The twisting lanes and pedestrian walkways suddenly opened out into parkland with a row of houses taller and more substantial than any Guy had seen on the way. Sally's house was not huge but it was impressive. From the front it looked like a doll's house, though a rather sombre one, the sort collected by antiques dealers rather than played with by children. It was built out of tiny bricks; Georgian, four storeys high with its windows and doors perfectly symmetrical and a neat white triangle above the front door. Guy could almost imagine the entire front opening on a hinge. Inside, a hallway and central staircase would be revealed with rooms of identical size positioned on either side. These rooms would have high ceilings and wooden floors and there would be plenty of them, with at least three bedrooms on the third floor behind the roof, and the

98

kitchen, from the look of it, in the basement. There was a front garden with two yew trees and a low metal gate separating it from the street. Guy wondered if Sally lived there with her mother. There would be room for a husband and several children too.

He walked through the gate and rang the bell. The door opened and he found himself being examined — rather coolly — by a woman who was about his own age. His first thought was that she was everything Kate wasn't. His second thought was that he'd only had the first thought because, as with Kate, he immediately fancied her.

She was fair rather than dark, small and slim rather than imposing, pretty rather than memorably beautiful. Her hair was straw-coloured and tied back with a band. She had grey-blue eyes that would have been attractive if they weren't so hostile. She was wearing a loose dress, pale green, with a pink cardigan. They weren't two colours that Guy would have put together but they worked on her. No jewellery, very little makeup. She had a pair of glasses perched on her head.

"Yes?" She stood in the doorway and had already made it clear that she wasn't going to invite him in. She was leaning against the architrave, her arm barring the way. He looked past her into a simply furnished hall with light falling across the floor, suggesting doorways beyond. It was like something by Vermeer. He wondered if there was a child asleep inside.

"Sally Lockwood?" he asked.

"Yes. Were you at the shop just now?"

"Yes, I was."

"Amanda saw you take my address off a private letter. Why did you do that?"

"You're right." Guy was surprised he had been caught out. "I'm sorry. It was wrong of me. But your assistant — Amanda — was busy and I just wanted to see you for a couple of minutes. My name is Guy Fletcher. I've come all the way from London."

"Come all the way for what?"

"I just want to ask you a question."

"What about?"

He made a decision and dived in. "About a joke. It was a joke you told at a public house, the Bear. You see . . . it's difficult to explain. I'm doing a thesis. I'm at London University."

"Which college?"

That floored him. Nobody had asked him that before. "Well, I'm not exactly in residence," he blustered. "I'm a postgraduate. Sort of freelance." He smiled, knowing he was making a hash of this. "I'm writing a paper on anecdotes and things like that. You know, jokes. I'm trying to find out where jokes come from. One joke in particular. I know it sounds mad, but I can promise you I'm harmless. Do you think I could come in for just a minute?"

She had noticed the helmet in his hands. "Where's your motorbike?" she asked.

"I left it near the shop."

She examined him carefully but her face gave nothing away. Then she said: "All right. I'll talk to you. But if you don't mind, I'd prefer it if you didn't come into the house. My mother is resting. She isn't well. If you wait a moment, I'll let you into the garden."

She closed the door in his face.

There was a second door at the side of the house. Guy only noticed it now. It was a door straight out of a children's book, solid and rectangular, half hidden by a sprawling mahonia bush that gave it an air of mystery, as if it might open onto Narnia or the Secret Garden. Guy went over to it. After what seemed like a long time it opened, and Sally stood on the other side, still sceptical but inviting him in. He followed her into the most perfect garden he had ever seen, neat and classical, with none of the hideous features — fountains, decking or Japanese pagodas — that now featured in every gardening programme on TV. There was a square of flat, manicured grass and a small patio laid with York stone. Most of the beds were filled with evergreens but they were spiky and dark-leafed; unusual varieties of plants he was unable to name. The garden was very private. It was impossible to see any neighbours' houses. Guy sat down underneath a giant umbrella, resisting the temptation to peer into the back windows of the house. The garden furniture was high quality: hand-crafted, not mass-produced.

"Would you like a drink?" Sally asked.

"Do you have a Coke?"

"I think so." She went into the house. There was a french window on the far side of the hall, opposite the front door. She came back a few moments later with a bottle and two glasses. "Only lemonade, I'm afraid," she said.

"That's fine." She must have brought it from her own shop. Guy didn't recognise the brand. "I'm not really at London University," he said.

"I didn't think so."

"It's just something I tell people to try and explain what I'm doing."

"And what are you doing?"

"I really am trying to find out where jokes come from. I know it sounds crazy." He drank some of the lemonade. It didn't quite taste of lemons. "I heard the joke in a London pub and I wanted to know where it came from. I had this idea that maybe I could write a play or something. The truth is that I'm an actor, currently out of work."

"I thought I recognised you," Sally said.

"Did you?"

"Why else do you think I let you into the garden? I knew your face the moment I saw you but it's only now I remember what from."

"*Manchester Murders*?" Guy suggested.

"No. You're in that advertisement, aren't you? The one for coffee. You're the whistling window-cleaner."

Guy nodded. It was recognition . . . of a sort. "That's right."

"It's one of my mother's favourites. She watches a lot of television and she pointed you out to me. You try to impress the girl by whistling and then she puts on a whistling kettle. My mother thought you were funny."

"Actually, it wasn't me whistling," Guy admitted. "I can't whistle. I was dubbed."

"Then why did they choose you?"

"I don't know. I suppose they liked my lips." He sighed. "To be honest, it was a bloody awful day's filming. I didn't get on with the actress playing my girlfriend and the director thought he was making something out of the *nouvelle vague*, not a thirty-second spot to go in the break before the *News at Ten*. And I don't even like coffee. I've never understood it. I mean, it seems such a strange thing to do. Roasting those little beans and then grinding them up and dumping them in hot water."

"It didn't show," Sally said. She examined Guy more carefully. "What was so important about this joke?" she asked. "The one that got you started?"

"Well . . . it was about someone I know."

"Is that so bad?"

"She died."

"I'm sorry."

He wanted to tell her. There was something about Sally that made him want to talk about Selina Moore, about being adopted, about needing to find his mother and losing her before he could. But he stopped himself. He had never told Kate. How could he talk about these things with someone he had only just met?

Instead, he told her about the Premium Bonds.

"I've always had these ideas," he said. "It's part of my nature. Something occurs to me and I just can't get it out of my mind."

"So what was it about Premium Bonds?"

"Have you got an hour?"

The sun had come out and suddenly the garden was warm and perfumed and reminded Guy of a scene in

Alice in Wonderland. Maybe that was the children's story the door had opened into.

"Well, it was a sort of conspiracy theory," he began. "I was thinking about Premium Bonds one day and it suddenly occurred to me that I'd never met anyone who'd won the top prize. That's a million pounds."

She looked at him curiously. "Is that so surprising?" she asked. "How many people do you know?"

"That's exactly the point. I probably know about a hundred people. I'd imagine that most people know about a hundred people when they really think about it. But the hundred people that you know also know a hundred people. So in fact there are probably about ten thousand people whom we all hear about from time to time. And it occurred to me that if, for example, your mother-in-law's neighbour's daughter knew someone who had won a million pounds on a Premium Bond, the chances are pretty high that you'd get to hear about it."

Sally gave a nod of agreement but Guy wasn't sure she was following him. He went on anyway: "Now, the government is meant to be giving a million pounds away every month, twelve months a year. And they're supposed to have been doing this for years and years." Guy drew a breath. "So it suddenly occurred to me that it was very strange that nobody I knew had ever heard of anyone who had actually won a million pounds on a Premium Bond."

"But you must know lots of people who've won smaller prizes."

"Of course. That's exactly what you'd expect."

Sally shook her head. "What are you getting at?"

"It was just a theory, but it occurred to me that the government could be lying. They throw out a few small prizes — twenty-five quid here, a hundred there — to keep people happy. But the big prizes don't exist. And the more I thought about it, the more I realised how easily it could all be done. I mean, commercial companies have to name their prize-winners. But that's not true of Premium Bonds. And what about all the people who have died or moved? What about all their tickets?"

"So, you think the government's swindling everyone." Sally poured herself some lemonade and, in that brief silence, Guy found himself wishing that he'd never begun. "But you didn't have any proof."

"No. But I was out of work and I didn't have anything else to do. So I started asking people."

"Oh." She understood now. "You mean like the joke."

"It was the same sort of thing, only it was more indiscriminate. I just wanted to find someone who'd won a million pounds on a Premium Bond. I was even going to advertise. I was going to put an advert in *Loot* or in the *Spectator*. 'Writer doing research seeks . . .' That sort of thing."

"So why didn't you?"

"I got a job and forgot about it. But, in a way, this business with the joke is the same sort of thing. I mean, it's more personal. It's a joke about Selina Moore and I knew her. I liked her . . . a lot."

"And do you really think that someone invented the joke? On purpose?"

"Why not?"

There was another silence. Sally seemed unsure what to say. "I think you're a bit of a conspiracy theorist," she said at last.

"I wouldn't say that," Guy replied. "Although it is absolutely true that the government has a top-secret department whose entire job is to keep an eye on conspiracy theorists."

That made her smile.

"I'm just interested in unusual things," he went on. "And for what it's worth, I have noticed something interesting about jokes. I know it's early days, but the joke has a definite direction. I've had to bounce around a bit, but most of the time I've been travelling north-east. I almost get the feeling that I'm heading somewhere, towards a specific point."

"What do you think you'll find when you get there?"

"I haven't got the faintest idea. I'm not even certain that there's a 'there' to get to. Maybe there's a fat stand-up comedian working on a pier in Lowestoft or somewhere. I once read somewhere that some of the older comedians — the ones who worked at the Palladium and all that — used to keep dozens of books full of jokes they'd invented."

"Maybe they swapped them. They could have had a library system."

"Yes. I quite like the sound of that."

And then everything changed. Guy heard a door open and at the same time saw the alarm in Sally's eyes. She was already getting to her feet as he turned round and saw a woman coming out of the house and into the garden . . . but a woman like none he had ever seen. She was huge. Not fat so much as massively, repulsively, impossibly swollen, with arms and legs that seemed to have been pumped full of water, a monstrous neck with chins melting across it, giant breasts that really were like water-melons in a sack. The woman was about fifty years old but her movement, as slow as a tortoise, made her seem older. She wore no makeup. Her skin was dead and disgusting, as if she had drowned and been pulled out of the river. Her eyes were bloodshot and seemed small, set in so much flesh. Her hair was grey and tangled. She was wearing a drab, flower-patterned dress that was shapeless, little more than a stretch of material hanging off her shoulders. Her feet were encased in pink, fluffy slippers that would slip on and off easily, a final humiliation.

"Mum!" Sally exclaimed.

"I thought I heard you talking to someone," the woman said. Her lips were so huge that they didn't quite seem to be shaping the words that she was actually saying, like a character in a cartoon. She waddled across the patio and slumped onto the bench. Her body had long ago lost its battle against whatever disease had invaded it. Now the fight was against gravity — and it was losing this one too. It wouldn't be long before Mrs Lockwood was unable to walk at all.

"I'm Sally's mother," she said unnecessarily. She was breathing heavily. The short distance had been all she had been able to manage.

"Hello," Guy said. He resisted the urge to stand up and shake the woman's hand. He couldn't quite bear the thought of touching it. "I'm Guy Fletcher."

"I haven't seen you here before. Are you one of Sally's friends? Not that she brings many of her friends here." She squinted at him. "I know you, don't I? What did you say your name was?"

"Guy is in that advert you like, Mother," Sally said, coming to his rescue. "The one for Nescafé."

"Nescafé?"

"He plays the window-cleaner."

"The cleaner!" She smiled, showing teeth that were slab-like and crooked. Wasn't there one part of this woman that God had spared? "I always thought you were very funny. And she was such an attractive girl! I sometimes think that the adverts are better than the programmes. What else have you done?"

"I was in *Manchester Murders*."

"I don't remember you."

"It wasn't my most memorable performance. I played 'man with puncture'. My character didn't have a name. He didn't even get murdered."

"Are you staying for lunch?"

"I'm afraid Guy has to leave," Sally said. "I'm going to walk him back to the shop."

"Why are you going back to the shop?"

"I have to cover for Amanda while she has an hour off."

There was some sort of ritual going on between mother and daughter. They were juggling half-truths between them. Sally was looking uncomfortable and

108

embarrassed. The mother was resigned. Neither of them would say what they really thought, not while Guy was there.

"Do you live in Cambridge?" Mrs Lockwood asked.

"No. I drove up from London."

"On a motorbike?" She had noticed the helmet. "They're such dangerous things. I'd never go on a motorbike."

She never *could* go on a motorbike. She must know that. Was she testing him in some strange sort of way?

"I'm a careful driver," Guy said. He stood up. He could see that Sally wanted to go.

"I haven't been to London for a very long time," Mrs Lockwood exclaimed. "I'd very much like to go there again. They've put a wonderful new roof on the British Museum — I've seen it in magazines. I used to spend a lot of time at the British Museum. In the Reading Room. I'd like to see that. Have you been?"

"No, I haven't." Guy was always embarrassed by how few of London's galleries and museums he had visited.

"You really should." She caught her breath. Even the act of speaking was limited to her. "Well, I'm very glad to have met you, Guy. I don't meet a lot of people these days and it's always a pleasure."

"Thank you, Mrs Lockwood."

"Daphne. Please call me Daphne. That's what all my friends call me."

Sally had stood up as well. "I'll only be an hour," she said. "Do you want me to help you back into the house?"

"No, thank you, dear. I think I'll stay out here. The garden looks so beautiful in the summer and after all that rain and fog . . . I never thought summer was going to arrive. Don't worry. I'll be all right. You take your time."

"Goodbye, Daphne," Guy said. "It was nice meeting you."

"And a pleasure to meet you."

He followed Sally back round the side of the house but he'd only taken a few steps when he heard whistling: a tune that he thought he recognised. Then he remembered. It was the tune from the Nescafé advertisement. He turned round. Mrs Lockwood was smiling at him.

"You see?" she said. "I can still whistle."

Sally walked with Guy back into the centre of Cambridge. "I'm sorry about that," she said.

"I'm the one who should apologise," Guy said. "I came to your house uninvited." There was a pause. He had to ask. "Has your mother always been like that?"

"No." Sally seemed distracted. "Only for the last six or seven years, but recently it's got a lot worse. She has elephantiasis. Do you know what that is?"

"I've heard of it."

"Lymphatic filariasis. That's its other name. That's what Mother calls it. She says she doesn't like being compared with an elephant. But what difference does a name make?" For a moment she was bitter. "Mother spent a lot of time in South America when she was young. My grandfather was in the tobacco business.

110

He's dead now. She was probably bitten by a mosquito carrying a parasite. That's how it's transmitted. The parasites hide in the corridors of the lymphatic system and reproduce until there are millions of them. You can have the disease for years without knowing it and then, suddenly . . ." She fell silent. "Well, you've seen."

"I'm terribly sorry," Guy said. "Isn't there a cure?"

"There are drugs. DEC and Ivermectin. But the doctors still don't know enough about the disease and nothing has worked on her. I'm afraid she can't go on very much longer. There's always a danger of kidney failure."

Guy shook his head. "I don't know what to say," he said. "I've come blundering into your life, asking you about a joke, and now this."

"Some people think Mother is a joke," Sally said, and in that moment Guy understood everything: her reluctance to let him into the house, her rapid departure, her assistant's protectiveness at the shop before they had even met. She was quietly angry. "And I suppose she is a joke, really. She's fat. She wobbles. She's a freak!"

"She's ill."

"You were talking about old-style comedians. 'I wouldn't say my mother-in-law is fat but when she falls over she rocks herself to sleep trying to stand up.' That's true in her case. If she falls over, she can't get up on her own. And I have found her asleep, once or twice, on the floor."

"Where's your dad?" Guy asked.

111

"He left. He couldn't stand it. You see, Mother was a very —" Sally stopped herself. "I've seen photographs and she was quite beautiful when she was young. She and Dad started the shop and got it running. He was an anthropologist, really. An amateur one. He wanted to write a book about ancient civilisations in Central America and Mum ran the shop to help him keep going. They used to spend hours together at the British Museum and places like that. I was their only child. I've always lived here in Cambridge."

"In that house?"

"No." She paused. There was something she wasn't telling him. "We only moved there a couple of years ago. That was after Dad left. He couldn't bear being with her. It wasn't just a question of being in the same bed. That was out of the question anyway. But watching her getting fatter and fatter. I think he loved her so much that it hurt him. I try to think the best of him anyway. One morning he just wasn't there. I got a postcard from him last year, from somewhere in Mexico, so I suppose he's happy. But as for Mum and me . . . well, we get on as best we can."

"Is there really no cure?" Guy asked.

Sally shook her head. "Elephantiasis usually only lasts four or five years. But with her it's different. She's had all sorts of treatments but it won't go away. One of the specialists even wrote an article about her. It was published in the *Lancet*. Mum said she was the page-three pin-up. I suppose it's a mercy she hasn't lost her sense of humour."

They had walked all the way back into Cambridge and suddenly they were in front of the shop.

"I never told you about the joke," she said. "The joke you were asking me about."

"Oh, yes . . ." Guy had already decided he wasn't going to mention it unless she did. It seemed horribly inappropriate now.

"A joke about Selina Moore. Why is Selina Moore like a Ferrero Rocher? I heard it about a week ago but I'm afraid I'm not going to be able to help you very much. It was about five o'clock in the evening. I'd just got back from the shop and there was a salesman in the house — you know, one of those door-to-door people. I was angry to begin with. I can't stand people cold-calling. We get them all the time in the shop but having them at home is even worse. I would have thrown him out then and there but I could see Mum didn't want me to."

"What was he selling?"

"Domestic appliances. Cleaning stuff. I don't know. I didn't really look. He was a pleasant enough man. About thirty-something. Quite well dressed. The thing is, Mum liked having him there. The way they were getting on, you'd think they'd known each other for years and, like I say, she doesn't get a lot of visitors. So I didn't ask him to leave. Not at once. And I have to be fair to him. He must have known that Mum wasn't going to buy anything from him but he wasn't trying to force any of his products down her throat. There was no hard sell. None of the sort of stuff you see on those TV programmes where old ladies suddenly discover

113

they've bought a time-share in Málaga or something. He'd even gone into the kitchen and made Mum a cup of tea. And he was chatting with her, telling her jokes."

"My joke . . ."

"Yes. That was one of them. To be honest with you, I didn't even think it was very funny. I don't like sick jokes. In fact, I don't really like jokes at all. I can never remember them and when I do tell them I always get the punch-line wrong."

"Me too."

"But then, a few days later, I found myself at the Bear. John Patterson is quite a good customer and he and Liz are always so welcoming. Whenever I go round there, he always insists that I stay for a drink. Anyway, there were quite a few people there and they were telling jokes and suddenly they were looking at me and I realised it was my turn and I didn't want to look like a stick-in-the-mud so I told the first joke that came into my head."

"Ferrero Rocher."

"Yes."

Guy considered. "What company was he working for, this salesman?"

"I knew you were going to ask me that. He gave me a business card but I don't know what I've done with it. I've probably thrown it away."

"You don't remember his name?"

"Bill something. I'm sorry. But I think the company was called Sphinx. It was either that or Sphinx Products or Sphinx Appliances. I remember the first

114

part because it was such a strange name for a company manufacturing vacuum cleaners."

"Are they local?"

"I can't tell you that either. I'm not being very helpful, am I? The man left about ten or fifteen minutes after I came in. And the funny thing is, in the end, we didn't even see any of his products."

"He didn't leave a catalogue?"

"Just a card."

Guy became aware that they were standing in the middle of the pavement, blocking the way for people going past. It seemed there was nothing more to say.

"If I find the card, I'll give you a ring," Sally said.

"Would you?" Guy gave her his telephone number. She wrote it in biro on the back of her hand.

She stepped into the shop. Guy noticed the assistant, Amanda, gazing at him suspiciously. Then Sally came out again. "Do you mind me saying something, Guy?" she asked. It was the first time she had addressed him by name. He shook his head. "I don't want to be rude — but I really can't see this idea of yours working. Jokes. I really think you're wasting your time."

"I know," he admitted ruefully. "I don't seem to be getting anywhere. Maybe I should go back to Premium Bonds."

"I wouldn't do that either."

They shook hands.

"It was nice meeting you," Guy said.

"Take care."

He walked back to his motorbike, hoping he could find a way to see her again.

CHAPTER
TEN

Guy's life returned to normal, for the next couple of days at least. He went shopping at Marks and Spencer. He went to the latest Tarantino with Jack and Paul. He joined a couple of workshops; one for movement, one for voice. He even went to the gym.

Like many actors, he tried to work out at least a couple of times a week although he hated every minute of it and felt a dull resentment against whatever forces in society had created the vogue for health and fitness. One day, inevitably, he would stop. Everyone did. And within a month all his hard work would have dissolved, quite literally, the muscles cheerfully returning to their former state of jelly and fat. That was another reason to hate the place. He looked forward to the time when everyone else woke up to the fact that no matter how much you flexed and strained, you would still grow old and die — and on that day every last Holmes Place and LA Fitness would be burned down in a nationwide fit of pique. Just what it deserved.

Still, he went and changed into his Nike shirt and shorts and even booked an appointment with Ryan, his occasional personal trainer who pretended to know everything about abs and pecs but still took ten minutes working out how to tie his shoelaces. Ryan was small and curly-haired and spent his whole life in the gym. He had virtually no life outside it. He was one of the saddest people Guy knew.

"Have you been working?" he asked, standing over Guy while Guy struggled with the chest press.

"No. I've been chasing a joke."

"Really? That's great. Keep those arms straight. What do you mean — chasing it?"

"Have you ever wondered where jokes come from?"

"No." Ryan waited until Guy had finished his set of eight repetitions. "I heard a good one the other day."

"Thanks, Ryan. I don't want to hear it."

"Right then. Ten minutes on the treadmill."

What was wrong with him? As he moved onto the carefully measured tedium of the treadmill, Guy realised he was still thinking about Sally Lockwood. He thought about her even as his feet counted out the thud, thud, thud of the exercise machine. Everything about her was improbable. The shop in Cambridge. Thud, thud, thud. That exquisite house. Her mother. He had liked her, that mix of assertiveness and vulnerability. He had been attracted to her too. He wished now that he had invited her out to dinner while he was there. But Cambridge was too far away for a relationship and although he had just run three point seven kilometres, he was no nearer. Anyway, she hadn't really shown any interest in him. He put her out of his mind.

"Have you got a girlfriend, Ryan?" he panted.

"Yeah."

"Where did you meet her?"

"The usual place."

The back pages of *Time Out*. Ryan had advertised so often, they probably gave him a discount.

And as he tramped back to the house, Guy wondered if the same fate would befall him. He hadn't had sex for weeks. Months, in fact. He would have liked to have had sex with Sally Lockwood. He could imagine her in bed. She would be lithe and mischievous. Sex with her would be a sort of naked hide-and-seek.

He arrived back at Mapletree Close and was sorry to be there. He knew now that if the flat had been a mistake when he bought it, it was well on the way to becoming a total disaster. He didn't want to be on his own — and he certainly didn't want to be on his own in a terraced, suburban house, sandwiched between a vicious spinster and a dwarf.

The telephone was ringing as he went in.

Guy reached it just in time, hoping, as he always did, that it would be Sylvie with good news. God, did that make him an actor or what? In fact it *was* Sylvie or, at least, her assistant, Eric. He was sounding flustered and weary. Eric always sounded weary, as if he couldn't stand being in the business. "Guy? How nice of you to answer the phone at last. Where have you been?"

"In the gym."

"For two days? Well, I'm glad you're in. Have the pages arrived?"

"What pages?"

"I biked them over this morning." A pause. "What happened to your answer machine?"

Guy glanced at the window-sill, at the space that the answering machine had once occupied. Now there was just a rectangle drawn in the dust. It was Kate, of course. She had come round to collect some of her stuff and, it was true, she had been the one who had paid for the answering machine. But he still felt a stab of irritation that it had gone.

"The pages should have been with you an hour ago," Eric went on. "We use a bike service and I was under the impression it was motorbikes they were referring to. Not the push variety. Anyway, you're wanted tomorrow morning: 8:30, Jacob Street studios. Do you know where they are?"

"They wouldn't by any chance be in Jacob Street?"

"That's very amusing, Guy."

"Eric, wait a minute. I don't have any idea —"

The doorbell rang. Guy was momentarily frozen, caught between the phone and the door. But Eric had heard it at the other end of the line. "That'll be them now. It's a straight offer. Two days' work. Read the pages and let me know if you've got a problem."

The line went dead.

Guy hurried downstairs and took a sealed brown envelope from a leather-clad dispatch rider. He signed for it, already testing the weight of the script in his hand. It was what everyone did with scripts: weighed them first. When he turned round, he found himself face-to-face with a grey, hunched-over woman in a very unpleasant cardigan. It was Mrs Atwood, his

119

downstairs neighbour. She had witnessed the transaction and, although she said nothing, her eyes were fixed on the package and her whole face radiated suspicion.

"How are you, Mrs Atwood?" Guy asked.

"Getting a letter?"

"Not a letter. No." Guy couldn't resist teasing her. She was always so bloody mournful. "I've decided to join the SAS and these must be my registration papers."

"The SAS?"

"Yes. But don't tell anyone or I'm afraid I'll be forced to kill you."

He left her on the doorstep and hurried back upstairs.

He discovered from the script and from the letters enclosed that he had been offered a walk-on part in a new television sit-com, which was being made for the BBC. Guy opened the script fearing the worst. There had been so many bad sit-coms on British television that the very word had become synonymous with something that was faintly embarrassing and unlikely to make you laugh. It felt as if several decades had gone by since much-loved actors in wobbly sets had delighted the nation. The unlikely couples. The remarried divorcees. The middle-aged rebels. Where were they now?

The answer seemed to be right there in Guy's hands. *Two in the Bush*, the producer wrote, was a homage to the innocent humour of the seventies but in a bright, contemporary setting. Homage, Guy wondered, rhyming with Bromwich? Or homage as in the French variety, *hom-arge?* Neither gave him much confidence. The story was set in Shepherd's Bush where Greg — a very strait-laced lawyer — found himself sharing a flat with Alan, a flamboyantly gay theatrical designer. As Guy had only been sent the second episode, he was unable to tell how this hilarious state of affairs had arisen. The two of them lived above a second flat owned by a married couple: Rosie, a nurse from Jamaica, and Charles, a dyslexic librarian.

The episode that Guy had been offered centred on Alan having a blind date with someone he had contacted through the Lonely Hearts section of *Time Out*. The date was coming to the flat on the same evening that Greg's right-wing, homophobic boss — Mr Baxter — was coming to dinner. Greg had arranged the dinner because he was about to be promoted to partner and needed to make a good impression. Guy would play Lawrence, Mr Baxter's personal assistant. He had been sent to the flat to pick up an article for a newspaper, which Mr Baxter had been commissioned to write. But Greg had mistaken him for the blind date.

Guy read:

17. Int. corridor outside Greg's flat evening

GREG *opens the door to find a young man, casually dressed. This is* LAWRENCE. *He works for* BAXTER. GREG *assumes he has come for his date with* ALAN. *He is determined to get rid of him!*
LAWRENCE: Good evening.
GREG: I'm really sorry. You can't come in.

LAWRENCE: Why not?

GREG: Why not? (*panicking*) We're feeling anti-social. We've changed our minds. We've got foot-and-mouth!

MR BAXTER *calls from the living room:*

BAXTER (o/s): Who is it?

GREG: It's no one. Just the pizza delivery man.

LAWRENCE: What?

GREG: Look. I'm sorry. You're going to have to forget the date.

LAWRENCE: (*puzzled*) It's September the fifth and I don't have any pizza.

GREG: No. I know. Look, I don't want to let you in.

LAWRENCE: Do you want to give it to me here?

GREG: (*aghast*) What?

LAWRENCE: How many column inches have you got?

GREG: (*to himself*) Alan — I'm going to kill you for this. (*to LAWRENCE*) Listen . . . I think you should know. I'm straight!

LAWRENCE: It doesn't bother me.

GREG: No. I mean — you've got the wrong person.

LAWRENCE: That's right. I'm looking for Mr Baxter.

GREG: (*horrified*) You mean . . .? (*He jumps to the wrong conclusion.*) I didn't know he was like that!

Guy read the script a second time, then he called Eric. "I've got a problem," he said.

"Oh, yes?"

"The script. It's terrible. It isn't funny!"

There was a brief silence. "Do you want to talk to Sylvie?" Eric asked. In his vocabulary, this was the ultimate threat.

"No, but —"

"It's two days' work. Four hundred pounds' engagement fee plus forty-five pounds for the second day."

"Why such short notice?"

"They didn't say. Do you want me to tell them no?"

It was four hundred and forty-five pounds. It was a job.

"I'll be there," Guy said, and rang off.

Guy went into the kitchen to make some tea, only to find that the kettle had gone too. Kate again. He put some water in a saucepan, and while it was boiling, he went round the flat, hoping there wouldn't be too many more unpleasant surprises. In fact, Kate had removed herself from his life with all the delicacy of a surgeon performing a life-saving operation. Two pillows had gone from the bed. There were faint patches on the wall where pictures had once hung, gaps in the CD stacking system and in the bookshelves. Odd items, including a bathmat, an ice tray, a stuffed wombat and a pretend Oscar, had been removed. It was like playing a new sort of parlour game. Separation, from Mattel. How much can you spot that's missing from the parlour?

He made the tea and read through the rest of *Two in the Bush*. It had been written by the successful team of Jeremy Samber and Don Reeve, the authors of *In for a Penny*, a sit-com set in the City, and *What Goes Up*, a British space station. It seemed that their entire oeuvre had been inspired by *Brewer's Dictionary of Phrase and Fable*. Guy tried to imagine the two of them working together, tossing ideas back and forth over their word-processors. Was this how jokes began, with two whiz-kids in a flat in Islington?

"How many column inches have you got, Jeremy?"

"That's great, Don. That's great. Do you want to give it to me now?"

But there weren't any jokes in *Two in the Bush*. Nobody could possibly find it funny, not until they put the canned laughter over the dialogue. Guy had heard it said that some of the people laughing at BBC sit-coms had been dead for thirty years. You'd have to be dead to laugh at material like this. Brain-dead, anyway.

Sphinx.

Sphinx Products. That was the name of the company that Sally's salesman had worked for and it had been whispering at the back of Guy's consciousness all day, even when he was at the gym. He was sure that it was familiar. Had he read about it? Had there been an advertisement in the paper? It was such an odd name. Sally had been right about that. Not the sort of name you'd forget and yet too oblique to be exactly memorable.

Sphinx. Sphinx. Sphinx. Sphinx. Sphinx.

It was still nudging at him now. He suddenly put down the script and went over to the telephone. At least that was still there. Now, what was the number for Directory Enquiries and what number did you ring to find out? Ever since they'd changed the service, Guy had had this problem. Eventually he remembered, and dialled.

"Hello? What name, please?"

"Sphinx Products."

"Can you tell me what town?"

"No. I'm afraid I don't know."

"I'm sorry, Caller. I need a town."

"It's a company. It could be Sphinx Appliances. I don't know where it's based. Somewhere near Cambridge?"

"Sphinx? How do you spell it?"

"S-P-H-I-N-X."

"I'm sorry. I don't have any listing in Cambridge."

He hung up and went into the bedroom. There was a table in the corner with a computer he used mainly for games, emails and surfing the Net. It was five years old, making its central processor a modern antique. It took an age to boot itself up and a small eternity to connect itself with AOL — but at last it was there. Guy had half a dozen emails but he ignored them for the moment. He chose a search engine and typed in the word.

There were four hundred and eighteen thousand files connected with Sphinx. Guy added the word "England", which brought the figure down to a mere twenty-three thousand but none of these seemed to be connected with domestic appliances. The first two hundred were related to Egypt, to Nile cruises, to hotels in and around Cairo and to the possibility that Luxor and the Valley of the Kings had been constructed by aliens. There were sixty or seventy companies advertising New Age products. And there were companies producing everything from hi-fis to gun-cleaning products to prosthetic limbs.

He scrolled down through several hundred websites but the truth was that the computer was so hopeless he could have moved faster if he had been turning the pages of a valuable antique book. In the end he got fed up and flicked it off. Then he went back into the kitchen to learn his lines, unaware that incredibly sophisticated eavesdropping technology had picked up his request on the computer, as it had a few minutes earlier when he said the two words "Sphinx Products" on the telephone.

It took Guy fourteen seconds to reach the kitchen. In that time, the information had been beamed twice round the world, setting off alarm signals in nine countries.

The sit-com still didn't make him laugh.

CHAPTER
ELEVEN

Two hundred miles to the north-east, a man in a dark suit was studying a file.

There was an extraordinary stillness about him as he concentrated on the closely typed pages, which, although word-processed, had been printed using such an old-fashioned typeface that they could have been thirty years out of date, perhaps uncovered by a historian under the Freedom of Information Act. That they were, or had been, top secret was in no doubt. Each page was stamped with the two words in red, and the heavy, dark green folder that contained them had attached to it a list of the personnel who were cleared to receive it. There were in fact only three names. The top one was Rupert Liddy and this was the name of the man in the suit.

He was of indeterminate age, somewhere in his fifties, although his jet black hair might have belonged to a younger man. Possibly it was dyed. He had the face of a businessman, all lines and angles, with very thin gold-rimmed spectacles, an aquiline nose and the merest suggestion of lips. The suit was an expensive one. He wore a very fresh white shirt with cufflinks and what looked suspiciously like an old school tie. He might once have been in the army. There was something about the way he sat, with his back straight, his shoulders perfectly in line, without any hint of comfort or relaxation. He was also totally emotionless. It was only when he turned a page that he proved with any certainty that he was actually alive.

He was sitting in a leather reproduction chair behind a large reproduction desk. Why anyone should have wished to reproduce the originals was a mystery for they were both hideous. The chair was black leather, the shiny sort, punched into the wooden frame with golden studs. It swivelled. The desk was huge and symmetrical with brass rings hanging on the drawers. The surface was almost empty. There was a single black telephone and, next to it, an in-tray and an out-tray. But that was not how they were marked. They were marked GOOD NEWS and BAD NEWS. There was nothing else on the desk; not so much as a pen, a paperclip or a family photograph. Only Liddy's reflection, reading the file, showed in the highly polished surface, a shadowy figure, a devil, rising up from some secret world below.

The room was rectangular with little ornamentation and a plain, beige carpet. There were two doors and most of the walls were taken up with bookshelves with books rising from floor to ceiling. There must have been over five hundred volumes but none of the spines showed titles or authors' names. Three wooden chairs had been placed opposite the desk. Dark green velvet curtains framed the only window and here was a surprise. Looking at the room and the man who occupied it, one might have expected a view of Whitehall or perhaps the City. Instead, the window looked out on a quite remarkably beautiful swathe of the English coastline: sand and water, wild grass blowing in the breeze, fishing-boats and dinghies moored round a ramshackle quay.

Rupert Liddy was holding a photograph of Guy Fletcher. Guy Andrew Michael Fletcher. All the names were attached along with just about everything else it was possible to know about the man. He had been trying to read the face but as the picture had been taken from *Spotlight* — the actor's Bible — it said very little apart from "I'm handsome — employ me!" It was a handsome face, certainly. It reminded Liddy of a young Robert Redford (and, indeed, the last time he had ventured into a cinema, Redford had been young). The picture was black-and-white but he could imagine the eyes were blue. They would go with the slightly boyish features.

An actor?

There were thirty pages in the file, beginning with Guy's age, his weight, his height, his postal address and the addresses of every building he had ever occupied. His foster-parents were in there, the date of his adoption, the identity of his true mother. This had particularly interested Liddy. Using a silver fountain pen, he had written the name, Selina Moore, on a piece of paper and circled it. Then he had added a question mark. His writing was very neat. The question mark was almost a work of art.

What else did Liddy know? He had Guy's email address, the registration number of his motorbike, the state of his current bank balance, all his direct debits, credit agreements and the details of the last three hundred payments he had made on Access and Barclaycard. His two police reports were there: the first for driving without due care and attention, the second a caution for the possession of half a gram of marijuana. There were also other photographs and facsimiles. Guy's passport photograph (enlarged and computer-enhanced) had been attached, along with a picture taken by a "traffic camera" near Alexandra Palace, the signature on his driving licence and a copy of his fingerprints. Guy had appeared in a local newspaper when he had played Horatio at the Clairemont and these clippings were enclosed. Finally, there were brief paragraphs about Jane, Torin, Jack and Paul, a slightly longer one about Kate and an inconclusive and rather unhelpful report from a psychiatrist.

All of this, Rupert Liddy had committed to memory. This was his great gift. He had a brain that was truly encyclopedic in that he could bring to the surface anything from the mating ritual of the aardvark to the back streets of Zanzibar if he had once come across them. That film with Robert Redford, for example, *A Bridge Too Far*. Written by William Goldman. Directed by Richard Attenborough. If he thought for a moment, he could probably tell you who did the set design. He had seen the film in a cinema in North London and he remembered buying a Kia-Ora from a girl who was wearing too much lipstick. It was a gift

130

and at the same a curse. Information screamed at him from morning to night. He couldn't look at anything without setting off a spinning, ricocheting series of associations. Sometimes he felt he carried the problems of the world on his shoulders. And he had a splitting headache.

It was obvious to him that Guy Fletcher was dangerous but the one question that the file had been unable to answer for all its meticulousness was, why exactly had he embarked on the course of action that had brought him this far? Clearly it had something to do with his mother but, according to the file, the two of them had never met . . . well, once if you counted the delivery room. Was he acting out of some misplaced sense of revenge? Liddy glanced at his watch. It was one minute to ten o'clock. He had requested a meeting on the hour and he knew that his associates would not be late.

Sure enough, just as the minute hand completed its long, tedious journey and began yet another, there was a knock at the door and, without waiting for an answer, three men came in from an outer office where they had evidently been waiting. Briefly, he glanced outside into a room that was more modern, more brightly lit than his own. It was divided by partitions, with blinds blocking the view outside. A young woman sat tapping at a computer keyboard. Surprisingly, she was scantily dressed with a bright pink top stretching across huge breasts and blonde hair falling carelessly to her shoulders. She was typing slowly with her tongue in the corner of her mouth, obviously having difficulty finding the letters. She was there for a moment and then she was gone. The third man closed the door and Liddy turned his attention to his visitors as they sat down in the waiting chairs.

"I'm rather afraid that we have a problem," he said. His manner of speech was military, the words clipped and very level. He had not wasted his time with any sort of welcome and none had been expected. "The person under examination originally claimed to be a university student. This turned out to be a lie. He is, in fact, an actor." He was unable to keep a note of distaste out of his voice. He continued: "His name is Guy Fletcher. He first came to our attention a couple of days ago when we received a report from our agent in East Anglia. I take it you've all read it?"

Two of the men nodded.

"I read some of it," the third man said. He spoke with an Irish accent. "But I only got it late last night, you know. And I wasn't well this morning . . ."

"It doesn't matter," Liddy interrupted. He drew a breath. "The fact that he was asking certainly unusual questions in a public house in Cambridge — the Bear, on Willow Road, originally Elizabethan — might have been nothing more than a coincidence. A quirk, a caprice, a vagary, a maggot, a capriccio, a whim-wham . . ." He forced himself out of that line of thought. "However, yesterday we received further intelligence. It appears that Mr Fletcher has been continuing his enquiries both on the telephone and through the Internet and that makes him very much a primary concern."

"Do you have any idea who he's working for?" one of the men asked. His name was Smythe and he was about fifty years old, with the face of an undertaker and the elongated body of a laid-out corpse. He was dressed in a made-to-measure suit with highly polished shoes.

"Not at the moment. No. It could be that he's acting independently. He has a curious connection with Selina Moore, actress, star of *The Interceptors*, Hollywood-based 1984 to 1991, recently deceased, as you will see from the report. But that is exactly what we have to find out. As far as we can tell, he has no links with the media or with any other interested party."

"You said that he's an actor," the second man said.

"Yes, Mr McLarrity. Reasonably well established in television, films and theatre, as you will have seen from his CV."

"Well, for fuck's sake, what sort of organisation would want to employ a fucking actor?"

McLarrity, as would have been suggested by both his name and his almost impenetrable accent, was Scottish — so he was probably over-egging it with his bright ginger hair, ginger beard and kilt. He was less than five feet tall with the body of a wrestler, his shoulders threatening to burst through his rather nasty worsted jacket. He was sitting in an aggressive position with his knees apart, showing bulging ginger-covered flesh between the bottom of his kilt and the top of his calf-length socks.

"It does seem unlikely," Liddy agreed. "But he has had occasional periods of unemployment, inactivity,

133

idleness, inertia, sloth . . . and anyone could have approached him in that time."

"Approached him to investigate us?"

"My instinct is that he's probably working on his own. But anything is possible."

"What do you want us to do?" Smythe asked.

"We have never had a situation like this before and I will naturally have to report to my superiors. In the first instance, however, I think we need to contain him. We'll need to keep him in a tight security network while we check him out, find out just what it is he thinks he's doing and why."

"What do you mean by 'contain' him?" the third man asked.

"Exactly what I say, Mr O'Neil. We need to be in control of the situation."

O'Neil was the youngest of the three and the only one who hadn't read the report. He was the least formally dressed, wearing a short leather jacket and jeans. He had yellow, wiry hair, sprouting out of a potato-like head. His eyes were pale green and lifeless. For much of the meeting, his attention had been fixed on a wasp, buzzing at a window. Suddenly he stood up and went over to it. He reached out and crushed it with his thumb. Then he sat down again.

Liddy opened the top left drawer of his desk and took out three further written reports. "These are the latest updates," he said. "Mr Fletcher is currently working on a new television programme, *Two in the Bush*, written by Jeremy Samber and Don Reeve. The latter is, incidentally, a member of the Communist

134

Party although I doubt that's particularly relevant. You'll find the shooting schedule here." He handed them across. "In essence, I trust you to handle the situation in whatever way you see fit. I'll be in London myself in a couple of days' time and you can report to me then. Do you have any further questions?"

There was silence. Smythe was already reading his report. McLarrity had rolled his up and was pounding it in the palm of his hand like a cosh. O'Neil was holding his upside-down.

"Very well. You can leave."

That was it. A decision had been made.

The Englishman, the Irishman and the Scotsman got up and left the room.

CHAPTER
TWELVE

It was strange how quickly Guy had forgotten about the joke. The events of the last few days — the Hungarian dentist, the Boy Scouts, the Bear at Cambridge — had faded from his consciousness as quickly and as completely as an old television programme. He still thought of Sally Lockwood though. He wondered if he should ring her and invite her down to London. She could come and visit him on the set.

Because he was working again.

It was wonderful being back, surrounded by lights, cameras and (spasmodically, this being the BBC) action. Guy still loved the world of television production, with its generators and lighting rigs, its trucks, its trailers, its twisting wires. He loved the way that nothing ever seemed to be happening when, in fact, so much always was. Once again, he was back on the double-decker bus, going home from school, instantly fascinated by the merest glimpse of location filming. What had he been? Nine years old? At that age, the trestle tables and tea urns had been nothing less than the twin pillars at the doors of the greatest church. No wonder he had become an actor. There had never been any chance he would be anything else.

And here he was back in the midst of it. He had been called at six in the morning and squeezed into a tiny compartment in an American Freeway. A table, a mirror and a fusty sofa. But it still had his name on the door. Or, at least, his character's name. And that was almost the same thing.

As so often happened, his scenes were being filmed back to front. He had already spent one day at the studio in Jacob Street where the permanent set had been built. He had collected the newspaper article from Mr Baxter, a five-minute scene that had taken not much longer — using multi-cameras — to shoot. Today they were doing exteriors. He would drive up to the house and meet Greg at the door. The unit was parked on a real street — not in Shepherd's Bush but in Vauxhall, and a few of the residents had come out to see what was going on. The sun was shining. So far everything had gone well.

While Guy waited for his scene to be shot, he read the *Sun*, the *Mirror*, *The Times*, the *Independent* and the *Stage*. He ate lunch on the catering bus and briefly met the actor who was playing Greg. Makeup and Costumes fussed over him. He was recognised by a spark who had worked on *E for Emergency*. In fact, everyone was so friendly that he found it easy to forget that he had only a small part in one episode and that the material was dire. By the end of the first day he had decided that *Two in the Bush* might, after all, be a comic masterpiece.

He still had no idea how the director, Mike Watson, had chosen him but that didn't matter. Mike was plump, smiling and easy-going. He had done his best work twenty years ago but his name was still a good one to have attached to a show. Guy's was the first scene to be shot after lunch and his notes were simple. Stand at the door, say the lines. Keep it cheerful. A master shot and two over-the-shoulder close-ups and it was done.

It all went very well. They were shooting on video, not film, which made the whole process faster, and Guy liked having members of the public on the opposite pavement. It was certainly more fun than being in a studio. After they had finished and the camera was being moved for the next shot, he strolled across the road. There was a Renault Mégane parked on the other side. This was the car he would be driving. He only had one shot left — his arrival.

But as he approached the car, he found his way blocked. There was three men standing in front of him. The one in the middle was short with ginger hair and, rather surprisingly, a kilt.

"Mr Fletcher?" the man asked.

"Yes?"

At first, Guy thought he must be another actor. The kilt, in the middle of London on a Tuesday afternoon, was somehow improbable, as was the ginger hair, sprouting untidily as if out of a gashed sofa. But he wasn't an actor. He was holding a pen and an autograph book.

"I'm a great admirer of yours," he said, but there was a malevolent twinkle in his eyes and his voice oozed menace.

138

"We all are." Guy noted the Irish accent almost immediately as the second man spoke. "In fact, we've been watching you for some time."

"Well . . . thank you." Even as he muttered the automatic response, Guy knew that something was wrong. He didn't have admirers. Not yet. Even so, he signed the book.

"Very kind of you. Very, very kind of you." This was the third man. He was much taller than the others. Skeletal was the word that sprang to mind.

"Thank *you*, Mr Fletcher," the first man purred. "You have given myself and my friends hours of pleasure. I personally cannot watch an episode of *E for Emergency* without recollecting your performance as — if I am not mistaken — the victim of a beating . . ."

"That's what it was," the Irishman said. "Beaten to a pulp."

". . . while your all-too-brief but enjoyable appearance in *Policemen's Wives* certainly provided me and my friends with an unforgettable viewing experience." Guy tried to withdraw his hand but the Scotsman was suddenly gripping it with fingers of iron. "And, of course, there were the *Manchester Murders*. Do you like murder, Mr Fletcher?"

"I'm sorry?"

"I've always enjoyed a good murder myself. That's why I was so keen to make your acquaintance."

"Look, if you'll excuse me . . ."

The Scotsman pumped his hand. The smile on his face was grim and humourless. "I want you to know that we'll be watching you, Mr Fletcher."

139

"We all will," the tall man said.

"What do you mean?"

Guy was suddenly nervous. Had he become the victim of three celebrity stalkers with a generous view of the definition of "celebrity"?

The eyes were boring into him: dirty blue beneath wispy ginger brows. But then there was a movement and normality returned in the shape of the first assistant: a cheerful and efficient girl who had come to fetch him. "We're ready for you, Guy."

The Scotsman let go of Guy's hand. "We'll see you again," he said. The three of them backed away.

Guy watched as they walked across the road and joined the small crowd on the other side. It occurred to him that all three looked more fake, more unreal than anything on the set. They were like extras out of another programme. A horror film. They were staring at him with a strange, brooding malevolence. He couldn't understand why they were there. And then it occurred to him. An Englishman, an Irishman and . . .

"Are you all right, Guy?" It was the first assistant again. She was worried about him. But it was her job to worry about everything.

"Yes. Sure." Guy tried to ignore the three men but even when he turned away he was still aware of them, watching him.

"The car's an automatic. Are you OK with that?"

"Fine."

Mike Watson came over to him. He was wearing the sort of puffa jacket that all TV directors seem to like. It was sleeveless, with "Trust me, I'm a Doctor" stiched across the back. He had a script in one hand. "You didn't drink at lunch-time, did you?" he joked.

"No."

"Well, we're just moving the car now. You drive it down and stop in front of the house. Do you see? We've drawn a chalk mark on the kerb. You park the car and get out. Then you go over to the door and ring the bell. We'll do the whole thing in a single shot."

"Right."

Makeup came over and dusted his cheeks. A girl took a Polaroid photograph of him for continuity. Meanwhile, the second assistant had moved the Renault a little further up the road and turned it round so that it was ready to drive.

Guy glanced round. The three men were still there.

"This way, Guy."

He was led into the car. The sun was beating down and it suddenly felt very hot. He forced himself to concentrate. A multi-racial group of fans had come to watch the filming. One had asked for his autograph. What was so strange about that? He was being ridiculous.

"All right, Guy. You can start the car. We'll be ready for you in a minute." The voice came from a transmitter on the back seat.

Mike Watson sat down on a folding chair in the middle of the road, opposite the house. The camera was next to him. Guy would drive towards it and it would pan round as he parked. Simple enough . . .

He turned on the engine. It seemed too loud.

"Seat-belt on, please, Guy," the voice said again from the back seat. He put it on.

And they were still watching him. The man in the kilt shook his head slowly, as if reprimanding him. "We'll be watching you." Guy remembered what he had said.

"Turnover. Be quiet, everyone. Sound running!"

The clapper-loader ran forward in front of the camera. "Scene fifty nine, take one!" she called out, and clapped the board.

It was all happening at once. The sun, the camera, the car, Mike Watson, the three men, all the different pieces seemed to have broken up and slowed down until they came to a complete halt. They hung there, disassociated. Guy felt as if he was having a massive attack of stage fright. What had happened to him? It was ridiculous.

"Speed!" the cameraman shouted. The single word referred to the movement of the film through the camera and had nothing to do with the car. Even so, Guy became aware that his foot was resting a little too heavily on the accelerator.

The three sets of eyes were fixed. Rigid.

"Action!" Watson called.

The car leaped forward.

It should have been the easiest thing in the world. How much acting talent did you need to drive a Renault Mégane ten metres down a street? But the three men had jinxed him. They had done it quite deliberately. Guy was aware only that he was hurtling too fast towards the camera. He tried to look for the chalk marking on the pavement but everything had become a blur. He forced himself to concentrate. The road whipped past him.

THUD.

Inside the car, the sound of the collision was incredibly loud. He thought he must have run into a lamp-post but then he saw, with a sickening lurch in his stomach, the limp form of the director hurtling past his windscreen. Disconcerted and not looking where he was going, Guy had accidentally run into him. He stamped his foot on the brake. Everything seemed to be happening in slow motion. In fact, it *was* happening in slow motion, he recalled. For some reason, Watson had told him he was going to shoot it that way. Now the body hit the pavement. The car shuddered to a halt. Everybody froze.

Guy was the first to react. He opened the car door and more or less spilled out on to the pavement. The assistant director, cameraman, grips, sparks and continuity girl were staring at him in total amazement. Guy closed his eyes. Why couldn't it have been a lamp-post? Why couldn't it have been anyone but him?

A St John's Ambulance man ran past. Watson sat up. At least he wasn't dead. Suddenly everyone was talking at once. The assistant director came over to him. "Are you all right?" she asked.

"I think so."

"You'd better stay where you are."

Guy nodded. He was feeling sick. He turned away and looked back into the crowd. The three men had gone.

On film and television sets, everyone treats everyone else with almost exaggerated politeness. This is partly because so many different talents deserve respect, but it also has a lot to do with the very large insurance claims that may be made when something goes wrong. So nobody said anything to Guy, apart from Watson who was screaming, "You fucking wanker!" as he was carried into the ambulance. The producer, hastily summoned from his office, could hardly have been more sympathetic. The other actors patted him gently on the back, silently thanking God and all His angels that they hadn't been the one behind the wheel. The rest of the crew said nothing and avoided his eye.

In fact, it could have been worse. Watson hadn't been badly hurt and was back on the set later that afternoon with a plaster on his forehead and one arm in a sling. Only three hours' filming had been lost and the insurance would definitely pay for that. Guy had already filmed the later scene and, unless there was any post-synching, he wouldn't be needed again. It had been decided that a stunt double could park the car for him and the second director had already completed the shot.

"I don't know what to say," he stuttered, when he found himself facing Watson just after they'd wrapped. "I'm terribly sorry."

"It doesn't matter," Watson said. He tried to smile but managed only a wince. Then he limped away.

"Don't worry," the actor playing Baxter observed, as the two of them were left alone. "I expect he'll see the funny side."

144

"You think it's funny?"

"Compared to this sit-com, I'd have said it was priceless. Shame the writers weren't here. They might have learnt something."

It was seven o'clock when Guy got home.

Johnny Peters, the dwarf who lived upstairs, was outside in the street when he arrived. "Your girlfriend gone?" he asked nonchalantly. He had a strange, strangled voice. Maybe it had something to do with his size.

"Yes," Guy said.

"Too bad."

That was typical of Johnny Peters. He was a little bastard — literally so. Guy had been living underneath him for three years but they'd never connected. Was size the issue? It was true that he and Kate had joked about Johnny — the nickname, for example, Grumpy. But that was what he was. On the couple of occasions they'd had a party, he'd complained about the noise. He'd even threatened to call the police. He'd stamped on the floor when they turned the music up too high. He wasn't a nice man and just because he'd been born small, that shouldn't have made any difference. But Guy still felt guilty about him. Even thinking of him as a dwarf. He was disabled. He was vertically challenged. There had to be a better word.

Johnny opened the front door and let the two of them in. Guy tramped upstairs, following his neighbour, who disappeared up the second flight. He was grateful to close the door of his own flat behind him. He wanted a drink, but there was nothing in the fridge and he'd finished the last bottle of whisky two weeks ago. Then he remembered the bottle of brandy, which had tasted so delicious when he drank it late at night on a Greek island with Kate but which had been kept hidden under the sink ever since. He found it and poured himself a glass. Yes, it was atrocious. Disgusting. But he needed it. He poured a second glass and slumped onto a chair, feeling sorry for himself.

And yet . . .

There was something wrong, a detail that was already fidgeting at his consciousness. What was it? He played back in his mind everything that had happened since he got back to the house. Johnny, the stairs . . . No. It wasn't anything outside. He'd come in through the front door, into the kitchen. And that was it! The brandy. The kitchen cupboard had been open when he took it out.

But it had been closed that morning when he left.

It was one of those details that you wouldn't normally notice. But Guy had taken out a dustbin liner just before he left the house and had noticed that the hinge on the door was coming loose again. He had had to push the door firmly to close it. And he *had* closed it. He remembered doing it.

Had Kate decided to make another sortie? Nothing else in the kitchen seemed to have been taken but, then, there wasn't very much else to take. And, anyway, she would never have come back without asking him first. Guy felt a growing sense of unease. He wondered if he had been burgled. Of course, that would be typical.

Mrs Atwood had been at her window the moment he got off his motorbike. He couldn't sneeze without her noticing. But when two kids from the local comprehensive were half-way up his drainpipe, the old bag had had to be out!

He went into the living room. But the hi-fi was there. So was the television. There was an ashtray full of loose coins. Nothing seemed to have been touched. And yet, at the same time, Guy was queasily aware that the room wasn't quite how he'd left it that morning. Was he imagining it or had things been moved? Surely that cushion on the floor had been on the sofa. Had the drawer been half open or closed? And the photograph of Kate. That should definitely have been face-down on the side table. It was standing upright again.

The telephone rang.

He snatched it up, at the same time not really wanting to trust it. Maybe it was the accident, but his nerves were jangling. He felt disconnected.

It was Sylvie. "I heard what happened!" she said.

"Sylvie —"

"What on earth is the matter with you, Guy? I mean, really, darling! I've just had Mal screaming at me down the phone."

"Mal?" Then he remembered. Mal Small was the BBC producer who had hired him for *Two in the Bush*.

"I'm not going to talk to you now because I don't want to shout at you. But you really are going to have to sort yourself out. I mean, first Nigel, now Mike

Watson. At this rate there aren't going to be any directors in London who are going to want to work with you. There aren't going to be any directors who are *able* to work with you!"

"I'm sorry, Sylvie."

"Sorry isn't good enough, Guy. You just have to take more care."

She rang off. Guy was left holding the telephone. And then he heard it. A click. And, faintly . . . "*I'm sorry, Sylvie . . .*"

An echo.

His own voice.

He stared at the telephone receiver as if the black holes in the mouthpiece were about to open up and suck him in. Then, very slowly, he lowered it. His own voice, recorded and played back to him. How was that possible?

There had been somebody in the flat.

He put two and two together and came up with a conclusion that simply couldn't be possible. Somebody had broken in. His telephone had been bugged.

No . . .

He searched the place, beginning in the living room. He opened every cupboard and every drawer. He looked behind pictures and under the sofas. The more he searched the more disruption he caused, making it impossible to tell if things really had changed since he had gone out that morning. But he didn't care. Somehow he was certain that somebody had been there, that his space had been violated. He wanted to find proof.

148

But there was none, not in the living room. He tried the bedroom. He tore the duvet off the bed and threw it on to the floor. He looked in the wardrobes, the bedside cupboard, the rather twee blanket box he had bought on that visit to Bath, which never had and never would contain blankets. He went into the bathroom, flushed the toilet, opened and shut the cabinet over the sink. He was on automatic now. What was he expecting to find? A signed business card from the burglars? But they weren't burglars. Nothing had been taken. The buggers, then. Police. MI5. The local council . . .

He was being ridiculous but he couldn't stop himself. In the cupboards — pots, pans — the microwave, the free-standing deep freeze. Someone had been here during the course of the day. What had they taken? What had they left behind? At last he forced himself to slow down.

This was absurd.

Three strange men on the set of Two in the Bush had rattled him and had caused a stupid, possibly ruinous accident. He had run over his director and even his agent was furious with him. He had just taken two slugs of poisonous Greek brandy. His entire system was in shock.

He was imagining things. Nobody had been into the flat because there was no reason for anyone to be there. A cupboard door had swung open. There had been an echo on the telephone line. And his overstretched imagination had done the rest.

Guy decided to forget it, to have a sandwich and then to go out. *Day for Night* was still showing. Now, more than ever, he needed the solace of a good film.

He opened the fridge. And that was when he found it. He was right. Somebody had been in the flat. They had gone into the fridge. The evidence was right in front of him.

There were footprints in the butter.

CHAPTER
THIRTEEN

"Footprints in the butter?"

Sylvie Graham blinked at Guy over the inevitable porcelain cup of tea. Eric was in the room with her — not a good sign. Eric very rarely came into the main office and never stayed unless he was expected to give moral support. When she was going to fire a client, for example. Eric was sitting on an uncomfortable wooden chair next to the desk. His trousers didn't come all the way down to his shoes. He was wearing pink socks.

"What sort of footprints?" she enquired.

"Well, obviously . . . little ones. They went diagonally from one corner to the other."

Sylvie glanced at Eric, demanding an explanation.

"A mouse," he suggested.

"You must know the old joke," Guy said. "I was told it when I was at primary school, for heaven's sake!" He sighed. "How do you know if there's an elephant in your fridge?" Sylvie and Eric looked at him blankly. "Footprints in the butter!"

Nobody laughed. Guy hadn't expected them to.

"So you're saying they were elephant prints!" Sylvie said.

"Well . . . yes. They were circular. With toes. But they were tiny."

There was a long, heavy silence. The red velvet curtains and solid walls blocked out the outside world. A grandfather clock — rumoured to have belonged to Noël Coward — ticked theatrically in the corner.

"What did you do with the butter?" Sylvie asked.

"I threw it out of the window."

"Don't you think that's a little extreme?"

"I was aiming for the bin. It's next to the window."

"A joke." Eric intoned the words with the same solemnity with which he had suggested the mouse.

"That's exactly what it is."

"Somebody played a joke on you. They went into your flat and they made little marks in the butter. Somebody with a key."

"Nobody has a key," Guy said, although that wasn't true. Kate did. And Martin probably had access to it. "Anyway, I'm telling you. The flat had been searched. And what about the phone?"

"Bugged?" Sylvie was sceptical.

"When you phoned me, there was an echo."

"Has anyone else phoned you since then?" Eric asked.

"Yes. A friend of mine, Torin, called. It's his birthday. He invited me to his party."

"And?"

"Nothing. The phone was fine."

Sylvie handed her teacup to Eric, who placed it silently on an unread script. Guy guessed he would never put anything on a polished surface. As far as he knew, it was Eric who did the polishing. Sylvie looked at him with a face that was half-way between concern and irritation. Guy was expecting a judgement and it came.

"I really don't think," she said, "that this business with the butter has any great significance. I agree with Eric. Maybe someone played a joke on you or maybe there is some sort of rodent in your kitchen but, either way, it's irrelevant. It seems to me that all this has much more to do with what happened the day before yesterday in Vauxhall —"

"It's got nothing to do with it," Guy interrupted. He stopped himself. "I mean, it's got everything to do with it. I told you. There were three men there —"

"They threatened you."

"Not exactly. But they were definitely threatening. That was why the accident happened."

"It happened because you weren't looking where you were going." This was Sylvie as brittle as he had ever seen her.

"I think the three men were sent by someone," Guy said. "And there's something else. Something I haven't told you." He paused. He hadn't wanted to bring this up but now he felt he had no choice. "Have you ever seen a blind man riding a bicycle?" he asked.

Sylvie and Eric looked at each other.

"One went past my house this morning," Guy said.

"How do you know he was blind?" Sylvie asked.

"He had a white stick. He was balancing it across the handlebars. And he had black glasses."

"And he went past your house?"

"Yes."

"Did he stop?"

"No."

"So why do you think he had anything to do with you?"

"He was probably partially sighted," Eric said.

"He had a guide dog, for Heaven's sake! It was running along beside him!"

This wasn't going well. Guy had never raised his voice in this room before. He had never interrupted. He wished now that he had gone to someone else with his fears. Jane was in Prague, but Torin wasn't working. Torin would have seen him. On the other hand, Sylvie was older and wiser. She was an authority figure. It was what he needed right now.

"Let me see if I understand you correctly," Sylvie said. There was a note of tiredness in her voice. "You decided to find out where jokes come from. For some unaccountable reason, you set off across England, asking questions. And now, you think, jokes have decided to come after you."

"An Englishman, an Irishman and a Scotsman. A blind man on a bike. Elephants in the fridge."

"Do you have any idea how mad that sounds?"

"Yes, Sylvie. As a matter of fact I do know it sounds pretty mad. That's why I'm here. I don't know what to do."

"I'd see a doctor," Eric said.

Sylvie gave a little sigh. Guy had been in the room now for more than half an hour and he hadn't had an appointment to begin with. She had had enough. "It

154

seems to me," she said, "that this all began with the joke you overheard in the pub. But actually it's got nothing to do with jokes at all."

Guy opened his mouth to speak but she stopped him with a raised finger.

"It was a joke about Selina Moore," she said. "Your mother. Now, I'm no psychiatrist although, goodness knows, you have to be sometimes in this job. But I don't think you were ever pursuing the joke, Guy. I think, obviously, you were searching for your mother. I know there was that business with the Premium Bonds but let's draw a discreet veil over that! No. This is a mother thing. I can't think of any other reason why you should have headed off the way you did. It makes no sense at all."

Guy wasn't sure she was right. He didn't feel that she was. But what she had said made sense. He had to admit it.

"It was only a few weeks ago that Selina died and I would think that you're mourning her. It must be very difficult for you. You never knew her and yet she was part of you — who you are and what you want to be. Sadly, she's gone. But the joke is still there, and by searching for it you're searching for the mother you never had."

Guy nodded. "I was upset by her death . . ."

"We all were but, of course, it mattered so much more to you. If I were you, Guy, I would forget about the Ferrero Rocher joke. It was just a bit of nastiness. It meant nothing. Maybe Eric is right and you should see a doctor. Maybe you need counselling. Or maybe you

155

should talk to someone who knew Selina. Her husband is still alive. And didn't I read somewhere that he lives in London? That might help."

She stood up. Eric slid off his chair and picked up the tea things. The interview was over.

"At any event, you've made a real mess of things and it's going to take us a while to patch them up. First Nigel Jones. Then, much worse, Mike Watson. You're getting a name for yourself, Guy, and it isn't a good one."

"I've forgotten about the bloody joke," Guy said. "I wish I'd never heard it in the first place."

"Don't we all?" Sylvie agreed. "I think you should take a holiday." Guy's face fell. "A short one. A couple of weeks. Have a rest and try to put all this behind you. Meanwhile, Eric will try to find you a bit of rep theatre. Something out of the way."

"There's a casting for *The Master Builder* in Inverness," Eric muttered gloomily.

"Something like that. Or maybe we can get you a foreign tour. Just try to stay out of trouble, Guy. We'll be in touch."

Don't call us. We'll call you. The inevitable cliché. But that was what she had meant.

Outside, in the sunshine, Guy tried to shake off the feeling of doom that had come over him. He knew it well. Whenever he was resting he felt it, the sense that he was no longer in control of his own destiny, that nothing would ever work out for him again. It was the worst thing about being an actor. On the one side was

156

desperation — lack of finance, lack of morale, lack of work. On the other there was chance. The colour of his hair, his height, a page happening to fall open in front of the right casting director. He was a cork bobbing about between the two. Helpless and hopeless unless the tide carried him the right way.

But he was determined. He would put everything behind him. He would act as if nothing had happened. Forget the joke. From now on he would concentrate on the future, a return to normality that was surely just round the corner. There was Torin, for example. Torin had invited Guy to join him for dinner on Friday. Danny would probably be there. Maybe Jack and Paul. It would be a loud, drunken, childish evening, just what he needed.

He would buy Torin a present. A Harry Potter mug-and-flannel set. Or something shaped like a penis. Anything that was either useless or obscene. That was what he would do. Right now.

He had left his bike at home so he took a bus up to Camden Town. The market was shut during the week but there were still plenty of small shops in the area that sold the sort of thing he was looking for. When he arrived there, ten minutes later, the pavements were crowded. Guy stepped off the bus and began to walk down towards the traffic lights. The sun was beating down on the high street, showing up the dust and the litter. The smell of traffic and kebabs hung in the air. This was normality all right.

He took out his wallet. He had five pounds and an old book token. The sight of them reminded him that this was something else to worry about. He would presumably be paid for *Two in the Bush* but, from what Sylvie had said, it would obviously be a while before he found himself in full-time employment and his savings were already running low.

He crossed the road and went to a cash machine. He fed in his card, keyed in his personal number and waited for verification.

The screen went blank.

Then a single letter appeared, sliding electronically from left to right.

H.

Guy looked at it, puzzled. Was this some sort of new advertising gimmick? He wasn't surprised. Advertisements had sprung up on the sides of taxis, on milk cartons, inside post offices and even on tube tickets. It could only have been a matter of time before . . .

A second letter appeared, this one moving from right to left to join the first. So now there were two of them, spelling out a word.

HA.

Ha? Was it somebody's initials? If Guy had banked with the Halifax it might have been the start of a message, but his was a different building society. Maybe the machine was out of order. But then, with a smoothness that could only have been programmed, the letters duplicated themselves, morphing into a pair like alphabetical amoebae.

HA HA.

Ha ha? What was going on?

158

Guy pressed the "Cancel" button. Nothing happened. He pressed it again. The entire screen exploded with the same pair of letters but now in a variety of colours, swimming, spinning, bouncing and colliding across the grey square. At the same time, fireworks burst and cascaded behind them. The screen flashed yellow and pink. The words streamed across, faster and faster.

HA HA HA HA HA HA HA HA HA HA HA.

The machine was laughing at him!

Guy pressed the button a third time and his card shot out with such force that if he hadn't ducked it might have cut him like a knife. For a moment he did nothing. Then he bent down and picked up the card. When he looked back at the cash dispenser, the screen was normal, inviting the next customer to log in.

A woman had appeared, pushing a shopping cart. She stopped at the machine.

"I think it's out of order," Guy said.

But she put her card in anyway, punched in her code and gave Guy a glance of disdain as the screen offered her the usual options. He watched her withdraw ten pounds. The machine was fine.

Guy felt sick. He had forgotten about Torin's present. He had forgotten everything Sylvie had said. This was part of it, whatever "it" was. The machine had been laughing at him. This was something to do with the joke.

He looked around him, certain that somebody would be watching. But the drift of pedestrians along the pavements seemed as mindless as ever. There were cars, queuing at the intersection by the tube station, but none of the drivers was looking at him. Camden Town was normal. It was only him who wasn't.

Suddenly he wanted to go home. He wasn't afraid but he was disoriented. If he went home, nothing more could happen. If he stayed out here, anything could.

Trying not to hurry, trying to persuade himself that everything would be all right, he went into the tube station and bought a ticket: the Northern Line to Highgate. Once he was there, he could catch another bus. The station had a long, double escalator and as he was carried down, Guy noticed two figures on the opposite side, talking together as they came up. They were nuns. There was nothing remarkable about that, although the fact that they were the only two people on the escalator made them more prominent than they might have been. But as they drew even with him, they suddenly stopped talking and both turned to look at him. Guy was struck by the disgust in their eyes. It was as if they were seeing some sort of minor demon. Were they really looking at him? He turned round, half expecting to see a lewd poster or perhaps a piece of obscene graffiti behind him. But, no, he was the one who had upset them. The three of them were side by side for just a few seconds. The nuns looked at him, deeply offended. And then they were gone, carried away, continuing their discussion as if nothing had happened.

Guy reached the bottom of the escalator and looked back, still unclear exactly what — if anything — had taken place. He just had time to see the two nuns step off at the top at exactly the same moment as four more

160

appeared and began to take the other escalator down. He stared at them. Unless somebody in the area was auditioning for *The Sound of Music* this sudden proliferation of nuns was very strange indeed. This new group was silent. Not one of them was talking. Their attention seemed to be fixed on him and with every second that passed they were getting closer. Suddenly, Guy didn't want to meet them. He turned and moved quickly but — he hoped — with no obvious display of panic, in the direction of the platform.

There were nuns everywhere on the platform. Hundreds of them.

In fact, there were only nuns. Before he knew what had happened, he was surrounded by them. There were nuns talking to each other. Nuns reading newspapers. Nuns with headphones. A nun with a dozen shopping-bags and another with a pram. Guy found himself frozen to the spot. He almost wanted to giggle. He felt like a character in a Woody Allen film, although even Woody Allen would never have been able to afford so many extras. There was, of course, a rational explanation for this. There was a conference on somewhere in London. An ecumenical gathering. The funeral of a well-known prelate. This had nothing to do with him.

It was only when the tube arrived and he saw that every carriage was also packed with nuns that Guy decided he would have to find another way back to Muswell Hill. He turned and ran, taking the escalator three steps at a time and vaulting over the ticket barrier to get back out into daylight and fresh air.

He had bad dreams that night. Kate was there, and Mike Watson and Sylvie and a woman he didn't recognise with a brightly coloured vacuum cleaner.

And nuns. There were plenty of nuns.

CHAPTER
FOURTEEN

The next morning Guy was feeling ill. Really ill. The pollen count must have risen because his eyes and nose were sore. He had suffered from mild hay fever all his life but his sleepless night and the stresses of the last few days had only made it worse. He remembered that Eric had suggested he see a doctor and Guy decided to take his advice. As it happened, he had a very good doctor, what he would call a solid doctor, one who knew you by name and who didn't ask you to wait nine or ten hours before he was ready to see you.

His name was Dr Khatami and he was every actor's dream, handing out mild sleeping pills and antidepressants without too many questions asked. It was possible that they were all placebos but they always worked. Guy called just before lunch.

"Can I help you?" He didn't recognise the voice. The receptionist at the medical centre in Crouch End — where he had been an occasional patient for the past five years — was a mother hen, the sort who always managed to make a visit to the doctor sound like a bit of a treat. This one sounded like Nurse Fletcher in *One Flew Over the Cuckoo's Nest*.

"Yes. My name is Guy Fletcher. I'd like to make an appointment to see Dr Khatami."

"I'm afraid that's not possible. Dr Khatami has left."

"Oh . . ." Guy felt deflated.

"Would you like to see his replacement?"

"Can I get an appointment?"

"You're lucky. There's been a cancellation. You can come in at half past four this afternoon."

"Thank you. Yes. That'll be fine."

"Four thirty, then. You'll be seeing Dr Doctor."

"I'm sorry?"

"Dr Doctor. That's his name."

It was with deep misgivings that, later in the afternoon, Guy went for his appointment at the double-fronted Victorian house just up the road from the clock tower. Sure enough, Dr Khatami had been painted out of the sign next to the door. He had been replaced by a new name: Dr A. Doctor. Guy spent five minutes making up his mind. Then he went in.

But in the end he never made it further than the waiting room. There were five other people there. The first was a middle-aged man with both arms so completely swathed in bandages that they had taken on the shape of party balloons. Next to him was a woman covered in brilliant red spots. Her disease was obviously contagious for the spots had spread across to the young man sitting next to her and now covered the left-hand side of his face. Next to him was an unhappy-looking mother with a small boy. Or it could have been a small girl. The child was sitting with a large saucepan jammed over its head.

164

As Guy took this in, a door opened and a voice called, "Next, please." He glimpsed an office with a bald, smiling man sitting behind a desk that was simply three straight lines. There wasn't even a telephone. The man was wearing a white coat and had a stethoscope round his neck. It was an image Guy had seen a thousand times. A cartoon image. He decided not to go in.

He went back to the flat.

But the truth was that, since the break-in, he no longer felt comfortable there. Whatever Sylvie might have said, he was sure the telephone had been tapped and if that was true then who could say what else had been concealed in the place? Anyway, Sylvie hadn't seen what had happened at the cash machine. She hadn't been in the tube station with a thousand nuns. Either he was going mad or he was being toyed with — in the grip of a power he didn't comprehend. He wished there was someone he could talk to. He wished Kate hadn't left.

He turned on the television. It was a quarter to six and he was surprised to see the face of Kenneth Williams leering at him from the screen, his famous nostrils flayed and quivering. "Infamy, infamy, they've all got it in for me." It was a Carry On film. *Carry On Cleo*, to be precise. The line was one of the very few memorable jokes that had been spawned throughout the entire series.

He flicked channels.

Channel 5 was showing *Carry On Spying*. An unusual error of programming: two Carry On films carrying on at the same time.

He flicked again.

And there was Charles Hawtrey, another Carry On regular, dressed in Foreign Legion clothes. It seemed that ITV was screening *Carry On Up the Khyber*. Guy glanced at the horrible, scrawny, dreadfully unfunny little man, wondering why it was that everyone seemed to be showing Carry On films. Had someone died?

He switched again.

And now he knew that something was seriously wrong. Channel 4 was showing *Carry On Doctor*. Or *Carry On Nurse*. Or *Carry On Something*. Because there was Sid James ogling Barbara Windsor with all the subtlety of a sixteen-year-old sex maniac just released from jail. "Cor, yuk, yuk, yuk, oi!" he was saying, or words to that effect . . .

. . . while on BBC 1, there was Barbara Windsor again, this time losing her bra in that famously mirthful moment in *Carry On Camping*, only this time it was Kenneth Connor leering at her while giving his famous impression of "man having premature ejaculation".

Guy turned off the television, forcing himself to accept that all five terrestrial channels had decided to scrap the news and show Carry On films instead.

But only on his television. He was sure of it. This was only happening to him.

He had to know.

He went out of the flat and went upstairs to Johnny Peters's floor. It wasn't something he wanted to do. In all the time Guy had been at Mapletree Close, he had only ever gone upstairs once. There had been a burst pipe, dripping down into the kitchen. Even then, Peters had been remarkably unfriendly — despite the fact that it was his pipe that was causing the damage. That was the truth about living in London. The best you could hope for, where neighbours were concerned, was that they would be out.

Now Guy knocked on the door and waited, nervously. A moment later it was thrown open and there was Johnny Peters in a dressing-gown and slippers, barring the way with all the ferocity that his four-foot frame could manage. He had a strangely plastic face. Black hair, grizzled and grey at the sides, round cheeks and brown, button eyes. Put him in a dinner jacket and he really would look like a ventriloquist's doll.

"I wanted to talk to you!" he snapped.

"What is it?" Guy asked.

"You threw a block of butter at me."

"What?"

"The other day. I saw it come out of your window. What's wrong with you?"

Guy remembered what had happened. "I didn't mean to throw it at you," he said. "I threw it in the dustbin and I missed."

"You nearly hit me!"

"I'm sorry!"

"I'm not used to being attacked when I'm coming home to my own house. If you want to throw your garbage out the window, that's your business. But if it happens again, I'm going to take action. Do you understand?"

He slammed the door. He hadn't even asked Guy what he wanted. But it didn't matter. Guy had seen past him into the room. Johnny's television had been on, tuned in to the BBC. But he hadn't been watching a Carry On film. He had been watching the news.

Guy made his way back downstairs. As he reached the door of his flat, he noticed Mrs Atwood looking up at him from below. She must have heard Johnny's door slam and had come out to see what was going on. He ignored her and went back inside. He really was going to have to sell the flat. Maybe he would move south of the river. Battersea or Streatham were somehow better suited to an actor living on his own . . . if he could ever find them. He had always found it almost impossible to find his way anywhere on the other side of the Thames. It was as if the signposting had been specially formulated to make sense only to people who were already there.

Thinking about this and much more, he threw himself on to the bed and fell, gratefully, asleep.

It was seven o'clock when he woke up, remembering even as he opened his eyes that this was the evening of Torin's birthday party, that he was expected in a restaurant in Soho in an hour's time and that in the end he hadn't managed to buy Torin a birthday present. He didn't want to go. He felt tired and looked dreadful. His hair had crossed the line from fashionably dishevelled to merely scruffy and there were dark rings under his eyes. He quickly showered, shaved and got dressed, aware that the television screen was watching

168

him all the time, a single, square, unblinking eye. He thought of turning it on but he didn't. He was afraid of what he would see.

There was no sign of either Mrs Atwood or Johnny Peters when he came out of the house. He really would sell. He had made that decision. He would call an estate agent first thing the next day. Once again, he left the bike behind. He was going to drink tonight. That much was certain. He took the bus down to Finsbury Park, passing the Cat and Fiddle where this had all begun. As he rode past, he found himself wishing that he had never gone in, that he had never heard the Ferrero Rocher joke, that he had never set off on his idiotic quest. But at the same time, he still couldn't quite accept that the joke really had been the beginning of all his troubles. Sylvie was right. It was mad.

Was he mad?

No actor was completely sane. How was it possible to be with so many different characters inside one head? Another truth: most actors were happiest when they were being someone else. When they were themselves, they were probably out of work. But that wasn't madness. It wasn't even schizophrenia. It was just the way it was.

What had happened to him in recent days had been something else. Basically, it was a philosophical question. Here he was, sitting on a bus, heading down to Archway. He knew these roads, the Irish pub on the roundabout, the station underneath North London's ugliest office block. Familiarity and sanity went hand in hand. But suppose the bus became an elephant?

Suppose the pub were surrounded by leprechauns? Suppose someone with enormous power (God, the government) were able to change everything on a whim?

How much would it take to persuade a sane man that he was mad?

Bugged telephones. A Doctor called Doctor. A laughing cash machine. Hundreds of nuns. Carry On everywhere.

Guy buried his head in his hands. He was sane. He had to believe it. It was the world that had gone mad.

The restaurant that had been chosen for Torin's birthday was called La Strada, a new Italian place near Soho Square. It was owned by a man who was passionate about the work of Federico Fellini with black-and-white photographs on the walls and music by Nino Rota coming out of the speakers. Even the cocktails were named after films — La Dolce Vita, the Casanova ... It was surprising how well they matched up.

Guy emerged from Leicester Square tube at ten past eight. The evenings were getting longer and a soft, grey light hung in the street as he made his way through Chinatown and across Shaftesbury Avenue. There were crowds pouring in and out of the Chinese restaurants but — he was glad to see — no nuns or blind men. He turned into Dean Street. The road was closed to traffic. A group of workmen was there, resurfacing. The air smelt heavily of tar. It occurred to Guy that ever since the congestion charge had been introduced more and more roads had been inexplicably closed off, part of the ongoing but undeclared war against motorists.

And then he saw them, coming the other way.

Greasy yellow hair and a lumpen face. Pinstripe suit. And kilt. It was the three men from the film set. He recognised them instantly — because, of course, they were instantly recognisable — and at the same time knew that it was no accident their being here, in this street. Somehow (well, of course, his phone was bugged) they had known where he was going and had arranged to be there, to intercept him. They were walking towards him now, the kilt in front, the other two on either side. Guy's mouth went dry and he felt his heart lurch and pick up speed. There was a sense of vacuum behind his eyes and between his ears. He had once tried to act this and knew only now how far he had fallen short of the real thing: raw, naked fear.

But why was he afraid? This was the middle of London on a Friday night. Nothing could happen. And these people — they were a joke! They were nothing. He drew himself up, refusing to be cowed. He would walk past them. He would ignore them. He would —

Suddenly it was too late to turn round and run away. He was right up against them. He couldn't brush past. The three of them were covering the pavement. A wooden barrier, placed there by the workmen, prevented him stepping into the street. He could hear the rumble of the steamroller, which had reached the top of the road and must have started its journey back. For a moment he was suffocated by the noise and by the stench of the tar. He felt himself collide with the man with the kilt.

"Why don't you look where you're going?" the Scotsman demanded, and what was strange, what was in its own way quite sinister, was that the man who had, only days before, claimed to be Guy's greatest admirer now pretended not to know him at all.

"I'm —" Guy began.

"Maybe you should look where you're going before you get there," the tall man in the suit said.

There was a pause. The two men turned to the third, the thug in the leather jacket, who appeared to have forgotten what he was meant to say. He blinked. "Or maybe you shouldn't go there at all!" He blurted out the words, finishing the sequence.

"Why don't you fuck off, all three of you?" Guy said, and pushed past them.

It had been what they wanted.

His foot came down on something soft and slippery and for a moment he thought he had stepped in a dog turd. But at the same time, he caught sight of a flash of bright yellow and as his foot slid forward, toppling his body backwards, he knew that it was — had to be — a banana skin. One of the three men must have dropped it even as they approached him. Guy tried to regain his balance but it was too late. The world swivelled, then turned upside down. He felt his shoulders hit the barrier and break through it. The road rushed up towards him as he fell, diagonally, away from the pavement. His right shoulder crashed into a surface that was still warm and soft. The smell of tar completely smothered him.

He started to get up but before he could move he heard a rumbling and a grinding and what was left of the evening light was blotted out by a huge, rotating cylinder. Guy screamed. The steamroller was heading towards him. He had fallen directly into its path and, though it was moving slowly, it had only centimetres to travel before it would crush him into the surface. He had a sudden vision of himself, paper thin, stretching from one side of the road to the other. He saw the pedestrians screaming, heard the ambulances arrive, watched himself being rolled up and carried to the morgue like a carpet. He had lived as an actor. He would die a cartoon. The thought made him angry and it was his anger that saved him. He felt a rush of adrenaline and then he was twisting away, different muscles interlocking, his body going through some amazing contortion to get him out of harm's way. The steamroller thundered past, indifferent to his fate. And then he sat up in the middle of the road. He was filthy. He stank of tar. The blood was still pounding in his head. People were staring at him. He looked round and saw the banana skin still on the pavement.

The Englishman, the Irishman and the Scotsman had disappeared.

The workmen ran over to him. The driver of the steamroller had turned off the engine.

"Blimey, mate! Are you all right?"

"What happened?"

"Jesus Christ — you could have been killed!"

173

They seemed genuine enough but suddenly Guy wasn't so sure. Any organisation that could fill a tube station with nuns could also hire a bunch of men to resurface a road. Guy ignored their solicitude, their offers of help, and hurried forward. He didn't stop or look back until he had reached the restaurant.

La Strada was almost full when Guy arrived, half an hour late. He thought he looked more or less presentable. Dirty and dishevelled, maybe, but surely not disgusting. The truth was otherwise. He knew the moment he walked in. The maître d' stared at him in horror. Waiters stopped and heads turned as the delicate scent of porcini mushrooms and prosciutto was elbowed aside by the smell of fresh tar. But he had come. It was too late to leave now. Fortunately, Torin had a table in a corner, slightly apart from the other diners. Keeping his head down, he headed straight for it.

They had been waiting for him. Torin, looking elegant in a white linen suit, was facing the door. Surprisingly, Jane was next to him. She must have flown back from Prague. The other guests were Danny and a short, spiky-haired girl he had met at Westcliffe-on-Sea, not an actress but the stage manager. There were cards and crumpled balls of wrapping paper in front of Torin, a book and a couple of CDs. Guy lurched forward and took his seat, the tar immediately sealing him into place. The apologies tumbled out of him. Late. No present. In a bit of a mess. He knew it was hopeless. They were all staring at him as if he had just jumped out of a birthday cake without his clothes.

"God, Guy!" Danny exclaimed. "You look terrible!"

"What's happened to you?" Jane asked, genuinely concerned.

"Nothing. I mean . . . I had a slight accident." Guy reached out for the wine and poured himself a glass, spilling some on the tablecloth. His hand was trembling. There was tar on his wrist and on the sleeve of his jacket. He was suddenly guilty. He was going to spoil the evening. He shouldn't have come. "I fell over," he added.

"You're covered in black paint," Torin said.

"It's not paint." Jane wrinkled her nose. "It's tar!"

"Yes. They were resurfacing the road and I slipped. Have you ordered without me?" Guy reached for a menu and made a great business of studying it. But it was written in Italian and the words wouldn't come into focus. He knew what they were but at the same time he'd forgotten what they meant. He lowered it again.

Everyone was still staring at him. The spiky-haired girl was biting her lip, as if she was trying not to laugh.

"What is it?" he said.

"What's been going on?" Jane demanded.

"Is this something to do with what happened to Mike Watson?" Torin asked. Of course, they would all know about the accident by now.

"No. Yes. I don't know." He drank some of his wine and made sure his hand didn't shake as he returned the glass to the table. He should have stayed at home.

Phoned them and said he was sick. This was all a terrible mistake. "It's just that a lot of very strange things have been happening to me recently."

"What sort of things?" Jane asked.

"Well . . . obviously that thing with Mike Watson . . ." Guy began.

And stopped.

He had been about to launch into the whole thing again: the joke, the quest, the bugged phone, the same story that he had told Sylvie. But it hadn't convinced her and he knew it wouldn't convince his friends either. He finished the rest of his wine, swallowing it in two large gulps. "I've just been having a rough patch," he said. "You know how it is. Kate leaving. Then the BBC thing . . . and all the rest of it. Anyway, here I am. A bit late. No present. Covered in tar. But otherwise it's delightful to be here. Any chance of a top-up?"

Nobody was convinced. "Your jacket's ruined," Jane said.

"I didn't expect to see you," Guy replied. "How's *Tale of Two Cities*?"

The maître d' approached, his own silk shirt and moustache impeccable. He wasn't looking happy. "Can I take your jacket for you?" he asked.

Guy shifted awkwardly. The jacket was firmly attached to the back of his seat. "No, thank you," he said. "But I'd like a bottle of house champagne for my friend. It's his birthday!"

It was the least he could do — and it broke the ice that his arrival had created. A waiter came and they ordered. The champagne arrived. Guy found himself

176

drinking heavily. The conversation bubbled and simmered all around him and he had to concentrate to follow what was being said. He was still thinking about what had happened outside the restaurant. They had tried to kill him. No. They had only wanted to scare him. But then again, the steamroller had been five centimetres from his head.

"*Blimey, mate. Are you all right?*"

A worker or an actor?

He, of all people, should have been able to tell.

The waiter returned with their first courses. Guy had managed to slip his arms out of his jacket, leaving it attached to the back of his chair. He hoped he looked normal now. He had ordered minestrone. Jane had a Caesar salad. Torin had risotto. Danny and his friend — her name was Gina — both had Parma ham.

There was the usual ritual with the Parmesan and the oversized pepper grinder. Danny launched into another anecdote about the horrors of Westcliffe-on-Sea.

Guy picked up his spoon.

Something moved in his soup.

He stared down, the spoon frozen in mid-air. The soup was a dark red colour with specks of orange where the olive oil had risen to the top. There were chunks of vegetable, maggot-sized lumps of barley and here and there small strips of pink bacon. Had he imagined it? Guy so hoped he had imagined it. But there it was again, pushing its way up through the surface, painfully crawling through the murky liquid, trying to make its way to the edge of the plate.

It was a fly. An enormous fly. Perhaps even a bluebottle. He could see the black, soup-streaked hairs on its neck and front legs as it struggled slowly towards him. Its black, shiny eyes seemed to be bursting out of its head. The thing was as big as his thumbnail, bloated as if it had gorged itself on the very food that was killing it. How was it even alive? It should have been scalded. But somehow it continued on its way, pushing between a lump of carrot and a slice of soggy, overcooked celery.

"Waiter . . ." he heard himself trying to articulate the word. He coughed. "Waiter . . ."

The waiter, in white shirt, black trousers and bow-tie, was at the table as if he had been waiting for his cue.

"There's a fly in my soup."

The waiter bowed low, and spoke so that only he would hear. He had an Italian accent but to Guy it sounded fake. "Don't say it too loud, sir, or everyone will want one."

Guy stood up. The chair came with him, clinging to the back of his tar-covered trousers. He caught hold of the tablecloth and dragged his own bowl of soup off the table. It crashed into him, spilling lukewarm soup over his feet. Then the bowl hit the floor and broke. All the glasses had toppled. Red wine and mineral water splashed into the risotto and the salad. The knives and forks rattled. The other diners fell silent, appalled.

"Guy . . ." Jane began.

"No!" Guy shook his head. He was tired of explanations. All he knew was that he couldn't stay here any longer.

178

He turned round and ran out of the restaurant, dragging the chair with him. One of the waiters grabbed hold of it and, for a moment, he was stuck, flailing at the air. Then there was a ripping sound. The waiter fell backwards. Guy was propelled out on to the street, the remains of his trousers flapping in the evening breeze.

The following morning he left for Stoke-on-Trent.

CHAPTER
FIFTEEN

Rupert Liddy sat in the back of his chauffeur-driven Mercedes S600, comfortably surrounded by soft grey leather with the air conditioning held at a perfect nineteen degrees. But he was going nowhere. They had barely driven half a mile in the last hour and were still surrounded by traffic, occasionally sliding forward an inch at a time. Nobody would be able to see into the car through the blackened windows and Liddy didn't bother to look out at the cars and trucks hemming him in on both sides. His eyes were closed. He had no newspaper with him but had read an edition of *The Times* a week before and he was able to summon up every story. The news never really changed. And it was always bad. He turned his mind to the crossword. Sixteen down: *Made by neat tailors?* (11). A childish anagram. Mentally he filled in the answer. *Alterations.* It gave him an *o* in twenty-two across, but no real pleasure. He had read the same clue six years before in the *Independent*.

This had been an appalling start to the week. A seemingly endless procession of caravans beating a retreat from the coast on the inadequate country lanes that twisted laboriously to the A12. Roadworks on the

A12 itself, and finally — just what he needed — a multiple pile-up on the M11. They had been diverted at junction seven and, with Liddy's permission, the chauffeur had picked up the news on the radio. It seemed that a coachload of old-age pensioners on their way back from Clacton-on-Sea had collided with a petrol tanker. There had been sixty-six people on board and every last one of them had died in the ensuing furnace. The motorway was closed until further notice.

Liddy briefly wondered if there might be something in it.

What does BP stand for?

Burned Pensioners.

What do you get when you cross a pensioner with an Esso tanker?

An old flame.

Why is an old-age pensioner like a lobster?

They're both cooked in the Shell.

Normally he would have picked up the car phone and relayed his thoughts back to the office. Of course, the office would already be on to it but he liked to keep himself on his toes. It was good for morale, too, showing that he was part of the team.

But not today. He had too much on his mind.

He had just received his orders from London referring to Guy Fletcher and the joke reference: J79985/SM3/0501B. Part of him had been dreading the letter that he knew would come in a brown A3 envelope marked FOR YOUR EYES ONLY. He had read the letter, digested the contents and then given it to his secretary — the blonde in the outer office — for destruction. An hour later, he had found her tearing it into tiny pieces, feeding each piece into the shredding machine beside her desk.

And now he had to deal with Guy Fletcher. Finally. Liddy did not think of himself as a bad man but the people who had written the letter, he knew, did not distinguish between good and bad. They simply demanded action. For reasons that were unclear, the out-of-work actor had chosen to become a threat to national security and it was Liddy's job to contain the situation. He thought of his father, who had served as a submarine captain during the Cold War. When Liddy was as young as six, growing up in the little house on the north coast of Devonshire, his mother had come into his room at night to tell him stories of life under the Arctic ice. She had explained how, one day, his father — if he opened the envelopes and found the right codes — might be expected to give the orders that might result in thousands of deaths. Commander Bill Liddy was not a bad man either. There was a black-and-white photograph of him on the kitchen dresser. He looked a little like George Formby. He collected stamps.

And now, one generation and thirty years later, Liddy found himself in the same situation. Press a button, give an order, pull the trigger of a gun. It made no difference. The orders had come and he was expected to act.

Somehow they reached the M25 and at last the Mercedes was able to break free of the mess, accelerating past the next three sets of speed cameras and getting each one of them to flash. This didn't bother Liddy or his driver. They wouldn't get a ticket. When the registration number was passed through the driving-licence centre at Swansea, it would be found that the car and its passenger didn't exist.

It was just after midday when the Mercedes drew up outside a shop on the Grays Inn Road. This was one of those corners of London where, if you half closed your eyes, you might still see a few shadows of Dickens — gabled windows, slate roofs, cobbled streets and pickpockets. A parade of shops sat back from the main traffic, selling nothing particularly useful to a handful of people who would have to be enthusiasts to know that they were there in the first place. There was a second-hand occult bookshop, a Polish delicatessen and, between them, a shop called Jolly's selling practical jokes and magic tricks.

These were arranged in two windows, one on either side of the door. To the left were the card packets, the linking rings, silk flowers and brightly coloured wooden boxes of the professional magician. The sight never failed to drag Liddy back — unwillingly — to his childhood. For a man who could remember so much, it was strange that he had built a mental block between himself and his early days in Appledore, on the Devon coast. But the sight of these tricks brought his defences crashing down and reminded him of the very solitary boy who had entertained his family on the days when his father came home on leave and who had dreamed of becoming a magician. His father had insisted he would go into the navy, but Liddy had surrendered himself to

183

the arcane world of Okido boxes, thumb-tips, rough and smooth and coin shells. How many hours had he spent perfecting the French Drop and the One-handed Pass? He had read Bobo — the greatest coin magician ever — from cover to cover. Not once but a hundred times. Before he was nine he could make a half-crown vanish and reappear, cartwheel across his fingers and turn into a sixpenny piece. His parents were concerned. They thought magic was an odd way to make friends. It never occurred to them that it was because he had no friends that the young Rupert had been drawn to magic.

But they had won in the end. A well-chosen English preparatory school had quickly squeezed out of Rupert any thought of becoming an entertainer. His entire *joie de vivre* had gone with it. By the time he came out of the obscure public school that had followed he had been well and truly stamped in his father's image, and his only defiance had been to opt for Sandhurst and the army rather than a life at — or under — sea. The army had been pure torture. In fact, that had been Liddy's speciality. Interrogation techniques. The application of pain, psychological or otherwise. It was never called that. There was no A level in torture. But it amounted to more or less the same thing.

He had seen action in Ireland, in the Falklands and the Gulf War. With his prodigious memory, he had learnt Arabic in just six months, although his was a limited vocabulary that ignored most of the social niceties, concentrating instead on the fairly specialised lexicon of information, electrodes and testicle. He left the army a year after his father died; the commander's ashes were sealed in a weighted-down box and dropped beneath the surface of the North Atlantic. But the army had never really finished with him. He had been transferred to the department where he had worked ever since. He was unmarried. He had no living relatives.

He had become what he had become.

The right-hand window of the shop was filled with practical jokes that, Liddy reflected, hadn't changed in forty years and which, for him, were just as evocative as the magic tricks. Fart cushions and vanishing ink, the nail through the finger, hot-pepper sweets. As a small boy, he had bought all of them and knew that very few actually worked. The famous make-your-face-black soap, for example, was unlikely to leave so much as a smear. The aid to ventriloquism, an oddly shaped piece of cardboard that fitted under the tongue, might at very best give the performer a slight lisp. Liddy had wasted his pocket money on both of these and more. If he had ever had children of his own they would doubtless have done the same. Miniature disappointments — that was how he thought of them now.

There was a bell, mounted on the door on a steel coil, and it rang as he went in. He found himself in a dark, cluttered space with tricks scattered on shelves and stored in cardboard boxes with the names handwritten in ink. The Three Card Monte. Pen Through Five-pound Note. Twisted Sisters. The shop smelt of varnish and coffee. Behind the counter, a rotund man with an arrow through his neck was

185

demonstrating the Svengali deck to a pair of young boys who must have been the only people left in the world who didn't know how it worked. Now it's an ordinary pack of cards. Now every one of them is a nine of hearts. The man hadn't looked up as Liddy came in but he nodded ever so slightly and reached for a button underneath the counter. This unlocked a door to one side. Liddy walked over to it and went through.

There was a staircase behind the door and this rose one floor to a reception area — grey carpet and bland, modern furniture — with an elderly woman sitting at a desk. She was dressed in a cardigan, with two pairs of spectacles, one on her nose, the other dangling on a chain across her chest. A security guard sat next to her. Armed.

"Good afternoon, Mr Liddy," she said, seeing him. It was only a few minutes past twelve but she would have noticed, of course. She would have wished him "good morning" if he had arrived five minutes earlier.

"Good afternoon, Miss Conduct."

She pressed a button on her desk and there was an audible buzz as a second, unmarked door unlocked. It led to a long corridor with offices on either side. As he walked forward, Liddy glanced left and right. Some sort of sales conference was going on in the first office. Through the half-open door, Liddy saw a man standing in front of a screen with a map of England projected on to it. There were half a dozen younger people — men and women — sitting at a long table, taking notes. The next office was empty. A pair of identical twins sat in the third, both talking on the phone. As Liddy continued along the grey-carpeted corridor, a tired-looking woman with a tea trolley turned a corner and began to move towards him, the wheels of the tea trolley squeaking as she went. He allowed her to pass and, without knocking, went into the last room. The Englishman, the Irishman and the Scotsman were already there. He sat down.

The room was an office, identical in every detail to the one he had left on the coast except that the view here was the Grays Inn Road. Nobody spoke as Liddy collected himself. He had been carrying a briefcase but he left it unopened. There was nothing inside it anyway.

"I am not happy," Liddy began. He was more than two hours late but he didn't apologise. The thought would never have occurred to him. "I have read your initial reports with, I have to say, incredulity. Would you mind telling me what the bloody hell you think you've been doing?"

The Englishman crossed his arms and said nothing.

The Scotsman scowled.

The Irishman shrugged. "We've been waiting for you, sir," he said.

"I don't mean what you've been doing in this office, O'Neil!" Liddy snapped. "I was referring to your management — or, I should say, your mismanagement — of the Guy Fletcher affair."

"Oh." O'Neil blinked.

"My orders to you were to contain him, to put a security ring round him while we had him checked out. Instead of which, you've thrown the book at him, acting on your own initiative and with no clearance from me.

187

I'm reliably informed that you have deployed no fewer than six operational teams — and I don't need to tell you what that's going to do to my annual budget." He briefly closed his eyes. "In the last forty-eight hours you've ploughed through our resources like there's no tomorrow. You've had nuns, waiters, road workers, blind men, cannibals, doctors. Yes? What is it, Smythe?"

The Englishman had coughed discreetly. "Actually," he said, "the cannibals didn't show up. I've already spoken to Accounts."

"Well, that's marvellous. But what about the rest of it? I'd like to know which one of you three is going to take responsibility for all this."

Smythe and McLarrity both turned to O'Neil. It took the Irishman a few moments to realise they were looking at him and he bowed his head, going a deep red. "Sir, if you want the truth now, it was my idea," he said.

"You're in charge of the operation?"

"Yes, sir."

"So tell me about your strategy."

"Well, it was pretty quiet, sir. Friday was very busy but strategy —"

"Your strategy, O'Neil!" Liddy's face was thunderous. "You know perfectly well what I'm talking about. And I'm warning you now that one day you'll push me too far." He drew a breath. "Anyway, who put you in charge of this particular operation?"

Smythe glanced down at his fingernails. McLarrity scowled and turned away. Once again, O'Neil realised he was on his own. He went a deeper shade of red. "It was my turn," he said, in a sulky voice.

"God in Heaven!" Liddy rolled his eyes. "It was your turn! Do you think we're playing games here? Do you think all this is done just to keep the three of you amused? I'm asking you again. What were you hoping to achieve?"

O'Neil had said enough. Smythe came to his rescue. "You did give us the impression," he said, "that this man could be dangerous to us. We took the decision that it might be sensible to disorientate him."

"Keep the bastard guessing," McLarrity added.

The Irishman was picking at an imaginary speck of dust on his knee but now he nodded vigorously. "Yes, sir. That's exactly what we were trying to do. We thought we might be able to frighten him off."

"Frighten him off. I see." Liddy paused. "And I don't suppose it occurred to you — to any of you — that everything you've done might have the opposite effect? That instead of concealing, disguising, enshrouding, ensconcing our existence — which was, I think, the general idea — you were advertising it? That instead of containing the situation, you were blowing it wide open?"

"No, sir." O'Neil shook his head. "I can honestly say that thought never occurred to me."

"Well that's exactly what's happened," Liddy said. He reached into his pocket and produced a folded sheet of paper, a copy of an email he had received while he was still in the car. "Fletcher is in Stoke-on-Trent," he said. "Do you know why he's there?"

Silence from the three men.

"He's following the joke. I'm not quite sure how, but he's picked up the trail again and this time he's following it south." Liddy slammed the paper down on the desk. "Maybe this whole business began as a whim," he went on, "but now you've given Fletcher a purpose. You blithering idiots! You've made him twice as dangerous as he was before!"

There was a long silence.

"Why don't we just kill the fucker and be done with it?" McLarrity asked.

"Because it's too late for that now," Liddy replied. "Fletcher has spoken to people. They know what he's doing. If something happens to him, even if it has all the hallmarks of a genuine accident, they may begin to wonder. Somebody else may put two and two together, and we can't risk that. What we have here is a germ. We can't allow it to become an epidemic."

"So what do you suggest?" Smythe asked.

"I haven't decided yet," Liddy said. "But first of all, we're going to have to make damn sure that the J79985 link is broken. You can see to that. And yes, reluctantly, we may now have to use extreme measures. As to Fletcher, the situation is already critical, which means we're going to have to be direct. We need to take him out quickly and cleanly, and in such a way that no more questions will be asked."

"I have an idea," O'Neil said.

"I'll have the ideas, thank you very much," Liddy replied.

190

* * *

Downstairs, the man with the arrow through his neck sold a bendy rubber pencil to a ten-year-old girl. She was smiling as she left.

CHAPTER
SIXTEEN

Guy had travelled many hundreds of miles since Stoke-on-Trent.

He had gone to Stoke-on-Trent in search of Michael Fairfax, the father of the chain-smoking landscape gardener who had heard the Ferrero Rocher joke twice, once from his father and once from his assistant, Harry Collins. This double telling had created a sort of T-junction in the joke's progress through Great Britain. Guy had taken what seemed to be the easier option but this had led to a dead end. He had got as far as Cambridge, where Sally Lockwood had heard the joke from an unknown vacuum salesman. But that was it. So he had decided to try the other direction — which meant heading north.

Michael Fairfax was a retired arboriculturist. He had heard the joke from his local newsagent, who had heard it from his brother who worked in the canteen of a police station and who had definitely heard it from a policeman, except that he couldn't remember which one.

In fact, twenty-nine policemen, two dog-handlers, half a dozen undercover detectives and a crowd of clamp operators, traffic wardens and lollipop ladies had passed the joke among themselves, although in the end Guy discovered that it was a criminal who had first brought it into their lives. Ray Jennings was a burglar, a habitual criminal, according to the police constable who had heard the joke from him. Fortunately Jennings was out on bail and Guy was able to visit him in his surprisingly pleasant, modern house. But he had to pay twenty pounds before Jennings would lead him to the next link in the chain.

Jennings had heard the joke from his girlfriend, who cleaned the offices of an estate agency in the nearby town of Cheadle. The chain then took Guy to Stubwood, Gratwich, Rugeley, Penkridge, then right over to Groby, on the outskirts of Leicester, before taking him south east through Wigston, Fleckney, Kibworth Beauchamp, Old Thrapston, Hadwick, Fandish, Wollaston, Harrold and Barnwell All Saints.

He noticed that he wasn't far from Cambridge and wondered if the joke would take him there for a second time. He wanted to see Sally Lockwood again. More than that. He wished that she was with him. When he had told her about the joke, she hadn't told him he was mad or stupid. She hadn't even laughed at his theory about Premium Bonds. Maybe that was why he had felt such an affinity with her. It would have been wonderful if she had agreed to come with him, sitting on the back of the bike. He wanted to feel her arms round him.

But he was alone, travelling ever further towards the Suffolk coast. Brandon, Hilgay, North Acre, Little Elingham, Morely St Botolph. Finally he came to Framlingham.

That was where he was now. Tired and stiff, with a crick in the small of his back. He had spent too long on the bike, driving too many miles of unrelenting motorway. He was beginning to wonder how much longer he could go on.

Framlingham was a Suffolk town that looked as if it had packed its bags and was planning to move somewhere else. It had a deserted feel, with several shops empty and deserted and the others displaying their goods with an enthusiasm that could only be called half-hearted. As Guy parked his motorbike outside the Swan Hotel, he saw windows filled with antiques that were little more than bric-à-brac, and white goods that were little better than antiques. The town had a medieval castle, a church, a square with a Saturday market and a few attractive alleyways, but these had been largely upstaged by a caravan park, a red-brick supermarket and a clutch of Barratt homes. It wasn't an ugly place yet. But until quite recently it might have been beautiful.

He had come in search of an antiques dealer called Brian Eastman, who had told the joke to one of his customers. There were no fewer than five antiques shops in Framlingham but for once Guy got it right first time.

The shop was on the edge of the town, just down the road from an Esso garage and round the corner from the castle. As Guy turned the corner, he was presented with the sight of two police cars and an ambulance parked outside what looked like a warehouse, with a few garden statues and rotting wheelbarrows on the pavement, secured by a rusting chain. A crowd of about twenty people had gathered on the other side of the road and, although nothing very much seemed to be happening, they were watching with that curious fixation — polite but determined — that the English have when confronted with violence and death. A uniformed policeman was standing outside the shop. Police incident tape fluttered in the breeze.

"What happened?" he asked.

"The man who owned the shop. He's been found dead!" The speaker was middle-aged with silver hair and an unfortunate parting. He evidently worked at Framlingham Castle. He was wearing an English Heritage jersey that was a little too small for him.

"Brian Eastman?" Guy had to be sure.

"Yes. I knew him. I used to see him out and about . . . you know."

"How did it happen?"

"They're saying that a clock fell on him."

"A clock?"

"A big grandfather clock. They say he was crushed."

Guy waited a few more minutes but nothing else happened. Nobody carried out the body — or even the clock. Even the crowd of locals was beginning to drift apart. He realised suddenly that there was nothing more for him to do. He would never find out who had told Brian Eastman the joke. His quest had come to a final, unavoidable full stop.

Guy turned round and walked back to his bike.

It was time to go home.

* * *

Had "they" killed Brian Eastman?

Of course accidents happened — but Guy had misgivings about any accident concerning an oversized grandfather clock. He still had no idea who "they" were but the death bore all "their" hallmarks. It definitely came from the same school as the steamroller and the banana skin. But would somebody, somewhere, really kill an innocent man just because he had told a joke? Was such a thing remotely conceivable? And if it was, where did it leave Guy?

He found himself driving more and more slowly. When he reached London, he took a roundabout route back to Muswell Hill and he avoided any street where there were roadworks. When he finally reached Mapletree Close, he turned the engine off and glided the last few metres as if the sound of the motorbike might tip off anyone waiting. He was getting paranoid, he knew. But after everything that had happened he was entitled to be.

And then he saw it. Sitting on the pavement, outside his flat.

A shaggy dog.

He gazed at it, irritated but not alarmed. It was an Old English Sheepdog, a virtually shapeless mass of grey and white hair. If it hadn't been sitting down, Guy would have been unable to tell which end was its head and which its arse. He looked up and down the street. The dog didn't seem to have an owner. There was nobody else in sight.

He got off the bike, removed his helmet and took a step forward. The dog didn't move. "Go away!" he shouted. "Go on! Fuck off!"

He waved the hand holding the helmet and a moment later the dog padded off. Mrs Atwood appeared at the window.

"And you can fuck off too!" Guy yelled.

He let himself into the flat.

It was no longer his flat — he knew that the moment he entered. It wasn't just that Kate had gone: whoever had bugged his telephone and put the footprints in the butter had never really left. They were still there, invisible and intangible but everywhere, hanging in the air. He took a beer out of the fridge and slumped on to the sofa, but even those movements felt strained, as though he were doing it for the camera. What camera? He looked around him nervously. He felt he was being watched.

For a moment, he sat. His feet were on the coffee table, the beer can perched on his knee. He looked out of the window but there was no sign of the dog. His motorbike was parked opposite. He could still feel it between his legs. It would probably be the middle of the night before his balls stopped vibrating. He sighed. He was in serious trouble. He knew it. His innocent, unpremeditated search for the source of the Ferrero Rocher joke had triggered something he didn't quite understand. Sitting quietly, thinking it through, he saw that there was only one way out of this mess, one thing he could do.

He had to tell everyone he had suffered a complete nervous breakdown.

It would be a public confession, starting with Sylvie, Mike Watson, Nigel Jones and his friends. If necessary, he would take out a full-page advertisement in the *Stage*. It was nothing new, nothing to be ashamed of. Actors were always having breakdowns of one sort or another, and for every voice coach, every dance instructor working in the business, you could find a dozen therapists. He would tell everyone who would listen; shout it from the rooftops. Splitting up with Kate had made him irrational. The strain had done something to him and he had become deranged. He was getting help. He was on Prozac. He was trying to get well.

It was the only solution. People would feel sorry for him and maybe the BBC and everyone else would forgive his recent misdemeanours. And the organisation that was persecuting him — the people who had presumably murdered Brian Eastman — would leave him alone. They would see he was no longer a danger to them. A public recantation. It was the only way out.

The telephone rang.

Guy hesitated, but only for a second. He had nothing to be afraid of. He answered it.

"Hello?" It was a woman's voice at the other end of the line.

"Who is this?" he asked. But even as he spoke he recognised the voice.

"It's Sally Lockwood. Do you remember? From Cambridge . . ."

"Yes, of course, I remember." He was absurdly pleased to hear from her. Sally had been the only good thing to come out of all this. He hoped she was in London. He desperately wanted to see her. "How are you?"

"I'm fine. I was wondering how you were getting on with that thing of yours. The jokes."

"Well . . ."

"I'm not sure I should be encouraging you, but I promised I'd ring and the other day I found the card."

"I'm sorry?"

"The business card that the salesman gave my mother. Sphinx Appliances. I thought I'd thrown it away but it turned up in the kitchen."

It was the last thing he had expected. And suddenly it occurred to him that she shouldn't be talking to him about it. Certainly not on the telephone.

But it was already too late. "His name was Bill Naughtie," she went on. "There's no address on the card. Just the company name. But there's a telephone number. I thought it might help."

"Listen, Sally —" Guy said.

"Have you got a pen and paper? I'll give it to you."

"No. Honestly. There's no need to. You see —"

There was a knock at the door.

That was strange. There was somebody in the corridor, which surely wasn't possible because you had to ring the bell in the street to get up to the first floor. It had to be either Mrs Atwood or Johnny Peters. Or possibly Kate.

199

"Guy, are you there?" Sally's voice was distant in his ear.

"Hold on a minute, Sally," Guy said. "There's someone here."

He put the phone down just as whoever it was on the other side of the door knocked again. Twice this time.

KNOCK KNOCK.

"Who's there?" Guy called out.

"Police!" came a muffled reply from the other side.

"Police?" Guy couldn't believe what he had just heard. "Who?"

"Please will you open the door, sir," the voice demanded. "This is the Metropolitan Police, Wood Green."

He opened the door.

There was a man standing in the narrow corridor, dressed in a smart navy blue suit with a white shirt and plain grey tie. He was about fifty years old, clean-shaven, black, with a round face and a lazy eye that made him seem not altogether there. He was a little shorter than Guy but he had a presence that filled the doorway. Without the police identification that he was holding in front of him, Guy would have taken him for an academic or perhaps a QC. A uniformed policewoman accompanied him. Limp brown hair and a pale face. She looked bored.

"Mr Fletcher?" he asked.

"Yes." Guy's head was spinning. There was a momentary rush of guilt. Did he have dope in the house? Had he paid for the TV licence? But then he was struck simply by the improbability of it. A black

200

detective and a uniformed WPC. What were they doing here and how had they got there? He hadn't noticed a police car outside.

"My name is Detective Superintendent Kilroy. Sergeant Carmichael." He indicated the woman standing next to him. "I wonder if we could have a word?"

"What's this about?"

"We're making a routine enquiry, sir. A missing person. Can we come in?"

He had asked so politely and his voice was so well modulated that Guy was taken unawares. It seemed that the two police officers were inside his flat before he knew it, looking around them, making a quiet appraisal of the furnishings as if they were old friends and he had invited them long ago.

"I was on the telephone," Guy said.

"Go ahead, sir. Finish your call. We don't mind."

Guy picked up the receiver. "Sally, do you mind if I call you back? I've just had someone at the door."

"I'm at the shop."

"I'll call you in five minutes."

He hung up and, in a way, he was grateful for the interruption. He would go out to a phone box to call her back.

"Nice place." Kilroy sat down without being invited. He moved very neatly, every muscle controlled. Guy had met people who had studied the Alexander technique and they were the same. Kilroy had chosen the sofa. Carmichael perched on the arm of a chair. "Do you live here alone?" Kilroy asked.

"Yes. I had a girlfriend but she moved out." Guy wasn't quite sure why he had offered this piece of information. He had the sense of not being in control.

"I understand you're an actor?"

"Yes." How did he know? "What is this all about? What are you . . ." Then he remembered. "You said this was something to do with a missing person."

"Yes, sir. There's a gentleman who lives on the floor above you. Name of Johnny Peters. I wonder if you could tell me, when was the last time you saw him?"

It wasn't what Guy had been expecting. He blinked. "The last time? It was a few days ago. I'm afraid I don't know him very well."

"Do you get on?"

"Is he missing?"

"Yes, sir. He hasn't shown up at work for the last two days and his employers have been concerned about him. He missed a number of significant meetings, which seems out of character."

"Significant." It was the first word Carmichael had spoken. She nodded gravely.

"We've checked his apartment and there's no sign of him there. The bed hasn't been slept in. He was also due at a ceremony last night, to pick up a humanitarian award. It seems very strange that he should have been absent, so we were called in."

Guy relaxed a little. This had nothing to do with him. "Well, I'm afraid I can't really help you," he said. "I spoke to him very briefly a couple of days ago. He seemed perfectly all right then."

"What did you speak to him about?"

202

"My television wasn't working. I thought it might be something to do with the aerial. So I went upstairs to see if his was all right. It was."

"Is your television working now?"

"No."

The remote control was lying on the coffee table in front of Kilroy. "Do you mind?" he asked. He reached out with a languid finger and pressed a button. The television flickered on. *Countdown* was showing on Channel 4. Kilroy changed the station. There was a cartoon on ITV. "It seems to be all right now," he said.

"It must have sorted itself out."

Kilroy turned the television off. There was an uncomfortable silence.

"There's nothing I can really tell you," Guy went on. "I saw him for less than a minute. He wasn't a particularly friendly person."

"Wasn't?"

"I'm sorry?"

"I'm just wondering why you're using the past tense."

"Wasn't. Isn't." Guy didn't like the way this was going. "I hardly know anything about him. We only spoke two or three times the entire time I've been here."

"Would it be true to say that the two of you didn't get on?" Kilroy asked.

"Well, we weren't friends. I've already told you that. Do you think something's happened to him? Is that what you're saying?"

Kilroy glanced at Carmichael. There was no expression whatsoever in the sergeant's face. "We understand that there was an altercation between you and Mr Peters a few days ago," she said.

"No. That's not true."

"Are you sure of that, sir?"

"Well, I've told you. He was always a bit on the grumpy side."

"Grumpy?"

"That was the nickname I gave him."

Kilroy nodded. "I assume that was a reference to his diminutive stature," he murmured.

"Yes."

"In the same way that you might refer to me as 'Blacky', perhaps?"

"No!" Guy was angry. The detective was provoking him on purpose, trying to get a rise out of him. "I'm not a racist. And I didn't have anything against Johnny Peters because of his size. He just wasn't very nice — that's all."

"Was that why you attempted to assault him?"

"What?" Guy almost laughed. "I never did anything of the sort."

Carmichael had taken out a notebook. It sat in her lap, poised, as if the handwritten notes could leap off the page and contradict everything Guy was saying.

"We've spoken to your neighbour downstairs, sir," Kilroy went on. "Mrs Atwood. She claims that you threw some sort of projectile at Mr Peters last Tuesday afternoon."

204

"I didn't throw a —" Guy stopped. "It was a piece of butter."

"Butter?"

"Yes. I threw a packet of butter out of the window. I wasn't aiming at anybody. I wasn't even aiming at the window. If you look in the kitchen, you'll see. The bin was next to the window and I missed."

"Why were you throwing the butter into the bin?"

"It was off." This was a lie, of course, but Guy had no intention of going into the truth. Not now. Not with this man.

"You threw the butter across the room?"

"Yes."

"It went out of the window."

"Yes."

"And it hit Johnny Peters."

"He said it nearly hit him."

"And this is what you spoke to him about, a couple of days ago."

"Yes."

Kilroy looked puzzled. "I thought you spoke to him about the television."

Guy was getting exasperated. "I went upstairs to speak to him about the television but he was upset because of the butter so we spoke about that. But I wasn't aiming at him. I had nothing against him particularly. It was simply an accident."

"A very unusual accident," Carmichael muttered, making her second contribution to the discussion.

"I understand you're thinking about joining the SAS," Kilroy said.

"What?" For a brief second, the room shifted and shimmered and Guy was back in Camden Town tube station, back in the Italian restaurant. He was beginning to see that this might all be part of the same thing.

"You told Mrs Atwood you were joining the SAS," Kilroy said.

"You threatened to kill her," Carmichael added. It was all there, in her notebook.

"I was joking!" Guy looked Kilroy in the eye. "It's the joke, isn't it? Have they sent you? Is that what's going on?"

"They, sir?"

"You know who I mean. The Englishman, the Irishman and the Scotsman."

Kilroy looked pained. "Let's talk about Johnny Peters," he began.

"No," Guy said. "I don't want to talk about Johnny Peters. I don't know anything about Johnny Peters. I hardly ever met Johnny Peters. I'm sorry. But I can't help you."

"I understand." Kilroy nodded imperceptibly and Carmichael put away her notebook. "I'm sorry to have taken up so much of your time, sir." The two police officers stood up and Guy thought it was over. But it wasn't. Almost as an afterthought, Kilroy added, "I wonder if we could take a quick look round?"

"Why?" Guy demanded.

"It's just a formality," Kilroy said.

"We can return with a warrant, if you prefer," Carmichael said. She was becoming increasingly menacing.

"You can take a look round if you want to," Guy said. Why not? There was nothing they would find.

"Thank you, sir."

They began in the bedroom.

It was a cursory search, as if they didn't really know what they were looking for and didn't expect to find it anyway. It was only as they glanced under the bed and inside the wardrobe that Guy began to see the pointlessness of the whole exercise. Did they really think they might happen upon Johnny Peters, bound and gagged, inside the blanket box? (They looked. He wasn't there.) Or did they think that he might have been here recently, that he might have conveniently dropped his bus pass or his invitation to appear in the Crouch End amateur production of *Snow White*? And if they did find such a thing, what would it mean? It wasn't as if they could arrest Guy on suspicion of kidnap just because his neighbour had been in his flat.

But still they went on. They looked in the bathroom, Carmichael peering suspiciously into the bath. At least they didn't lift up the lid of the toilet. Then they tried the kitchen. A brief glance across the surfaces. Carmichael seemed interested in the cork noticeboard, another nastiness from Ikea. She opened the free-standing deep freeze chest.

"It's a big deep-freeze for a small flat," Kilroy said. He was looking intently at Guy. But the lazy eye was elsewhere.

"Kate's mother gave it to us," Guy said. "My girlfriend. Her mother —"

"Sir!"

There was something about the way she had spoken the word, the single syllable. Kilroy walked over to the deep freeze. Guy followed him. The two of them looked in.

And there he was.

Johnny Peters had been strangled. The belt was still round his neck. He had been squeezed into the deep freeze and was lying in a foetal position with his head resting on a pillow of frozen peas. His face had gone blue. His eyes were frozen open.

"What . . .? I . . .? How . . .? No . . ." Words somehow floated into Guy's mouth and slipped out again, making no sense.

He couldn't tear his eyes away from the figure. Was Johnny dead? Of course he was. He didn't look quite human any more. He was like a wax model. An exhibit at the Saatchi Gallery.

"It's Johnny Peters," Carmichael said, quite unnecessarily.

"Can you explain this, Mr Fletcher?" Kilroy asked.

"I . . ." The air wasn't reaching Guy's throat.

"Did you kill him?"

"No!"

"Is that your belt?"

Guy stared past the ice, past the chiselled lips. It was his belt. "Yes."

"I am arresting you for the murder of Johnny Peters. You are not required to say anything but anything you do say . . ."

208

The words faded out. Guy could hear the sound of his own heart, thudding, impossibly, inside his head. Carmichael had produced a chair and he sank on to it. There was a wind rushing into his ears and the chill of the deep-freeze reached out and slithered round his neck. Ten minutes passed. Or maybe twenty. Or maybe only one. Suddenly there were more policemen in the kitchen staring in disgust at the figure in the freezer. Someone was taking photographs. Flash. Flash. Flash. Guy felt the light hammering into his eyes. More policemen were dusting the place for fingerprints. Why? Maybe it was just something they did. For the moment Guy was being ignored. He was the cause of all this. He was the centre of it. But he was sitting motionless while it all went on around him.

"We can't get him out, sir."

"We're going to have to defrost him."

The voices came from somewhere else. Guy was in shock.

Eventually they led him out on to the street. They were surprisingly gentle with him. He could have been an invalid or a very old man, someone who needed help. He made his way down the staircase of the house and somehow he knew he was seeing it for the very last time. There were more policemen waiting at the bottom. They stared at him, but at the same time avoided his eyes.

There was a small crowd of people outside the house. It was hard to know where they had come from or how they had got there. Mrs Atwood was there, of course, and a couple of people Guy thought might be neighbours. The others must have just been passers-by although he had never noticed pedestrians in Mapletree Close before. And there were three people he recognised. A tall man in a suit. A grey-haired Irishman. A thug in a kilt.

And that was when he decided. A police car was waiting for him on the other side of the road, its back door open, and Guy knew that once he had allowed himself to be led into it, he would never again be free. He was in the grip of an organisation that was at once all-powerful and yet incomprehensible. They had set out to discredit him and to destroy him and they had been prepared to kill — twice — to achieve their aims. First Brian Eastman. Now Johnny Peters. He would be next. Once he was in prison he would be in their control. An accident in the showers or another convict with a knife — anything could be arranged. The click of the door on the police car would be as final as the click of a coffin lid. He had only one chance to get away and that was now.

He acted.

There were two policemen escorting him and he took them by surprise. In a sense, he had taken himself by surprise. He twisted round and kicked out. One of the policemen fell, gasping, his hands clutching his crotch. Guy flailed out at the other one. His fist crashed into the side of the policeman's face and he went down with a spray of blood. He ran forward to the police car and threw himself over it, rolling his back across the bonnet. He had seen a stuntman do something similar in *Policemen's Wives*. Then he was on the other side of

210

the street with the crowd staring, more policemen running, his heart pounding.

He ran on, into the garden of number fourteen. He knew something they didn't. There was a gap in the fence. Burglars had got in that way three months before and it still hadn't been repaired. Across the lawn and into the rhododendron bushes. Guy didn't dare look back. Surely the police were only centimetres behind.

He found the fence. The gap was still there, the wires hanging limp between two posts. He lunged through, cutting his hand, then slithered down the slope through weeds, nettles, long grass and litter. It led to a disused railway line that ran between Muswell Hill and Alexandra Palace. A man walking a chocolate Labrador stared at him as he emerged from the undergrowth and threw himself along the path. The dog barked. Guy plunged into a dark, graffiti-covered tunnel that led underneath the main road. At the same instant, a police car, its siren screaming, passed over his head.

He had often walked in the area, he and Kate. He knew just about every footpath, every twisting alley. He ran past a school and into park land, then along a path that sloped down between evenly spaced trees and dog poo-bins. How long would it take the police to call in helicopters? Once he had been spotted from the air he would have no chance.

But, in fact, he was lucky. Even as he regained the road and ran, breathless towards Crouch End, a bus pulled in and he jumped on to it. He had an old ticket in his back pocket. He flashed it at the driver, who took no notice. The bus carried him to Finsbury Park. Three more police cars shot past, but nobody noticed the sweating, trembling figure on the upper deck.

The police closed Finsbury Park station ten minutes after Guy had jumped on to a Victoria Line train to central London. His choices had multiplied and multiplied again. There had only been two or three ways he might go in Mapletree Close. There were four lines at Finsbury Park and therefore eight routes. When he emerged at Oxford Circus, there was no telling what direction he might take.

He had got away. But not for long. By six o'clock his face was on every news bulletin for, it now turned out, Johnny Peters had not been his only victim.

CHAPTER
SEVENTEEN

It was a story with all the ingredients to make a tabloid editor happy to be alive. A bizarre murder in a North London suburb. Police incompetence. A sensational escape. And — the icing on the cake — a well-known actor at the centre of it all.

It didn't matter that nobody had ever heard of Guy Fletcher. He had been in *E for Emergency, Policemen's Wives* and the *Manchester Murders*, and they were all very well known indeed. He had even starred in a Nescafé commercial. Suddenly Nescafé found themselves receiving the sort of publicity they could have done without. COLD BLEND ran one of the punning headlines in the press, a slightly forced reference to the deep freeze. This led to a po-faced press release from the coffee company, and, three weeks later, the sacking of their advertising agency.

And at the same time there was the character and the background of the murdered man. Johnny Peters, it now turned out, had worked for the NSPCC and various other charities, visiting sick children in hospitals up and down the country. He would dress up in a bright orange and green three-piece suit with dyed hair and a bowler hat and enter the wards, cartwheeling down the corridors with a cry of: "Here's Little Johnny!" He would juggle with the fruit brought by the visiting parents — three apples and a banana. He was a comedian, a ventriloquist, a magician and — according to many of the doctors and nurses who had encountered him — he had been personally responsible for the recovery of many children who might otherwise have perished.

"He was wonderful," Marsha Brown, of the Whittington Hospital in Archway, told the *Daily Mail*. "The children all adored him — even the ones who weren't fully conscious. The moment he arrived, everyone cheered up. I can't believe there's anyone on the planet who would want to do him harm. Little Johnny was a saint."

She caught the national mood. Suddenly everyone was talking about Little Johnny. He effortlessly stole all the front pages, even that of the *Financial Times*. Even the imminent publication of the Sanderson report — an enquiry into government corruption — was, for the time being, forgotten. Then Oxfam stepped in. Little Johnny had worked for them too, entertaining children in the third world. He had been in New York after 9/11. It was no wonder that Guy had rarely seen him in Mapletree Close. He had been tireless.

At first nobody knew why Guy Fletcher had murdered his upstairs neighbour. Mrs Atwood, of course, appeared in every single newspaper. This was to be the crowning achievement of her life: gossipmongering on a national scale. But despite what she said, a "domestic" seemed unlikely. Neighbours argued in

Muswell Hill but, by and large, they didn't kill each other — not unless they were Dennis Nilsen (who, by coincidence, had lived just round the corner). And there was something strangely at odds between the leafy surroundings of Mapletree Close and the grotesque nature of the killing: the belt round the neck, the body in the deep freeze. But then the detective superintendent called a press conference and, in the packed, neon-lit room he had commandeered in the Wood Green town hall, he dropped the next bombshell into the laps of the slavering press crowd.

He had, he said, received information that might tie in this death with several other murders that had taken place across the country, all of them involving little people. Choosing his words carefully, he told the journalists that three more vertically challenged men had been found murdered in St Albans, Wimbish Green and Stoke-on-Trent, while a fourth was still missing from his home in Groby, on the outskirts of Leicester. Guy Fletcher had recently visited all these places for no apparent reason and his behaviour had become increasingly eccentric. In St Albans, for example, he had managed to insinuate himself into a pack of Boy Scouts, passing himself off as a postgraduate student. It could be, Kilroy said, that he was sizing up his next victim. And size was what it was all about. He might have killed anyone, provided they were less than four feet tall.

It seemed that no dwarf in England had been safe. So ran the headline on the front page of the *Sun*. Meanwhile, the *Mirror* published a helpful five-page

215

supplement: famous dwarves across the centuries. There was General Tom Thumb, who worked at Barnum's Circus, Toulouse-Lautrec, Alexander Pope, the actors Kenny Baker (R2D2 in *Star Wars*) and David Rappaport, the founder of the Dwarf Athletic Association, Arthur Dean, and Napoleon, who hadn't technically been a dwarf but who had been very short and who brought up the number of dwarves on the spread to a convenient seven. Suddenly everyone was talking about dwarfs. It was a good time to be small.

But not a good time to be Guy Fletcher. He was a figure of contempt: a serial dwarf-killer, his guilt certain less than twenty-four hours after he had disappeared and long before he had appeared in court. He was the main subject in Internet chat rooms and on radio phone-in shows. The police were warning that he was extremely dangerous and not to be approached. It was the sort of fame he had always hankered for, but it had gone horribly wrong. He had wanted to be in the spotlight — not in searchlights. This was not going to help his career at the BBC.

Sylvie Graham was interviewed but said little. She stood by her clients, no matter what they had done. The press moved on and found Alistair and Ruth Fletcher, who had by now retired to Bournemouth and who could only get the crowds of journalists and photographers out of their tiny front garden by disowning Guy altogether.

And that was the next explosion in the story, which seemed to be getting better and better with every passing hour. DWARF KILLER IS SELINA MOORE'S SON.

216

It was a headline almost on a par with the stand-up comedian who had once swallowed a small mammal.

The press investigated and finally, after thirty years, the reason for Guy's adoption became known. It was entirely predictable. Selina had become pregnant when she was in her mid-twenties, the result of an affair with an actor she had met doing rep outside London. She had never revealed his name and it was possible that he was unaware even that he was responsible. She had given up the child because he was in the way. Her career came first.

The press had never been able to knock Selina off her pedestal while she was alive. They did so now that she was dead. She was implicated in Johnny Peters's murder. Her selfishness had, quite definitely, contributed to the crazed, dwarf-hating maniac that her son had become. Faced with a growing public outcry, the Bishop of Rochester was forced to appear on *Newsnight* to defend her name.

He was a very elderly man with the long white hair, ruddy cheeks and patronising smile that seem peculiar to many senior figures in the Church of England. He was interviewed by Jeremy Paxman, the two of them face to face across a table in the sombre lighting of the *Newsnight* studio.

"Did Selina Moore have many relationships?" Paxman asked.

"Not at all," the bishop replied. "To a very large extent, Selina kept herself to herself when she was in Los Angeles, you know. Of course, she did have wonderful friends. She learnt to fly a helicopter and spent a great deal of time with her instructor. She often spoke to me about Harry and his big red chopper."

"She must have been close to a lot of actors, though," Paxman said.

"Indeed so." The bishop nodded. "There was one young man who had a big part in *The French Lieutenant's Woman* and she mentioned another with whom she once performed in *The Cherry Orchard*. She didn't spend all her time with actors, though. There were writers and artists. And also an architect . . . He often visited her at her house. In fact, she told me she had inspired many of his erections. Selina was a wonderfully gregarious person. She loved a party or a night out and, at the end of the day, she was happy to see anyone who would give her one."

"Yes, yes, yes." Paxman was characteristically impatient. "What sort of life did you have together?" he continued, brashly invading the privacy of their marriage.

"Well, as I'm sure you know, Selina came to religion late in life," the bishop said. "But she said she hoped to spend a lot of time on her knees. She enjoyed running her fingers over the church organ. Bach was her favourite composer. She loved a good fugue."

"It must have been strange, being a bishop married to an actress."

"Not at all, Jeremy. We understood each other perfectly."

Selina's life was suddenly in the public domain. As was Guy. Hated, reviled, feared as a sizeist and serial

218

killer, his face was in every newspaper and on every television screen.

But where was he?

Guy had emerged from the tube system to discover that a teeming metropolis was very much a twin-bladed weapon if you were a wanted killer on the run. There were a million faces to hide among, but they were also a million faces that might recognise him at any time. He might have thousands of hotels and hostels to choose from, but what good were they when he would need some sort of ID to book himself a room? He could lose himself anywhere outside, but getting indoors was going to be a problem. For the first time in his life he felt himself at one with the homeless, those lost souls selling the *Big Issue* or sleeping rough in office doorways. He was surrounded by wealth and by comfort but it seemed to exist in a separate dimension. All around him and yet a million miles away.

He had twenty-seven pounds in his pocket and a bunch of credit cards that would have been cancelled even if they worked. He wondered what would happen if he tried to use a cash machine, and decided not to bother. The last time, it had laughed at him. This time it might call the police. At least the weather was dry. But even so he knew he couldn't stay on the street much longer. He had no survival skills. It could only be a matter of time before he was recognised and taken back into custody.

But he was an actor. He had to remind himself that he did have at least some resources he could draw on. He went to a chemist and bought hair-colouring and cheap sunglasses, then tried to find a toilet he could use to effect his disguise. This wasn't easy. He needed a sink and a mirror but the toilets at Charing Cross Station and the surrounding pubs were too busy while the ones at McDonalds were locked, presumably to discourage the local drug users. In the end, he walked up Piccadilly and ducked into the Ritz. He had been to a function there once and remembered a toilet in a basement corridor, tucked away at the end of half a mile of plush carpet. It took him twenty minutes to apply a chestnut wash to his hair, and although it had made him look like the world's most optimistic rent-boy, he was reasonably sure that he would no longer be easily recognised.

He solved the problem of where to spend the first night by finding a cinema in Brixton with an all-night screening: five Marx Brothers films. Early in the morning, he found himself in an old-fashioned auditorium — velvet-covered seats and a proscenium arch — watching *Duck Soup* with about half a dozen other film buffs and insomniacs.

"You can leave in a taxi. If you can't leave in a taxi you can leave in a huff. If that's too soon, you can leave in a minute and a huff. You know, you haven't stopped talking since I came here! You must have been vaccinated with a phonograph needle."

He had loved the Marx Brothers. He had watched them every Christmas, late at night, usually on Channel 4. But *Duck Soup* didn't make him laugh. Groucho as Rufus T. Firefly. Margaret Dumont as the stately Mrs Teasdale. The black-and-white figures flickering in front of him meant nothing at all. They were like ghosts. Or maybe it was he who had become the ghost. It was a dreadful feeling. It was as if something in him had died.

And so to the next day. Guy had lunch in a café near the cinema and tried to work out what he was going to do.

He had become a fugitive, in the classic, Hollywood sense of the word. He could almost see the newspapers spinning round and round to the appropriate orchestral accompaniment. It was like something out of *The Thirty-nine Steps*, the film he had been shooting when this all began. But this wasn't Hollywood. This was South London. Nobody was going to yell, "Cut", and let him go back to his trailer. His feet were hurting, he was tired and beginning to smell. This was real.

Part of him was scared. Part of him was angry with himself for wilfully walking into this in the first place. Nobody had asked him to go chasing after jokes. But it was the fact that he could see no way out of it that frightened him. At least Richard Hannay had known what he was up against. Guy was trapped inside some sort of huge labyrinth with the lights turned off. He wouldn't be aware of the walls until he walked straight into them. Or until they closed in and crushed him. That was how he felt. Claustrophobic, miserable, just wanting to get out.

He wished now that Kate had never left him. Kate would have stopped this happening from the start. If he had come back from the Cat and Fiddle and told her the joke he had heard, she would simply have got rid of

221

it. It was nothing. It meant nothing. She would have made him see that.

But perhaps she could still help him. Thinking about Kate made him want to see her. Even now she might be able to get him out of this mess. At the very least she would be able to offer him a change of clothes, a roof over his head, a sense of stability under his feet. Did he dare get in touch with her? She was living with Martin and Martin was a famous actor now, a personality with a reputation to protect. But he and Martin had been friends too. Guy couldn't think of anywhere else to go. He didn't dare spend another twenty-four hours out on the street, even with his disguise. He thought of ringing but he had forgotten the number and, anyway, he knew that it would be easier to reject him over the phone. Martin had a flat in Hoxton. That was where he went.

There was nobody in. The flat backed on to a canal in a part of London that had barely had a name five years ago but which had become suddenly trendy. It looked like a converted warehouse but it was, in fact, a brand new development designed to look like a converted warehouse. This was Sunday-supplement living: bare brick, exposed girders, electronic gates and lots of glass. Art critic on the first floor, celebrity chef on the second and that actor with all the buggery on the third. Guy rang the bell half a dozen times before he gave up. Perhaps Martin and Kate were away. He spent the rest of the afternoon browsing in bookshops and came back in the early evening, determined to give it one last try.

222

This time he was lucky. He rang the bell and a voice answered almost at once. That was the good news. The bad news was that it was Martin's voice.

"Yes?"

"Martin, this is Guy."

"Who?"

"Guy Fletcher."

There was a pause. The receiver, built into the gateway, stared blackly. Then: "Jesus Christ, Guy! What the fuck?"

He knew, of course. There wouldn't be a person in the country who didn't.

"Please, Martin. Will you let me in?"

"Guy —"

"I was set up, Martin. I'm in a lot of trouble. I need help."

There was another pause; at least a minute this time. Guy could imagine his old friend sweating on the other side of the speaker-phone. Martin never had been much good at moral dilemmas. Then there was a buzz. He pushed open the gate and crossed the courtyard to the front door.

The interior of the building was all angles: triangular hallways and narrow, rectangular windows. The lift doors were silver polished to a mirror finish. When Guy stepped out on the third floor, Martin was already waiting for him, framed in a doorway, yellow light spilling over his shoulders. He seemed both alarmed and surprised to see him, as if the voice that had come over the intercom might, despite everything, have belonged to someone else.

"What the hell are you doing here?" he demanded, in an over-theatrical whisper. "I just saw you on the news. The police are looking for you!"

"Do you think I could come in, Martin?" There were two other flats on the same floor. Someone could come out at any time.

"Why?"

"Why do you think?"

"I don't know."

"For God's sake, Martin. I've walked half-way across London. I've been up all night. I need something to eat. What's the matter with you?"

"It's not what's the matter with *me*," Martin muttered, but he stood aside and let Guy in.

Guy found himself in a large, open-plan room with a double-height ceiling and a galleried first floor. There was an open-plan kitchen — gleaming clean — and a black leather suite arranged round a plasma television screen that had been built into the brick wall. The lighting was halogen and expensive, the floor polished wood with scattered rugs. It was a far cry from the rooms Martin had shared in Kilburn when he had been at the Clairemont. The only things that had been scattered there were old socks and underwear and the rest of it had been Formica-topped furniture and damp. And yet there had been a warmth, a sense of identity in the Kilburn flat that was entirely missing here. Kilburn had been lived-in. This was more a backdrop for a life that was happening elsewhere. It said nothing about Martin, everything about his aspirations.

224

Guy examined his old friend. The last time he had seen him had been more than a year ago, after the first night of his play. For a moment he was confused, unsure whether Martin looked completely different or exactly the same. In a way he was both. He had the same fair, unruly hair, the same lazy blue eyes. He was still twenty pounds overweight and haphazardly dressed. But now the clothes were designer-made. He had a deep and slightly unattractive tan: the sort you get skiing early or late in the season when everyone else is at work. He was tauter, more sure of himself. In short, he was richer. That was what showed.

"Is Kate here?" Guy asked.

"She was in the shower when you rang the bell," Martin said, adding, accusingly: "We were about to go out."

"Does she know I'm here?"

"Yes. I told her."

"Could I have a drink?"

Martin grimaced. It was obvious that letting Guy in at all had been bad enough as far as he was concerned and he was afraid of committing himself any further — even as far as giving him a drink. "We've got some beer," he said.

"Not alcohol, thanks. Just juice or coffee. And I don't suppose you've got anything to eat?"

They went into the kitchen — if it was possible to enter such an open-plan space. Martin opened the fridge and took out a carton of apple juice, ham and cheese. He found bread and butter, some leftover salad, and put it all on the table, leaving Guy to help himself. "You look awful," he said.

"Thanks."

"What happened to your hair?"

"I put some dye in it."

"I suppose that's one way to draw attention to yourself."

"That wasn't the idea." Guy poured himself a glass of apple juice. "So, how are you getting on, Martin? How's the career?" He had smoothly switched the conversation, hoping to divert Martin with every actor's favourite subject — himself.

"It's good. I've got a film starting next week — starring Ewan MacGregor."

"Have you met him?"

"Yes. He's really nice."

There was the sound of a door closing and Kate appeared, first on the gallery, then making her way down the spiral staircase. Guy felt a familiar flutter in his stomach and knew that he was still attracted to her. At the same time, a series of images flashed into his mind like picture postcards spilling out of a drawer. A visit to Paris, falling about laughing in the tiny garden of a house in Battersea, the Aztec exhibition at the Royal Academy, trying to assemble the Ikea bed — things they had done when they had been most together. The images came in a rush and vanished. They were all gone now. He had lost her. No. It wasn't as easy as that. She had walked out on him.

He tried to look at her more dispassionately. She had changed her hairstyle. That was Guy's first impression.

226

Her black hair was short now and made her look more adult. He didn't like it. She was wearing a simple grey dress with a silver necklace that looked Mexican and which she'd certainly never had when she lived with him. Martin must have bought it for her unless she'd gone out and got it herself. She reached the bottom of the stairs, trailing a hand on the banister. Her fingernails were painted silver. That was new too. She had never polished her fingernails before.

And suddenly there they were. Guy sitting at the table with a plate of food. Martin leaning with his back against the fridge. Kate standing alone, watching them both with eyes that had recently become more serious. "Hello, Guy," she said.

"Hello, Kate."

"I can't believe you're here. I can't believe what's happened to you. What's been going on?"

"It's a long story."

"We don't really have time for a long story," Martin said, forcing a smile as if it could make up for the bitterness in his voice. "We're going out."

"We're not expected until eight," Kate said. "And it doesn't matter if we're late."

"This is Marc and Peter!" Martin countered. "They said eight o'clock and I think we should be on time."

"Look, I don't want to hold you up —" Guy began.

"It's all right." Kate's voice was quiet and measured. It was a sure sign, Guy knew, that she was annoyed. She turned to Martin. "Why don't you go and get changed?"

"I am changed."

"I think you should wear a suit."

"A suit's too formal."

"Then wear a suit with a T-shirt. Please?"

Martin looked sulky. He wanted to argue but decided against it. He pushed himself upright with his shoulder-blades, then lumbered over to the stairs. He turned back once more. "I don't think Guy should be here," he said. "I think it's a bad idea." Then he climbed up, leaving Kate and Guy on their own.

Kate moved to the table and sat down. "Are you all right?" she asked and, hearing her voice, being so close to her, Guy wanted to take hold of her and kiss her just one last time.

Instead, he asked, "Who are Marc and Peter?"

"They're the producers on Martin's new film."

"What's it about?"

"It's a gangster movie."

"Another British gangster movie? Just what the world needs."

"It's a good script."

He had put her on the defensive, hardly sensible, given the circumstances. He changed the subject. "How are you, Kate? I mean . . . you and Martin?"

"That's none of your business." Now she was brittle. "What the hell is going on, Guy? You didn't really kill him, did you? Johnny Peters? He was a horrible little creep but strangling him! And then putting him in Mum's deep-freeze!"

"I didn't strangle him. I had no idea he was there."

"Then how did he get there?"

"I don't know."

"And why did you run away? Why did you attack a policeman? On the news this morning they said he might lose a testicle."

"They were exaggerating." Guy looked around him. "Nice place."

"Thank you."

"Can I stay here?"

"I don't know, Guy." Kate sighed. "Martin didn't even want to let you in. He wouldn't have if I hadn't made him."

"That's nice of Martin."

"This is his flat. And, anyway, he's got a point. You've put him on the spot. You shouldn't really have come."

She went to the fridge and poured herself a glass of wine. The glass had an absurdly long stem — it was the sort designed to make an effect at a dinner party and Guy recognised it. Someone had given Kate a set of six when they moved into Mapletree Close but she had hardly ever used them. They couldn't go into the dishwasher and every time they were used they hung around for days, waiting to be washed up. She had been so afraid of breaking them that they had simply become an annoyance. But she was using them now.

"What are you going to do?" she asked.

"I don't know. I haven't thought."

"Do you have any idea who it was?"

"Who?"

"Little Johnny."

Guy had known he would have to explain eventually. He had already decided that he wasn't going to tell her

229

the truth. She would only snap at him. "I have no idea," he said.

"And what about the others? They're saying you've been all over the country. They say there are other victims."

"It's all a lie, Kate. For God's sake. You know me. I wouldn't want to kill anybody."

"I do know you. And of course you wouldn't kill anyone. But if anyone was going to get caught up in something totally insane, it would have to be you."

"That's not fair."

"Is this something to do with one of your conspiracy theories? Did you get something in your head to do with dwarves?"

"No."

She could see right through him. He should have known that. He didn't want to tell her the truth but he couldn't lie to her. "I was trying to find out where a joke came from," he said.

"What?"

"It's a long story."

"What joke?"

"It doesn't matter any more. I was asking questions about a joke. Maybe it hasn't got anything to do with it. All I know is that somebody killed Johnny Peters and put him in the flat. They called the police and I had to get away. If I'd let them arrest me, I'd still be in prison now. What else could I do?"

"I don't think you should have run away. If you didn't do it, the police would have found out."

"Tell that to the Birmingham Six." He sighed. He was suddenly miserable. There was a lot of food spread out in front of him but he hadn't touched any of it. "I wish you hadn't left me, Kate. If you hadn't gone, none of this would have happened."

"So it's my fault?"

"That's not what I'm saying."

"Tell me about this joke."

"All right."

It took him only a few minutes to tell the story. Kate listened to him in silence. He didn't know if she believed him or not. She wasn't giving anything away.

He finished. And now the reaction came.

"Guy! For God's sake — this is so typical of you!" Kate was looking at him not with anger but with so much dismay that he was taken aback. "Don't you understand why it didn't work out with you and me? Why I left you?"

"You left me because Martin had more to offer."

She almost threw her wine at him. He saw her hand tighten. For a moment she was really angry. "You think I'm sleeping with Martin just because he's got money and a career?"

"I didn't mean that."

"Yes, he's got a nice flat. Yes, he's got contacts. He's doing well. But do you really think that's why I'm here? I mean, what does that make me? Is that how you see me after all our time together?"

"No, Kate. I'm sorry. It wasn't what I meant."

"You might as well know, it didn't have anything to do with Martin. I would have gone anyway."

Guy felt his throat closing. "Why?"

"I loved you, Guy. I really did. I wanted to be happy with you. You're funny and you're kind and you're intelligent —"

"Why don't you just stop there? Quit while I'm ahead."

"— but I never knew where I was with you. I could never tell what was going on in your head. The way you saw things — you were completely unpredictable."

"I was never unpredictable!" Guy exclaimed. He sighed. "You knew I was going to say that, didn't you?"

"Sometimes you could be really irritating. If you didn't get a job it was because the director knew somebody who knew somebody who had a grudge against you. It was never because you weren't good enough. And it was almost impossible living with you when you were out of work. Why couldn't you just go out and wash dishes like everyone else? You had all these crazy ideas. I mean, following a joke! You were following a joke? Only you could come up with something like that."

"Why did you never say any of this to me before?"

"I did say it to you but you didn't listen. You were too busy wondering about Premium Bonds and the traffic and the weather-forecast men and traffic humps. Sometimes you almost drove me mad. You were the only person I ever met who could spend an hour talking quite seriously about why four-finger KitKats taste better than two-finger KitKats. We had fun together. I'm not saying we didn't. But there were times when you didn't seem to be living in the real world. Nothing real seemed to matter to you."

"What about you and me?" Guy said. "Moving in together. That was real. That mattered to me."

"I thought it was. I hoped it was. But in the end, you were just play-acting then too. Trying to turn us into . . . I don't know what. Happy Families. It wasn't you and me in that house, Guy. It was a cartoon version of you and me."

There was a sophisticated telephone system in the flat. The receiver was attached to the wall. Out of the corner of his eye, Guy saw a little light come on. It glowed red.

"Was she really your mother?" Kate asked suddenly.

For a moment he was thrown. "What?"

"I heard it on the news. Selina Moore."

"Yes. She was."

"Why didn't you tell me?"

"I don't know, Kate. I should have. It was one of those stupid things. I didn't tell you when we started going out and later on there never seemed to be a right moment. I didn't mean to keep it a secret from you. It's just the way it happened. Would you have been impressed?"

"I don't know. Maybe I'd have understood you a little more."

They fell silent. The light on the telephone went out.

"What do you think I should do?" Guy asked.

"You could start by taking off the sunglasses. They don't suit you."

Guy took off the glasses. He had forgotten he was wearing them. "And now?"

"I think you should go to the police."

"You mean, turn myself in?"

"No, Guy. Don't 'turn yourself in'. Now you're talking like someone in a Jimmy Cagney film. Walk into a police station and tell them who you are. Are you still with Sylvie?"

"Yes."

"Call her. You can use the phone here. She'll get you a solicitor. Everyone who knows you will speak on your behalf. The police will know it wasn't you."

There was a newspaper lying on the table. Guy turned it towards him and glanced at it. His picture was there, spread over three columns. He felt sick. He was wishing he hadn't come here. "They're saying that the dwarves who were killed lived in St Albans, Wimbish Green and Stoke-on-Trent," he said.

"Yes."

"I was in all those places." His voice was heavy.

"Why?"

"I told you. I was following the joke."

And then Martin came back down the stairs. He had changed into a dark blue suit with a white T-shirt. He was looking very handsome. He seemed annoyed to see Guy still there but he nodded at the half-empty wine-glass on the table. "I'll have some too," he said. Kate didn't move so he went over to the fridge and opened it.

"Who did you telephone?" Kate asked.

"I didn't," Martin said.

"I saw the light go on on the upstairs extension."

Martin took out the wine bottle and closed the fridge door. It was an American fridge, of course. Well stocked, with three or four bottles on the shelves. "Oh. You mean just now? I called the restaurant to tell them we might be late."

It was a lie. Martin wasn't such a good actor, after all, Guy reflected. He couldn't keep the liar out of his eyes.

Kate knew it too. "Tell me who you called," she said, like a mother talking to a difficult child.

Martin said nothing. He poured himself some wine, studying the glass as if it were a holy relic.

"Did you call the police?" she asked.

"No."

"Did you call the police?"

Martin bit his lip. He nodded.

Guy's stomach turned. He pulled himself to his feet.

"Why?" Kate wanted to know.

Martin avoided her eye. He turned to Guy and it all came out in a rush: "I'm sorry, mate. I really mean that. But you've got to understand. I don't know what happened, but they're calling you a serial killer, for heaven's sake! If they found you here I'd be in deep shit, and I'm really sorry but I have to think of my career." He glanced very quickly at Kate. "The film! You saw the contract. You know what the Americans are like. All those fucking morality clauses. If I get pulled in because of him . . . I don't want to lose the part," he concluded weakly.

"How long did they say until they'd be here?" Kate asked, coldly furious, and Guy was grateful to her because of it. Martin didn't answer. "Give me your wallet," she said.

He didn't want to. Guy could see the hesitation in his face and understood the miniature power struggle that was taking place. At the same time he knew that if Kate won this fight, she would lose in the end because Martin wasn't the sort of person who could live with someone stronger than him. He felt guilty. Kate didn't deserve this.

Martin passed his wallet across and Kate took out all the cash, about two hundred pounds. She threw the wallet back, its emptiness somehow contemptuous, and handed the money to Guy. "Take this," she said. "If you've got any sense, you'll do as I say and go to the police. But if you need more time, well, maybe it will help."

"Just don't say where you got it," Martin added.

Kate ignored him. "I can't believe this is happening," she went on. "I can't believe I'm seeing you like this."

"I'm sorry, Kate." Guy meant it. "I shouldn't have come."

"There's a service door down in the basement. It comes out at the back. I think you should take it."

"Thanks."

"Good luck." She stepped forward and kissed him, lightly, on the cheek. And then, close to him, she spoke quietly so that only he would hear: "For what it's worth, you were right about one thing. I've noticed recently . . . maybe four-finger KitKats do taste better than two-finger ones."

Real police sirens joined the imaginary ones. Guy could hear them, perhaps a mile away. He hurried out of the flat, down four flights of stairs and out, into the uncertain night.

CHAPTER
EIGHTEEN

It stormed that night in London.

Guy did indeed have a theory about weathermen, as Kate had mentioned. As far as he was concerned, the entire science and practice of meteorology might be, and probably was, nothing more than a gigantic fraud. After all, despite all their charts and computer-generated isobars, and for all their pretence at sophistication, the forecasters were wrong just about as often as they were right and the cold front coming in from the Atlantic bringing rain to the south later in the afternoon could just as easily turn left over Ireland and go and bother someone else.

The forecasters themselves seemed an odd bunch, media celebrities who regularly turned up on quizzes and reality shows. But what was the reality? Perhaps it was the actor in him, but Guy couldn't think of them as anything more than geography graduates who'd struck lucky: men and women with reasonable looks and no lisp. They reminded him of ancient Inca priests. People believed them. They had the same authority. But analyse their results and all those arrows and wavy lines would turn out to be as reliable as the entrails of a chicken.

Not one of the bastards had managed to predict this storm, for example, although some had said it might drizzle and one or two had gone as far as heavy showers. Heavy? The rain was torrential. It slammed into buildings, gushed out of pipes and formed spreading puddles in the street. The sky was black. And the wind howled up and down the pavements, turning the few pedestrians unlucky enough to be out into bent old men, leaning forward to prevent themselves being scattered away.

But it was a good night to be a fugitive from justice. In a sense, the storm had made fugitives of everyone and Guy travelled through London in the certain knowledge that nobody would be looking out for him. Nobody was looking at anybody. They were just battling to get to where they had to be. He quickly made it to King's Cross station and only here did he experience any doubts. It was quite possible that the police would have every mainline station under surveillance. Hoxton was not very far away and they had been only minutes behind him when he set out. But, once again, the weather was on his side. Commuters were arriving with their hair plastered down, their shoulders hunched over, their collars turned up. How could anyone spot him in a crowd like this? Even so, he bought his ticket from an automatic machine and waited until the last possible minute, jumping on to his train just before it left the station.

He was going to Cambridge. He had decided to go back to Sally Lockwood.

It was, he knew, his last chance. If she couldn't help him, he might as well do as Kate had said and turn himself in. For a brief moment, he reflected on a life sentence at Broadmoor. At least he'd meet some interesting people. They might know some good jokes.

But Sally had been on the telephone when the police arrived. She had found the next link in the chain, a salesman called Bill Naughtie. If all else failed — and now that he thought about it, it had — he could pick up the trail again, continue his search for the source of the joke. Because it seemed obvious to him that whoever was responsible for the Ferrero Rocher joke had to be behind what was happening to him. He had once thought of a fat boy in an attic. Well, for "fat" read "psychotic". He had to find him.

A conductor passed through the carriage. Guy glanced down as if half asleep, passing his ticket over his shoulder. The conductor took it, punched it, handed it back. Raindrops ran in panic, horizontally, across the windows. The train was already in the suburbs and picking up speed.

There was something else worrying him. Sally had offered to help him and she had been speaking on a phone that had been bugged. He was suddenly afraid. He had put her in danger. First Brian Eastman, then Johnny Peters . . . now her. It seemed impossible that she would be the next target but, then, everything that had happened in the last few weeks had been impossible and he couldn't just abandon her, no matter how small the risk. He felt responsible. He had to warn her.

240

She probably wouldn't believe him. She would have read the newspapers, seen the television reports. She wouldn't even want to talk to him. But he had to see her. He wanted to see her. The truth was that he had nowhere else to go.

An hour later, they arrived in Cambridge and Guy got up and left the train, trying to look relaxed. As far as the police were concerned, there was no reason why he should have come here and so, he hoped, nobody would be looking for him. He went straight to the house on the edge of the green but when he got there he stopped. It was after eight o'clock and already it was dark. There were no lights showing behind the windows and he wondered if anyone was in. Sally could have taken Daphne Lockwood to the hospital. And that reminded him. He knew how she felt about her privacy, how protective she was of her mother. This wasn't the right time.

No. It wasn't just that. If he rang the bell, she might not even open the door. He wouldn't be able to reason with her, explain what had happened, not with a slab of wood between them. He wasn't thinking about her. He was thinking about himself. He was wet, tired and afraid. He couldn't bear to be rejected by her — not tonight. He would approach her in daylight, and somewhere neutral. At the shop.

And until then? He had two choices. He could spend the night on the street, sleeping rough. Or he could find some sort of guesthouse or hotel. Neither option was particularly appealing. Although the rain had stopped, it was still damp and suddenly cold, the British winter determined to linger on, even in the month of May. Guy couldn't spend twelve hours outside. He didn't know where to go and, besides, it would be one sure way to bring himself to the attention of the police. On the other hand, a hotel would be a terrible risk. If he was recognised, he would be arrested while he slept. He walked back to the station and examined himself in the mirror in the toilet. He looked ridiculous. The cheap hair colour, diluted by the rain, had gone a strange, unnatural orange. His clothes were crumpled. So was his face. He put the glasses back on and tried to rearrange himself. He had to admit that he looked nothing like his normal self. He had the money Kate had given him. He decided to take the risk.

He found a pub with rooms to rent about ten minutes from the station. There were only a few people inside in the reassuringly dark and gloomy atmosphere. The landlord was elderly and a little deaf, the sort of man who didn't ask too many questions because he had got fed up with being unable to hear the answers. Guy told him that his name was Wim Wenders, that he was a Danish student visiting the university and that his luggage had been stolen on the train. The landlord didn't need persuading. Guy handed over forty pounds and received in return a key, tied with a piece of rough twine to a heavy wooden fob. Somehow it told him what sort of room to expect.

He wasn't wrong. The key opened the door to an amazingly nasty room on the second floor. Not small but somehow poky, it had nylon sheets, curtains that stopped an inch short of the sill, a dripping tap and a

242

view over the car park. There was a chill in the air, as if the room had been unoccupied for weeks or even months. But Guy didn't stop to examine the décor. He pulled off his clothes and fell on to the bed; instantly, deeply asleep.

The following morning he was outside Sally's Pantry half an hour before it actually opened, safely tucked away in the little cemetery just opposite. Amanda, the stern assistant, arrived at nine o'clock on the dot, riding a bicycle. She unlocked the door, carried the bicycle in, then reappeared at the window, arranging the display. There were several deliveries in the next half-hour but no sign of Sally, and at ten o'clock, Guy decided to phone her. He couldn't go into the shop until she was there. Amanda would certainly remember him from the last time — the stolen address. She hadn't trusted him then. She would scream the place down if he showed his face.

Sally had not given him her private telephone number and it wasn't listed with Directory Enquiries. But the number for Sally's Pantry was written above the front door. He called from a telephone box.

"Sally's Pantry." It was Amanda who had answered.

Guy deepened his voice. "May I speak to Sally?" he asked.

"Who is this?"

"I'm calling from the Bear." That had been the pub where Guy had first heard Sally's name.

"Sally's not here," Amanda said. "Can I get her to call you?"

"No. Do you know when she'll be back?"

"She's gone to London . . ."

So he had been right the night before. She hadn't been in the house. Guy felt a wave of disappointment.

". . . but she said she'd be back this evening around six. Do you want to leave a message?"

"Are you expecting her at the shop?"

"No. I think she'll go straight home."

"Thank you." Guy hung up. He was annoyed — but it could have been worse. He just had another eight hours to kill in a town with more than its fair share of cafés and bookshops.

He bought himself a baseball cap, which both masked the orange hair and, with the sunglasses, made a perfect, simple disguise. He might look like a very minor celebrity or a nerd but he certainly didn't look like a criminal on the run. He started at another bookshop, but when he got bored with that he went on a tour of Cambridge museums, choosing the ones that he thought would be least crowded: the Whipple Science Museum, with its collection of navigational instruments, the Folk Museum (eel snares and drainage equipment) and the Museum of Geology on Downing Street. He had lunch in the anonymous surroundings of a fast-food restaurant and in the afternoon he went to the cinema and sat through two screenings of a film directed, coincidentally, by Wim Wenders. He was almost alone in the dark.

At five o'clock, he was sitting on a bench in the park opposite Sally's house, waiting for her to return. Despite everything, part of him was looking forward to seeing her again for reasons that had nothing to do with Bill Naughtie, Sphinx or the joke. A girl with an invalid mother, running an upmarket delicatessen in Cambridge: in normal circumstances she would have been the last person he would have expected to meet. Just about all his friends were actors. It was sad how much of his life had been spent in the same, rarified circles. London, theatre and television, auditions, cheap restaurants, gossip. Perhaps everyone was the same. And yet actors were more than usually inward-looking. They were what they were. And what they were was everything to them.

Could he have lived with Sally, been part of her life? He wondered again how she managed to make ends meet: the expensive house supported by an obviously failing business. And even with the NHS there must be some medical expenses too. Did she have private medical insurance? He could never have afforded it himself.

And then he thought about what Kate had said. Quite a few home truths had emerged during his brief visit to her Hoxton flat.

"The way you saw things . . . you were completely unpredictable."

Those were her words. She hadn't meant to hurt him. She had only said what she must have been thinking all along. Was she right? Perhaps. But what was so wrong with that? Was it really such a character defect, to look at life from a different angle, to dare to ask stupid questions? The entire country was reading *Harry Potter*, for God's sake! The books had sold a billion copies because people had had enough of face values, enough of the tough, matter-of-fact, cradle-to-grave existence that twenty-first-century life offered. They wanted to fantasise again.

In the end, it was hardly surprising that his relationship with Kate had gone off the rails. She always had been too much of a realist, too aware of the gap between what she had and what she wanted and unable to dream the difference between the two. Sally was different. Living with her improbable mother in the oversized doll's house that was their home, running a shop that sold nothing useful, she was much closer to Guy's world. The more he thought about her, the more he wished that he had met her years ago. If there was anyone in the world who would believe him — believe everything that had happened to him — it was her. He was certain she would want to help.

The traffic was getting heavier as the day ended and now and then the house was obscured. At a quarter to six, a line of buses rolled past like circus elephants, nose to tail. The lights changed and the line moved on. And suddenly it was there, revealed behind the red metal curtain.

A dog sitting outside Sally's house.

A shaggy dog.

Guy recognised it instantly. He got to his feet, clutching the bench for support. His head was swimming. It was the same dog that he had seen outside his own house, minutes before he was arrested. He knew why it was here.

And then, before he could do anything, a taxi drew up and Sally got out. She was wearing a pale grey raincoat with the belt hanging loose. Her fair hair was also untied. She must have been to a business meeting. She wore a shirt, buttoned up to the collar, and she was carrying a briefcase. He saw her pay the driver and wait while he gave her a receipt. At the same moment, the shaggy dog stood up and padded away. The taxi drove off. Sally straightened up, tucking the receipt into her pocket. She turned and began to walk towards the house.

"Sally!" Guy shouted out her name as he ran across the park. But there was a busy street between her and him and she didn't hear. "Sally!" he called, a second time, waving his arms. He knew now that he had been right and that she was in danger. The dog was a warning. Either that or a signal. It had been sent to the house, just as it had come for him.

He stepped into the road but the lights had turned green and the traffic was moving in a steady stream. Nobody wanted to stop. "Sally!" This time she heard him and turned round at the gate. She looked alarmed. And no wonder. Here was a man in sunglasses and a baseball cap on the other side of the road, waving as he tried to duck and weave between the cars. Guy had to reach her. He dodged behind a taxi-cab and ran forward. A white Transit van slammed on its brakes. There was a crunch and a tinkle of glass as the car behind it went straight into its back, then a second collision, then a third. Horns blasted. The doors of the van flew open. Somebody shouted.

But Guy had reached the other side of the road. He grabbed hold of Sally, pulling her away from the gate. "You can't go in!" he said.

"What?"

"It's me. Guy." He pulled off the glasses and the baseball cap. "Guy Fletcher. Do you remember me?"

"Guy?"

"You have to come with me. Please."

He was pulling her away but she refused to move. Behind him, he heard the driver of the white van. "Hey — you!" He didn't know who Guy was but he knew who had caused the pile-up. The two words were loaded with anger and aggression.

"What are you doing? Let go of me!" Sally was trying to break free.

"You're in danger!"

"What are you talking about? Go away!"

A policeman on a motorbike pulled up on the other side of the road. Any moment now, Guy knew, someone was going to recognise him. That was all he needed.

"Sally, please —"

"No."

The van driver was walking towards him. The policeman got off his bike. The other car owners were arguing with each other.

And then Sally's house blew up.

It seemed to tear itself apart in slow motion — or in a series of freeze-frames that defied time and common sense. For one fantastic, elongated second, it simply bent out of shape like an inflating balloon, the bricks and tiles twisting impossibly, unable to resist the

248

pressure inside. Then came the flame, a brilliant orange fireball with a black heart, bursting through the windows and doors, shooting out of the chimney, ripping apart the brickwork, in an instant larger than the house that had contained it. The blast was so deafening that it was actually inaudible. Guy didn't hear it. He felt it. Bricks, shattered wood and spinning fragments of glass exploded in an angry swarm that filled the sky and blotted out the sun. At the same time, he was lifted off his feet and thrown carelessly into the side of the white van, its metal panels buckling under his shoulders. His face felt as if it was on fire. There was a wind rushing in his ears. For a moment he was blind. But then his vision cleared and he found himself sitting on the road in total, absolute silence, watching helplessly as debris from the house rained down all around. There was no sign of Sally. The dog, too, had gone.

He got to his feet, stumbled, fell, got up again. Still there was no sound. Nobody seemed to be moving. He pressed his palms together, wondering if there was any feeling in his body. There was blood on his hands. He had scraped them on the road. He looked at the house. Very little of it was left. Black smoke and fire were pouring out of the remains. One of the yew trees in the front garden was burning. The other had been snapped in half. He realised that the two trees, the wall and the gate had protected him from the worst of the blast. Otherwise he would have been killed.

Sound returned and with it came heat from the flames, tears from the smoke, pain from the cuts on his arms and hands. Somebody was screaming, short, rhythmic screams, like some sort of hysterical Morse code. The van driver who had been about to attack him was sitting on the road, one side of his face blackened, blood pouring out of a cut above his eye. Guy wondered what he himself must look like, why he hadn't been more badly hurt. He began to look for Sally and saw her almost at once, lying on the pavement, her clothes torn and her hair in complete disarray. He staggered over to her as she tried to sit up. Her raincoat had been torn to shreds. There was terror in her eyes.

"Mother!" It was her first word, almost inaudible in the noise and confusion all around.

"Sally —"

"She was inside."

"Oh, God, Sally, I'm so sorry." This was his fault. Already he knew that. He didn't know what to say to her.

"Where's Mother?"

Guy looked at the house, what was left of it. "She's dead, Sally. I don't think she could have —"

"No!"

But there was the proof of it, in what had been the front garden, lying among the tangled wreckage of furniture and decoration. Two extra large fluffy slippers, one of which was on fire. Sally saw them and stared. She was too shocked to cry. Her mouth was wide open. Her skin was white.

"I'm so sorry, Sally." He tried to help her to her feet.

"No." She was afraid of him, as if he had been the one who had set the bomb and detonated it. Then she remembered what he had said, moments before. "You knew this was going to happen."

"I came here to warn you."

The two were completely disoriented — as if it wasn't just bricks and mortar that had been blown apart but emotion, perception, reality. There was just too much to take on board. Guy was here. He was wanted by the police. Sally had lost her mother. Her house had been destroyed. There was a crowd. There were police. And this was Cambridge. This was meant to be the end of just another day.

Guy didn't know whether to stay with her or to leave her. Any minute now he might be recognised and arrested — he had lost the baseball cap and glasses. Someone was coming towards them.

"Sally . . ." he began.

Her tears started to flow. Silently, overwhelmingly.

But then he looked again at the two men who were approaching and saw that they weren't paramedics or policemen. They weren't even ordinary passers-by. They were walking too slowly. Their pace hadn't faltered. When a house blows up in the middle of a provincial town, you don't walk towards it. Not unless you expected it to happen and have some reason to be there.

And these people were rabbis.

Guy saw the long black coats, the wide-brimmed hats, the hair hanging down in ringlets, the beards. Hassidic Jews. And he knew.

"Sally," he said suddenly, and his tone of voice was so different that she looked up and he knew he had her attention. "I can't explain to you now but you're in terrible danger. You have to come with me. Right now."

She wiped her eyes. "What?"

"Please. Believe me. We have to go."

The rabbis were fifty metres away. He looked across the road, back at the park where he had been sitting, waiting for Sally to arrive. There were another three rabbis moving together across the grass. What were the chances of a Jewish convention taking place in Cambridge on this very day? It was always possible that a large number of rabbis, meeting together, had heard the explosion and come out to help.

Possible. But unlikely.

"Mother . . ." Sally was too shocked to understand what was happening.

"There's nothing you can do for your mother, Sally, but if you don't come with me, you're dead."

Somehow he got her to her feet. He put an arm round her and began to pull her with him, back up King Street towards the city centre. There was an open-topped tourist bus in the middle of the road straight ahead of him, not moving. It must have come to a halt when the explosion happened, leaving the top deck full of tourists stranded between a row of almshouses and a shopping parade. They'd certainly got more than they'd bargained for in their evening tour of Cambridge. He looked beyond them. There were rabbis appearing everywhere, weaving behind the stationary cars, hurrying along the pavements. He'd already had *The Sound of Music* when he was at Camden Town station. This was a malign chorus from *Fiddler on the Roof*. The rabbis were ignoring the chaos, the motorists who had been injured in the blast. That told Guy all he needed to know. He ran, dragging Sally with him.

They went past the tourist bus. There was suddenly no traffic and Guy guessed that the explosion must have been heard throughout Cambridge, that everyone had stopped moving until they found out what had happened. But for the emptiness, the lack of crowds, he would never have seen the four men walking towards him from yet another direction. It also helped that they were holding hands.

They were homosexuals. There were two pairs. A man dressed in tight-fitting jeans with a white singlet. Another, like Liberace, in pink jacket and sequins, an orange silk scarf round his neck. A third with a Freddie Mercury moustache, dressed entirely in black leather, showing a bare chest beneath his open leather jacket, both nipples pierced. The last, limp-wristed to the point of absurdity, with a bag over his shoulder, mascara on his eyes.

It was this man who saw them first. "There they are!" he screeched, drawing a curve through the air with a painted fingernail.

"Hurry! Hurry!" Liberace wailed, sounding like a demented shopper on the first day of a Harrods sale.

Guy looked back. The rabbis had congregated and were closing in rapidly. The road was blocked. But to one side there was a passageway, too narrow for cars.

Sally still didn't seem to be aware of what was happening. Probably she was in shock. He took hold of her again and pulled her violently with him.

The passage led to another park with a path bending to the right, past some tennis courts and a group of sixteen-year-olds, slouched on the miniature roundabout, smoking. He headed for the open space, but now Sally stopped, digging her heels in.

"What's happening?" she demanded. "What are you doing?"

"There's no time to explain."

"I'm not coming with you. I don't understand —"

"Listen to me, Sally. Please. We're in danger but I can't explain to you why. There are people chasing us. They want to hurt us."

"What people?"

"Stereotypes."

"What?"

"Racial and sexual stereotypes."

"What are you talking about?"

"I know it sounds mad —"

"We're being chased by stereotypes?"

"Yes!" Guy pointed across the park. The rabbis had found their way on to the grass and were moving faster now, their robes and prayer shawls flapping in the breeze. "I'll explain everything to you. I swear. But not now. We have to find somewhere safe."

He had been right about Sally. Kate would have argued. Kate would have stood her ground and been killed. But Sally nodded and came with him. More than that. She took the initiative, steering him away from the park and past the tennis courts. "We can get to the bus station," she said. "This way."

The path brought them past the back of a row of houses with overhanging windows and ivy. Ahead of them, the bus station loomed up — an ugly modern building in the town's commercial heart. But they couldn't reach it. Once again the way was blocked only this time it was black people. No. That wasn't the right word. They were hideous parodies of black people with their roots in 1950s pantomime and television programmes. They had thick, protruding lips, wide eyes. Their tight, brightly coloured trousers had been deliberately cut to emphasise the enormous size of their sexual organs. There were about a dozen in all, some with huge ghetto-blasters balanced on their shoulders, others wearing knitted hats, all moving in an elaborately rhythmic way, hips swaying, arms gyrating as if at a New Orleans funeral rather than the middle of Cambridge on a busy shopping day. They seemed to spot Guy immediately. Several whooped and yelled. One, a woman with a fruit arrangement balanced on her head, jiggled her ample breasts, paddled her hands in the air and sang out: "Thank you, Lord!"

Sally had seen them, and if she had had any doubts about what Guy had said they vanished at once. She turned off the path and down a second alleyway, this one running behind a parade of shops with dustbins and air-conditioning ducts on both sides. It led nowhere. It was blocked by a high wall and before they could think of climbing it, a Chinaman whose eyes could only be described as slitty, dressed in a black

255

T-shirt and coolie-style hat, popped up in front of them, snarling and snapping incoherently. There was a door open to one side. They ran in and found themselves in the storeroom of a shoe shop, just about to close for the night. They ran straight through, into the showroom and out on to the high street.

The homosexuals had somehow got ahead. Three of them were pushing their way through crowds of people who had been making their way home with tired kids and shopping bags. The fourth had been diverted by a shirt in the window of a shop selling designer clothes. A group of Arabs was storming down the high street, white robes sweeping behind them, gold jewellery flashing. Their wives followed, at least half a dozen for each man, and they, too, could have been described as slitty-eyed in that only their eyes could be seen through the slits of their burkhas. The Jews and the black people had been left behind. Guy and Sally ran up another passageway, which brought them to a corner where the shopping street divided into two, with a taxi rank on one side, a bank on the other and bicycles everywhere.

"In here!" All Guy knew was that they had to get out of the open, find somewhere to hide until this new nightmare had run its course. What he had seen was the entrance to Christ's College and perhaps it was the name that made him decide to seek sanctuary here. They ducked in through the open gate, past the porter's lodge, across one courtyard and into a second where at last they came to a halt in a circle of perfect green grass in an equally perfect square of ivy-covered buildings and open stairwells. They had left the town itself, outside. A few students walked past but otherwise they were alone.

Neither of them spoke for a very long time. The sun was already low and soon it set. Darkness fell on the courtyard.

At last Sally spoke. "This is all about jokes, isn't it?" she said.

And Guy knew he had found the love of his life.

CHAPTER
NINETEEN

"Poor Mother," Sally said. "She wouldn't have lived very much longer anyway. She knew that. Her heart couldn't take all the weight. But she did enjoy her life, Guy, and she was so looking forward to the summer. I can't believe I didn't say goodbye to her. I left very early this morning and she was still asleep. And now . . ."

They knew she was dead. They could see the body being carried out on *News at Ten* in front of them, two paramedics struggling under the weight. Was it Guy's imagination or was the newscaster finding it difficult to retain his *sangfroid*? The sight of the great bulk underneath the grey blanket, the strain on the faces of the stretcher-bearers, was out of kilter with the context . . . as if Benny Hill had somehow wandered into the Gaza Strip. Otherwise it was all there: the smoking remains of the house, all shattered windows and jagged walls, the blue-and-white police tape fluttering along the pavement, policemen and women and firefighters inspecting the damage, the twisted carcass of a brass bed, half covered in broken bricks and plaster.

"The university town of Cambridge was brought to a standstill this evening, following an explosion in the

Maid's Causeway, close to the town centre," the newscaster said. "The cause of the explosion, which destroyed one house and damaged several others, is still unknown, but the police have ruled out terrorism. One woman was killed."

Guy looked at Sally to see how she was taking this, but she seemed distant, unmoved. "One woman was killed." He was amazed how the news, with its voracious, all-consuming appetite for tragedy and disaster, could reduce a whole life and a vast network of friendships and shared histories to just four words.

Because terrorism had been ruled out, the bulletin had come second on the evening news. The first spot had been taken by the long-awaited publication of the Sanderson report which had, surprisingly, exonerated the government from any wrong-doing in its dealings with big business despite the enormous sums of money that had clearly changed hands. The press, which had itself been castigated, was not amused.

Guy himself had dropped to fourth place. Only now did it strike him how very similar the news was to the music charts or the bestseller lists. You were up one minute, down the next, and unless another dwarf kicked the bucket soon, he would be out all together. Not that he would be sorry. It seemed that nobody had seen him in Cambridge but the police were still looking for him and once again his photograph appeared on the screen. He recognised the picture. It had been taken from *Spotlight*, the actors' register, but something was wrong. His eyes weren't as close together as that and surely, when the photograph had been taken, he had

259

been smiling. Had they air-brushed it to make him look more sinister?

He turned off the television.

"I should have been there," Sally said.

"Where were you?" Guy asked.

"I went to London. There was a launch by the Cheese Council. Isn't that silly? All that way to sip cheap wine and eat lumps of cheese in the Earls Court exhibition centre. It wasn't even very nice cheese —" She broke off. Guy was surprised that she hadn't cried any more — but, then, too much had happened in too short a space of time. She was still wearing the shirt and the black, ankle-length skirt she had worn to London, although she had discarded the coat. Sitting there, pale and quiet, with her hands crossed and her grey-blue eyes still fixed on the blank television screen, she reminded him of a Victorian doll. Perhaps he was thinking of the Victorian doll's house that had been her home. She looked exhausted.

They were back in the room Guy had stayed in the night before. He would have liked to stay almost anywhere else but they were safer there. He could pay with cash. The landlord thought of him as a Dutch tourist. With the police everywhere in Cambridge, he didn't dare move yet. They hadn't eaten but Guy had gone downstairs and bought two large whiskies and a packet of cigarettes. He hadn't smoked in ten years.

"What will happen about the house?" Sally asked.

"What do you mean?"

260

"It's gone. It's all gone! And everything inside! All my clothes — everything I ever owned. I suppose it's insured. But there's nothing left!"

"I'm so sorry, Sally," he said. "This was my fault."

"Why do you say that?"

"You were on the telephone to me when I was arrested — and I'm afraid it was bugged. I was trying to tell you. But then the police arrived and, anyway, it was already too late."

"Why?"

"They must have heard you telling me that you had the number I wanted. They knew we'd met and you were trying to help me. So they decided to kill you. And I don't even think you were the first."

It took her a moment to understand what he was saying. "They've killed already?"

"Well, there was Johnny Peters, obviously. Somebody killed him and put him in my deep-freeze and it certainly wasn't me. But there was also an antiques dealer called Eastman. I was going to see him in Framlingham. But by the time I got to him, he was dead. There was an accident. At least, they said it was an accident. A clock fell on him."

"How could that kill him?"

"It was a big clock. A grandfather clock."

There was a long silence. Sally sipped her whisky. She was taking all this very calmly and Guy guessed she must still be in shock. She was sitting on the bed. He was on the other side of the room, in a chair. He wanted to be closer to her. He would have liked to put an arm round her . . . but this wasn't the right time.

261

The way he was feeling, one thing would only lead to another — or at least, a fumbled attempt at the other — and that would be disastrous.

"Are they killing everybody who told the Ferrero Rocher joke?" Sally asked.

"No." Guy shook his head. "I imagine that would mean massacring half the country. They'd be killing people left, right and centre. No. It's only me that they're interested in. They just wanted to break the line —"

"Wait a minute. Wait a minute." Sally put down her glass. The whisky had restored a little of the colour to her face. "You keep on talking about 'them'. 'They' do this and 'they' want that. But do you have any idea who 'they' are?"

"No. None at all."

"So what you're saying is . . ." She tried to collect her thoughts. "Somebody somewhere doesn't want you to find out where jokes come from. And it matters so much to them that they'll frame you and they'll kill my mother and me just to stop you."

"That's right. And whoever they are, these people have enormous power. They can bug my telephone. They can access my bank account, break into my flat . . . They seem to have the police on their side. And they have a lot of people working for them. They can set up roadblocks, and you saw all those people today . . ."

"The rabbis."

"People dressed as rabbis. I've already had blind people and nuns."

Sally glanced down at her empty whisky glass. "I need another of these. Do you mind going down?"

"No."

He stood up. But then she changed her mind. "No. I'll go. It's safer if you stay in the room. There's always a chance someone will recognise you."

"I expect the police will be looking for you too by now."

"Not in the same way."

She left. Guy went over to the bed and sat down. He ran a hand over the indentations — still warm — that she had made in the cover. He had never met anyone quite like Sally Lockwood. That strange mix of softness and strength. Right now, for example. Her mother was dead. She had lost everything. All in all it was astonishing that she could be so level-headed in the face of such overwhelming calamity. She seemed to have taken it for granted that he was telling the truth, that he had never killed anyone. Any other woman would surely have been afraid of him. Thinking about her, waiting for her to return, he supposed that all those years of living alone with an invalid had not only protected her from the real world but steeled her against it. Sally had been taught to hold her own. Now she was on her own. But she was mentally and emotionally prepared.

He waited for her and as the time passed he became uneasy. He looked at his watch. It had been ten minutes since she had left the room. He opened the door and stepped into the corridor. There was nobody there. When, after fifteen minutes, Sally still hadn't come back, he went to the window and looked out over the car park, listening for the sound of approaching cars. It suddenly occurred to him that he could have been quite wrong about her. Had she only been pretending to go along with him while she waited for an opportunity to slip away? Even now she could be calling the police. How could he have been so stupid?

Then the door opened and Sally stood there, balancing a tray with two more double whiskies and a plate of sandwiches on her knee. "I'm sorry I took so long," she said. "I realised that we'd neither of us eaten. They didn't have very much, but I hope it'll do."

"Come in!" Guy hurried over to take the tray. There were also two bags of crisps and a KitKat. The four-finger variety. He hated himself for what he had been thinking. Kate had been right: sometimes he saw things completely the wrong way.

The sandwiches were white, factory bread with processed cheese and chutney, but they wolfed them, chasing them down with the whisky.

Then Sally began again: "While I was waiting for the food, I was thinking," she said, "and this is what I thought." She paused. "I don't know why you started all this, Guy, but you decided to find out where jokes came from . . ."

"I wish I never had started it," Guy said.

"I'm sure. Anyway, I'd have said that jokes didn't come from anywhere. I've never really thought about it — but surely jokes come out of books and television and, I suppose, films. Don't people like Woody Allen invent jokes? People see the films and then they pass on the jokes."

"Not sick jokes."

"Well, there are lots of sick jokes in films. But that's not the point. You asked a stupid question and really you should have got a stupid answer. But you didn't. All these things started happening to you, and just because I telephoned you and said I could help, they've also happened to me. So it's obvious that someone really is determined to stop you and, as you say, they're very powerful and they seem to have unlimited resources. Which means that maybe you're right. Maybe jokes are controlled in some way — although I don't know why — and there is a machine or something . . ."

"A fat boy in an attic," Guy said. "That was what I first imagined."

". . . a fat boy in an attic, then. Maybe that's the secret that everyone is trying to hide."

"I have to find him," Guy said. "I think you'll be safe now. They've tried to kill you once and they've failed so maybe they'll leave you alone."

"I very much doubt it," Sally replied. "Anyway, it doesn't make any difference because I'm coming with you."

"Where?"

"Down the line." She reached for a purse, which was lying on the bed and which she must have taken out of the pocket of her ruined coat, although Guy hadn't noticed it before. She opened it and took out a small white card. "At least we've got this," she continued. "I happened to have that business card with me. The salesman. Here's the number."

She handed the card to Guy. It read:

WILLIAM NAUGHTIE
Sphinx Appliances
0880–450–513
Your friend around the house

"There's no address," Guy said.

"I know. And it's an 0880 telephone number. That could be anywhere in the country. But it's a start. We can call them tomorrow and maybe they can put us in touch with Naughtie and then we can start following the line."

Guy loved the sound of that "we". He had found a like mind in a lunatic asylum. He was no longer alone. "We should get some sleep," he said, adding, "I'll take the chair."

"You don't have to. This isn't a double bed. It's two singles. We can move them apart."

Later, they lay side by side in the twin beds, like a brother and sister sharing a room.

"Mother would have been game for this," Sally said, her voice drifting up in the darkness. "She loved anything that was unusual. She loved puzzles and riddles and things that couldn't be explained. When the illness took over and she was stuck in the house, she didn't have many pleasures in her life. But there were still the little things. Like that advert you were in. And

266

things like a good clue in a crossword. She couldn't wait to tell me about it when I got in.

"We never argued. Well . . . just once. But she didn't have any interest in ordinary things. She couldn't stand politics. She thought that was a waste of time. She was completely stuck in that great fat body of hers but she could let her mind wander and that's what she did. She liked to look at the patterns the birds made when they migrated. She loved the insects she found in the garden. She'd sing that song, 'Ladybird, ladybird, fly away home. Your house is on fire, your children are gone,' and she'd let it fly off as if there really was a little house and a family of ladybirds. People could be so cruel to her. But she never let life get her down. She always looked for the little things . . ."

Sally fell silent. Lying so near to her, Guy knew that she had finally given way and allowed the cover of darkness to conceal the flow of her tears.

The next morning, he telephoned the number on the card. It was engaged. He tried again. It was still engaged.

On the twenty-first or twenty-second attempt, he got through.

"Thank you for calling Sphinx Appliances, your friend around the house. For reasons of security and customer efficiency, this call may be recorded. You have reached our automated answering-service. Please begin by pressing the star key on your telephone now."

It was a woman's voice. Guy pressed the star key.

"Thank you. You are now going to be given seven options. If at any time you misdial or would like to return to the main menu, you can do so by pressing the star button twice. If you are interested in making a purchase from our range of vacuuming products, press one. If you have a question regarding an existing warranty or insurance policy, press two. If you require technical support, press three. If you wish to purchase accessories, press four. If you are dissatisfied with a Sphinx product and wish to make a return or an exchange, press five. If you have an invoice enquiry and would like to be connected to our accounts department, press six. For all other enquiries, please stay on the line and one of our customer-service personnel will be with you shortly."

DEE DEE DEE DEE DEE DEE DEE DEE
DUM DIDDLY DUM DIDDLY DUM DIDDLY DUM DIDDLY
DEE DEE DEE DEE DEE DEE DEE DEE
DUM DIDDLY DUM DIDDLY DUM DIDDLY DUM DIDDLY
DUM DIDDLY UM DIDDLY
DUM DEE DEE DEE DEE DEE
DUM DEE DUM DEE DUM DEE DUM DEE DUM

Vivaldi's "Four Seasons" played for the next seven minutes. Mercifully, it was finally ended by a second voice.

"You are through to the Sphinx Appliances Customer Centre. Every call is valuable to us and we hope to be with you as soon as possible. If you are a retail customer, please say the word 'retail' now."

Guy said nothing.

"If you require customer support, please say 'support' now."

Guy wasn't sure about that one. He still said nothing.

"If you have a general enquiry or would like further information about the company, say 'information' now."

"Information," Guy said.

"I am sorry. Your request has not been understood. If you are a retail customer, please say the word 'retail' now. If you require customer support, please say 'support' now. If you have a general enquiry or would like further information about the company, say 'information' now."

"Information!" Guy said, more loudly. "Information. Information. Information."

"What is it?" Sally asked.

Guy pointed at the telephone and shook his head.

"You have come through to the Sphinx Appliances Customer Centre," the voice told him.

"But I don't want the customer centre," Guy groaned. "I want —"

"If you have either a complaint or a comment to make about your products, please press one. It would help us expedite this call if you could have your Sphinx product close at hand and be ready to quote the twelve-digit number which you will find next to the barcode. If you wish to make an enquiry about our product range, please press two. If you would like to make an appointment for an engineer to visit your house, press three. If you know the name and the department of the person you wish to speak to, you can at this stage dial the direct number, starting with a seven if they are in Scotland or Ireland or a six for England and Wales."

Guy didn't have William Naughtie's personal number so he dialled two.

DEE DEE DEE DEE DEE DEE DEE DEE
DUM DIDDLY DUM DIDDLY DUM DIDDLY DUM DIDDLY
DEE DEE DEE DEE DEE DEE DEE DEE
DUM DIDDLY DUM DIDDLY DUM DIDDLY DUM DIDDLY
DUM DIDDLY UM DIDDLY
DUM DEE DEE DEE DEE DEE
DUM DEE DUM DEE DUM DEE DUM DEE DUM
DEE DEE DEE DEE DEE DEE DEE DEE
DUM DIDDLY DUM DIDDLY DUM DIDDLY DUM DIDDLY
DEE DEE DEE DEE DEE DEE DEE DEE
DUM DIDDLY DUM DIDDLY DUM DIDDLY DUM DIDDLY
DUM DIDDLY UM DIDDLY
DUM DEE DEE DEE DEE DEE
DUM DEE DUM DEE DUM DEE DUM DEE DUM

This time, Vivaldi's "Four Seasons" played for a full fifteen minutes before the cheerful female voice returned.

"We are sorry to keep you waiting but we are currently experiencing higher than normal volume. However, your call is important to us and we hope to connect you very shortly. Thank you for your patience."

270

DEE DEE DEE DEE DEE DEE DEE DEE

DUM DIDDLY DUM DIDDLY DUM DIDDLY DUM DIDDLY

DEE DEE DEE DEE DEE DEE DEE DEE

DUM DIDDLY DUM DIDDLY DUM DIDDLY DUM DIDDLY

DUM DIDDLY UM DIDDLY

DUM DEE DEE DEE DEE DEE

DUM DEE DUM DEE DUM DEE DUM DEE DUM

DEE DEE DEE DEE DEE DEE DEE DEE

DUM DIDDLY DUM DIDDLY DUM DIDDLY DUM DIDDLY

DEE DEE DEE DEE DEE DEE DEE DEE

DUM DIDDLY DUM DIDDLY DUM DIDDLY DUM DIDDLY

DUM DIDDLY UM DIDDLY

DUM DEE DEE DEE DEE DEE

DUM DEE DUM DEE DUM DEE DUM DEE DUM

DEE DEE DEE DEE DEE DEE DEE DEE

DUM DIDDLY DUM DIDDLY DUM DIDDLY DUM DIDDLY

DEE DEE DEE DEE DEE DEE DEE DEE

DUM DIDDLY DUM DIDDLY DUM DIDDLY DUM DIDDLY

DUM DIDDLY UM DIDDLY

DUM DEE DEE DEE DEE DEE

DUM DEE DUM DEE DUM DEE DUM DEE DUM

DEE DEE DEE DEE DEE DEE DEE DEE

DUM DIDDLY DUM DIDDLY DUM DIDDLY DUM DIDDLY

DEE DEE DEE DEE DEE DEE DEE DEE

DUM DIDDLY DUM DIDDLY DUM DIDDLY DUM DIDDLY

DUM DIDDLY UM DIDDLY

DUM DEE DEE DEE DEE DEE

DUM DEE DUM DEE DUM DEE DUM DEE DUM

Eight minutes later . . .

"You are being held in a queue for our next available operator. Sphinx Appliances apologises for this delay, which is due to an unusually high demand for our services. You are currently number nine in the queue."

"We're number nine," Guy told Sally. She was beginning to look concerned.

DEE DEE DEE DEE DEE DEE DEE DEE
DUM DIDDLY DUM DIDDLY DUM DIDDLY DUM DIDDLY
DEE DEE DEE DEE DEE DEE DEE DEE
DUM DIDDLY DUM DIDDLY DUM DIDDLY DUM DIDDLY
DUM DIDDLY UM DIDDLY
DUM DEE DEE DEE DEE DEE
DUM DEE DUM DEE DUM DEE DUM DEE DUM
DEE DEE DEE DEE DEE DEE DEE DEE
DUM DIDDLY DUM DIDDLY DUM DIDDLY DUM DIDDLY
DEE DEE DEE DEE DEE DEE DEE DEE
DUM DIDDLY DUM DIDDLY DUM DIDDLY DUM DIDDLY
DUM DIDDLY UM DIDDLY
DUM DEE DEE DEE DEE DEE
DUM DEE DUM DEE DUM DEE DUM DEE DUM
DEE DEE DEE DEE DEE DEE DEE DEE
DUM DIDDLY DUM DIDDLY DUM DIDDLY DUM DIDDLY
DEE DEE DEE DEE DEE DEE DEE DEE
DUM DIDDLY DUM DIDDLY DUM DIDDLY DUM DIDDLY
DUM DIDDLY UM DIDDLY
DUM DEE DEE DEE DEE DEE
DUM DEE DUM DEE DUM DEE DUM DEE DUM
DEE DEE DEE DEE DEE DEE DEE DEE
DUM DIDDLY DUM DIDDLY DUM DIDDLY DUM DIDDLY
DEE DEE DEE DEE DEE DEE DEE DEE

DUM DIDDLY DUM DIDDLY DUM DIDDLY DUM DIDDLY
DUM DIDDLY UM DIDDLY
DUM DEE DEE DEE DEE DEE
DUM DEE DUM DEE DUM DEE DUM DEE DUM
DEE DEE DEE DEE DEE DEE DEE DEE
DUM DIDDLY DUM DIDDLY DUM DIDDLY DUM DIDDLY
DEE DEE DEE DEE DEE DEE DEE DEE
DUM DIDDLY DUM DIDDLY DUM DIDDLY DUM DIDDLY
DUM DIDDLY UM DIDDLY
DUM DEE DEE DEE DEE DEE
DUM DEE DUM DEE DUM DEE DUM DEE DUM
DEE DEE DEE DEE DEE DEE DEE DEE
DUM DIDDLY DUM DIDDLY DUM DIDDLY DUM DIDDLY
DEE DEE DEE DEE DEE DEE DEE DEE
DUM DIDDLY DUM DIDDLY DUM DIDDLY DUM DIDDLY
DUM DIDDLY UM DIDDLY
DUM DEE DEE DEE DEE DEE
DUM DEE DUM DEE DUM DEE DUM DEE DUM
DEE DEE DEE DEE DEE DEE DEE DEE
DUM DIDDLY DUM DIDDLY DUM DIDDLY DUM DIDDLY
DEE DEE DEE DEE DEE DEE DEE DEE
DUM DIDDLY DUM DIDDLY DUM DIDDLY DUM DIDDLY
DUM DIDDLY UM DIDDLY
DUM DEE DEE DEE DEE DEE
DUM DEE DUM DEE DUM DEE DUM DEE DUM

Another twelve minutes passed.

"You are now number five in the queue. Sphinx Appliances are made in Britain to be sturdy, lightweight and reliable. We are proud to have been awarded a Duke of Edinburgh Award for Industry. Whatever the

273

job, Sphinx Appliances are your friend around the house."

DEE DEE DEE DEE DEE DEE DEE DEE
DUM DIDDLY DUM DIDDLY DUM DIDDLY DUM DIDDLY
DEE DEE DEE DEE DEE DEE DEE DEE
DUM DIDDLY DUM DIDDLY DUM DIDDLY DUM DIDDLY
DUM DIDDLY UM DIDDLY
DUM DEE DEE DEE DEE DEE
DUM DEE DUM DEE DUM DEE DUM DEE DUM
DEE DEE DEE DEE DEE DEE DEE DEE
DUM DIDDLY DUM DIDDLY DUM DIDDLY DUM DIDDLY
DEE DEE DEE DEE DEE DEE DEE DEE
DUM DIDDLY DUM DIDDLY DUM DIDDLY DUM DIDDLY
DUM DIDDLY UM DIDDLY
DUM DEE DEE DEE DEE DEE
DUM DEE DUM DEE DUM DEE DUM DEE DUMDEE DEE
DEE DEE
DEE
DEE DEE DEE
DUM DIDDLY DUM DIDDLY DUM DIDDLY DUM DIDDLY
DEE DEE DEE DEE DEE DEE DEE DEE
DUM DIDDLY DUM DIDDLY DUM DIDDLY DUM DIDDLY
DUM DIDDLY UM DIDDLY
DUM DEE DEE DEE DEE DEE
DUM DEE DUM DEE DUM DEE DUM DEE DUMDEE DEE
DEE DEE
DEE
DEE DEE DEE
DUM DIDDLY DUM DIDDLY DUM DIDDLY DUM DIDDLY
DEE DEE DEE DEE DEE DEE DEE DEE

274

DUM DIDDLY DUM DIDDLY DUM DIDDLY DUM DIDDLY
DUM DIDDLY UM DIDDLY

DUM DEE DEE DEE DEE DEE

DUM DEE DUM DEE DUM DEE DUM DEE DUMDEE DEE
DEE DEE

DEE

DEE DEE DEE

DUM DIDDLY DUM DIDDLY DUM DIDDLY DUM DIDDLY
DEE DEE DEE DEE DEE DEE DEE DEE

DUM DIDDLY DUM DIDDLY DUM DIDDLY DUM DIDDLY
DUM DIDDLY UM DIDDLY

DUM DEE DEE DEE DEE DEE

DUM DEE DUM DEE DUM DEE DUM DEE DUMDEE DEE
DEE DEE

DEE

DEE DEE DEE

DUM DIDDLY DUM DIDDLY DUM DIDDLY DUM DIDDLY
DEE DEE DEE DEE DEE DEE DEE DEE

DUM DIDDLY DUM DIDDLY DUM DIDDLY DUM DIDDLY
DUM DIDDLY UM DIDDLY

DUM DEE DEE DEE DEE DEE

DUM DEE DUM DEE DUM DEE DUM DEE DUMDEE DEE
DEE DEE

DEE

DEE DEE DEE

DUM DIDDLY DUM DIDDLY DUM DIDDLY DUM DIDDLY
DEE DEE DEE DEE DEE DEE DEE DEE

DUM DIDDLY DUM DIDDLY DUM DIDDLY DUM DIDDLY
DUM DIDDLY UM DIDDLY

DUM DEE DEE DEE DEE DEE

DUM DEE DUM DEE DUM DEE DUM DEE DUMDEE DEE
DEE DEE
DEE
DEE DEE DEE —

"Thank you for your patience. All our operators are
currently engaged on other calls. We apologise for this
delay in answering your call. You are now second in the
queue. Have you got an old appliance that you would
like to exchange? Sphinx Appliances will offer you a
discount of up to twenty-five per cent when you trade
in your old model for a new one."

DEE DEE DEE DEE DEE DEE DEE DEE
DUM DIDDLY DUM DIDDLY DUM DIDDLY DUM DIDDLY
DEE DEE DEE DEE DEE DEE DEE DEE
DUM DIDDLY DUM DIDDLY DUM DIDDLY DUM DIDDLY
DUM DIDDLY UM DIDDLY
DUM DEE DEE DEE DEE DEE
DUM DEE DUM DEE DUM DEE DUM DEE DUM
DEE DEE DEE DEE DEE DEE DEE DEE
DUM DIDDLY DUM DIDDLY DUM DIDDLY DUM DIDDLY
DEE DEE DEE DEE DEE DEE DEE DEE
DUM DIDDLY DUM DIDDLY DUM DIDDLY DUM DIDDLY
DUM DIDDLY UM DIDDLY
DUM DEE DEE DEE DEE DEE
DUM DEE DUM DEE DUM DEE DUM DEE DUMDEE DEE
DEE DEE
DEE
DEE DEE DEE
DUM DIDDLY DUM DIDDLY DUM DIDDLY DUM DIDDLY

276

DEE DEE DEE DEE DEE DEE DEE DEE
DUM DIDDLY DUM DIDDLY DUM DIDDLY DUM DIDDLY
DUM DIDDLY UM DIDDLY
DUM DEE DEE DEE DEE DEE
DUM DEE DUM DEE DUM DEE DUM DEE DUMDEE DEE
DEE DEE
DEE
DEE DEE DEE
DUM DIDDLY DUM DIDDLY DUM DIDDLY DUM DIDDLY
DEE DEE DEE DEE DEE DEE DEE DEE
DUM DIDDLY DUM DIDDLY DUM DIDDLY DUM DIDDLY
DUM DIDDLY UM DIDDLY
DUM DEE DEE DEE DEE DEE
DUM DEE DUM DEE DUM DEE DUM DEE DUMDEE DEE
DEE DEE
DEE
DEE DEE DEE
DUM DIDDLY DUM DIDDLY DUM DIDDLY DUM DIDDLY
DEE DEE DEE DEE DEE DEE DEE DEE
DUM DIDDLY DUM DIDDLY DUM DIDDLY DUM DIDDLY
DUM DIDDLY UM DIDDLY
DUM DEE DEE DEE DEE DEE
DUM DEE DUM DEE DUM DEE DUM DEE DUMDEE DEE
DEE DEE
DEE
DEE DEE DEE
DUM DIDDLY DUM DIDDLY DUM DIDDLY DUM DIDDLY
DEE DEE DEE DEE DEE DEE DEE DEE
DUM DIDDLY DUM DIDDLY DUM DIDDLY DUM DIDDLY
DUM DIDDLY UM DIDDLY
DUM DEE DEE DEE DEE DEE

DUM DEE DUM DEE DUM DEE DUM DEE DUMDEE DEE
DEE DEE

DEE

DEE DEE DEE

DUM DIDDLY DUM DIDDLY DUM DIDDLY DUM DIDDLY
DEE DEE DEE DEE DEE DEE DEE DEE

DUM DIDDLY DUM DIDDLY DUM DIDDLY DUM DIDDLY
DUM DIDDLY UM DIDDLY

DUM DEE DEE DEE DEE DEE

DUM DEE DUM DEE DUM DEE DUM DEE DUMDEE DEE
DEE DEE

DEE

DEE DEE DEE

DUM DIDDLY DUM DIDDLY DUM DIDDLY DUM DIDDLY
DEE DEE DEE DEE DEE DEE DEE DEE

DUM DIDDLY DUM DIDDLY DUM DIDDLY DUM DIDDLY
DUM DIDDLY UM DIDDLY

DUM DEE DEE DEE DEE DEE

DUM DEE DUM DEE DUM DEE DUM DEE DUMDEE DEE
DEE DEE

DEE

DEE DEE DEE

DUM DIDDLY DUM DIDDLY DUM DIDDLY DUM DIDDLY
DEE DEE DEE DEE DEE DEE DEE DEE

DUM DIDDLY DUM DIDDLY DUM DIDDLY DUM DIDDLY
DUM DIDDLY UM DIDDLY

DUM DEE DEE DEE DEE DEE

DUM DEE DUM DEE DUM DEE DUM DEE DUMDEE DEE
DEE DEE

DEE

DEE DEE DEE

DUM DIDDLY DUM DIDDLY DUM DIDDLY DUM DIDDLY
DEE DEE DEE DEE DEE DEE DEE DEE
DUM DIDDLY DUM DIDDLY DUM DIDDLY DUM DIDDLY
DUM DIDDLY UM DIDDLY
DUM DEE DEE DEE DEE DEE
DUM DEE DUM DEE DUM DEE DUM DEE DUMDEE DEE
DEE DEE
DEE
DEE DEE DEE
DUM DIDDLY DUM DIDDLY DUM DIDDLY DUM DIDDLY
DEE DEE DEE DEE DEE DEE DEE DEE
DUM DIDDLY DUM DIDDLY DUM DIDDLY DUM DIDDLY
DUM DIDDLY UM DIDDLY
DUM DEE DEE DEE DEE DEE
DUM DEE DUM DEE DUM DEE DUM DEE DUMDEE DEE
DEE DEE
DEE
DEE DEE DEE
DUM DIDDLY DUM DIDDLY DUM DIDDLY DUM DIDDLY
DEE DEE DEE DEE DEE DEE DEE DEE
DUM DIDDLY DUM DIDDLY DUM DIDDLY DUM DIDDLY
DUM DIDDLY UM DIDDLY
DUM DEE DEE DEE DEE DEE
DUM DEE DUM DEE DUM DEE DUM DEE DUMDEE DEE
DEE DEE
DEE
DEE DEE DEE
DUM DIDDLY DUM DIDDLY DUM DIDDLY DUM DIDDLY
DEE DEE DEE DEE DEE DEE DEE DEE
DUM DIDDLY DUM DIDDLY DUM DIDDLY DUM DIDDLY
DUM DIDDLY UM DIDDLY

DUM DEE DEE DEE DEE DEE

DUM DEE DUM DEE DUM DEE DUM DEE DUMDEE DEE
DEE DEE

DEE

DEE DEE DEE

DUM DIDDLY DUM DIDDLY DUM DIDDLY DUM DIDDLY
DEE DEE DEE DEE DEE DEE DEE DEE

DUM DIDDLY DUM DIDDLY DUM DIDDLY DUM DIDDLY
DUM DIDDLY UM DIDDLY

DUM DEE DEE DEE DEE DEE

DUM DEE DUM DEE DUM DEE DUM DEE DUMDEE DEE
DEE DEE

DEE

DEE DEE DEE

DUM DIDDLY DUM DIDDLY DUM DIDDLY DUM DIDDLY
DEE DEE DEE DEE DEE DEE DEE DEE

DUM DIDDLY DUM DIDDLY DUM DIDDLY DUM DIDDLY
DUM DIDDLY UM DIDDLY

DUM DEE DEE DEE DEE DEE

DUM DEE DUM DEE DUM DEE DUM DEE DUMDEE DEE
DEE DEE

DEE

DEE DEE DEE

DUM DIDDLY DUM DIDDLY DUM DIDDLY DUM DIDDLY
DEE DEE DEE DEE DEE DEE DEE DEE

DUM DIDDLY DUM DIDDLY DUM DIDDLY DUM DIDDLY
DUM DIDDLY UM DIDDLY

DUM DEE DEE DEE DEE DEE

DUM DEE DUM DEE DUM DEE DUM DEE DUMDEE DEE
DEE DEE

DEE

DEE DEE DEE
DUM DIDDLY DUM DIDDLY DUM DIDDLY DUM DIDDLY
DEE DEE DEE DEE DEE DEE DEE DEE
DUM DIDDLY DUM DIDDLY DUM DIDDLY DUM DIDDLY

"We are experiencing unusual delays due to the high volume of customer enquiries. We apologise for the delay. You are now third in the queue —"

"That's impossible!" Guy exclaimed. "I was second in the queue and now I'm third! What do they think they're doing?"

He had now been on the telephone for almost an hour.

Vivaldi played for the seventh time.

"You are through to the Sphinx Appliances Customer Centre. Every call matters to us and we apologise for the delay in answering. If you know the name and the department of the person you wish to speak to, you can at this stage dial the direct number, starting with a six if they are in Scotland or Ireland or a seven for England and Wales. If you are an existing customer and have either a complaint or a comment to make about your products, please press the star key twice. It would help us expedite this call if you could have your Sphinx product close at hand and be ready to quote the twelve-digit number which you will find next to the barcode. If you wish to make an enquiry about our product range, please continue to wait."

"Wait a minute. They've already said this," Guy said. He noticed that the hand holding the telephone had gone white as the blood had drained out of his knuckles. Sally was sitting in a chair, watching him. "It's gone wrong."

"Hello?" This time it was a real human voice.

"I'm through!" Guy crowed.

"How can I help you?" It was a man — young from the sound of him.

"Yes. I'm trying to get through to someone in your sales department."

"I'm sorry? Who is this speaking?"

"It's — my name is Guy Smith. But I'm trying to get in touch with —"

"We don't have a sales department."

"I'm sorry?"

"I think you've got a wrong number."

"That's not possible. I've been on this number for almost an hour!"

"I'm afraid you've come through on the wrong extension. You have to call our London office."

"What do you mean?"

"Don't worry, sir. I can connect you."

"No —"

But it was too late. There was a click and then:

"Thank you for calling Sphinx Appliances, your friend around the house. For reasons of security and customer efficiency, this call may be recorded. You have reached our automated answering-service. You are now going to be given seven options. If you are interested in making a purchase from our range of vacuuming products, press one. If you have a question regarding an existing warranty or insurance policy, press two. If you require technical support, press three. If you wish to purchase accessories, press four. If you are dissatisfied with a Sphinx product and wish to make a return or an exchange, press five. If you have an invoice enquiry and would like to be connected to our accounts department, press six. For all other enquiries, please stay on the line and one of our customer-service personnel will be with you shortly."

DUM DIDDLE UM DIDDLE UM DIDDLE UM
DIDDLE IDDLE IDDLE IDDLE IDDLE IDDLE EE DEE
DUM DIDDLE UM DIDDLE UM DIDDLE UM
DIDDLE DIDDLE DEE DEE

This time it was Paganini. It played for eleven minutes.
Guy slammed the receiver down.
"It's a fucking joke," he said, and realised that maybe that was exactly what it was.

CHAPTER
TWENTY

They missed breakfast the following morning. Surprisingly, they had both overslept, and when they went down, the chef was standing in the doorway of the kitchen. He was a young man, barely out of his teens, dressed in dirty white trousers and a T-shirt, smoking a cigarette. "I'm sorry," he said. "We stop serving at nine."

Guy looked at his watch. It was two minutes past. But looking into the kitchen, which was dilapidated and covered in grease, he decided not to argue.

Sally agreed. "Let's go out," she said.

It was a bright morning. The storm of forty-eight hours before had cleaned both the streets and the sky, and even in this shabby end of the town something of the summer was in the air. They walked back into Cambridge . . . not quite hand-in-hand but almost. Guy still hadn't quite worked out how Sally could have come through so much and still be so unaffected. In the sunlight, she looked serene. At the same time, he felt nervous being with her. He was walking purposefully, a short distance away. The police were still looking for him and he didn't want to put her in any more danger. He couldn't let them find her with him.

284

As if reading his mind, she smiled and reached out to him. Their hands met. He would always remember the moment when they touched. "They're much less likely to notice you if you're with someone," she said. "They think you're on your own."

Guy said nothing. It felt wonderful, no longer being on his own.

They found a coffee bar. Cambridge was full of them: American imports that had seemed comfortable and pleasant when they arrived but which had already become intrusive. They ordered cappuccino and croissants and carried them to a table at the back.

"How are you feeling?" Guy asked.

"Grimy. I'm going to need a change of clothes."

"I don't think you should use your credit card."

"Why not?" She thought for a moment. "You think they'll know we're together?"

"Probably. I don't think we should underestimate them."

They sat for a while in silence. Then . . .

"Why did you do it?" she asked.

"What?"

"The joke. Where do jokes come from? It seems such an odd question to ask."

Guy shrugged. "It wasn't just a joke. It was about my mother."

"Selina Moore?"

"Yes." He hesitated, but only for a moment. He had never talked about this with Kate. But Sally had a right to know. Anyway, it wasn't a secret any more. The story had been in every newspaper. "You must have read that

Selina Moore was my mother. I never met her. I was adopted before I was even a year old."

"It said in the papers . . . it was her career."

"I know. I always wondered why she abandoned me and now I know. I got in the way."

"Did you never try to contact her?"

"I often thought about it. I mean, I wanted to be an actor and maybe she could have helped. She must have had hundreds of contacts. And, of course, she was rich."

"So why didn't you?"

"For all the reasons I've just said." Guy was playing with the crumbs of his croissant, drawing circles with the tip of his finger. "A lot of actors are bloody selfish people," he said. "We only ever think of ourselves. And now it turns out that's exactly why Selina dumped me. I think I'd have despised myself if I'd tracked her down just for me and my career. Anyway, she probably wouldn't have wanted to know. It would have just been embarrassing."

"You can't know that."

"Well, I was afraid of it. The strange thing is, you see, I admired her so much. She was everything I wanted to be and in a way she *was* me. I mean, biologically, we were really the same. I'd have loved to know who my father was, how I was born. He was probably an actor too."

"You could have asked her."

Guy shook his head. "I really loved her, Sally. I had all her films on video and I had all her press clippings. I saw her on the stage once. I thought about her all the time. And after she retired . . . I was going to write to her. I thought that once she'd left the business we could meet, like ordinary people." He shrugged. "I just left it too late."

"You heard a sick joke about her. You wanted to be her champion."

"Only when it was too late. Too late for her. Too late for me. If you want the honest truth, I should never have been an actor. I was never much good and I was never going to be famous. Not like her."

"You were good in the coffee advert."

"I was dubbed."

There was a women's fashion shop on the other side of the road. Sally left Guy on his own while she slipped out to buy a change of clothes. She was only gone about ten minutes and when she returned she was wearing blue jeans, a loose lumberjack shirt and trainers. She looked like a street urchin, a modern-day Oliver Twist. She had also bought him a new baseball cap.

She sat down next to him. "So, what are we going to do?" she asked.

"Sphinx Appliances," Guy said. He had worked it out while she was gone. The revelation hadn't come in a jump-out-of-the-bath moment of inspiration. It hadn't even taken much thinking about. It was simply there and, once Guy had seen it, he had realised that, really, it had been blindingly obvious all along.

"What about them?"

"OK. Let's start with the name. What sort of company is going to call itself Sphinx? Half its customers wouldn't be able to pronounce it, let alone spell it. I mean, it's completely stupid. It's meant to be making vacuum cleaners. What's that got to do with some ancient Egyptian monument missing its nose?"

"Maybe the vacuum cleaners are manufactured in Cairo."

"I doubt it. But think about it, Sally. The riddle of the Sphinx. Maybe that's the clue."

"The company's a riddle. And a riddle is a sort of joke."

"Exactly." Guy slipped on the baseball cap. It fitted perfectly. "And think about the telephone call," he went on. "I know everyone's got automated answering systems and they're all a pain in the neck. But that business last night. That was something else. I think it was deliberate."

"They don't want people to contact them."

"They don't want to be found. They're not on the Internet. They've got a telephone number that doesn't lead anywhere. And their sales reps carry business cards that don't have an address."

Sally nodded. "Are you saying that Sphinx . . . make jokes?" she asked.

"No. I don't think I am saying that. I think they make vacuum cleaners."

"I don't understand."

"Mrs Galton had one," Guy said. This was something else he had worked out while she was gone. "I saw it when I was at her house."

"Who is Mrs Galton?"

"She was the mother of the Boy Scout, Bobby Galton. When I went to see her, she was vacuuming her hall and she had this weird gadget. It was like nothing I'd ever seen. It was modern but it looked old-fashioned. And it had loads of attachments . . . all different colours."

"So this woman — Mrs Galton — could have heard the joke from one of their salesman. Just like —" She stopped.

"Like your mum," Guy said.

"It could be a coincidence, Guy. They've probably got salesmen travelling all over the country. What are you saying? That they're deliberately telling the same jokes?"

"Maybe Sphinx isn't a real company." Guy realised he had just contradicted himself. "What I'm trying to say is, maybe the vacuum cleaners are just a cover for what they really do. Think about it, Sally. You said the salesman didn't really try to sell your mother anything. He made her a cup of tea. He chatted. He was a nice man. But did he have any brochures? Did he leave any behind?"

"I didn't see any."

"Did he leave anything — besides his card?"

"No."

"That's weird in itself. But I've seen a Sphinx appliance. At least, I think I have. It's odd. It's clunky. It's badly designed. Nobody in their right mind would want to buy one."

"Mrs Galton did."

"The exception that proves the rule."

"So you're saying . . . that the salesmen aren't really interested in selling anything at all?"

"They travel the country. The jokes go with them. That's how they spread them around!"

"But that still doesn't tell you where the jokes originally come from."

"If we can track down Sphinx Appliances, we can find out."

There was another silence. Sally's face was screwed up in concentration, one hand pressed against her forehead. She was a very expressive person. If she'd ever been at the Clairemont, she'd have been told off for overacting.

Eventually she spoke. "You were arrested just after you got back from Framlingham," she said.

"Yes."

"The antiques dealer, Mr Eastman, had been killed. That was the end of the second trail."

"That's right." He couldn't see what she was getting at.

"How many trails did you actually follow?"

"Three. The first one got as far as the Boy Scout in St Albans. His name was Robert Galton but his father wouldn't let me speak to him so that was that. The second one was the longest. It got me all the way to you. Then I started again in Stoke-on-Trent and went all the way to Framlingham." He sighed. "I suppose we could look around and find someone else who knows the Ferrero Rocher joke and then start all over again. But it's not going to be so easy. They know about me now and they're almost certainly looking for us. Assuming the police don't find me first."

"Mrs Galton lived in St Albans," Sally said.

"Yes."

"That's north of London, isn't it?"

"Yes. Why?"

"It's just occurred to me. Every time you followed the joke, it took you in the same sort of direction. From London to Cambridge. And then from Stoke-on-Trent to Framlingham. You've always been heading towards the same point."

Guy reached out and grabbed Sally's arms. "Sally! You're brilliant!"

This time it was he who left her sitting on her own. He hurried out, hardly caring if he was seen or not. It only took him a few minutes to find what he wanted. When he came back, he was carrying a pen, a ruler and a road map of Great Britain.

He laid out the map on the table.

"This is the first trail," he said. He marked, with crosses, the places he had visited in pursuit of the joke: the City of London, Enfield, Hertford, Sandridge, Redbourn, Chaul End, Bishop's Stortford, Royston, Wimbish Green, Saffron Walden, Duxford, Stapleford, Great Shelford, Rampton and Cambridge. The crosses made a definite pattern. There were blips. Rampton, for one, didn't fit into the picture. But the movement north-east was unmistakable.

"Do the second trail," Sally said.

He put a cross on Stoke-on-Trent. Then another on Cheadle, Stubwood, Gratwich, Rugeley and so on all the way to Framlingham. He noticed his pen passing close to Cambridge and remembered that, while he had been driving, he had thought he might be led back to the city. Now he saw why. The second line slanted towards the first: two sides of an arrow.

"Now join them up." Sally said.

He laid the ruler so that its edge took a direct path between the majority of the crosses he had made. He drew a line. One or two of the crosses came nowhere near connecting. But there were enough remaining to make the direction of the line obvious. He did the same with the second set of crosses.

The two lines intercepted on the Suffolk coast.

"There's nothing there," Sally said. She was disappointed that her idea hadn't paid off.

"There's no town marked," Guy agreed, "but that doesn't mean anything. First of all, this is very rough. It could be any one of these places." He pointed with his finger. "Southwold, Dunwich, Walberswick . . . even Sizewell."

"At the nuclear plant?"

"We still don't know what we're looking for. It could be a factory or an office or even a series of outbuildings in a farm. Sphinx Appliances could be in the middle of nowhere. We need to get a map with a bit more detail. And we're going to need a car." Guy's motorbike, of course, was in London. Sally's car had been parked outside her house and was now either in pieces or a police pound. "We're going to have to rent one," he said.

"Without credit cards?"

Guy frowned. "You're right. But we can't risk it. They've known about every single move I've made. They got into my bank account. If either of us paid for a car with a credit card they'd soon know about it, which means they'd know the number-plate and —"

"You sound really paranoid," Sally said.

"I feel like Robert Redford in *Three Days of the Condor*."

"I loved that film."

"Me too." He had watched it on television with Kate. But Kate had got bored and gone to bed.

Sally thought for a moment. "I might be able to borrow a car," she said. "I've got a friend. At least, he isn't exactly a friend. He helps out with some of the deliveries from the shop. He's got his own business and he rents out cars. He might accept cash."

They left the coffee bar together. As they stepped on to the pavement, three police cars raced past, lights blazing. They watched as the cars spun round the corner, heading back the way they had come.

"Do you think . . .?" Sally began.

Guy nodded. He had no doubt that the police were on their way to the pub they had left just a few hours before. "The phone call," he said. "We made that call to Sphinx Appliances. They must have traced it."

"But you didn't give them your name."

"I was calling from Cambridge. Maybe they have voice-recognition software. I don't know." Guy shivered. He was surprised the police hadn't got there sooner but even so it had been a narrow escape. He could feel the net closing. "Let's find this friend of yours," he said.

The car-rental place that Sally knew was outside Cambridge. They took a bus there, travelling together in silence. A taxi would have been easier but they were afraid of being seen. The car-rental company was called Frank's. It was on the Fulbourn Road, not far from the airport. There was a garage at the front with three pumps that clearly hadn't seen petrol since the days before lead-free, a semi-derelict showroom and a sign reading FRANK'S CAR RENTAL, hand-painted on what looked like a piece of driftwood. There was, however, no sign of any cars.

Frank himself was a short, dark-haired man with two days' stubble and a lifetime of failure etched into his face. Everything about him was run-down: the soiled, shapeless clothes he was wearing, the plastic chair on which he was sitting, the rags and debris in the dilapidated garage that surrounded him. He was behind a counter, listening to the radio, the *Sun* newspaper in front of him, a mug of tea in one hand, a cigarette in the other. The nicotine had spread up his middle and index fingers. His skin was an unhealthy mix of yellow and black.

He seemed pleased to see Sally, and nodded at Guy, who was lingering behind her, trying not to show too much of his face.

"What are you doing out here, Sal?" he asked. "You want a cup of tea?"

"No, thanks, Frank. I want to ask you a favour. I need to borrow a car."

"Borrow — or rent?"

"Rent. But it'll have to be cash."

Frank wiped a sleeve across his mouth. It was hard to say whether he made his mouth cleaner or dirtier. "Cash," he said.

"I can give you a hundred pounds."

"How long do you want it for?"

"I don't know. A few days. Maybe longer. I'll be able to pay you more later."

"You in trouble, Sal?"

"No."

Frank glanced over his shoulder. There was a line of key hooks on the wall underneath the inevitable girlie calendar. The calendar was still open on Miss January, a girl wearing fur gloves but nothing else. A single key dangled above her head. Frank seemed to examine it, then turned back to Sally. "Who's your friend?" he asked.

Guy felt his chest tighten.

"He's just a friend."

"He's Guy Fletcher." Frank turned the newspaper and there was Guy's photograph, quite small, on page six.

Sally looked him straight in the eyes. "He didn't kill anyone, Frank. He's been framed. I'm trying to help him." Frank said nothing so she went on: "There are people chasing him, not just the police. They're looking for me too. Yesterday they blew up my house."

"That was your house?"

"Yes."

Frank nodded but still didn't speak. The radio was playing an old Beatles song. "The Fool On the Hill."

"We need a car. I thought of you because you helped at the shop. Will you help us?"

Frank thought for a moment. It seemed that a moment was all he needed. Then he leant back and unhooked the key.

"The whole bloody business is going to pot," he said. "The wife's walked out on me and I've got the solicitors on the phone telling me she's going to take the house and everything else."

"I'm sorry."

"Don't be. I'd prefer to give you the car than see her get her hands on it." He stubbed out the cigarette and lit another. "I sometimes wonder how people manage. I don't know why we don't all go mad. I've got two kids who can't stand me. A wife who's just left me. And a bank manager who wants to shove me down the toilet. You can have the car and you can keep your hundred pounds. It probably isn't worth half that."

The car was a Skoda. It was at the back of the garage, parked behind a row of oil drums as if it was hiding there. It looked grey but in fact it was mauve, with a thin coating of dust. One of the wing mirrors was cracked. It was covered in rust and all the tyres were flat. The Skoda had a car sticker in the back window. The sticker read: "My other car is a Skoda." Frank handed Sally the key. "It's a 1989 Skoda Favorit, GLXi," he told her. "You ever driven one?"

"No."

296

"The rust isn't as bad as it looks. They get a lot of rust, these old Skodas. The engine's all right but it needs a bit of work. I was going to take a look at it but I didn't have the time. Wheels need air. There's a garage down the road. You'll have to fill it at the same time. There's only just enough petrol to get you there."

"Thank you." Sally wasn't sure what to say.

Frank looked past her at Guy. "I hope she's right," he said. "I hope you didn't kill them. The little people."

"I didn't," Guy said.

"But I'd understand. I mean, when you look at it, life, you've got to do something. I'd have liked to be an inventor. I was always mucking around with bits and pieces when I was a kid. I'd have liked to have invented something, but I never did. At least if you're a serial-killer you get your name in the papers. People know about you. It's something I'd have liked."

"Thank you for the car," Guy said.

"Don't mention it. You're welcome."

Sally handed him the key and he opened the driver's door. It creaked and he had to force it most of the way. The two of them got in. The inside of the car smelt of ash and old plastic and both the front windows refused to open. Guy looked for the ignition. He noticed that even the key was rusty.

But, surprisingly, the Skoda started first time although the engine sounded feeble and sick. Guy wrenched the gear into reverse and they backed out of the garage and into the yard.

Frank had followed them out in order to see them off. He stood in the sunlight for a moment, watching as the Skoda shuddered onto the main road. The last Guy saw of him was in the rear-view mirror. Frank raised a hand, then turned back and walked into the darkness from which he'd come.

CHAPTER
TWENTY-ONE

From Cambridge they headed east, through Bottisham and on to the A14 around Newmarket. After that, they continued across country that was empty and uninteresting, but with the promise of the sea ahead. They could have been, Guy thought, an elderly couple off on holiday . . . elderly because the Skoda was only capable of thirty miles per hour and belched black smoke when he tried to go any faster. It was raining again, but when Guy turned on the windscreen wipers, only one worked, grinding uselessly against the glass. One of the brake lights was broken. The brakes themselves were only intermittently effective.

"What are we going to do?" Sally asked as they wheezed, very slowly, up a slight incline.

"You mean when we get there?"

"Yes." She turned to him. "And where exactly *is* 'there'? Where are you going to start?"

"I've been thinking about that." Guy signalled but nothing happened. The indicator lights had gone too. "The two lines on the map met just underneath Southwold so we might as well start there. We'll spend a day in Southwold and then we'll continue down the coast."

"Doing what?"

"Just hanging around. Nothing happens in the countryside without people knowing about it. So we'll spend time in pubs. We'll listen to conversations. Perhaps someone will mention Sphinx. We can ask a few questions — if we're careful. We can go into local electrical shops and ask about buying a vacuum. Maybe we can ask at Tourist Information. I don't know. If that doesn't work, we can go along footpaths. We'll look at any interesting buildings. If we meet anyone out walking, we can say we're lost and we're trying to meet a friend at the factory where they make vacuum cleaners, that sort of thing . . ." His voice trailed off. He knew that it wasn't much of a plan.

But Sally didn't seem disheartened. "Maybe we'll get lucky," she said. "Suffolk is a small county. And there's not a lot there."

The Skoda hated being on the A14, which was more like a motorway as it curved south towards Ipswich. It crawled along the hard shoulder, the engine coughing, rust cascading out of the bodywork. The rest of the traffic rushed past, a blur in the window. Guy no longer knew how fast they were going. The needle in the speedometer had fallen off. He was getting nervous that a police car might pull them over and demand to see their MOT. Sally twisted in her seat and he heard one of the springs snap somewhere underneath her.

He glanced at her. She appeared remarkably relaxed in her lumberjack shirt. She was wearing no makeup and her pale hair hung loose and unbrushed. "You've taken all this very well," he said.

"I'm sorry?"

"Nothing." He realised he had spoken his thoughts out loud without meaning to.

But she had heard him. "You mean . . . my mother," she said.

"Your mother. Me. You're suddenly on the run with someone you've only ever met once. We've got the police looking for us. And jokes —" He broke off. "You've hardly said anything. I don't even know why you agreed to come."

"Because I believe you," she said.

"Nobody else would."

"I saw what happened." She thought for a moment. When she spoke again, her face was utterly serious as if she was saying something she had rehearsed for a long time. "In a way, I was waiting for you to come along," she said. "There's a film I saw a long time ago. I think it was *Slaughterhouse 5* — you know, based on the Kurt Vonnegut story about the bombing of Dresden. I don't think it was very good and I don't remember very much of it. But I do remember a scene near the end. The hero, the main character, is sitting on his bed and a meteor appears. It's a light in the sky that gets nearer and nearer and suddenly it's there in the bedroom with him, and then it takes him away and carries him off to another planet. And the thing is, the character is surprised by what's happened. But at the same time he knows he's been expecting it all his life. That's how I feel now. You're the light in the sky —"

She would have gone on but there was a loud bang under the bonnet and the Skoda slowed down.

"What's happened?" Sally asked.

"I don't know," Guy said. "But it doesn't sound good."

They came off the A14 at the next turn and began to follow country lanes on the far side of Halesworth. Their speed had dropped to fifteen miles per hour and the Skoda's temperature gauge was creeping up. It was also getting harder to change gear. The clutch was slipping and the whole car was vibrating in a way that made them both feel nauseous. To add to their woes, it had suddenly become very dark. It looked as if there was going to be a storm.

"What do you want to do?" Guy asked.

"I think we're going to have to stop for the night. We'll have to sleep in the car."

Guy thought for a moment. Steam was hissing out of the radiator. "Let's keep going while we still can," he said. "Maybe we can find a barn or something."

Five minutes later the Skoda made the decision for them. They had just turned into a narrow, pretty lane with grass banks and wild poppies when the engine simply stopped and they rolled to a silent halt. Guy turned the key but the car was quite dead. "That's it," he said.

Sally pointed. "Look!"

The Skoda had brought them to an impossible funfair.

It was in a field next to the road, somewhere on the outskirts of Halesworth, and there couldn't be a reason in the world for its being there. At first sight, there was something almost shocking about the vivid colours

302

standing out against the flat, dark green of the surrounding countryside. The rides looked new: the merry-go-rounds, the dodgems, the House of Fun, the swing-boats, the helter-skelter. There was no sign of decay, no broken lightbulbs or obviously flaking paint. This wasn't a funfair that had been abandoned and left to rot. It was somehow more nightmarish than that, inexplicably missing the crowds and the noise that would have justified its existence. It was a funfair that had been stripped of the fun.

They got out of the car and climbed up the grass bank and into the middle of the field. Now they could see that all the rides had been locked or disabled, the electricity disconnected, the generators removed. There was no sign of the caravans or trailers that would normally surround such a place although there were tyre tracks in the grass suggesting they had been and gone. At last they came to a simple if incomplete explanation, typewritten on a sheet of paper and pinned to the side of what must once have been a rifle range.

FAIRGROUND CLOSED
By order of Suffolk County Council

"What do you think?" Guy asked.

"I don't know." Sally looked around her. "Maybe the rides weren't safe. Or maybe they didn't have the right licence."

Guy felt a splash against the side of his neck. The wind was blowing hot and cold. The darkness was more intense. The clouds were about to burst. "I think we should stay here," he said. "We can find somewhere to shelter."

"The dodgems?"

"I've had enough of cars for one day. Especially small tinny ones."

In the end, they broke into the House of Fun. It was at once the most solid of the fairground structures and the one with the least security, probably because there was nothing inside to steal. In most travelling funfairs, the Haunted Castle or the House of Fun was nothing more than a parked lorry and a plywood façade — with a gnarled woman or a spiv in a glass box charging a crazy amount for the questionable pleasure of going in. More care had gone into this attraction, which was semi-permanent, two storeys high and built to resemble a gingerbread cottage as designed by a children's illustrator, a clown or an architect on acid. The doors and windows slanted in every direction. The chimneys bent. The flower-boxes were on springs and drainpipes looped everywhere like multi-coloured snakes. A single padlock and chain hung on the front door and Guy kicked it open easily. He felt bad doing it, like a small bully with a gigantic toy.

The inside of the house contained the usual paraphernalia: areas of floor that shuddered or swung, a staircase divided into moving sections, false doors and cartoon pictures. There was no electrical power and it was almost pitch black.

"Wait here," he said.

He ran back to the car. There had been a large supermarket at the garage where they had bought petrol and pumped up the tyres. Guy had already seen that it might be too dangerous to book into any more pubs and hotels, with his picture still everywhere in the press, so he had bought basic supplies: food and wine, sleeping-bags, candles, a torch with spare batteries. The rain was beginning to come down as he collected everything from the back of the car. The Skoda looked indescribably sad with the raindrops hammering on its bonnet and roof. It seemed to know it had died. Guy slammed the door and ran back to rejoin Sally.

She was still waiting in the House of Fun. He turned on the torch and fifty beams of light shafted across the interior, reflecting off mirrors that hung on every wall. They were distorting mirrors, turning Guy and Sally into dwarves or giants — depending on where they looked. There was also a children's play area with a ball pond and a climbing frame. Guy spread out the sleeping bags over the ball pond. He opened the supermarket bags and took out plastic knives and forks, sandwiches, salads, yoghurts and fruit. Finally, he opened the wine. "Your table is ready, madam," he announced.

She joined him, sitting on the balls and the sleeping-bags, which shifted quite comfortably beneath them. They ate together quietly. They were both hungry. They'd had nothing to eat since the coffee bar in Cambridge. Guy had filled two plastic tumblers with red wine.

"Cheers," he said.

"Your health."

Plastic clicked against plastic. They drank.

"I don't think things can get any weirder than this," Sally said. "This funfair! Just abandoned in the middle of nowhere. And this place. The House of Fun. It's like being in a dream."

"A dream dreamed by a surrealist," Guy said. He pointed at the reflection of a candle in one of the distorting mirrors. It twisted and stretched inside. "This is the sort of dream Salvador Dalí probably dreamed."

There was a soft growl of thunder outside, silence, then the harsh rattle of rain hitting wood, amplified all round. It was really coming down now.

"I am so sorry," Guy said.

"Why?"

"I feel guilty, Sally. I know what you said in the car, but even so . . . I had this idea about jokes but it didn't give me any right to come knocking at your door. And look what I've done! I've destroyed everything."

"That's what I meant," Sally said. "Maybe my life needed destroying. Or, at least, shaking up a little. My mother certainly thought so. She didn't want me looking after her. She wanted to go into a home. It was the only thing we ever argued about . . . but in a way she was right. She didn't really need me. At least, she could have managed without me. I was using her as an excuse."

"An excuse?"

"It goes back to when Dad left us. We had no money. We had nothing, and he just walked out on us. I think I was even more shocked than she was. I really adored him, you see. He used to tell me about the Aztecs and the Mayans . . . the history, the mythology. He would come into my room when I was little and tell me stories until I fell asleep. Sometimes I think I can still smell his aftershave. He was my whole world and I couldn't believe he would do that. And after he went . . . I was twenty. I was in a relationship. I was going to do so many things but I just let it all fall apart. I hid behind Mother and I stayed hiding behind her. Of course, her illness was getting worse so I had an excuse but it was only an excuse. The real truth is that I was scared to come out. I didn't have a life. I haven't had a boyfriend for three years. If you hadn't come along with all this madness, I would have turned into one of those awful spinsters you see bicycling around Cambridge, doing good works."

She had finished her wine. She held out her plastic glass and Guy refilled it.

"Even the shop was a waste of time," she went on. "I only looked after it because Mother said I needed something to do. But it wasn't really a good idea. Most of the things we sold were too expensive for students so most of the people who came in were tourists, and all they wanted was local fudge or presentation packs of tea. The rent was always going up and if it hadn't been for Mother and Amanda, I'd have packed it in ages ago."

"I could still get you killed," Guy said. "If you hadn't gone to London yesterday, you'd be dead already."

"I'm still glad you turned up. I know I shouldn't say it, but I am. And maybe this will have a happy ending.

307

We'll find out what Sphinx are doing and they'll leave us alone."

"What if there is no happy ending, Sally?"

"We'll just have to make some happy moments along the way."

It was still raining, but more gently now. The sound of the water hitting the roof was softer and more distant. The candle flames bowed and twisted in rhythm. Guy reached out to Sally and drew her towards him, the plastic balls nudging each other and rolling aside to make space. For the first time she was close enough for him to smell her scent. Her hair, falling over his hand, was fine — almost weightless. He kissed her, feeling her lips against his. The lips questioned her and she pressed herself against him, giving her answer.

They undressed.

In one of the mirrors, Guy saw his shirt travelling further and further as he attempted to pull it over his head, perched far away at the top of his giraffe neck. In the next, Sally had become as massive as her mother had been, pulling off her bra and jersey and releasing monster breasts. She was, in fact, made almost entirely of breasts with half a head, slanting eyes and stubby feet poking out below. She reached down for her skirt and her body concertinaed amazingly. The breasts vanished. Her hips ballooned. The hips vanished. Her breasts ballooned. She managed to rid herself of the skirt and her legs poured out, zig zagging into the distance.

Guy unfortunately had the sexual organs of a one-month-old child. They were trapped, sucked into the endless corridor of his own legs. He shifted his position on the sleeping-bag and was relieved to see them explode outwards, leaping over his shoulder. Sally's head had shrunk to the size of a pea but he seized hold of her and drew her towards him, their bodies rippling into each other and becoming one living thing. It was no longer possible to tell whose arms were whose or even if they were arms at all. They had become an unrecognisable pink shape that throbbed, shimmered, twisted and constantly redefined itself on the equally liquid bed of plastic balls.

They kissed — and their lips knotted and melted into the shape of a heart. She rolled on top of him and sucked his entire body into hers, two Russian dolls, one emerging from the other. The candle flames had become magnified. The whole building was on fire. Guy threw back his arms and his hands leapt from one mirror to the next and the next and the next and the next. Sally's head splashed over him, her lips stretching, still glued to his. Tentacles of flesh erupted in every direction. The painted clowns on the walls and ceilings looked down and laughed.

Afterwards, they lay together, sandwiched between the sleeping-bags, listening to the last of the rain.

"There's something I have to ask you, Sally," Guy said. "I've been wondering about it ever since I met you."

"What?" She was half asleep.

"You said that when your dad ran off, he left you with almost nothing. And the shop wasn't earning you anything. So I was wondering how you managed to survive. How did you buy that lovely house you were living in?"

She stiffened very slightly and he wondered if she had some secret she had been trying to keep from him. He was right.

"I'm glad you asked," she said. "I wanted to tell you."

"It's none of my business."

"No. You might as well know." She rested her head on his shoulder. Her hair brushed his face. He felt her drowsiness. It was communicating itself to him. "It's true," she went on. "After Dad left, everything was disastrous. He'd left us a little money, but not enough to live on. We didn't know what we were going to do."

A long pause.

"But then I won a million pounds on a Premium Bond. They'd been given to me by an aunt and I didn't even know I had any. It just came out of the blue and completely saved us. I'm sorry, Guy."

"There's no need to be sorry. It's marvellous."

Together, they fell asleep.

CHAPTER
TWENTY-TWO

The Skoda was finished so the next day they set off on foot, leaving the fairground behind them. They followed footpaths through cornfields and woods carpeted with bluebells. The spring weather had changed once again, and although it was wet underfoot, the sun was shining. They walked for ten miles until at last they arrived at a village that had both a bus stop and, only an hour later, a bus. That was how they finally arrived in Southwold.

"It's beautiful here," Sally said. "I always wanted to live on the coast."

"Me too."

"Then why didn't you?" she challenged him.

Guy considered. "There's no work for actors on the coast," he said, "unless they're doing Punch and Judy. What was your excuse?"

"Mother."

Southwold was perfectly beautiful, an English seaside town that remembered when the English seaside was somewhere everyone wanted to go. It reminded Guy of an old lady on her way out of a hairdresser's: sedate and slow and proudly aware of herself. He loved the perfectly restored pier, the lighthouse — improbably — right in the middle of a street, and the beach huts with their brilliant colours defying the endless grey of the North Sea. He and Sally walked the full length of the beach, then sat down and had a picnic on the shingle. They had found out absolutely nothing about Sphinx but a fair bit about each other.

They had a lot in common. They both liked the music of the Eagles, the films of David Lean, Greek food and white chocolate Magnum ice-creams. They both disliked politics, conveyor-belt Japanese restaurants and anything by Tracey Emin or Damien Hirst. There were differences. Sally never went to the theatre. "I think it's boring," she said. "You have to pay so much for a ticket and then you sit there, cramped and uncomfortable, and the plays just go on and on."

"Shakespeare? Boring?"

"My bum always goes to sleep around Act Four. I'm sorry, Guy. I love the sonnets and there's some wonderful poetry in the plays. But I prefer reading them to seeing them."

"That's sacrilege!"

Guy leapt on to one of the groynes and stood there, balancing on one leg. "All the world's a stage," he shouted. "And all the men and women merely players: they have their exists and their entrances; and one man in his time plays many parts . . ."

Sally applauded. The waves crashed down beneath him.

Guy jumped back on to the shingle. When he had been with Kate, he had always felt himself challenged. That was the truth of it. She had set certain standards and he had always been afraid of falling short. Looking

312

back, he saw that the relationship had been doomed from the start. He had only been with Sally for a short time but he already knew that he could relax with her. Every time he looked at her, a hundred clichés sprang into his mind. The woman of his dreams. Love at first sight. Made for each other. He felt as if he had known her all his life and he had already forgiven her for winning a million pounds on a Premium Bond.

They finished their picnic and shoved the bags into a litter bin. Then they walked back into Southwold and made their way down the high street, looking for an electrical shop. There was only one. It was a small, low-ceilinged place with bow windows, so old-fashioned that it made the goods it was selling look old-fashioned too. They went in.

The owner was a seventy-year-old man in a brown coat. He had bad eyesight and there was no chance he would recognise Guy. He more or less had to feel his way to the front of the shop.

"Yes?" He gazed at Sally through bifocal glasses. He was virtually bald with a head that craned backwards in a way that reminded Guy of a baby bird waiting to be fed.

"We want to buy a vacuum cleaner," Sally said.

"We've got vacuum cleaners," the old man assured her.

"But we want a Sphinx vacuum cleaner."

"Sphinx? Never heard of it. I've got Dyson and Electrolux."

"No. We really want a Sphinx."

"Sphinx? What's that, then? Is it French? We've got Miele. They're French. And we've got one on special offer."

Guy took over. "We were told that Sphinx was a Suffolk company," he said. "We understood they produced household appliances somewhere around here."

"There's nobody making anything electrical in Suffolk that I know about," the old man said. "In Ipswich, maybe. But certainly not around here."

They went back out on to the street. It was a Wednesday afternoon and many of the shops had closed early. There weren't many people around.

"Well, that was a waste of time," Guy said.

"We've only just started."

"I know. But . . ."

Guy already saw the impossibility of the task he had set himself. Here he was in the middle of Southwold. How was he to find something that might not even exist, that might still be fifty or a hundred miles away and that might look like a factory but, on the other hand, might be disguised as almost anything? The Adnam's brewery was on the other side of the road, towering over the shops. Who was to say that Sphinx wasn't concealed inside? A joke distribution service masquerading as an appliance manufacturer masquerading as a distillery. Guy couldn't ask too many questions without drawing attention to himself. Even in Suffolk the police were probably still on the look-out for him. So what was he to do? Where was he meant to go next?

And, secretly, he was also worried about the method he had used to get here — the lines on the map. At the very least it was imprecise. It might also be fatally flawed. The lines seemed to meet on the Suffolk coast — but who was to say that they didn't continue all the way over to the Netherlands? Could it be that the Ferrero Rocher joke had arrived in England on a boat? The real problem was that he had no idea what he was looking for. A single word. Sphinx. It could be anything. It could be nothing.

They looked in the shop windows but there was nothing among the advertisements for second-hand prams and Jobs Wanted that seemed remotely relevant. They asked people indiscriminately in the street. "We're looking for Sphinx. What is it? We think it's some sort of production plant. You haven't heard of it? Thank you very much." Sally bought another set of clothes in a Southwold shop and came out looking like a sea captain. The owner had never heard of Sphinx. There was nothing like that around here.

They stayed the night in another pub. It seemed to them that the people of Southwold were so cut off from the rest of the country that they might not have heard of Guy Fletcher, the serial dwarf-killer, and that if they had they probably wouldn't be interested. Anyway, there was little chance of his being recognised. A seaside town like this was surely the last place anyone would expect him to come.

That night, Guy and Sally lay in bed, holding each other.

"This is hopeless," Guy muttered.

"Do you want to give up already?"

"Sally, we don't know what we're looking for."

"Have you got any better ideas?"

"No."

"Then shut up and come here . . ."

From Southwold to Walberswick via Blythburgh, with its unreasonably grand church dominating the marshes, they spent the next two days exploring the Suffolk coast. They took buses some of the time but otherwise they were happy to be on foot. It allowed them more time to spot anything that might be worth investigating. But farmhouses, barns, industrial units, pumphouses and semi-derelict towers proved to be just that. The countryside was innocent of anything to do with Sphinx Appliances and everyone they spoke to responded with an increasingly familiar shake of the head.

Thorpeness was more promising. Here, about a mile to the north of Aldeburgh, was a totally weird Victorian holiday resort that had been created by Victorian patriarchs for their workers and it was, of course, extremely sinister. Everything had been landscaped. It was all fake, including the great expanse of water that looked like a natural lake but was a careful half a metre deep. The houses in Thorpeness were black and white and seemed to have been borrowed from Switzerland. There were archways and piazzas, crumbling tea-rooms, the famous "House-in-the-Clouds", a water tower disguised as a levitating cottage. In a way, the tower could have been seen as a bad joke.

The whole place reminded Guy of an episode of *The Interceptors*. He and Sally spent half a day there, expecting to see men with bowler hats and umbrellas or fur-clad women in fast cars. Surely to God if Sphinx was going to have a secret headquarters anywhere, it would be here. But the place was virtually empty. A lot of the houses were now owned by weekenders. The residents who were left seemed blameless. It was just another seaside town, minding its own business on the east coast.

Aldeburgh was less than an hour's walk away.

They spent the rest of the day there, starting with lunch: the best fish and chips they had ever eaten, wrapped in paper and carried over to the sea wall. But Guy knew at once that they were wasting their time.

"Aldeburgh's much too posh," he said. "I mean, all the people who live here are rich Londoners or ex-Londoners. I've never seen so many art galleries in one street. We're wasting our time."

"What else can we do?"

Guy had been seriously thinking about it. Ever since they had left Southwold, part of him had been facing up to the future . . . whatever future he could make for himself if he couldn't prove his innocence. "Sheep farming," he said.

"What?"

"I'm serious. You've got money. And you're not wanted by the police. You could buy a sheep farm somewhere in Scotland. A croft. You said you wanted to live by the sea. Maybe we could move to the Shetlands."

"And farm sheep?"

"At least we'd be together."

Sally leant over and kissed him on the cheek. "I'll go wherever you want to go, Guy," she said. "But let's not give up yet."

Guy sighed. "I wish we could forget this whole business," he said. "Or I wish this business would forget us. I'll tell you one thing. When this is all over, I'm never going to tell another joke."

"If you're going to be a sheep farmer in the Shetlands, you'll need a sense of humour."

They explored Aldeburgh. Once again there was a single electrical shop and a clutch of newsagents but nobody knew anything about Sphinx. There was an information centre and, in the same office, a reservations desk for the Snape Maltings concert hall. Both were run by charming elderly ladies. Both were unable to help.

And so, the next day, they continued south. They had got used to seeing the gleaming white dome of the Sizewell B nuclear power station on the edge of the sea and Sally wondered if they should take a closer look. It might have a visitor centre but, apart from that, it was one of the very few buildings on the coast that was officially and seriously off limits. Guy was against it.

"If we get caught trying to break in, we'll both get arrested. And, anyway, you can't have a vacuum-cleaner factory hidden in a nuclear power station. That's just mad."

"And being chased by rabbis through the middle of Cambridge isn't?"

318

"Forget it, Sally. We'll just keep going down the coast and if we don't find anything we can always come back."

And so at last they came to Kelford, a fishing town not quite on the sea but on the river Ore, just the other side of Butley Creek. It was immediately different from the other Suffolk villages they had visited, more cut off, at the end of a single road that was surrounded by an endless sprawl of woodland. Guy and Sally walked for a whole hour before they were picked up by a farmer with an open-backed truck and it was still a while before the trees came to an end. They saw no houses, no open vistas and no signposts but, then, there were no other roads. At last they emerged into a perfect piece of English countryside. Fields as smooth as carpets. A church, a farmhouse and a haystack straight out of a Hornby railway set, placed on the landscape with the same meticulous care. A pale blue sky dotted with cotton-wool clouds. Warm sunshine, a gentle breeze. The farmer dropped them off and headed back towards Snape.

There were not many hills in Suffolk, but Kelford found itself at the bottom of one. The whole place sloped, getting older and more eccentric the further down it went. At the top were the modern houses, the bungalows and Tudor-style cottages, the acne on the face of every English village. There was a small garage with just two pumps and, opposite, a library and a furniture shop that had closed ten years ago with a single flowery sofa still sitting, optimistically, behind a rectangle of plate glass. About half-way down came the village square, which wasn't square at all but long and rectangular with a pub, a chandler's, a bookshop and a post office-cum-general store. Next came a church — St Sebastian's. And this was where Guy and Sally saw their first sight of village life . . . or, rather death. They had arrived in time for a funeral.

As they walked past, a coffin was carried out of the church and into the cemetery by four young men dressed in dark suits, and ties that hung awkwardly, too long or too short, with knots straining at the collar. These were not people who wore ties often. About thirty men and women followed behind. First came the vicar, his arms wrapped round him as if to protect himself from the cold, his head turned to the ground, his concentration fixed on something to the left of his feet. He was an old man and, Guy thought immediately, an ineffectual one. He was ignoring the widow. She was all in black, her face veiled, trailing two teenaged sons — pressed unwillingly into suits — and a seven or eight-year-old daughter. The rest of the villagers made up a typical funeral crowd, shuffling forward uncomfortably as much as unhappily, constrained to silence, probably thinking about anything other than the reason they were there.

"Do you notice anything odd about that cemetery?" Sally asked.

"No," Guy said. He watched the procession make its way along the church path.

"It's got an awful lot of graves."

It was true. The graveyard was overcrowded, with too many headstones fighting for the limited space and too little grass in between. Some of the graves were old. They were the ones whose stones were weathered and not quite perpendicular to the ground. But the majority were new and the slabs of modern marble with their machine-made lettering seemed unsympathetic and intrusive. Guy was reminded of two packs of cards, badly shuffled together. This was not a graveyard of elegies and solace. It was a mess.

Guy watched as the coffin was carried to its final resting-place. A dark slit had been cut perilously close to a large, spreading oak. Surely the roots would get in the way. Sally tugged at his arm. She didn't want to stay there and neither did he. Together, they moved on.

The road turned a corner just past the church and continued downhill again, with a row of terraced cottages on one side and grander, Georgian houses on the other. Some of these had bushes cut into strange shapes: peacocks, archways, seashells and boats. They came to a crossroads with a sign warning them that they would come to a dead end if they continued straight ahead. On one side, there was a second pub, bow-windowed and ivy-covered, seemingly sinking into the grass. It was called the Anchor and advertised rooms to rent.

"We can get a room here," Sally said.

Guy wasn't sure, but he nodded. They had walked far enough and getting back out of Kelford would take them hours. That was what worried him. If they were found here, there really would be no escape. He had never been to a more isolated place. The surrounding forest had cut it off completely from the modern world.

They walked across the car park. The pub was open and they stepped down into a low, cosy room with a flagstone floor, a sagging wooden bar and a grate that smelt of soot and long winter evenings. It was half past twelve and there was nobody else in there but opening the door had rung a bell on a spring and a moment later the barman appeared, stooping as he passed through an archway that must lead to the kitchen. He was a thin, balding man with a down-turned face and empty eyes that gazed at the two of them as if they were intruders rather than customers.

"Yes?" He managed to make even that one-worded question almost hostile.

"We'd like a room," Sally said.

"Oh." The barman might have forgotten that the place had rooms.

"Do you have any vacancies?" Sally asked.

"How long are you staying?"

"Just tonight."

The barman pulled an old and grubby exercise book off a shelf and looked inside it. He was clearly disappointed to discover that nobody at all was staying at the Anchor. He snapped it shut again.

"It's thirty pounds a night," he said. "Including breakfast."

"That's fine." Sally glanced at Guy, who nodded. There was no chance of the barman recognising them. So far, he hadn't even looked them in the eye.

The barman produced a key — heavy and a little rusty, attached to the slab of wood that all country pubs seemed to favour, this one with a figure 2 carved into it. "Top of the stairs on the right," he said.

They made for the stairs but, at the last moment, Guy couldn't resist turning. The barman was leaning — or slumping — against the bar, his head resting on his hand. He was the picture of misery. "We saw a funeral on the way in," Guy asked. "Was it a friend?"

The barman shook his head. "No. I didn't know him."

"Well . . . I'm sorry."

The barman shrugged. They went upstairs.

The room was much as they would have expected from the outside of the pub: small, old-fashioned, uneven. The floor sloped one way, the walls another. The ceiling and the four-poster bed bulged in sympathy with one another. There were chintz curtains, framed watercolours of Aldeburgh and Snape by an amateur artist and an armchair too big for the corner in which it had been placed, making it impossible to walk round the bed. Guy opened the window and looked out at the crossing they had come to with the cul-de-sac running off to the right.

"Thank God! There's a shower!" Sally said. She had opened a second door that led into a bathroom not much larger than a telephone kiosk. She came back into the room. "Why did you ask that man about the funeral?"

"I don't know. I suppose I wanted to know why he looked so bloody miserable."

Sally thought for a moment. "Don't ask him about Sphinx Appliances," she said, suddenly.

"Why not?"

"I don't know. Just don't!"

Sally took a long, hot shower — leaving Guy with a short, cold one. They had a quick lunch in the pub, served by a woman even more funereal than the landlord or, indeed, the funeral. She was short, dumpy, wearing a muddy dress, and reminded Guy of one of those extras in an old *Hammer* film, serving *bratwurst* in a Transylvanian inn. There was still nobody else there. The food was not good.

They spent the afternoon walking around the village. Kelford was actually larger than it looked. The intersection where the pub stood offered roads heading east and west out of the village and on towards two new estates that must have been built in the last ten years. This was surely a conservation area and both Guy and Sally were surprised by how many new houses had been built. Walking out of Kelford, they soon arrived at the first estate. It contained about two dozen modern houses, mainly two-up-two-down, painted Suffolk pink or blue. Each house had a neat garden and a garage but there was nobody in sight.

Everywhere they looked, in fact, the streets were empty. But they still got the feeling that Kelford was more truly lived in than either Aldeburgh or Southwold — in the sense that it had fewer tourists and weekenders. There were more cars parked in the driveways, more clothes hanging out to dry on washing-lines. A glance through front windows revealed rooms that were untidy. Smoke could be seen, here and there, coming out of chimneys.

They found a network of alleyways snaking between old wisteria-covered walls and allotments. These led them back up to the main square, past a smokehouse and a café. Both of these were open. The first had a bearded man feeding mackerel into an outdoor oven, handling each one as if he had a personal grievance against it. There were a few people sitting in the café and Guy thought they might have come from the funeral. None of them was talking. One was reading a newspaper and, from the look of it, the news was all bad. The café was dark and undecorated. It was the sort of place where even the welcome mat seemed vaguely threatening and they decided not to go in. Instead, they crossed the square and went to explore the church.

St Sebastian's was, like so many English country churches, impressive from the outside but a little depressing once they were in. It needed money spent on it and a congregation would have helped. The windows had lost their stained glass — perhaps they had been bombed out in the war — and a cold afternoon light slanted down on to grey stone and grey wooden pews huddled together in front of an unforgiving cross. Next Sunday's hymns were already posted on a board: two, eleven, twelve, twenty-one and twenty-two. Guy wondered if the vicar had managed to lose all the figures apart from the ones and the twos, condemning his parishioners to a lifetime of the same few hymns.

They were glad to get back out into the sunshine. The cemetery was now deserted but, walking among the graves, they came upon a gravedigger, still filling in the hole that had been dug that morning. He did not look like a gravedigger — quite different from the ones Guy had met at Ickleton . . . or was it Saffron Walden? He was young, with spiked-up hair and an earring. He was listening to a radio tuned into the local news.

"Good afternoon." It was Sally who had addressed him. The gravedigger looked up with a flash of annoyance but said nothing. "Are you busy?" It was a daft question but asked with such warmth that anyone would have forgiven her.

The gravedigger shrugged. "I'm always busy," he said. He had a true Suffolk accent.

"We saw the funeral as we drove in. Was it someone local?"

"It was Ray Clarke." The gravedigger looked down at his handiwork as if including Ray in the conversation. "He's the butcher assistant. Or he was."

"A young man?"

"I couldn't tell you that. I suppose he was about the same age as me."

That would have made him about twenty-one.

"What happened?" Sally asked.

"Cut his wrists in the bath."

"That's horrible!"

"Yeah — well, if you're going to do it, I suppose it's one way." The gravedigger sliced down with his spade. The earth was moist and sticky. The new grave looked very ugly.

"Did you know him?" Sally persisted.

"I met him once or twice. When I was in the shop."

"Why did he do such a thing?"

"Why do you want to know?"

"You're right. It's none of my business. But I just happened to see the funeral and . . . it seems so sad!"

"Well, he must have been right pissed off about something but don't ask me what it was because I wasn't the one who found him. I'm just the one who has to fill him."

The gravedigger went back to his work. Guy and Sally moved on. "Why were you so interested in the butcher's assistant?" he asked her.

"I don't know. But there's something odd about this place."

"You said. It's got a lot of graves."

"It's not just that." Sally looked around her, at the crosses and lozenges, the kneeling angels and slabs. "Look how many of these graves are new," she said.

Guy had already noticed it. He read some of the inscriptions.

In loving memory of DORA
A wife taken before her time.
1950–1999
HARRY BAKER.
A good husband and father. Sleep well.
5 April 1958–5 April 2000
REX AND PHYLLIS UNDERWOOD.
The Lord called and they answered.
12 September 2001

"All these inscriptions tell different stories," Sally said. "Harry Baker was only forty-two when he died and it's interesting that it happened on his birthday. Dora must have died of illness or in some sort of accident too. She was only forty-nine. And what about the Underwoods? How come they both died on the same day?"

"Maybe it was a car accident," Guy said.

" 'The Lord called and they answered'. What's that supposed to mean?"

"Why don't we get out of here?" Guy suggested. "This place gives me the creeps."

They left the cemetery, but not without noticing Jane, who had died when she was twenty-seven and Stephen who had only been twenty-five. Two more husbands and wives had managed to go together and someone called Jim Beavis had "chosen to leave his cares behind", which made him sound as suicidal as Ray Clarke had ultimately been.

"If you ask me, the whole lot of them could have committed suicide," Guy said. "And I wouldn't blame them."

"What do you mean?"

"Only that this is a fucking miserable place. I've only been here a few hours and I'm feeling depressed."

They walked back down to the Anchor, but this time they crossed the main road and continued to the quay. This was without question the most beautiful part of Kelford, although even here they felt a note of melancholy, gazing at the wide, empty horizon, the iron grey river, the already darkening sky. The quay was a square of concrete with a broken wooden jetty and water on three sides. The river ran parallel to the road, east to west, with yachts and dinghies moored haphazardly and more boats tied up on the shingle beach. There was an island on the other side of the river, long and narrow with a scattering of brick buildings that surely dated from the last war. Some were quite large, the size of airport hangars. Others were barely more than sheds. All of them looked abandoned. At the far eastern point of the island was a lighthouse, bright red and white and presumably automated. It looked as unreal as the models of it they had already seen in the Aldeburgh souvenir shops. Nothing was moving apart from the reeds bowing in the wind and a few birds circling overhead. Guy could make out a second jetty, which suggested that a ferry might make the crossing from time to time but there was no sign of a ferry and no other way to get there.

A boat pulled in at the quay. It was manned by two fishermen who had been out catching lobsters. As Guy and Sally watched, they unloaded a basket of slowly moving claws and twitching antennae. The fishermen could have been any age. They were wrapped in oilskins and went about their work in total silence, like sleepwalkers.

Guy went over to them. "Excuse me," he said. "Can you tell me how we can get over to the island?"

"You can't," one of the fishermen answered, at the same time heaving another basket up on to the quay. This one was filled with flat fish of some sort. "It's protected."

"I'm sorry?"

"Seals. It's a seal sanctuary."

"My wife and I are both keen seal-watchers."

"Well, you'll have to do it from this side of the river. There's no one allowed."

The evening was drawing in and it was getting colder. Guy and Sally walked back up towards the Anchor and were about to go in when Guy froze, grabbed hold of her and pulled her back into the shadows. A car had just pulled out of the car park. As they watched, it turned left and continued up towards the church and the village square. Guy had recognized the driver instantly, and although he had only glimpsed the two passengers, he had known them too.

The Englishman, the Irishman and the Scotsman. The three men who had come to the film set, who had tried to kill him on his way to the Italian restaurant and who had been there when he was arrested.

He was unsure now whether to go into the pub. Had they been there searching for him? Had they told the barman to warn them if he came back? Guy quickly added up the possibilities and decided that they couldn't have known he was there. If they had, they would have waited for him and grabbed him the moment he walked in. Seeing the three men had been a coincidence, but not a remarkable one. It simply told him that his methodology had been right and that the two lines on the map had indeed brought them to where they ought to be. Sphinx Appliances had to be close.

They went in. The barman ignored them. He was just opening for the evening, going about his business in exactly the same way as the fishermen, the gravedigger, even the man outside the smokehouse,

330

with the same sense of sullen determination. Guy and Sally went upstairs and Guy told her what he had seen outside.

"What do you want to do?" Sally whispered.

"I don't know. We might as well stay here tonight. I don't think they know we're here. But tomorrow I think we ought to move somewhere safer."

"But maybe the answer's here in Kelford."

"We can keep looking. But let's just base ourselves outside."

They lay on the bed but didn't make love. They were too unsettled, and not just because of the three men. There was something about the whole village that was hard to define, but which was still almost tangible. Guy had been thinking Hammer Horror when they first arrived but now he wondered if it wasn't more Stephen King: less obvious and more genuinely creepy. He thought about the people he had seen at the funeral. Of course they had looked sad. But there had been something more than that. They had seemed as lifeless as the man they were following to the grave. And then there had been the man with the fish . . .

He fell asleep. The next time he opened his eyes it was dark and Sally was sitting at the window, looking out over the street.

"What time is it?" he asked.

"Nine o'clock. I didn't want to wake you."

"Have you eaten?"

"No."

"Let's go down."

They went downstairs. There were a few logs glowing in the fireplace but there was no other cheer to be had at the Anchor. The barman was back in his place, his elbows on the bar, his head and shoulders hanging between them like washing on a line. Half a dozen customers had come in and were scattered at the tables with pints and cigarettes, but either they had all been at the funeral that afternoon or, by coincidence, they were on their way to another one because their mood was utterly bleak. When they spoke it was in clipped sentences, their voices low. Much of the time they were silent. A television was on in a corner. Nobody was watching it.

Guy ordered a pint of beer for himself, red wine for Sally and dinner for both of them. The pub had a menu but no choice. Everything was off except for the lamb curry and the barman seemed doubtful about that too. They took a table in the darkest corner, furthest from the fire. Nobody had taken any notice of them. They were glad about that.

"Nice place," Guy muttered, raising his glass. He always hoped beer would taste better in the countryside even though it never actually did.

"Aren't you afraid they'll come back here?" Sally asked.

"Who?"

"The Englishman, the Irishman and the Scotsman." She had accepted the three men — the fact that they existed — immediately and without question. That was what was so wonderful about her.

"I suppose it's possible," Guy said. "If they do, I'll just have to dive under the table or something."

"Maybe we should ask about them. We don't have to mention Sphinx but the barman might know them. If they come drinking here regularly, he could even know where they work."

"Let's ask him tomorrow, Sally. In the daylight."

And then one of the men sitting at the bar turned and stared at Guy in a way that told him, at once, that he had been recognised. The man was dressed in a very old tweed jacket. He was about fifty, his face beaten about by the wind and the rain and by life. When he spoke he showed a gap where his two front teeth should have been. "You're on TV!" he said.

Guy's heart sank. A news bulletin! He gripped the side of the table, preparing to make a break for the door. But then he looked at the screen, and although it took him a few moments to work out what he was seeing, he finally realised. It wasn't the news. It was the episode of *Two in the Bush* that he had been filming when the Englishman and his two friends had first appeared and when, in a sense, all his troubles had begun. It seemed very soon for the programme to have been edited and screened and he wondered if the producers had decided to use the publicity of his arrest and escape. But, of course, the BBC didn't work like that. As a corporation, it was almost certainly unaware that there had been an arrest and an escape involving one of its erstwhile employees, or even that it had made a programme called *Two in the Bush*. No — this smacked of a last-minute dash to fill a gap in the

333

schedule. The series had been put out in a hurry and here was his episode — here, indeed, was he.

"That's you, isn't it?" the man asked.

"No," Guy said. "It's someone else."

They watched the episode together and Guy was astonished to see that Sally appeared to enjoy it. She smiled throughout and even laughed out loud twice. This seemed incredible to him. Not only were they on the run from the police and from a bunch of unknown psychopaths, not only had her mother been violently murdered just a week ago, but *Two in the Bush* wasn't and never had been in his mind even remotely funny. He remembered reading the script without a flicker of amusement and as the credits rolled he turned enquiringly to her.

"You were good," she said quietly. "You were funny."

"If you thought I was funny then, you should have seen me when I ran over the director," Guy replied. The lamb curry arrived. Guy tasted his. It wasn't as bad as he had feared. "You didn't really enjoy it, did you?" he asked. "I thought it was awful."

"That's because you're in it. I agree that it was old-fashioned, but it wasn't any worse than most of the things you see these days. I thought the scene with the Pavlova was hilarious."

"I wasn't in that scene!"

They were talking about it at the next table too.

Two men and a woman were sitting there. They were all middle-aged. Two of them might have been married but, if so, it was hard to say which two. They probably met there often.

"You'd think he'd have known," the woman was saying.

"Who?" her husband or friend asked.

"Mr Baxter. He was meant to be homophobic so he must have known that the theatre designer was gay. I mean, there's no way he wouldn't have known."

"Maybe he did know but he didn't like to say," the other man suggested.

"Of course he'd have said something. I mean, he wouldn't have stayed! He'd have walked out of the house."

"My own feeling was that he was the sort of person who'd speak his mind," the second man said. "He was, after all, a tax barrister. I used to know a tax barrister and these people are very forthright."

The other two nodded.

"I thought it was disgusting, the way they treated the young man who came to the door," the woman said.

Guy's ears pricked up. They were discussing his character.

"He'd only come round to pick up a newspaper article and they did everything they could to get rid of him!"

"Greg thought he was homosexual too," the first man reminded her.

"Well, yes. But only because of that misunderstanding about the column inches. Lawrence was talking about the newspaper but Greg didn't understand. He thought Lawrence was talking about his genitalia."

The second man nodded. "It was a very strange mistake to make. I'd never make a mistake like that."

"Well, Greg was panicking. He thought the dinner was going to be spoiled."

"Greg was meant to be intelligent. If you ask me, that was a definite fault in an otherwise quite enjoyable script. On the subject of which, I found the scene with the Pavlova quite unnecessarily violent. It actually went straight into Mr Baxter's face! That could have been very painful . . ."

And so they went on. Guy listened to them with a certain horrid fascination. They had taken the half-hour completely seriously. Alan's situation, the fact that he was a strait-laced lawyer sharing a flat with the impossibly flamboyant Greg, seemed to them inconvenient to the point of being untenable and they were surprised that he hadn't moved out. As they continued to discuss the finer points of the relationship, Guy wanted to go over and scream at them. "It's not Ibsen! It's a sit-com! If Alan moved out there wouldn't be any sit so you couldn't have any com! Can't you see that?"

But by then the news had come on and the three of them turned to watch the continuing arguments about the Sanderson report, another explosion in Tel Aviv and a walk-out by nurses protesting at conditions in a flagship hospital on the south coast. If the sit-com had failed to cheer them up, the news positively destroyed them. When the reporter mentioned the latest incidence of an old man who had died after being mugged by two twelve-year-olds, the men fell silent and stared into their beers. The woman began to cry. Neither of the men comforted her. Either they hadn't noticed or they were too upset themselves.

Guy glanced at Sally. "This place . . ." he began.

She shook her head. He could see the uneasiness in her eyes, the sense of being in the wrong place at the wrong time. She didn't understand what was happening. But she didn't want to interfere.

Guy examined the other people in the pub. The news seemed to have upset them all equally. There was a man rapping his knuckles again and again against the bar. Another covering his eyes. A third swearing silently to himself, rolling the obscenities over and over in his mouth. The barman, wiping a glass, had the sly, turned-down-mouth look of someone who had heard it all before. But he was upset too. The glass he was drying shattered. He barely noticed. Blood dripped down from his hand.

What did it all mean? Guy didn't know but he suddenly had an idea. Sally still had a full glass of wine but his was empty. He picked it up and went over to the bar.

"I'll have another half," he said.

The barman had wrapped a tea-towel round his hand. He filled the glass.

"You've got a nice place here," Guy said.

"We do all right by it."

"Can I offer you a drink?"

"I'll have a pint, thanks."

The barman didn't actually pour himself a pint, but he took the money for it and tipped it into a pint glass beside the till.

"I heard a great joke today," Guy went on. The barman looked up enquiringly. "What do you call a fish with no eyes?" It was a very old joke. He had thought of it remembering the basket of fish that afternoon.

The barman considered. He seemed put out by the question as if Guy were challenging his IQ. "I don't know," he said at length. "I think most fish have got eyes, haven't they?"

"Fsh," Guy said.

"I'm sorry?"

"What do you call a fish with no eyes? Fsh!"

The barman frowned. "Oh, yes," he said. "I'm sorry. When you asked me, I assumed you meant a fish that was unable to see. I didn't realise you meant the letter *i*. But you're absolutely right. If you spelled fish without the *i*, I suppose you would be left with fsh although I doubt anyone would understand what you were going on about."

Guy paid for his beer and went back to Sally. "Nobody in Kelford has got any sense of humour," he said.

"What?"

"The barman. The people at the next table. Everyone we've met. They've got no sense of humour. That's what so weird about this place."

"I haven't seen anyone laughing," Sally agreed.

"I don't think you ever will. I think they've forgotten how to."

Half an hour later they went to bed. Sally had nightmares that night. Guy himself barely slept. At four o'clock in the morning they were wrapped round each other, a tangle of arms and legs and shared warmth. Guy had never needed anyone more.

338

CHAPTER
TWENTY-THREE

At half past six the next morning, Guy stood at the window of his bedroom at the Anchor looking out at the grey light of morning. The church of St Sebastian's rose up in the distance, watching over the village as it had done for centuries. There was nobody moving in the street but Guy heard a sound, an approaching vehicle. Sure enough, a brightly coloured truck appeared, with a huge, smiling chicken painted on one side and the legend SUFFOLK FRESH POULTRY written underneath. It reached the crossroads and continued forward in the direction of the quay. Guy waited a few minutes, thinking about what he had just seen. Then he quietly got dressed.

Sally was still asleep. There was something almost childlike about the way she lay there with her head in the crook of her arm, her fair hair spread across the pillow. As Guy went over to the door, she stirred and asked, sleepily, "Where are you going?"

"For a walk. I'll be ten minutes." He kissed her on a cheek that was warm from the bed and went out.

The pub was empty, the bottles now locked behind a wire mesh. Guy let himself out, his feet crunching on the gravel, the cold morning breeze blowing away the last memories of sleep. It took him just a few minutes to walk down to the quay. Once again he found himself surrounded by the river, grey and choppy, with the island about fifty metres away and no way of getting there. There was a single boat, an oyster catcher, moored to the jetty but it looked as if it had been there forever. He examined the ground. It had rained at some time in the night and he could see tyre tracks running the full length of the quay, stopping only at the end where a pair of metal ladders climbed down into the uninviting water. Guy suddenly felt very alone. He also felt as if he was being watched, which was impossible as it was obvious that there was nobody around for miles.

There was no sign of the truck.

Deep in thought, he turned round and went back to the pub.

Sally had gone back to sleep. He watched breakfast TV with the sound turned down. The fat presenter and the pretty presenter were sitting next to each other on the couch, mulling over the morning news in a way that somehow extracted any relevance from it whatsoever. Guy's own story was no longer on the agenda. Two suicide bombers had blown themselves — and sixteen Israelis — to smithereens in Tel Aviv, putting a kink in the American road map for peace. A hundred doctors had resigned from the NHS. The Prime Minister was angrily denouncing those who insisted that the Sanderson report was a whitewash — and was demanding the resignation of several newspaper editors. An old-age pensioner had been murdered somewhere or other. At eight o'clock someone turned up to make breakfast. Guy heard a door open and close, the clatter of a pan. The smell of frying seeped up through the floorboards. Sally stirred and woke. "Why are you up?" she asked.

"I couldn't sleep. Are you hungry?"

She nodded.

"Let's go down."

Sally washed and got dressed, and then they went downstairs. A woman from the village had come in to make breakfast and she served eggs, bacon and toast at a table in the room next to the bar. Guy and Sally were the only guests. The woman was short and solid, and Guy thought he had spotted her the day before in the graveyard. She gave them a newspaper. The NHS doctors were on the front page.

"You wouldn't want to be ill," the woman said. She looked disgusted. Her face had a folded-up quality with hard, watery eyes. "The NHS. It makes you sick." She wasn't joking. She meant what she said and spoke the words with venom.

"It is a problem," Guy said. It was too early for this.

"A problem? You pay your National Insurance all your life but the moment anything goes wrong they don't want to know. I've got rheumatoid arthritis. I'm in pain all the time. But I had to wait five hours in Ipswich hospital and then they wouldn't do anything about it. My dad died on a trolley in a corridor. The wheels had gone rusty before they noticed he was there. I was fifty-three years old last week. Fifty-three, and what have I got to look forward to? More pain, more problems, and then I suppose I'll drop dead and that will be the end of it. And the cost of funerals! I want to be cremated and my ashes scattered at sea but I can't even afford the ferry. I don't know . . ."

She stamped off back into the kitchen. Guy had lost his appetite.

There was a long silence.

Guy waited until she had gone. "I think I may have found something," he said.

"What?"

He told her about the truck he had seen. "The question is," he said, "why did the chickens cross the road?"

"The chickens in the van, you mean?"

"Yes. Suffolk Fresh Poultry. It came into the village early this morning, before anybody was awake. It came down the high street and then crossed over. It was only out of my sight for a couple of minutes but when I got there it was gone." Sally looked blank so he continued: "It crossed the road, Sally, but there is only a cul-de-sac on the other side. The track goes down to the quay. And if it wasn't on the quay when I got there, it must have somehow crossed the river on to the island."

"Did you see a ferry?"

"No. But why would there be a ferry if the island really was a seal sanctuary, off-limits?"

"Unless . . ." She left the rest of the sentence unfinished because it was really too obvious. If a truckload of chickens had gone over to the island, it was because there was a restaurant or a cafeteria on the island with chicken on the menu. Which meant that it

342

was less deserted than it seemed to be — and certainly nothing to do with seals.

They finished their breakfast quickly, walked down to the quay and looked across the water to the land on the other side. It really was very desolate, a last barrier against the North Sea. The furthest buildings seemed to be perched on the edge of the world, standing out against the great white nothing of the sky. A few boats went past, fighting against the current. Seagulls swooped overhead, breaking the silence with their mournful cries.

"There are radio masts," Sally said.

Guy hadn't noticed them before. There were three of them on the other side of the lighthouse, seemingly taller than it was although that might have been a trick of perspective. He looked across the quay. The oyster-catcher that he had noticed tied up earlier was now occupied. A man in a dirty leather jacket was doing something to the engine and Guy walked over to him. "Excuse me," he said, "I wonder if you'd give us a lift over to the island?"

"The Flat?" The man in the boat wiped his hands with a rag dirtier than his hands had actually been. "No way, mate. You can't go over there. It's off-limits."

"We just want to walk round. My wife and I are photographers. We'd like to get some shots of the seals. We'll pay you to take us."

"I take you over there, I'll lose my licence and my mooring. It's protected. Sorry. You want photographs of seals, you should go to Colchester Zoo. They've got plenty."

They didn't go to Colchester. They went to the library that they had passed, next to the furniture shop.

It was a tiny place with swing doors and a musty smell. Inside, there were a few low tables with newspapers and magazines, about twenty shelves of books and a woman in a cardigan, knitting behind a desk. There was nobody else in there.

The woman nodded at them and went on with her knitting. Guy and Sally walked past the different sections, each of which had been categorised. First there was Fiction, then History, Biography, Science and Leisure. Guy stopped abruptly and felt Sally do the same.

"Do you see?" he said.

Sally nodded.

They had come to the Humour section — but it was the least crowded shelf in the building. It had only a dozen books, some of which had fallen over. Guy picked up an old copy of *Jeeves and Wooster*. The pages had yellowed. He blew and dust rose in a cloud. There were books by Ben Elton, Bill Bryson and Stephen Fry. He picked one up. *Moab Is My Washpot*. He opened it and looked at the first page. Nobody had ever taken it out. The book had never been read.

"Let's find what we came for," Sally said.

They continued to the Local History section. This was better populated. There were several books on Kelford and one that concerned itself specifically with Kelford Flat.

This was the official name of the island which was eight miles long and which had been formed by the

344

movement of Shingle around the twelfth century. There had been a lighthouse of some sort on Kelford Flat since 1600 and it was said that Queen Elizabeth I had once picnicked there although there was no historical evidence of this. Margaret Catchpole, the famous pirate, had briefly used it as a base. The island was home to many wild flowers, including the famous yellow horned poppy. It was apparently a breeding ground for avocets and at one time it had been home to a family of rough-legged buzzards. There was only one mention of seals. They were occasionally sighted at its northernmost point.

Kelford Flat had become more prominent in the years leading up to the Second World War. Guy had been right about this. The radio masts had been part of a research facility where — in conditions of great secrecy — the development of radar had first taken place. There were other facilities further down the coast at Orford and Bawdsey. Various other weapons had been tested there, including the tail design for the nuclear bomb that was used at Hiroshima, and it was said that the American Stealth fighter had been put through its paces in the skies overhead — although the Americans had always denied it. The military had only left in 1962 at which point the island had been closed, leaving behind scores of unexploded bombs still half buried in the wild grass. Some of these had been cleared in the mid-seventies when the island had passed into the hands of the National Trust but the place was still considered to be too dangerous for anyone to visit.

345

"How come the seals never managed to blow themselves up?" Guy said. "And what about these rough-legged buzzards? They'd be no-legged buzzards if they landed in the wrong place."

"Meaning?"

"I bet there aren't any unexploded bombs at all. They probably just say that to keep people away."

"Do you want to find out?" Sally asked.

"Yes." Guy closed the book. "We're going to have to get across. I wonder if we can swim?"

"The water looked freezing. Anyway, there could be currents . . ."

"We need a boat."

"Where are we going to get a boat from?"

"There are plenty of boats."

"We're going to buy a boat?"

"No. We're not going to buy a boat."

That night, they stole a boat.

Guy felt strange doing it. He had never stolen anything in his life and he hated the fact that it was so easy, that the people who lived in the country were still so trusting that they still left their doors open and their property unlocked. And here was he, fresh up from London to prove them wrong. He felt he was damaging something sacred, a last memory of an England that had once been. It wasn't just theft that he was committing. It was a small sacrilege.

There was a little dinghy sitting on the beach and he dragged it down to the water while Sally kept watch. Oars were a little more difficult. The owner had at least thought to lock these away but only in a wooden shed that wouldn't have defeated a nine-year-old delinquent in Muswell Hill. Guy prised open a door and found oars, rowlocks, a torch, even a waterproof chart of currents and tides.

"We'll return all this when we get back," he said to Sally.

"Of course we will."

Why were they trying so hard to reassure themselves? Partly they were ashamed of themselves. But there was also the unspoken thought . . . They might not make it back. There were the tides to consider. And whatever might be waiting for them on Kelford Flat.

"Look!" Sally pointed. The lighthouse was flashing on and off. It had been dark when they set out. "Someone's there."

"No." Guy shook his head. "It's probably automated. Almost all of them are."

There were no lighthouse keepers any more. It was another part of Britain that had gone long ago.

The boat seemed to make a tremendous amount of noise as they pulled it over the shingle but at last it was floating, the oars were in and nobody had surprised them, walking along the shore. They climbed awkwardly aboard. Anyone watching would have known at once that they had never been in a rowing-boat before. For the next minute or two, their body language was foreign to them as they tried to find their centre of gravity and stop the dinghy tipping up. Guy tried to get to one end. Sally nearly fell off the other. They embraced, clumsily, in the middle, a slow dance as they tried to get past each other. At last they had got themselves sorted out. Sally was at one end, Guy — facing her — at the other. He lifted the oars and dropped them into the rowlocks. He pulled back and the boat slid away from the shore.

And just for a moment, unexpectedly, everything was perfectly beautiful. This was the moment that he would never forget, when everything that had happened actually became a proper adventure with a hero and a heroine and a quest and a possible resolution. It was the moment when they left Kelford and entered *A Thousand and One Nights*.

The sky was very black, the water calm and silver. A tiny, delicate slice of moon, a Turkish crescent, hung over them. There were no clouds and a million stars. The boat made a wonderful sound as it pushed forward, the oars suddenly rhythmic, cutting through the river like scissors through silk. All around them, the water seemed to be singing. In the far distance, the beam from the lighthouse blinked, beckoning them on and somehow assuring them that the way was safe. It was a warm night, the breeze behind them. The other boats were rocking gently at their moorings and the great bulk of Kelford Flat, reaching out rapidly around them, was not threatening so much as enticing, the frontier of another land.

They landed with a thud. Now they were trespassers. They might be in danger. Guy glanced at Sally, checking with her that she wanted to go ahead. She nodded. He got out and swore breathlessly as cold water and mud rose over his ankle and almost up to his knee. With difficulty he managed to swing the boat round and Sally was able to climb straight on to dry land. He tried to follow her but found that he was stuck fast. The water had risen almost as far as his crotch and he couldn't move forwards or backwards. He could only corkscrew round.

"Guy," Sally hissed. She couldn't see what was happening and didn't like being left on her own.

"One minute!" He twisted round and pulled with all his strength, using the side of the dinghy to lever himself up. He felt his shoe and sock being sucked off his foot. His leg came free and he managed to throw himself, sprawling, on to the bank. But his footwear would be lost for ever in the mud and he had also managed to push the dinghy back out into the river. It was already drifting away, and by the time he noticed it was too late.

They were stuck on Kelford Flat. They couldn't go back.

"What now?" Sally asked.

He was surprised she hadn't bitten his head off. Kate would have. Guy looked around. Nothing seemed very promising. "Let's try this way," he said.

They set off, over the grass and towards the first of the buildings. The unexploded bombs, which had seemed so unlikely in the comfort of Kelford library, had suddenly become horribly real in Guy's mind and he found himself stretching out before every step, as if he might be able to feel the metal casing with his bare, twitching toe and hopefully step round it before setting it off. The island seemed enormous now that they were on it, the mainland all too far away. At the far end, the lighthouse continued to blink on and off as it would all night. Nothing else moved. There wasn't a sound anywhere — not so much as a peep from a nesting avocet or a splash from a passing seal.

They came to the building. It was nothing more than a shed, less interesting and more broken-down than the one from which they had stolen the oars. There was an old net inside, impossibly tangled, and some pieces of rotting wood that might once have been a boat.

"There's nothing here," Guy said. He had added to his woes by stepping on a stinging nettle. He had, of course, chosen the foot without the shoe and sock.

"Guy, what are we going to do?"

"What?"

Sally had been thinking things through. She looked worried. He could see her face, pale in the moonlight. Her hair hung low over her eyes. "We've lost the boat. That means we can't get off the island."

"We can find somewhere to sleep."

"But tomorrow morning! We're going to have to call for help. And we're not meant to be here. They might call the police."

She was right. There didn't seem to be any sign of life on the island and the whole expedition had been ill-planned and hopeless. Why couldn't he have hung on to the boat?

"We'll worry about that tomorrow," Guy said. "Let's just take a look round for now. One of these buildings must be open."

350

The two of them crossed the island. Nothing moved. They were making for the nearest of the hangar-sized buildings they had noticed from the shore . . .

. . . and then a light came on.

Guy and Sally stopped exactly where they were, looking for somewhere to hide. But there was nowhere. They were in the middle of a wasteland, following a rough track. Ahead of them, no more than twenty metres away, a door in the side of the hangar had opened and this was the source of the light. As they watched, a man stepped outside. He seemed to be searching for something which he was holding in front of him. Then he opened his legs and they heard the sound of water pattering on to grass. He was urinating. They could see him, silhouetted against the light, but fortunately he hadn't seen them. They stood where they were until he had finished. Then he turned round and walked back into the building. The light went out.

They were not alone.

"I was right," Guy whispered. "I think we've found them. Sphinx . . ."

"We've found someone," Sally agreed. "Do you want to take a look?"

What else could they do? They were trapped on the island.

"Just a quick look. Yes."

They crept forward. Guy's left foot crunched on the gravel. His right foot, without the shoe, was silent. Anyone listening would think they were being stalked by a man with one leg. He looked back over his shoulder, still certain that he was being watched. There was no one. The grass bent in the breeze. Beyond, the water rippled, reflecting the moon.

They reached the door where the man had come out. It was solid metal, fitting flush to the brickwork. Guy really could imagine Second World War scientists working here. It was the sort of door built to hide secrets. He glanced at Sally, who nodded.

He opened the door and they slipped inside.

The door led into a corridor, illuminated with industrial neon lights hanging on chains. Thick pipes ran in parallel lines along walls painted military green. At the end was a lift, a heavy steel box with all the workings showing, like something in a mine or a nuclear bunker. The letters C-1 were painted in orange on the wall.

"What do you think?" Sally whispered.

"There must be a basement," Guy whispered back. He had seen the building from the outside. The lift could only go down. "Let's see if we can find some stairs."

There was a second door by the lift and behind it a flight of concrete steps — a fire exit. With a sense of dread, they made their way down. The island, then the hangar, now the basement. It was a series of traps within traps. Guy thought of Brian Eastman and Johnny Peters. Sphinx was an organisation that killed indiscriminately. If they were found here, they would die. It was as simple as that. He glanced at Sally, hoping she hadn't reached the same conclusion. He wished he hadn't brought her here.

352

The staircase continued for three levels but Guy and Sally left it at the first — C-2 — one level below ground. It was far enough. They found themselves in another corridor, this one carpeted and with more ornamental lights. But for the complete absence of windows and the sense of fear and claustrophobia, they could have been in a modern hotel. Classical music — Chopin — was coming from somewhere round the corner.

Guy took Sally's arm. There didn't seem to be anyone around — it was a quarter to eleven at night — but all in all it was probably better not to dawdle. They set off briskly, as if they had every right to be there. Guy was limping, one shoe on, one shoe off. His right trouser leg was completely soaked. He stopped and kicked the other shoe off. That made things easier.

Sally pointed. "Look."

There were doors on either side of them. She had stopped in front of one of them. There was a sign reading: KNOCK KNOCK BEFORE ENTERING.

"I think we're in the right place," she said.

Guy tried the handle but the door was locked.

They continued towards the music. The corridor turned sharply and became a bridge, a gallery that crossed a large chamber. The chamber rose all the way to the surface with shelves full of books along two walls and narrow, horizontal windows, high up, just below the ceiling. Twin portraits of the Queen and the Duke of Edinburgh hung opposite them. There were about a dozen people in the room, casually dressed. Some were sitting in comfortable armchairs, reading books or

353

magazines. Some were talking softly among themselves. There was a widescreen television in the room, the volume turned down, and a snooker table with the balls scattered over the green baize. Apart from the fact that the people were of different ages and ethnic groups, it reminded Guy of a London club.

"What are these people doing here?" Sally whispered.

"God knows. Let's keep going . . ."

They hurried across the gallery. Fortunately they were high up and in shadow. Nobody saw them pass. Ahead of them, the corridor widened with four more lifts, modern ones this time, facing each other in pairs. There was a "ping" and one of the lift doors opened. Sally grabbed hold of Guy and drew him back. They watched as a crowd of people emerged. There were two very old ladies, supporting themselves on zimmer frames, then a doctor, a fireman, a monk and a ventriloquist. They knew the last man was a ventriloquist because he was carrying a dummy, an exact replica of himself. The crowd moved off in the other direction. Guy and Sally started forward again, following them.

They came to an archway and, on the other side of it, a fully operational restaurant with waiters in white jackets serving about thirty diners — the night shift — sitting at circular tables. The people from the lift had joined white-coated scientists, clerks, secretaries and other personnel. Guy nudged Sally and pointed. The Englishman, the Irishman and the Scotsman were sitting at a table by themselves. They were eating fried chicken.

It was difficult passing the restaurant without being seen. Guy noticed a dessert trolley and pushed it in front of him with Sally walking at his side. Anyone glancing in their direction might take them for kitchen staff — that was how Richard Hannay had escaped from the Fascists in the BBC adaptation of *The Thirty-nine Steps*. In fact, nobody looked their way. They abandoned the trolley outside a toilet and hurried down the corridor ahead.

This corridor led them past a plate-glass window framing what looked like a language laboratory: individual booths, headphones, computer screens. As Guy and Sally peered in, a door opened somewhere behind them and they ducked behind a folding information board as two men, dressed in white coats and carrying clipboards, walked towards them, talking together.

"What's the difference between the Pope and a washing-machine?" the first one was saying.

"I don't know. What is the difference between the Pope and a washing machine?"

"Don't ask me. I'm asking you."

"Well, I don't know."

"I thought you might have heard. It came in today from Rome. I heard someone in R and D — Wilson — he said it was going out this week."

"So, what is the difference between the Pope and a washing-machine?"

"Search me. Something to do with spin cycles? Vibrations?"

The conversation continued as the two men turned the corner and disappeared through a pair of swing doors. Guy and Sally came out from behind the screen.

"We're definitely in the right place," Guy whispered.

"I think we should go back outside," Sally said.

But that wasn't so easy. They had somehow made their way through to K-2 — the letters were stencilled on the wall — but there was no sign of a lift or a staircase going back up. Guy examined the information board. There were regulations: what to do in the event of a fire, duty officers, telephone numbers. A bridge tournament between Creatives and Distribution. Excursions to concerts in Aldeburgh and Snape. But no map. No useful information.

They went through the swing doors, passing a series of uniform offices with identical tables, chairs and filing cabinets. Guy wondered how anyone could work underground, with no daylight, no view. He was feeling increasingly uneasy, knowing that their time — and luck — had to be running out. The corridor came to a dead end but at least there were more lifts: two sets of steel doors. Guy pressed the call button.

"This place is unbelievable," Sally said.

"Yeah. Like something out of a fucking James Bond film."

"It must have been built in the war. It said in the book they developed radar here." She paused. "What are we going to do?"

"Swim back to the mainland." Sally glanced at him. "The current can't be that strong," he said. "I think we can make it."

She grimaced. "I should have told you. I can't swim."

"You can't swim?"

"I'm sorry."

"Why didn't you tell me before?"

"Are you angry?"

"No. Of course not." Guy shrugged. "We'll just have to think of another plan."

The lift doors opened. There were three guards standing there with Heckler and semi-automatic guns pointing at them. They came out of the lift, fanning forward, taking up their positions. A fourth man, dressed in khaki, stepped out. He was young and looked apologetic. "I'm afraid you're going to have to come with me," he said. He had a polite, rather upper-class voice.

"Why?"

"This is government property. You're not authorised."

"We got lost," Sally said. "We came to see the seals."

"I'm sorry, but I'm afraid that won't wash. We've been watching you on TV. You've been snooping around for quite some time now."

"Who are you?" Guy asked.

"My name is Sanderson. You're Guy Fletcher, aren't you?"

"Yes."

"I thought as much. You'd better come with me."

They were led back into the lift. There wasn't a great deal of room with so many men and machine-guns. The man called Sanderson pressed the bottom button and Guy felt his ears compress as they were carried several levels further down.

"You really shouldn't have come here, you know," Sanderson said. Guy got the feeling that he was probably quite a pleasant man. He couldn't have been more than twenty-five years old. He had sticky-out ears, accentuated by the fact that his hair was cut so short.

The lift stopped. K-7. Guy wondered how far down the complex went. He allowed the soldiers to lead him along a final corridor, this one with doors that were more prison than office. Naked lightbulbs punctuated the way. At last they stopped.

"You're going to have to spend the night here," Sanderson said. He still sounded apologetic. "We'll talk to you in the morning."

"Can we stay together?" Sally asked.

"No. I'm afraid that's not possible."

Sally was shown into the first cell, Guy into the second. His was a small, bare room with two bunks, a toilet and — of course — no window. Sanderson stood for a moment in the doorway. "Is there anything you need?" he asked.

"A cup of coffee and a sandwich would be nice," Guy said.

"I'll see what I can do."

But in fact he didn't come back. The door closed and Guy heard the key turn and after that he was left on his own.

CHAPTER
TWENTY-FOUR

"I would like to tell you a joke," Rupert Liddy said.

"I don't like jokes," Guy said.

"You'll like this one."

Guy had been brought up — alone — to Liddy's office: the Whitehall office with the Suffolk view. It worried him that he and Sally had been separated. So did the presence of Smythe, O'Neil and McLarrity, which, he now knew, were the names of the Englishman, the Irishman and the Scotsman. But nothing worried him more than the man who sat like a soldier, dressed like a businessman and talked like a public-school headmaster. Even when he had been pushed under the steamroller or chased by the stereotypes, Guy had felt himself to be in less danger than he was now. There was a stillness about the man and about the room that felt somehow inescapable. At the same time, he knew that he had reached the end of the road that he had first imagined, then found to be real.

This was where jokes began. With this man. Here.

"Where is Sally?" he demanded.

"She's downstairs."

"I'd like to see her."

"I'm sure you would. But you don't need to concern yourself with her. At the moment, I'm afraid, you should be rather more concerned about yourself."

That didn't sound so good. Guy glanced round at the three men who were sitting behind him. They were perched on uncomfortable chairs that had been brought in from the room next door — unmoving, like toys waiting to be turned on. This was the fifth time he had seen them and it occurred to him that they were wearing the same clothes they always wore. The kilt, the suit and the leather jacket were their uniforms, defining them and at the same time masking whoever they really were. He wondered how much they were paid. Where had they come from? It was unlikely he would ever know.

There was a brief silence while Liddy composed himself. Guy knew that when he told his joke he would be word-perfect. He would tell it exactly the way it had been set down.

"One day," he began, "all the children at school are told they're going to give a talk about what their fathers do, and to make their talks more interesting they should come in dressed, if possible, like their fathers. Now, it happens that one little boy's father is a welder so the little boy comes to school wearing a welding mask.

"Unfortunately, he can't see very well with the mask. As he comes out of the house, he bumps into a lamp-post. He bumps into a parked car in the street. He's late for school and he bumps into the school gates, and going into the school he bumps into the wall. In fact, he spends the whole day bumping into things

360

and he's glad when four o'clock comes and it's time to go home.

"Anyway, he bumps into the classroom door on the way out and he bumps into the teachers and he bumps into the school gates a second time. And now he's running for the school bus but he bumps into a bus-stop and misses the bus so now he's got to walk home. So he's walking along the pavement bumping into things when suddenly a Mercedes pulls up and a man leans out of the window and says," Liddy put on a slimy voice, "'Little boy! Little boy! Would you like me to give you a lift home?' Now, the little boy has been told lots of times that he shouldn't accept lifts from strangers but he's tired and he's fed up with bumping into things so he says yes and he gets into the car. The door closes and they drive off together.

"The two of them drive on for a while, and then the man leans over and he says: 'Little boy,' he says. 'Do you know anything about homosexuality?'

"The little boy shakes his head.

"They drive on a bit more. Then the driver leans over a second time. 'Little boy,' he says. 'Do you know anything about paedophilia?'

"Once again, the little boy shakes his head.

"And the driver leans over once again. 'So tell me, little boy,' he says, 'do you know anything about buggery?'

"And the little boy says, 'No. Actually, I think I should tell you. I'm not really a welder.'"

Liddy sat back, pleased with himself. Guy hadn't laughed. But, then, he hadn't really been expected to. "I know twelve thousand, five hundred and fifty-two jokes," Liddy said. "Many of those jokes are, of course, variations on the same joke. But the one I have just told you is, I think, my favourite. I would like to explain to you why."

"If you must."

"A good joke almost always contains an element of surprise," Liddy said. "I think of the punch-line of a joke as a collision at the end of a road that you were following only because you had nowhere else to go. Take the oldest joke in the world, the joke told by the Sphinx. Some say this is the first joke ever created. 'What is it that has four legs in the morning, two legs in the afternoon and three legs in the evening? The answer is a man. He crawls as a baby, walks as an adult and uses a stick, as an old man.' It is, strictly speaking, a riddle rather than a joke, although the two are related. But the humour is in the surprise. This creature, which seems impossible, is in fact the most obvious one of all. It is you.

"A similar formula applies to another very old chestnut. 'When is a door not a door? When it's ajar.' Why is this funny?"

"I don't think it is," Guy said.

"It is not hilarious, Mr Fletcher, I agree. But it is none the less a well-established joke, first told on November the twelfth 1923 — the same day that Hitler was arrested following the abortive beer-hall *putsch*. I mention these two circumstances for a reason. Hitler's arrest — another step along the way to the Holocaust. The arrival of a new joke — a tiny grain of salvation.

362

But we shall return to this. The point I am trying to make is that the joke is slightly more than a play on words. It is another visual surprise, very similar to the appearance of the man in the riddle of the Sphinx. You are asked to consider a door and you are given a question that seems impossible. This is the road along which you are invited to travel. At the end of the road, in your thoughts, the door is transformed almost magically into a jar. Do you know the world's shortest joke? 'A blind man walks into a bar . . .' Once again, the effect is exactly the same. The bar full of drinks is transformed into a metal bar — and we can add the pain and the shock of the blind man who has injured himself. This, too, amuses — even if it shouldn't. This is the surprise.

"In this instance of the joke I began by telling you, another type of transformation comes into play. You are led ever further down a path that you are sure is going to be distasteful, embarrassing, unpleasant. But, in fact, the punch-line delivers something quite different. It is sweet and completely innocent. The little boy may be in considerable danger after he has entered the perverted man's car, but we end up celebrating his innocence. We laugh. And the danger, the feeling of disgust, is dispelled."

"Did you hear the one about the lunatic on the island?" Guy asked. He wanted to put a pin into this man, into his sense of self-worth.

Liddy ignored this. "For me, even more important than the punch-line is the environment in which a joke takes place. The perfect joke creates its own, complete world. In a joke, we do not need to ask the colour of the Jaguar, the size of the school, the city or the country in which the joke takes place. All this is built in. My joke perfectly creates the little boy's world and we know immediately where we are. Note also how the logic of that world is self-contained. It would, of course, be sensible for the little boy to remove the welder's mask so that he will no longer bump into things. A teacher would surely tell him to do so. But that idea does not occur to him and neither does it occur to us. The rules of the world are created at the same time as the world itself and those rules are never disobeyed.

"Finally, the joke has a wonderful rhythm about it. The repetition of the word 'bump' carries us along and lulls us into a sense of familiarity that will strengthen the power of the punch-line. I wonder if you noticed that the climax arrived in three stages, like the declamations of a politician. 'Do you know anything about homosexuality? Do you know anything about paedophilia? Do you know anything about buggery?' Each level is slightly worse than the one before until your expectations are punctured and the rug is pulled out from beneath your feet.

"There are jokes about children that frankly sicken me. The 'Mummy Mummy' jokes for example. That particular format was invented by a Russian in April 1955. The Russians can be tremendously cruel with their humour although Elevonich was undoubtedly a master. Ivan Elevonich. He began writing jokes the day he was given a translation of his name.

364

"Many jokes concerned with children *are* distasteful, and you laugh because of the destruction of innocence, the hurting of one human being by another. I have to remind myself that such jokes have their place in the great panoply of humour that is spread out before us, and we must remember that the oldest jokes in the world — the custard pie, the cat chasing the mouse, the man falling into the hole in the pavement — are based on the cruelty of one being to another. Why is this? Let us go back to Hitler who showed us, all too recently, the darker side of our nature. We know what we are. We have seen the monster inside us. But how to tame the monster? What better way than by laughing at it? The little-boy joke surprises because it rejoices in the innocence of children and reminds us of the other side of humanity, the side that I have always, in my own way, tried to support."

"Well, I still didn't think it was funny," Guy said. "And it's even less funny now that you've explained it."

"Jokes are never funny once they are explained," Liddy retorted. "Describe a Marx Brothers film in the third person and you will bore an audience rigid. Analyse an episode of any comedy programme and you will reduce it to inertia. There used to be people who were able to recite entire sketches by the Monty Python team. They were as popular as acne. Try to explain why you find anything funny and you will discover that it never actually is."

"May I say something?" Guy asked.

"Please go ahead."

"I think you should let Sally go. She's done nothing wrong. You've got absolutely no right to keep her here."

"You're quite wrong," Liddy replied. "I have every right to keep both of you here because I have been entrusted with enormous, far-reaching and very significant powers. It is unfortunate that Miss Lockwood chose to become involved. But, as I've already said, it's your own position you need to worry about." He looked up suddenly. "Who are you working for?"

Guy blinked. "I'm not working for anybody."

"Who sent you here?"

"I wasn't sent by anybody."

"Then how did you find us?"

"I don't have to answer your questions," Guy said. "I want to see a lawyer. I want to make a telephone call."

"You may be allowed to make a telephone call in a television drama, Mr Fletcher, but this is not a television drama." Liddy sighed. "I hoped you would be more co-operative."

"Do you want to take him to J-5?" O'Neil asked. The soft words came from behind Guy's shoulder.

"Yes. We'll go down there now."

Liddy stood up and gestured at the door. Guy had no choice but to do as he was told. McLarrity opened it and Guy allowed himself to be escorted out and down yet another staircase. He was beginning to see that the installation was something of a puzzle box . . . and one that could have been designed by Escher. It seemed to go on for ever. "What is this place?" he asked.

366

"We inherited Kelford Flat in the late sixties when it was decommissioned by the Ministry of Defence," Liddy replied. "It was constructed during the war although there have always been secret things here at Kelford. In the eighteenth and nineteenth centuries, smugglers were active on the Flat and it was they who constructed some of the passages that are still here to this day. There are American air bases hidden in the woods. Parts of the atom bomb were tested here. It's strange, isn't it, how some areas seem to attract mysteries? Kelford Flat was a perfect base for us. It is not easy for more than a hundred people to go about top-secret business without being noticed but we have more or less managed it here."

"You make jokes," Guy said. "I was right. You made the Ferrero Rocher joke. You made it here."

"The Ferrero Rocher joke — J79985/SM3/0501B — is actually a variant on a joke invented by an Italian clown called Bembo. There are some who say that he was the only humorous clown who ever lived. He created the original version the day after the assassination of Archduke Ferdinand. But otherwise you are correct. We adapted it and redistributed it earlier this year."

"So this is a joke factory!" Guy exclaimed. He was still having to come to terms with the fact that he had been right from the very start. It made his head spin.

"That is exactly what we are. Yes." A pair of armed guards walked past them, coming the other way. They both saluted Liddy. He nodded in return. "You might like to know that this is not the only country with a joke factory . . . if that's what you want to call us," he went on. "They exist in almost every civilised country in the world. Germany is, in fact, the only country that I can think of without one, although the Danish also have only a very small and, to my mind, ineffective joke-production centre concealed in an old bicycle factory just outside Copenhagen. Generally speaking, Mr Fletcher, Great Britain still leads the world in the quality and variety of its jokes. At a time when there are so many detractors, when our self-esteem is often so low, I take great pride in that."

They had reached the gantry that Guy and Sally had crossed the night before. Guy found himself looking down into the club room with its books, its snooker table, its portrait of the Queen. There were more people there now, talking quietly among themselves. None of them looked up as they passed.

"This is the Creative Department," Liddy said, speaking in a whisper. "The very heart of our operation. These fine people spend their time inventing, adapting and reworking jokes. I'm afraid we're a little short-staffed today. The others are away on a field trip."

"Nobody's laughing," Guy said.

Liddy looked at him with disdain. "They're professionals."

"Where do they come from?"

"We recruit from a number of areas including the psychiatric and ethnology departments of certain universities, as well as the secret service." Liddy pointed at a bald-headed, middle-aged man wearing a suit and bow-tie. "Tom Cunningham," he muttered, proudly.

368

"He was a huge hit at the 1978 Edinburgh Fringe." He waved a hand. "These are the boffins, the white-coat boys, as we like to think of them. The joke that I just told you was created here by one of them, John Winterbotham, in June 1985. Winterbotham was one of the great joke writers. There are those who say he could hold his own against Elevonich. He unfortunately died in a roadrage incident two years ago but his own death inspired nine very fine jokes so at least nothing went to waste."

Guy hesitated, and one of the three escorts pushed him hard in the back. They came to another lift, this one old-fashioned and ugly, like something in the service area of a hotel. Liddy pressed the button.

"Working closely with the creatives is a second department," Liddy continued. "They come under the heading, the name, the soubriquet of Research and Overseas Development, and their job is to monitor the airwaves, taking what they can from television and radio — although it will come as no surprise when I tell you that the vast majority of jokes they hear and see began their life here anyway. They are also in constant communication with our friends across the sea, exchanging jokes and, where necessary, adapting them. Jokes do travel, Mr Fletcher, but they change. To take an obvious example, the English consider the Irish to be the most stupid people on the planet. For the Americans, however, it is the Poles. The Dutch people sneer at the Belgians. The Russians make jokes about the Chukchi; and the Van der Merdwe South Africans for some reason find anyone with the surname irresistibly hilarious. We recently turned up a tribe of headhunters in the Amazonian basin who considered a second tribe, just a few miles away and every bit as primitive as themselves, to be in every way inferior, and although they were still too primitive to have actually formulated jokes, they still liked to point and laugh. New Zealanders tell jokes about the Australians and Australians tell jokes about the British. And on it goes."

The lift arrived. It was empty. Liddy nodded at Guy politely and they all got in. McLarrity pressed the button for level five.

"It goes without saying that the same template can be adapted to create many jokes," he continued, as the lift doors closed and they shuddered down. "The Selina Moore joke was most recently used about the late Princess Diana. You may recall that, following her tragic accident, she also came out of France in a box."

"But why would anyone want to laugh at that?" Guy demanded. "It was sad and horrible."

"It was precisely because it was sad and horrible that the joke was required."

The lights in the lift blinked slowly on and off. Level two, then level three.

"Level three is distribution," Liddy muttered. "I'm afraid I don't have time to show you round."

"Distribution?" Guy wondered what he meant. "You distribute the jokes using salesmen," he said.

"That's right. Travelling salesmen. There are other ways, of course. The Internet, for example, carries hundreds of jokes every day. However, in my opinion, jokes belong to the oral tradition and lose something

370

when typed on the screen. Travelling salesmen are ideal ambassadors. They travel and they go into people's houses and they gossip. We have the country divided into territories and our people go out to every town, every village, every street. They are known and they're liked. They stay in guest-houses where they meet other salesmen who become unwitting accessories. The taskforce of salesmen was developed twenty years ago and, in my view, it was a stroke of genius. Of course, it was necessary to give them a *raison d'être* in other words, a product to sell. At the same time, we didn't want to waste time and resources. So we came up with a vacuum cleaner — the Sphinx. It was actually developed here and was carefully designed to be at once credible yet almost one hundred per cent non-viable. Even the name has an unattractive quality. The machine is over-priced and difficult to use, and I am proud to say that in twenty years, we have only sold two dozen models. It is strange how there is always someone, somewhere who will buy something totally worthless. The point, of course, is because they are selling a domestic appliance, our people are able to penetrate almost every type of household. They try to persuade but inevitably they fail to sell. But in so doing they tell jokes. It really is the most natural thing in the world to punctuate a conversation with an amusing story. The only difference is that we work out with some care which particular story we wish to disseminate. Our strategy is planned with exactly the same precision as that used by a real sales force."

The lift slowed down. Guy felt a weakness in his knees and hoped it wasn't fear. The doors opened. There was an elderly, round-faced woman on the other side, dressed in a white coat and with her hair in a net. She was holding on to a tea trolley with two silver urns, milk cartons and several packets of twin-wrapped Jaffa Cakes. A name-tag, pinned to her blouse read: Mrs C. Lingus.

"Good morning, Connie," Liddy said, as he stepped round her.

"Good morning, Mr Liddy."

"How are you?"

"Very well. No tea this morning?"

"I'm afraid we're off to Interrogation."

"Oh dear."

"This way . . ." Liddy was talking to Guy now. There was only one way to go: a corridor with white tiles and a curving ceiling, like something in a London Underground station. Guy's heart was thumping. The single word "Interrogation" drummed in his ears.

"Who do you work for?" he demanded. "Is it the government?"

"Whatever gave you that idea?" Liddy replied, a little primly.

He stopped for a moment. The tea-lady had disappeared as the lift doors closed and she was carried to the upper levels.

"A great many of our jokes do have a political purpose," he admitted. "At the time of the Iraq war, for example, there was a great deal of concern about nuclear and biological warfare. People were afraid. We therefore put into circulation several dozen Saddam Hussein jokes. These were all drawn from a computer database — large moustache, oil wells, sex with camels, nepotism, black beret and so on. Partly as a result of that war, we detected a certain amount of anti-American feeling out on the street so we immediately set to work on American jokes. Presidents who are either sexual athletes or morons. Fat Americans. Rich Americans. All in all, it is better to laugh at Americans than to insult them. Certainly better to laugh at them than to fear them."

"So they're government-controlled."

"Jokes are regulated, but they have a much wider function." Liddy sighed. "Perhaps it would be easier to explain if you allowed me to make a philosophical observation, Mr Fletcher. It is at the very heart of what we at Sphinx are about. It is this. Man is the only creature on this planet with a sense of humour. Man is also the only creature with an awareness of his own death."

"I don't think I see the point," Guy said.

"What keeps us sane? How do we survive with the knowledge that every passing second brings us closer to our own extinction? The richest man on the planet knows that all the money in the world cannot buy him one more second, one breath more than he has been allocated. The poorest one lives in daily, hourly knowledge of how little he has been given and how little his life is worth. Think of the dog, the cat, the rabbit that simply gets on with its existence until it falls over dead or is shot or crushed by a car. Envy it! We humans

373

are cursed in that we alone are aware that our life consists almost entirely of shortcomings and that, moreover, it is short."

They had begun walking again. Guy and Liddy went first. The three others followed behind. The sound of their footsteps clattered rhythmically in the empty passageway.

"The immensity, the inevitability of death has to be countered. We have to have something to set against the extremely high chance of our succumbing to cancer, AIDS, Alzheimer's, Parkinson's, MS, motor-neurone disease or simply being run over by a drunk driver who will end up with a six-month suspension and a five-hundred-pound fine. As we get older, we will see all our friends disappear, one by one. We will watch our own bodies begin to fail us. Our life will contract. What will prevent us going mad?"

"We'll tell jokes."

"Exactly. Stories that make us laugh. Stories that make us forget. We need protection — and not just from the big issues, the matters of life and death. There are also the smaller complexities of day-to-day living. The stresses of urban life. The emptiness of country life. Bills piling up on the doorstep. Taxes . . .

"We pay exorbitant amounts of tax. How do people live with the fact that a huge amount of what they earn is forcibly taken away from them, often before they even receive it, that they spend thousands of hours, a great chunk of their lives, working to support a state that is at once invisible, incompetent and mean-spirited? We are taxed from the moment we first draw

374

breath to the moment we die — and even beyond. And what happens to all this money? You mentioned the government, Mr Fletcher. Our governments are lazy and corrupt and waste much more money than they spend wisely. They choose to live in a luxury that they would deny everyone else, but it is everyone else who pays for it. The chauffeur-driven limousines, the country houses, the first-class flights, the favours they pay their friends and allies. We all know it. Western democracy is rotten to the core.

"Look at the government we have at the moment. They treat the electorate like fools. The Sanderson report . . . everyone in the country knows it's bollocks but they sit there, untouchable, unaccountable, and worse than all this, smug. The endlessly changing targets and figures. The pretence that everything is fine when anyone who is sick or in need knows otherwise. There is a modern word . . . *spin*. The word itself is actually a spin because the real word is *lie*. We are lied to all the time. But why is it that there has only been one attempt to blow up the Prime Minister and everyone else in the Houses of Parliament — and that was four hundred years ago? Why do we put up with the day-to-day incompetence of these grinning, overpaid idiots?

"The answer is simple. We don't kill our politicians. We laugh at them.

"We laugh at everything. It's our most vital defence system. Every minute of every day throws something hateful at us but we simply bat it aside. There are jokes about terminal illness, about the disabled, brain damage, poverty, sexual abuse, racial prejudice, the Inland Revenue, old age, paedophilia, 9/11, the unnecessary death of a much-loved princess or an actress. I know this because we invent them. And we invent them because they are needed. Life would be insupportable without them."

"But you don't need an organisation to make jokes," Guy said. "People make jokes. Jokes just evolve!" He heard himself speak and wished he had been listening weeks ago when this all began. He had answered his own question but the answer had come too late.

"Some jokes do simply evolve, it's true. But what sort of person could sit down and invent a joke like the little boy and the man in the Mercedes?" Liddy replied. "Were you really so unable to respond to its sheer artistry, the perfection of its construction? Winterbotham was a true artist — albeit an anonymous one. There is a library here with more than seven hundred jokes created by him. They all have the same trademark. Are you telling me the woman in the launderette or the fat taxi driver in the traffic jam could dream up, invent anything as good?"

"There are comedians on television."

"And the bulk of them are unoriginal hacks who steal their material from wherever and whomever they can get it and who, at the first taste of success, become too full of themselves and too drugged out even to deliver it properly. There are people working here for a tenth of what your so-called comedians earn, Mr Fletcher. They have no egos, no insatiable desire to be adored by all and sundry. They are good, quiet people, serving their country. Patriots."

They had come to a door. Solid wood. Unpainted. A barrier that seemed somehow final. Guy hesitated, wondering whether to lash out and make a run for it. But the three men had gathered close behind him and he knew he had nowhere to go. Liddy opened the door.

It led into a square, whitewashed room with no windows, no decoration, no possibility that it could be anything other than a torture chamber. There was a butcher's block table with leather straps and buckles dividing it into three. To one side was a metal counter, empty but for an ebony box that might have contained a set of cutlery: place settings for six, perhaps. The fact that the box was black and surrounded by so much space made it terrifying. Guy felt his bladder open involuntarily and was glad that he had been given nothing to drink.

"I'm not a danger to you," he said.

"I disagree."

"Why have you brought me here? I've already told you. I'm not working for anyone. Your fucking joke was about my mother. That's the only reason I'm here."

"I have to know how you found us."

"I worked it out. It was just luck. I haven't told anyone about you. You can hurt me as much as you like, but I haven't got anything to tell you."

"I don't like hurting you at all. But I'm afraid I have no choice."

"Please . . ."

Guy wasn't just going to walk in. The civility of it all — the gracious explanation, the lift, the tea-lady — revolted him. He screamed and lurched backwards, away from the table and the straps, away from the black box, hoping to find the strength to break through them, to get back out into the corridor. But now Smythe and O'Neil grabbed hold of him. They were incredibly strong. They must have targeted his nerve points. He couldn't move at all.

"Take his clothes off, will you, please?" Liddy said.

He had no shoes. While the Englishman and the Irishman kept him pinned between them, the Scotsman reached out and seized hold of his trousers, tearing open the flies and dragging them off his legs. It was all over so quickly that he realised they must have done this before, many times. With his trousers trailing on the floor, he was yanked backwards on to the table. He felt his jacket being swept off his shoulders the socks pulled off his feet. He was writhing and shouting but it was expected and did him no good at all. McLarrity pulled the straps over him and tightened them. It took only a few seconds and then he was lying on his back in his shirt and boxer shorts. He couldn't move at all.

Liddy watched all this with disinterest. He barely seemed to be listening as Guy let loose a torrent of swear words. There were tears streaming down the sides of his face. Smythe walked over to the door and closed it.

At last, Guy fell back, exhausted. He wondered what they were going to do to him. He wondered what was inside the box. He didn't want to know.

378

"You may be interested to know that jokes became institutionalised as long ago as the sixteenth century," Liddy said, continuing as if nothing had happened. "You have heard, I'm sure, of Walsingham. Sir Francis Walsingham, 1530-1590, secretary of State to Elizabeth I, her spymaster. It was he and his people who wrote many of the jokes in Shakespeare's plays. But in fact people in power had recognised that jokes were an essential part of life long before that. The king in his thirteenth-century castle, surrounded by plagues, famines, cold and the probability of a short life followed by an extremely violent death, employed a jester. It was the jester's job to keep his sovereign happy — often in the face of insurmountable odds. We at Sphinx Appliances are the jesters for modern society. We are here for everyone but, at the same time, we have been successful in what we set out to do because nobody suspects we exist. We are invisible. It has to be that way."

Guy struggled to find the strength to speak. His heart was pounding so hard that the breath was having difficulty reaching his throat. "If people knew about you, they wouldn't laugh any more," he said.

"Exactly. And that is why you find yourself in this unfortunate position now. If it became common knowledge that jokes are not in fact spontaneous and somehow self-creating, the result would be catastrophic. You were in Kelford. Most of our ground force — catering, administration, security and so on — are drawn from that village. We only have limited accommodation here and the new housing that you may have noticed had been constructed for their benefit. Not everyone in Kelford works here and those that do have been obliged to sign the Official Secrets Act. Even so, there is still a tacit and widespread understanding of the nature of our work. This has had an extremely unfortunate result.

"Kelford has the highest suicide rate in the country. In the winter months, suicides can sometimes be as high as one a week. Our own turnover is unparalleled. We have tried to offer counselling, but it doesn't work. The local populace are terminally depressed and nothing will cheer them up. Sadly, they are no longer able to tell jokes. They have lost their sense of humour. I suppose it's to be understood. People in this country have a natural dislike of government. It's the reason why government campaigns against cigarettes, for example, nearly always lead to a rise in smoking. Why attempts to improve the British diet will have people queuing up to eat hamburgers and chips. Tell people that something is good for them and they will avoid it like the plague. We cannot let it be known that jokes fall into the general category of public service.

"And that is why I am obliged, forced, compelled to bring you here to this room. It may well be that you are what you say you are. An out-of-work actor who was offended by a joke — but one who took the highly unusual step of trying to find out where it came from. To be frank with you, Mr Fletcher, I do believe that to be the case. But I have to be sure. Apart from anything else, there are international protocols I have to observe. If it's any consolation to you, your irrational pursuit of the Ferrero Rocher joke has been discussed at top level in six countries. We have had to take enormous and very costly steps to contain you. You are not being subjected to this because of some whim on my part. Our international partners demand and expect no less."

Liddy walked over to the box and ran his hand over the lid.

"I have just three questions," he said. "How did you find your way here? Did you tell anyone where you were going? And did anyone, apart from Miss Lockwood, give you any help?"

"I've already told you. Jesus Christ — I've already told you. Nobody knows. I came here on my own. And I only found you by joining the dots together on a map."

"Who gave you the map?"

"I drew it myself! I just worked it out. There's no need to do this. You've got to believe me!"

"I do have to believe you. Exactly. But you must help me believe you."

Liddy opened the box.

Guy craned his neck and saw that the inside of the box was lined with red velvet and that there was an indentation, a space for a single object. Liddy removed it. When he turned round, he was holding a single, multi-coloured feather.

"This comes from a bird-of-paradise," he said, "*Paradisaea raggiana*, from the forest highlands of eastern New Guinea, a tree-dweller subsisting largely on fruit and berries. This is male plumage, of course. We find it most effective for our purpose."

"Go fuck yourself!" Guy shouted.

"I rather fear I'm about to fuck you," Liddy replied. "Figuratively, anyway."

He walked over to the butcher's block and stopped. Then he reached out and drew the feather across Guy's bare feet. Guy felt an extraordinary shiver of white-hot non-pain. His whole body twisted as it travelled up his legs and into his chest.

He laughed. He couldn't stop himself.

"Three questions," Liddy repeated.

Again he touched feather to skin but this time he didn't stop and the shivers came in waves, one after another, pulsating from one nerve ending to the next, fanning outwards, throwing Guy's entire nervous system into chaos. Guy laughed and laughed. His shoulders contorted. He could feel his head wrenching itself off his neck. He was screaming with laughter, screaming with laughter. But then he was only screaming.

The Englishman, the Irishman and the Scotsman watched, unamused. They had seen it all before.

CHAPTER
TWENTY-FIVE

Guy opened his eyes.

He tried to move but there were more straps holding him down — this time in a sitting position. He looked down and saw that his trousers were back on, although they hadn't been fastened round the waist. His whole body was drenched with sweat. He could feel it running under his arms and down his back. His shirt was soaking wet. His throat was on fire. His eyes were swollen, his sight out of focus. He felt as if he had been punched and kicked for a week by a professional rugby team.

He lifted his head. His neck could barely manage it. He saw Sally sitting opposite him and knew from the expression on her face that he must look as bad as he felt. He opened his mouth to speak to her but the words wouldn't come. His vocal cords seemed to have been shredded. He could hear his every breath, rasping inside his head.

"Guy . . ." Sally said.

"You all right?" He whispered the three words.

"They haven't hurt me. I've been so worried about you."

He closed his eyes tight, then opened them again, forcing himself to take in his surroundings.

He was in another room, a glass box about the size of a sauna. The floor and the ceiling were made out of modern pine slats. Sally was sitting in a wooden chair. Her arms and legs, like his, were tied down with padded bands that fastened with Velcro strips. He looked up and saw a light enclosed in a glass panel. It was attached to a sensor of some sort. He also noticed a small grille set in the floor.

Liddy stepped forward into his line of vision. He looked apologetic. "I believe you," he said.

Guy didn't waste his breath swearing. It hurt too much.

"What have you done to him?" Sally demanded.

"I have ascertained that he was telling the truth," Liddy said. He stood in front of Guy. He seemed to be swaying but in fact he was quite still. "I owe you an apology," he continued, addressing Guy. "I am not, whatever you may think, an uncivilised man. My father was in the services and I learnt from him that sometimes one has to put duty before personal inclination. You gave me no choice. I have no choice now."

"What are you going to do to us?" Sally asked, more quietly.

"First, let me assure you that I am not going to cause either of you any more pain. Unfortunately, for reasons I have already explained at length to Mr Fletcher, I cannot allow either of you to leave this island. I could, of course, keep you here for ever, in some sort of

384

confinement. But that would be barely more humane than the course of action on which I am now decided."

"You're going to kill us," Guy rasped.

"In a few moments, I am going to leave this chamber and my associates will take over. You will, at least, have a little time together before the end. I hope that will be of comfort to you."

"What are you going to do?" Sally couldn't keep the fear out of her voice.

"This is a gas chamber. It is based largely on those used by the American penal system. We will seal the doors and pump gas through the grille in the floor. It is odourless and will cause you no discomfort. You will simply go to sleep. You may have noticed the light above you in the ceiling." He pointed. "When the amount of gas reaches a lethal level, the light will go out. At that moment, you will die. It's as simple as that. Your bodies will be taken out and buried at sea. To the rest of the world, it will simply be that you have disappeared. People disappear every day. They are quickly forgotten. You will be too. I am really so very sorry."

He walked over to the door and disappeared. Guy wanted to be alone with Sally — even here, even now — but it wasn't yet to be. The Englishman, the Irishman and the Scotsman had taken over the final operation.

O'Neil checked the bindings, kneeling down beside Guy. Guy looked down at the yellow, lifeless hair, noticing that he had bad dandruff. It was all over the shoulders of his leather jacket. "They're all set," O'Neil said.

385

"Check them again," Smythe said.

"I just said —"

"Please?"

O'Neil went over the two chairs a second time and noticed that one of Sally's feet had in fact come loose. He scowled at Smythe and pulled the strip across. Smythe gestured and he went over to the door where McLarrity was waiting.

"Well, this is goodbye," Smythe said. "As Mr Liddy said, this won't be an unpleasant experience. We're not monsters, you know."

"I don't agree," Guy said. His voice was coming back to him. "I think you're fucking lunatics."

"Well, I suppose you would think that. After I close the door, you'll have a couple of minutes before it starts. Time to say goodbye to each other. Do you have any last requests?"

"I'd just like you to leave," Sally said.

"I'm going now. Goodbye."

He followed O'Neil out. McLarrity was already waiting on the other side, gazing through the glass with something like a snarl on his face. The door closed electronically. As it swung silently shut, Guy noticed that it had a heavy rubber seal round the edge. The room was now airtight. He tried to move his hands and legs but the bonds were scientific, exact. His arms and legs were comfortable but there was no yield at all. He and the chair were one.

For what felt like a long time neither Guy nor Sally said anything. He knew that he was wasting precious seconds but, at the end of the day, what was there to say? What did it matter when, in a few minutes, there would be no record, no memory of it anyway? He wished now that he had made a last request. He wanted to hold Sally in these final moments, to kiss her and to feel her close.

"What did they do to you?" Sally asked. "Did they hurt you?"

"It doesn't matter. Forget it." He paused. "I'm sorry, Sally," he said.

"Is this really the end?"

"Yes. I suppose so."

"Well . . ." Sally sighed ". . . these things happen."

"Do you really think so? I was thinking how unlikely it all was, really . . ."

"They happened to us."

"It was all my fault."

"It's a bit late to start all that again, Guy."

"Are you angry with me?"

"I'm not sorry I met you. The more I knew you, the more I liked you. I think we could have been happy together. But I'm not altogether delighted that things turned out the way they did. First Mother. Now me."

"I got your mother killed. It was my own mother who started all this. I was only trying to — I don't know — protect her, I suppose. Her memory. And this is the result." He tried to smile. "It wasn't what I expected."

"Me neither."

There was another silence. Guy tentatively smelt the air but nothing seemed to have changed. He looked over his shoulder and saw Smythe, O'Neil and

McLarrity watching him through the glass. He quickly looked back again. He didn't want the three of them to be the last thing he ever saw.

"Listen!" Sally said.

He cocked his head. There was a very faint hissing coming from the floor. He knew what it meant. They had started to pump in the gas. In a few minutes the light would go out. In his case, for ever.

"I love you, Guy," Sally said.

"I love you too, Sally. The funny thing is, if I hadn't started chasing the joke, I'd never have met you."

"That's true," Sally agreed. "But it isn't what I'd call funny."

"I meant funny peculiar."

Guy's head spun. Was it the gas? It seemed to him that the conversation at a time like this could have been a little more profound — but he couldn't think of anything to say. "Do you want to pray?" he asked.

"No." Sally shook her head, and for the first time Guy saw that she was crying. A tear had left its trail, glistening down the side of her cheek. He struggled again, desperate to reach out to her. "I don't believe in God," Sally said. "And if more people believed in God, they wouldn't need jokes. If we only had faith, we'd be able to put up with everything."

"I suppose you're right," Guy agreed. "Maybe that's why there are no jokes in the Bible."

"The Bible doesn't need jokes."

The hissing was louder.

"They're killing us, Sally!" He almost choked on the words. He felt his own tears, welling up in his eyes.

"Goodbye, Guy."

"Goodbye, Sally."

They sat looking at each other. Guy so wanted to touch her one last time. He pulled with his arms and found that suddenly he had no strength left.

"Sally?" he called out.

Her head had rolled forward. He realised that he was alone.

"God rot the lot of you," he shouted out. Perhaps there would be a transmitter in the room. Perhaps they would hear him.

The room swam. His eyes closed.

Thirty seconds later, the light behind the glass panel went out.

He was dead.

He opened his eyes for a second time and found himself floating in a great, white world. He looked down and saw that he was dressed in long robes that fell all the way to his bare feet. He was holding something. A harp. To his astonishment, he also had wings. He looked around, but there was no sign of Sally.

Ahead of him, a pair of silver gates loomed out of the cloud. Brilliant sunlight streaked through the bars, shafting out into the sky. He knew where he was, of course. He walked forward a little self-consciously. For some reason he was embarrassed by his robes, bare feet and wings, although he had to admit they were preferable to a tail and horns. There was a figure waiting at the gate, a man with an enormous white beard and an open book. That had to be St Peter, hadn't it? The elderly — indeed eternal — saint beckoned with his hand, calling Guy forward. Somewhere, a choir began to sing.

There was the blast of a funnel.

Guy opened his eyes yet again and found himself lying on his back, staring at white clouds far above. He was on the deck of a ship, heading out to sea. It took him a moment or two to realise that he had been dreaming — and then he had to work out exactly when the dream had begun. Could it be that the builders at the Cat and Fiddle, the search for the joke and the terrible consequences had never happened? He turned and saw Sally lying next to him. He could tell at once that she wasn't dead. He could see the rise and fall of her chest and there was a pink glow in her cheeks.

So everything that had happened had happened. Except something had gone wrong. The gas chamber hadn't killed them.

He wasn't feeling well. He wanted to throw up and he had a headache that was making his eyeballs throb. The floor seemed to be going up and down. No. He was on a ship. The floor actually was going up and down. He looked over the side and saw that they were already well out to sea. God! Buried at sea. That was what Liddy had promised. They must be on their way.

Sally groaned.

He had to act before she woke up. He was suddenly afraid that they would be discovered, overcome a second time and thrown overboard, alive, with an anchor tied to their legs. He looked around him and saw a heavy, rusting spanner. He picked it up.

The boat was a trawler, an old fishing-boat. Guy waited until his strength had returned and made his way down the deck, crawling on his hands and knees. There was a cabin in the middle with a single, bearded man — the captain — in an oilskin coat, standing behind the wheel. Guy crept up behind him, hit him with the spanner and was mildly gratified when he fell down unconscious, just like they did in the movies. Then he was sick over the side.

He had no idea where they were. He could see no sign of land in any direction and no other ships. He quickly checked that there was nobody else on the boat, then turned the engine down to its lowest setting. There was a small galley underneath the cabin. Guy dragged the captain inside and locked him in. Then he went back to Sally.

She was sitting up. Her grey-blue eyes were dazed.

"What happened?" He couldn't hear her over the sound of the engine, the waves, the rushing breeze. She shouted the words again.

"Something went wrong. We're not dead."

"Where are we?"

"On a boat. God knows where. Somewhere in the English Channel."

There were two sacks on the deck. Also a length of chain. Guy knew with certainty that at some time they would have been loaded up and dumped overboard. That would have been Captain Birdseye's job.

"Don't worry," he shouted. "There was only one other man on the boat and I've locked him in the cabin."

"What are we going to do?"

"Do you know how to read a compass?"

Sally nodded.

"Good." Guy looked ahead of him. The boat rose and sank, on the crest of a wave. "Then let's head for France."

Back in the office, a grim-faced Rupert Liddy was behind his desk, facing Smythe, O'Neil and McLarrity, who were once again in their chairs, arranged like naughty schoolboys.

"So you're saying they weren't killed," he said.

Smythe glanced at O'Neil. O'Neil looked at McLarrity. But McLarrity was already looking accusingly at him. He scowled. "Well, sir, we can't know that for sure."

"But —"

"But we've just been told, it seems that the machine, you know, the gas chamber thing . . . it malfunctioned."

"You mean, there was no poison gas?"

O'Neil refused to say any more. Smythe took over. "There was poison gas," he continued, "but maybe there wasn't enough of it."

"I don't understand."

"Well, sir, it's quite —"

"It was the light," McLarrity broke in impatiently. "The bloody thing's meant to be calibrated. When the light goes out, it means they're dead. You turn the gas off and when it's cleared, you put them on the boat and they're taken out for burial at sea."

"Is that where they are now?"

"Yes, sir."

"Have you spoken to the skipper?"

"We've tried to reach him on the radio, sir, but there's no answer."

"Go on."

McLarrity took a breath. "The light went out so we assumed the process was complete and we turned the gas off but then one of the maintenance people took a look at it and it seems that it may have been that the light was faulty."

Smythe shook his head in exasperation. "This is Maintenance's fault," he said. "I'd already put an order in, asking them to look into it."

"And why hadn't they?" Liddy asked.

"They said they were short-staffed."

"For God's sake!" Liddy cried. "How many top-secret government technicians does it take to change a lightbulb?"

By this time, Guy and Sally had dismantled the radio and turned the boat round, steering a course for Calais. Neither of them heard the hysterical cries of the real fat boy in the attic, the man they had left behind.

CHAPTER
TWENTY-SIX

Anyway.

Guy and Sally somehow manage to get to the French coast and nobody notices them so now they're in Normandy and they're having a fantastic time, even though they're on the run. And somehow they find themselves outside this château in the Loire Valley and the sun is shining and Guy says to her, "I want to live with you for the rest of my life." But they're worried they won't have a life if Sphinx gets hold of them. So they steal a car and head south, disguised as tourists.

But the thing is, they don't actually know if anybody's still looking for them. After all, there's nothing on television or in the newspapers so it could just mean they've been forgotten or it could mean that every secret service in Europe is looking for them. They just don't know.

So they decide to go to South America because they think they'll be safe there. The South Americans, generally, have an underdeveloped sense of humour and of course Sally's father . . .

Sorry.

I should have mentioned this earlier. You remember Sally's father, the archaeologist who'd worked in South

America? He's phoned her from this beautiful Caribbean island, just off the coast of Venezuela and, after Daphne got killed, Sally rang him and the two of them had a sort of reconciliation and had asked him to come and live with her. Complete paradise.

I should have mentioned that.

So Guy and Sally manage to get on a plane at Marseilles and . . .

Wait a minute.

Passports and money. Of course, they haven't got their passports, and they don't have any money. But there's always their friend, Jean-Pierre.

Didn't I mention him?

Damn.

Damn, damn, damn, damn, damn . . .

I seem to have completely ballsed this up. I'm really sorry.

Do you mind if I start again at the beginning?

Yes. That's probably best.

Yes.

CHAPTER
TWENTY-SEVEN

There's this guy, goes into a bar . . .

Also available in ISIS Large Print:

Mister Fabulous and Friends

Celia Brayfield

Funny, sad, moving, hilarious — a social comedy that touches the heart of modern middle England.

What do you do when the kids you work with have never heard of the Bonzo Dog Doo Dah band and your mates think 'Lady in Red' is a really quite a good song? For Percy George Hodsoll, the answer was easy. You drive your motorbike over the central reservation and go out in a blaze of glory.

George leaves behind four members of his classic R&B band: Mickey, star commercials director who has a career on borrowed time; Rhys, conscientious doctor, in love with Mickey's wife; big-hearted Andy is married with kids but has a dangerously sexy new neighbour; Sam, the egotist supreme, is leaving home for a woman who thinks she's an Egyptian goddess. Men for whom life, love and masculinity has caught them up and then passed them by. It's time to move on, but where to?

ISBN 0-7531-7091-4 (hb)
ISBN 0-7531-7092-2 (pb)

Aberystwyth Mon Amour

Malcolm Pryce

Schoolboys are disappearing all over Aberystwyth and nobody knows why. Louie Knight, the town's private investigator, soon realises that it is going to take more than a double ripple from Sospan, the philosopher cum ice-cream seller, to help find out what is happening to these boys and whether or not Lovespoon, the Welsh teacher, Grand Wizard of the Druids and controller of the town, is more than just a sinister bully. And just who was Gwenno Guevara?

ISBN 0-7531-6883-9 (hb)
ISBN 0-7531-6884-7 (pb)

The Eyre Affair

Jasper Fforde

There is another 1985, somewhere in the could-have-been, where Thursday Next is a literary detective without equal, fear, or boyfriend. Thursday is on the trail of the villainous Acheron Hades who has been kidnapping characters from works of fiction and holding them to ransom. Jane Eyre has herself been plucked from the novel of the same name, and Thursday must find a way into the book to repair the damage.

She also has to find time to halt the Crimean conflict, persuade the man she loves to marry her, rescue her aunt from inside a Wordsworth poem and figure out who really wrote Shakespeare's plays. Aided and abetted by a cast of characters that includes her time-travelling father, a pet dodo named Pickwick and Edward Rochester himself, Thursday embarks on an adventure that will take your breath away.

ISBN 0-7531-6821-9 (hb)
ISBN 0-7531-6822-7 (pb)